TWO RUNS OF STONE

HEART'S DESIRE

Book III

STEVEN D. NIELSEN

TWO RUNS OF STONE

Volume 1: A Beckoning Call
Volume 2: Windships America
Volume 3: Heart's Desire

Although *Two Runs of Stone—Heart's Desire* is based upon historical facts and refers to actual people and events, the work as a whole is a work of fiction, and the dialogue and characterizations of individuals reflect the author's interpretation.

Published and Distributed by:

Granite Publishing and Distribution, LLC
868 North 1430 West
Orem, Utah 84057
(801) 229-9023   Toll Free (800) 574-5779
Fax (801) 229-1924

Cover Design: Steve Gray
Page Layout and Design: Lyndell Lutes

ISBN: 978-1-59936-041-6
Library of Congress Control Number: 2009927320
First Printing 2009
10 9 8 7 6 5 4 3 2 1
Printed in the United States of America

Table of Contents

Acknowledgments

Aileen Jardine Larson remains the first name to come to mind where this series of novels are concerned. Aileen introduced to me the vast work done by the Daughters of the Utah Pioneers in compiling the history of the noble women, and men who laid the foundation of the Church of Jesus Christ of Latter Day Saints. Aileen is the past president of the Weber County Chapter of the Daughters of the Utah Pioneers, my mother-in-law and a more unique, kind, generous and strong individual I do not know.

I am truly grateful to Joëlle Yetive Greenhalgh for excellent advice, editing and technical assistance also to Lauri Humphreys for editing and many valuable suggestions. For inspiration I will always be indebted to my kind and honorable mother Carma May Monsen Nielsen, to Martha Hire of Ogden, Utah for believing in me, to Dean Grover, also of Ogden, Utah for his teaching and love of literature; Peter Jorgensen (deceased) of Houston, Texas for historical assistance, translation, friendship and moral support; and Patrick D. Nielsen, a technical writer, for his encouragement and editing assistance.

I remain indebted to Ronald E. J. Börgstedt for creativity, honesty, and technical assistance, to Judy Niederhauser for continued strength and encouragement and also to Don Enders of the L.D.S. Church Historical Department for all of the above.

Last, but not least, I would like to thank two people I hope to meet one day: my great-great-grandfather, Niels Peter Nielsen, who at eighteen converted to the Church of Jesus Christ of Latter Day Saints in Holbaek, Denmark and was beaten severely for his trouble and then left for dead. And finally to Kate B. Carter, author, teacher, journalist, historian, publisher, and long time President of the Daughters of the Utah Pioneers.

Synopsis

With her son Peter's conversion to Mormonism and his subsequent departure from Denmark for the heathen infested plains of Western America, the foundation of Catherine Jensen's otherwise secure life began to crumble. She'd attended crowded firesides at the home of her friend Casten Pedersen, listened intently to the missionaries and genuinely tried to understand their message. Oddly enough in the middle of her struggles, her uneducated, quasi' daughter-in-law Krista had embraced the Gospel of Christ with something akin to a bonfire. Krista's reading, painfully awkward and very sluggish nevertheless she gained a solid testimony of Christ that literally transformed her from Gypsy to Saint.

An attitude of humility followed Krista that touched Catherine deeply resulting with intensified investigation of the Church of Jesus Christ of Latter-day Saints and even taking up the Book of Mormon again. But she hadn't progressed very far before being emotionally knocked back when her foreman, Torkil Olsen quit the mill and with his uncles and their families immigrated to New York City! By now Catherine felt her world coming apart at the seams; even her dear friend Casten Pedersen was talking about leaving Denmark. What did she have left? Her mill with only Ferdinand to run it and lately he drank as heavily as his deceased father.

One quiet morning in her overstuffed chair near a sunny window Catherine sat reading from Third Nephi where it spoke of the Lord Jesus Christ appearing in the Americas just after his crucifixion—the spirit of God gently poured over her soul like sunshine, her faith soared to new heights and Catherine's mind glowed with a clear understanding of what she'd just read. Jesus Christ lived! In His resurrected form He'd come to visit His 'Other Sheep'. Tears of joy streamed down Catherine's face. Her soul filled with light and her heart felt at peace.

Two Runs of Stone is an epic in historical fiction set in the late 1800's and is the result of fifteen years of concerted effort. Actual journals of the women and men who lived and died during the era provide the foundation for the work not to mention life histories of their Danish, English and American ancestors. Under the inspired leadership of the Prophet Brigham Young, second president of the church, Latter Day Saints colonized over 300 cities in Western America, not to mention laying the foundation for the restored Gospel of Jesus Christ. Here's to good reading!

Preface

Maren and Peter Jensen, Gunda and Claus Wangsgaard and company of Latter-day Saints led by Trevor Wells, have somehow survived the cholera plague that killed 85 church members on Arsenal Island near St. Louis and now find themselves deposited on the banks of the frozen Missouri River in January of 1866, near Atchison Kansas. Twice quarantined by authorities before finally being allowed to pursue their goal of wintering near Omaha Nebraska (before traveling to Zion) the 528 survivors, their belongings and livestock are now refugees smack in the heartland of America and feeling altogether lost.

Nevertheless welcomed by a kind hearted, yet somewhat nervous populous of the tiny Kansas settlement, and finding few if any accommodations for so great a number, the European Saints are forced to continue their journey but before doing so procured a few wagons and ox teams from local farmers, just enough to carry their heavy trunks and other bulky belongings. What couldn't be loaded they carried on their backs.

Meanwhile, Torkil Olsen and his Uncles, Sebastian and Jonathan Olsen have escaped the iron grip of New York City and after a hazardous trip that included freezing cattle-cars, and worn-out wagons have finally landed amid hundreds of frozen and snow bound lakes near Madison, Wisconsin on their way to Morehead, Minnesota. On the outskirts of town they found a cluster of abandoned cabins and barns littered with old hay—remnants of a small settlement formerly the home of employees of a now defunct lumber company. Spared from the freezing weather, yet with starvation knocking at their door, driven to survive the former residents of Holbaek Denmark have beaten the odds as Torkil luckily found employment working in—of all places—a small cheese factory.

A riveting surprise within the pages of Book III "Heart's Desire" in the series "Two Runs of Stone" concerns Catherine Jensen (Peter's mother); however, so profound are the events of her fascinating life that to introduce details here would ruin the story. So travel along with us during the late 1860s, as immigration and a call to Zion sounds throughout England, Europe and Scandinavia eventually washing a wave of choice souls upon the shores of the Civil-War torn yet again United States of America. Experience first hand the lives of those who braved the oceans and prairies, cleared the land, conquered the desert wilds of our nation paving the way so that you and I might enjoy the light of freedom, prosperity and the right to worship almighty God and His only begotten Son the Lord Jesus Christ according to the dictates of our own conscience—so far, without fear of tyranny.

Section One

Chapter 1

A Troubled Wind

January 25, 1866.

It's been six days since the riverboat steamed away leaving us near the small settlement of Atchison, Kansas. We bought a few oxen there and any supplies they would sell us. Tonight we're camped five miles past the settlement of Mormon Grove. The ground is frozen and lightly covered with snow; driving tent stakes was extremely difficult but we're now snug in our tent.

Mormon Grove was an outfitting place for immigrants before America's Civil War and completion of the rails from New York to Omaha. Few people still live in the small town and between them and those in Atchison we were able to buy eight wagons to carry our tents, trunks and the heavy crates of muskets we purchased at Fort Leavenworth.

The trading post at Mormon Grove was poorly stocked; we only found flour, beans, leather strips and army tents. Our visit was brief as we had to get moving or freeze to death. The settlers of the town were frightened by our numbers.

I am currently penniless. It became necessary to donate all my money to help buy the wagons and teams. Nobody wanted to sell, and those who did robbed us; everyone gave heavily. We had no choice. Brother Wells says we should be reimbursed once we arrive in Zion. He also said there wouldn't be need of additional supplies as Winter Quarters is well stocked. If not, I'll sell a pendant[1] to buy from locals; I will not allow Maren to do without.

Terrin Forsgren hooked his milk cows to two of the wagons, saving us the cost of additional teams. Their udders are dry but it's still an unusual sight. We used every resource possible and started off into the wilderness; humbled because of Arsenal Island, few complained—they're so grateful at last to be free!

Claus Wangsgaard butchered one of Dewey Farnsworth's sows shortly after we made camp tonight. The big old sow had its last litter a year ago and wouldn't have made it another week out here. Claus shot it just behind the ear with a pistol, then we hung the carcass by the hocks from a stout branch and Dewey slit its throat. After the carcass bled out Dewey gutted and skinned it. He handles a knife like our family butcher in Holbaek. The smell of fried pork cheered the entire camp and most everyone got a piece.

Our tent is warming up. The kerosene lantern hangs from a rope down the center of the tent and Maren brought in an iron pot filled with hot coals. My feet are beginning to thaw; they scream painfully.

Each day we travel from seven to eight hours before stopping to make camp; there isn't much time for cooking and so we are back to eating hard tack and beans.

Night falls quickly out here—we pitched our tent as the last light faded and crawled in with our blankets. Outside the wagons are parked in a half circle and the oxen and horses are roped off to forage as best they can . . .

♥   ♥   ♥

Peter stopped writing to gaze at Maren; heavy coat, woolen stockings, thick, wooden clogs; every part of her bundled except her small hands. He felt a loving, protective urge toward her and wanted to take her in his arms, lay with her on their bedroll, and kiss her lovely mouth!

Maren was knitting so intently she barely glanced up at him.

"Everything all right?" he asked.

"Yes," she lied. She held up her work to examine it. "Other than missing a loop back there! I've got to undo two full rows to fix it."

She truly looked angry, and Peter wisely decided to return to his journal.

Most of these people were city dwellers; few among them can handle animals, but because of my farm experience I have been given charge of a team of horses. Maren rode on my wagon at first; however, being with child, she actually prefers walking. Her dress drags the snow and rubs her legs and I fear she'll become sick. But she's a stubborn girl and insists walking makes her feel better; once she sets her mind on a thing there is no arguing with her.

My wife is very prudent and while walking wears a big wooly coat and high buttoned shoes. All wrapped up and wearing thick mittens she appears very stout, but still leaves a tiny footprint! Conditions are harsh and women of this company have buried many a child. I've quit counting, but if I could I'd have the baby for her.

A hard wind slowed our progress today; stung our faces. Though it's gray and overcast we appear like we've been in the sun. We put an elderly couple and five little children aboard our wagon; we've no chance of getting lost from the others as the frozen river guides us. It appears a smooth white winding road lined with snow—covered bushes. Captain Osmond also gave us an old yellowed map.

We're camped in a valley out of the wind and as it's the Sabbath tomorrow, there will be no travel. Everyone needs rest, our oxen and horses too. All the animals are roped off and staked out among the trees. Dead grass is plentiful there; we gathered a few armfuls for bedding in our tent. There have been no deaths since we left the riverboat; it appears we're finally free of the cholera.

We should be in Winter Quarters in a week or better. I close this entry chilled to the bone, very tired but grateful to God for our blessings.

Peter leaned back slowly and stretched out his stiff limbs. He'd been sitting cross-legged, crouched over his writing, and had the overwhelming desire to stand straight but the tent was too low. He placed the journal in a leather pack, fastened the straps tightly then turned to face Maren again. She was likewise sitting cross-legged on the other end of their bedroll.

Except for her hands, which were still knitting, she was wrapped head to toe in a blanket.

"Needlework certainly keeps the hands warm," she said as she held up her work to inspect the place where the needle pierced.

"A sweater for the baby?" he asked.

"It's a blanket," she nodded.

"*JEG elske jer skat*. I love you, treasure." She didn't answer immediately. "Are you sure you're all right?" His breath hung in mid-air and he gently touched her cheek.

"I'm tired, Peter," she answered somewhat curtly. "I won't lie. But you are too."

"It was a long hard day," he agreed. "Hard on everyone."

The army surplus tent they had purchased was heavy canvas, claustrophobic and smelled of oil, but kept the weather at bay. It had been snowing for half an hour. Heavy flakes thickly blanketed the tent top, muffling the sound of their voices, and for a moment they were the only two people on earth.

"Why don't we get into our bed roll before we freeze to death," he said giving her a faint smile.

"I want to finish another row or two," she said somewhat distantly, "I want to finish this as soon as possible."

Certain that Maren was exhausted from the day's ordeal, Peter wondered why she hadn't crawled into their blankets long ago. Rarely short with him he sensed something amiss.

"The day's trek actually left me exhilarated," she sighed. "I'm unable to sleep just now . . ."

"There's something troubling you, isn't there?" he asked cautiously. Lowering her head even further Maren wouldn't look at him. Knit one, pearl two, her long knitting needles clicked rapidly. Peter marveled as he watched her deft little hands fly. He loved her hands; loved to hold them and loved when she held his.

"I've got to step outside for a minute," he said looking away. She didn't say anything.

Quickly opening and closing the tent flaps to keep the snow out, his footprints led behind a thick tree next to where the cattle were roped off.

While he relieved himself Maren put her knitting away. The damp, unfriendly close walls of the heavy canvas tent made her move cautiously so as not to bump them. Goose bumps pimpled down her body as she took off her coat, long dress and petticoats down to her underclothes. Only when in cotton underwear did she slide between the wool blankets. She lay like a marble statue in the cold, rough blankets patiently waiting for warmth to slowly pace itself through her body.

She wished for once it would hurry!

Shortly Peter was back inside and rubbing his hands together. "Burrr!" Peter exploded as he kicked off his snow-covered boots. "It's freezing out there!"

He hit them together to knock off the snow in a corner of the tent, then with his stiff fingers awkwardly fastened the ties of the tent flaps, cutting off the chill air. He then turned the wick down on the kerosene lantern and by its faint light undressed to his red flannel long-johns. Next he put his pants and Maren's long damp dress under his side of the blankets to dry. It was an old trick Torkil Olsen taught him and Hans back when they'd camped together. Many times Peter slept next to wet clothing only to wake up next morning not only to find it dry but warm as well.

Peter then slid in beside Maren and rolled his coat for a pillow, feeling as he did for Catherine's necklace in the lining. It was as natural to him as breathing and he was never satisfied until he was certain of his treasured inheritance's presence. Nor could he have slept!

"I feel so sorry for those ladies who have to sleep alone," Maren said absently as he lay close to her.

"It can't be pleasant," he agreed yawning wide and shivering. His eyes watered, his face was numb with cold and his feet felt like icicles. He moved as close to Maren as possible and at first her body felt so stiff he thought she was frozen. She seemed barely conscious of his presence.

"I feel sorry for *anyone* who has to sleep alone on a night like this," he said. "Even with the layer of dead grass you put down, the cold seeps right up through our blankets."

"Next time I'll gather leaves to put on the grass," she said a bit sarcastically.

They lay quietly together for a time, allowing their stiffened limbs to relax and for the goose bumps to smooth. If he hadn't have been so cold Peter would have noticed his wife wasn't snuggling affectionately against him, but just laying there as stiff as him.

"Peter," she said at length.

"Umm?"

Maren didn't respond immediately.

"What is it?"

"I have a question . . ." another lengthy pause. "Have any of the brethren been encouraging you . . . to . . ."

"To what?"

"T- to take an additional wife?" she blurted.

If it had been buried under ten feet of snow the tent couldn't have been more silent.

"Well," she pressed when Peter didn't answer, "have they?"

"Not exactly . . ." he answered reluctantly.

"That's what I thought," she said, the hurt plainly in her voice. "Gunda was telling us that Brother Wells had discussed that very thing with Claus and some of you men around the leader's camp fire last night and she's extremely upset, I don't mind telling you! She says Brother Wells flat out told Claus to consider taking one of the widows for a second wife. Is that true?"

"Brother Wells did speak with us about Celestial marriage," Peter offered reluctantly. "But it wasn't the first time. We men heard plenty about it aboard ship. It always sounded to me that only a few leaders practiced the principle. I never paid that much attention; there was little apparent need . . . but after what happened on Arsenal Island . . ."

"I know, I know . . . there are many widows amongst us!"

"That's not the compelling reason for celestial marriage and you know it, Maren. "You've heard the teaching same as I."

A long silence ensued. Like Peter, she *had* heard about "the new and everlasting covenant of marriage" before her baptism; it was written in the "Book of Commandments."[2] But she'd never read or studied it because there was no Danish translation of the book. And also like Peter, Maren believed plural marriage was only practiced by a few select Church leaders . . . but now it was beginning to sound like "they wanted every worthy man" to live the awful principle! And to Maren, sharing her life and her husband with another woman was indeed awful.

"It seemed so distant when I first heard about the principle," Maren admitted. "But now when it comes slapping me in the face . . . well . . . it's just too much!"

Peter nodded, but she wasn't looking at him. "Gunda told us there's a terrible contradiction in what we're being told and what is scripture! The Book of Mormon clearly states that a man shall have but one wife!" Maren fairly barked the last and didn't care if any of the tents pitched nearby could hear.

Peter lay there in misery and not just because he was cold. He knew that the Book of Mormon and the Holy Bible taught strict moral chastity but that during certain times during the development of mankind God had imposed plural marriage upon *certain people, and for a certain length of time,* (not upon everybody and not throughout time) and that under His law, God's law, plural marriage was chaste! He had to say something; Maren expected and deserved an answer, but this was all new territory.

"In the history of man there weren't a more righteous and chaste group of men than were Abraham, Jacob and Isaac," he started authoritatively. "All three men were completely loyal to their wives; there was no philandering, and no adultery. God instructed Sarah to give Hagar to Abraham, and God also gave Leah and Rachel to Jacob, and Isaac, who God also favored, had even more wives than Jacob. In no case did any of these men violate the laws of God and so the scriptures indicate, they always provided amply for their families."

Suddenly he sounds like a scholar on the topic, Maren thought to herself. *Peter **has** been thinking about it!* She felt like screaming at him.

"That wasn't the case with David, however," Peter continued knowledgeably. "David of old had also been given plural wives, but he *did* commit adultery when he lusted after Bathsheba. He even had her husband sent to the front lines of a hot battle where he was killed thus opening the way for him and his intended."

"I know the story," said Maren listening intently for even the slightest hint of desire, self-interest or pride from her husband at this point. He showed absolutely none but she could also tell he'd almost said his piece.

"David committed adultery, and murder as well by his actions, and consequently lost his eternal crown . . . a sad ending for such a brave man."

"For certain people living in Old Testament times plural marriage must have been sanctioned[3] by God," she stated, indicating she was still full of questions. "I'm sure of that Peter . . . but was it an order practiced only by the children of Israel and only for a specific time?"

"I'm not sure, but I certainly think so . . ."

"Did God ever command Israel to stop the practice Peter?"

"Umm, that sounds logical, then again I don't remember seeing that in the scriptures . . . but following your reasoning . . . which I believe is very sound; I'd say yes. And it stands to reason that if the practice was in fact removed from the earth by God, then He could certainly restore it again. Apostles, prophets, teachers, evangelists . . . the true order of things in the Lord's true church; and I suppose that includes plural marriage . . . are you cold, Maren?" he added.

"I'm fine," she said evenly, although the tent felt like an icebox and frosted breath accented her words.

"I'm sure that plural marriage wouldn't be restored to mankind in general Maren," Peter went on after a lengthy silence. It's supposed to be sacred, not to be trampled on by selfishness and lasciviousness." Then knowing how hollow, preposterous and pious this next might come out he added: "Just as in biblical times, only Israel is expected to live the law of plural marriage today; only members of the church guided by the Holy Spirit through God's chosen Prophets . . . now, just as in days of old."

"Humph," said Maren somewhat icily. The tent being as cold as her thoughts, she longed to snuggle up to Peter but her ragged feelings and torn emotions prevented her.

"Only a certain righteous few, will even attempt plural marriage Maren," he went on digging a pit he knew he'd never be able to climb out of. "And only men with the proper priesthood *authority* can perform the sacred ordinances. Men called, chosen, and set apart by General Authorities of the Church."

"Humph," she repeated barely audible.

Peter could scarcely imagine what must be going through her mind but Peter sincerely believed Joseph Smith was the Lord's chosen Prophet in the latter-days and he trusted that God Himself had revealed and sanctioned the doctrines Joseph taught as pure revelation, and true and correct principle. Plural marriage was clearly supported by God during certain times in the history of mankind and recorded in the Holy Bible; but furthermore, a single verse in the Book of Mormon also made the doctrine crystal clear: Jacob, Chapter 2 verse 30:

For if I will, saith the Lord of Hosts, raise up seed unto me, I will command my people; otherwise they shall hearken unto these things.

Peter now knew that particular scripture by heart. Trevor Wells had been teaching him and many others in the group.

Regardless of the above he loved Maren with all his soul and had no desire whatsoever to take a plural wife. God would have to reveal it to him and if that were ever to happen, agreement must also come from Maren. So he didn't worry, much less think about plural marriage. He knew Maren would never hear of such a thing, therefore neither would he.

"So what has all this talk from Gunda, have to do with me?" He asked Maren flatly.

The tent was again silent for a time. All that could be heard was the steady and rapid breathing of the occupants.

"Oh Peter," blurted Maren and very despondently. "Why would God impose such a law upon us?! I say it's simply *too* much to ask!"

She could feel Peter's discomfiture with her attitude, but Maren wanted to get things out in the open and put the distasteful subject behind them once and for all. Yes she had known plural marriage to be a teaching of the Church; and so had Peter, but it was such a distant thing, something that happened in a far away place, and certainly to other people. Neither she nor Peter had ever considered the principle would become an issue in their marriage. But now here they were in America and the principle of plural marriage was staring them smack in the face!

"In various times and sundry places," Peter went on, "God, as he sees fit, has imposed the doctrine upon the people of Zion, Maren. That's either true, or we're just like anybody else . . . ordinary people in an ordinary church rationalizing the laws we like and casting out those we don't."

"But I think plural marriage will bring misery upon our people," Maren interrupted.

"Perhaps," he said. "Human beings are what they are. No marriage is without problems," he added, yawning against the cold and bringing the covers up tighter under his chin. "But Trevor said that rich blessings are there for the church and its members for being obedient."

"Plural marriage will obviously build our numbers," said Maren, relenting slightly. "There's no doubt and I'm sure that's mostly what's behind it, but . . ."

"I don't think so, Maren. I'm told . . ."

"I don't want to hear it, Peter! Who can know the Lord's true purpose?"

Silence.

"Maren . . ." Peter said at length. "I can hardly keep my eyes open. Can we . . . discuss . . . this another time?"

"Will you want another wife, Peter?" She asked flatly.

"No. I have a wife," he said sluggishly, then kissed her on the fore-head. Rigid as a rock, she barely acknowledged the gesture. "I married a beautiful and intelligent lady . . ."

No comment.

"I've just got to get some sleep, Maren. Claus blows that bugle ear-lier every day . . ."

"We don't travel tomorrow," she reminded him.

Peter closed his eyes. This time he didn't respond. He knew Maren was far from satisfied, but his eyes felt like lead and he was having trou-ble finding words.

"I don't intend to take another wife, Maren. I love you more than life and am very happy the way things are." He rolled over and his bare hand touched the wet clothing beside him. He shivered and inched away.

"These clothes couldn't possibly be dry in the morning. Could they?"

She ignored him but reluctantly snuggled against him. Thick as the wool blankets were, she was still cold. "We need to get some Buffalo robes . . . I heard about them in Atchison."

"Don't have money," said Peter fading away. "High drifts today. We pulled those horses . . . through several high drifts . . ."

Peter fell dead asleep. Only his rising and falling chest told Maren he was alive. She should have been exhausted herself as she'd walked the entire way, but sleep evaded her. Her mind raced with wonder and fear. She lay in pitch-blackness for another hour wondering how a young girl from Copenhagen could have gotten herself into such a difficult situation.

Tears rolled down her cheeks, uncertainty surrounded her, and Maren offered a silent yet angry prayer to God asking how He could expect women to accept such a terrible teaching! No answer came, and had there been one, she was too troubled to receive it.

She tucked her chin and nose under the blankets, exposing just her eyes to the arctic night air, freezing her tears into tiny wisps of frost. A crack of light split the tent flaps, barely revealing diamond white snow-flakes disappearing silently. Other than an occasional snort from Peter breaking the silence, all was quiet.

She snuggled tightly against him. His hairy, muscled masculinity gave her a false feeling of security; she embraced him, smelled him, settled into his breathing rhythm; holding on to what belonged to her! She wanted to be under his skin, be one with him, and she didn't want to share him. With anybody! Physically a very strong individual, Peter was always so gentle with Maren; to her he epitomized righteous manhood.

Maren was warm now, but sleep still evaded her; too much to think about! With all the death and sickness they'd seen, with all they'd endured over the past two months, few thought of little else but survival.

Now this *principle* as Brother Wells had called it. Maren feared plural marriage more than she did cholera because with cholera came death, whereas with plural marriage life would be constant pain. Endured, bound to children and bound to a man who was bound to other women, not going anywhere, constantly serving . . .

Why would the Lord try women this way? she thought bitterly. *Ever since I heard about the principle—as members have began calling it—I've wished it would go away. But not so; it's here . . . I just pray I don't have to live it!*

That day as they'd trudged along, Gunda had said, "Just you watch, the leaders will have us all sharing our husbands!"

"Not me!" Maren had answered hotly. "The men aren't compelled to take more than one wife."

"She's right," Marjouri Coffey had piped in. "It isn'a for everyone."

Out here Maren wasn't certain. Everyone had to pull together and become like one huge family.

As she lay there, in her mind she suddenly saw the widow, Talitha Kjars, struggling with one of the tents. Then she saw Peter and Terrin helping her. Maybe she just imagined it, but hadn't Talitha been overly friendly with them as they made her camp? Wasn't she a little *too* appreciative to Peter after the tent was standing taut and ready for the night?

I've never seen them talk alone . . . maybe they have though . . . when I'm not around. With her platinum blonde hair and those lovely pale blue eyes, Talitha's such a beautiful woman. I'm certainly no match for her . . .

"I'll bet he's noticed!" she said aloud.

Maren bolted upright, astonished at her outburst. Frigid air immediately wrapped its arms around her, and Peter's hand groped absently for the blankets. Maren covered him and slid quickly back under the blankets hoping she *had* awakened him. She wanted to beat his chest and demand an answer, beg him to tell her how much he loved her and promise her he only wanted her.

"What ever is the matter with me!?" She said, again aloud.

Maren's possessive thoughts poisoned her, startled her; a quiet voice reminded her softly, distinctly, that as much as she wanted Peter only to herself—body and soul—he first belonged to God. *One cannot possess another; our bodies belong to Father in Heaven.* For just a brief moment Maren understood this. And if Father in Heaven had a purpose for something then she must trust it, and the only way she could trust in His purpose was to really know Him. The only way she could do this was to let go of rage, fear and jealousy.

If this thing, this religion, was something she couldn't deny—then it must be all or nothing. She must pour this toxic anguish upon the Lord. In this endless frigid night, she could not endure the idea of plural marriage a single moment longer. She needed to give her anguish up to Him!

Maren's tortured thoughts had exhausted her and suddenly, abruptly, she quit thinking all together. All mind activity ceased. Laying there in the stillness she became aware of herself, aware of her soul, and a deep feeling of peace, of truly letting go, washed over her.

Maren . . . peace be unto you . . . You are a most precious daughter unto me. A noble woman; I go before you; I am your rearward . . . You shall bare five souls with Peter during your sojourn in life and shall raise them unto me. Thy children will rise up and bless you.

Peter loves you. He will only bring good upon you, never harm. Walk with him, trust him . . . trust in **me.**

♥   ♥   ♥

Maren didn't hear a voice; rather a powerful, electric communication had engulfed her very being. It came from within her mind and heart powerfully, instantly becoming part of her. Like her rock-solid testimony of the restored gospel and the Book of Mormon, she owned her communication with God and could count upon it always.

He had spoken to her and she lay in awe, scarcely daring to breathe. She was wide awake and totally at peace with the world.

At length Peter mumbled something unintelligible. She put her arm around him, held him tight and at long last drifted off into sleep.

Outside the snowfall had nearly stopped. Fires were only black dents in the ground where they'd gradually sunk and died. Clouds thinned and a random star twinkled in the night sky. Snow-covered wagons sat patiently awaiting the day, and near the grove of trees overlooking the small tent city, cattle were laying with their legs curled up beneath them. Standing nearby, horses breathed steam into the night, raising a hoof now and again as they slept.

Chapter 2

Castle Gardens

atherine stepped off the rowboat on the shores of Castle Garden in New York Harbor and would have knelt and kissed the ground if she could have seen it! Crowds of people jammed the docks and more were stepping out of rowboats by the minute. There were five times more immigrants than she'd seen in Liverpool. A crushing throng; alarming! Top hats, round derbies, leather caps and bonnets bobbing like corks in the water, the packed crowd did serve to ward off the chill of early March.

Catherine Jensen, Evette Ericksen, little Hans, Casten and Otto Pedersen, Krista Holsen, and Anna Katrina Jensen, Catherine's granddaughter were bunched together in a knot holding tightly to each other as they were swept along toward an enormous rotund red granite building that once housed a fort[4].

Their trunks had earlier been taken by steam tug to a huge warehouse behind the fortress to be picked up after everyone had registered. Soldiers in Union Blue uniforms were everywhere, and the next thing Catherine knew they were ushering the people from her ship *The Carthage* toward the entry of the thick-walled fort and into a huge auditorium-like area in the center. From there everyone was squiggled into one of four long lines with a nurse and two official-looking men standing on opposite sides of a small table.

Catherine and company felt like potatoes mashed together in an enormous pot with more potatoes streaming through the double doors by the minute. The open area sounded exactly like the trading pit of the London Exchange; men shouting at their wives and children, babies crying, people with claustrophobia panting and gagging, while on the ground amid mothers nursing infants were elderly people looking as though they had given up hope.

Back a few rows of people, Catherine heard a retching and instantly smelled the inevitable sour stench of vomit. "Mercy, she's lost her breakfast!" a woman shouted. "Get some rags!" Instinctively the crowd parted like a small red sea, while dotted throughout the huge building with its arched entry ways, other immigrants stood on tip-toes looking for the source, somewhat bewildered, entirely suspicious and extremely protective.

How many times had they counted the heads of their children? "Where's Kathleen, where's little Jenny? Have you seen the baby?!" The building was dimly lighted by a large glass dome in the center and though it was still daylight, gas chandeliers around the perimeter were being lit by men with long lighted wick poles shouting, "Make way, make way!"

Catherine's legs felt like jelly in a jar, mush, and she felt trapped as she struggled to get her bearings; for a moment she thought she might be going mad. "I've never felt so confused," she confided to Evette.

"It's unbelievable," was her daughter in-law's reply. Catherine looked around and gratefully there was Otto Pedersen; tall, wide-shouldered, sure-of-himself Otto had become the strength of their little unit, a father figure to Evette and Krista and grandfather to both little Hans and Anna Katrina, their children. Pushed to and fro, Catherine felt somewhat helpless and she was becoming angry. Casten Pedersen on the other hand seemed to be enjoying herself.

What a huge new land! What an enormous and high ceiling! Nothing like this building existed in all of Copenhagen; the general feeling it gave was that of a huge carnival.

"How many ships have landed today, for heaven's sake?" Catherine demanded of Casten.

"I have no idea, but isn't it wonderful? Is there room enough in this country for all these people?"

"We should wonder!" Catherine answered, surprised at the volume in her tone.

All of a sudden a bald-headed man with a huge mustache cranked up a siren. People strained to see the source of the high-pitched scream, but shortly it became loud enough to shatter glass. Everyone put their hands to their ears, especially little children.

When the siren finally faded into a low growl, the little man picked up a long speaking trumpet. "All right then ladies and gentlemen . . . welcome to the United States of America!" The crowd stood still; a thrill swept across them, and a ripple of applause erupted into what sounded like a downtown playhouse in Copenhagen at the crescendo of a *Romeo and Juliet*. Thunderous applause!

The little bald-headed man looked around triumphantly; then as the noise abated, his demeanor changed to that of a storm warning. "You must show identification!" he barked. "Your birth certificate or christening document, your destination and occupation. After you pass the recording officers, women and girls to the left, men and boys to the right for medical scrutiny!"

What looked to have been a simple matter of making it through the long line ahead now became four hours on their feet, but at last Catherine, Evette, Casten and Krista with granddaughter Anna Katrina, collapsed on a long hard bench against the far wall of still another large room, waiting for Otto and little Hans to emerge from the medical examining area. Across from them was a long sign with letters plainly printed:

a b c d e f g h i j k l m n o p q r s t u v w x y z

A B C D E F G H I J K L M N O P Q R S T U V W X Y Z

Learn to read and speak English!

Catherine was just settling down when a lady seated exactly next to her said, "Mormons, eh?" She was Danish, therefore Catherine was taken back.

"I didn't see you on *The Carthage* did I?"

"No. I come on *The Yorkshire*. We anchored four ships away from yours, waitin' on the tugs like all the others."

Catherine felt ill at ease with the woman but decided to try and be cordial. "Yes, we're Mormon," she said pleasantly. "These are my friends, Casten, Evette, Krista, and my little granddaughter Anna Ka . . ."

"I really don't care to know any of you people," the stocky woman interrupted. "An' you won't find your welcome much better in America, either."

Catherine's eyes widened then she closed them and shook her head. When she looked up again not only the rough speaking lady, but several other women leaning forward on the bench, were waiting for Catherine's reply. The abrupt lady had allies, and before Catherine, Casten, or Krista—themselves leaning forward staring at the woman— could speak, the she continued her verbal assault.

"You people were once run outta' New York here, run outta' Ohio and Illinois too . . ." She next let fly a stream of foul language conclud- ing with: ". . . because you folks think you're so high and mighty, sooo exclusive!"

"Now wait just a minute here," Catherine had literally pushed up the sleeves of her coat. "You don't even know us! What do you mean we think we're exclusive?"

"You act so self righteous, pushin' your religion in everybody's face . . . that's what she means, lady!" a woman three places down blurted. In their dark heavy coats and winter bonnets the women bore a slight resemblance to a row of penguins.

"I'll handle this, Sarah Marie," the lead penguin stated as she abruptly turned to her. "I'll tell ya what I'm talkin' about..." she had turned back to Catherine, "...you people claim to be the Saints of God, exclusive somehow, an' I'll tell you that we're all God's children... every stinkin' one of us... and He answers our prayers same as he does yours!"

Every woman seated down from her vigorously nodded to each other then turned back to watch the action. There were also a number of little girls cross-legged on the floor with their arms folded glowering at little Anna.

Catherine had taken a deep breath. Where she at first felt she was back at the mill standing up to son Ferdinand, she had reached deep into her soul and knew she was about to speak for the Savior.

"That is true, dear sister," she said mildly. "We *are* all His children." And that's all she said. Catherine would never allow herself to even feel anger where any discussion concerning the Lord took place.

"An' there you are sitting like plump pigeons ready to head out West and become the brides of Brigham Young!"

Casten and Krista blanched at that. Catherine flushed; that didn't warrant a response and she gave none. Her eyes developed a softness rarely seen just one year ago. Evette, with her face in her hands, leaned over and cried softly while tough little Krista watched her daughter's grandmother with admiration. Casten Petersen grew sick of the whole thing and was about to rise from her seat and throttle the attacker. Catherine, sensing her dear friend's anger, reached back and placed a firm hand on Casten's knee.

"An' your cursed Gold Bible!" the woman spat. "We got a Bible; we don't need another Bible!" Her pinched face cut her circulation enough that veins bulged in her neck as the woman bore down. "Where do you people get off havin' another Bible? Answer me that!"

"We use the same Bible as you do," Catherine rebutted gently. "King James."

But her attacker would have none of it. She already had her speech memorized and one way or the other she was going to give it! "An' you don't drink wine, or chew . . . or smoke . . . you think you're so . . ." another ugly stream of profanity, "self righteous!"

"Alcohol causes more women to be beaten than any other single cause, dear sister." Tears fell gently from Catherine's eyes at that point. She couldn't speak for a moment and when she did her voice became even softer. "My husband is dead because of alcohol."

Verbally recalling Elias' drunken demise had the immediate effect of silencing her attacker momentarily, and the lady actually teared up . . . slightly. She took a breath to hold back tears. More women than she *or* Catherine realized slowly crowded around the debate, watching and waiting for more hostility. Realizing she was on stage the lady steeled herself.

"An' you Mormons think Joe Smith talked to God hisself, and now you think you're the only ones going to Heaven." The stout lady's voice had risen perceptively. "It just ain't so!"

"We don't think that at all, dear friend," Catherine stated mildly. "We believe every single man, woman and child will hear the Gospel of Jesus Christ. Even those who have died . . ."

"Humph." The lady's hair was streaked with gray and she wore it tightly in a bun. Her long dress and dark woolen coat buttoned clear to the neck mirrored a closed mind. She didn't understand what Catherine had just said at all, and many other women standing around missed it altogether. Perhaps it struck something familiar, something they longed to know, but were afraid to hear. Catherine instantly regretted making her last statement; that ground being far too sacred.

She'd said it a little too flippantly, this crowded zoo of a place being the wrong setting to even mention work for loved ones departed. Luckily nothing came of it. The women gathered around had all seen tears streaming gently down Catherine's cheeks. That was enough.

Being reminded of temple ordinances, a sacred and precious part of what the missionaries had taught her before being baptized, emotions swept over Catherine, and she knew the only answer was to be quiet. Little Anna Katrina was also red eyed as she watched her grandmother stand up to the mean lady.

"All I can say is it's going to go hard on you folks here in America," the woman pressed. "You'd do well to forget about your prophets and such an' get down to makin' it the same as us . . . any way you can."

"I know it's going to be hard on all of us ladies here in America," Catherine stated broadly, striking a chord in every woman present. At that she stood and picked up her granddaughter. "Good day to you madam . . . and good luck to you as well." The conversation was over. Catherine's attacker felt like melting into the crowd. She muttered something unintelligible and slunk down on her bench.

With her back to all of them, Catherine looked around at the high portholes in the thick walls of the castle or fort or whatever the British had built here in 1812. A battle had been fought on the premises this day without a shot being fired. Women's voices all around were soon chattering about what papers they had to sign to enter America, finding lodging for the night, wondering what people ate in New York and would their men find work in this crowded city. It was as if nothing had transpired.

Chapter 3

Peter and Maren

The morning broke clear and blue above an empty countryside as wide and far as the eye could see. Peter parted the canvas flaps of the tent and stuck his uncombed head out to survey the situation. Powdered snow crystals flew about glittering in the sun; the temperature was well below zero and the wind wasn't blowing. It would be a good day.

Returning inside, he stepped into his pants. One pant leg was still damp and would rub his leg raw before the day was over, but he and Maren had survived another night in the wilderness and everything else was minor.

With great effort he pulled on his unforgiving boots, awkwardly lacing their rawhide strings up the eyelets then tucking his pants into the tops military fashion. Peter pushed his calloused hands through wool gloves, grabbed a double-bit ax from the tent corner and stepped into the morning, leaving Maren curled up in a ball under the blankets.

Shortly a crisp *whack* sounded through the grove as he found a dead tree suitable for fire. A rapid succession of *whacks* followed, then a distinct cracking noise, followed by a muffled thud, which echoed slightly off the hillside. Other men were approaching the grove and soon their axes were likewise busy.

Peter split a few logs, cut up some kindling, then stopped chopping and took in several deep breaths of air. His heart was pumping rapidly; he felt strong and fully invigorated. It was good to be alive, to be away from the Mississippi River and from Arsenal Island!

While he rested on his ax, Peter's breathing slowed, the sweat on his face began to evaporate, and he looked over the vast territory surrounding him. What a beautiful land —wild, untamed and beautiful; untouched. He knew he could fall in love with America. He stooped down, loaded his arms with wood, and returned to the tents and knelt near a burned-out fire. With a gloved hand he scooped away the top layer of ash until he felt warmth from the deep embers.

Peter dug further, being careful not to burn his gloves, and noted with satisfaction the coals were still hot enough from last night's fire to start another. Placing some fine kindling shavings first, he built a small tepee of sticks and blew carefully until an orange glow developed, igniting the shavings.

Soon a strong fire crackled and spat, needing several trips back to the grove to feed it. *Better to travel on such a cold day,* he mused as he crouched by the fire. His leg muscles were beginning to tighten and his back stiffen. *Better to keep moving,* he thought.

"*Goddag God Morgan*, good morning," Jergen Madsen called from the tent he and Trevor Wells shared. Ten yards from the fire it looked like a little house with its roof sticking out of the snow. "Can I join you?"

"Bring your coffee pot," said Peter.

Madsen ducked inside the tent and rustled about, knocking snow off the top, exposing olive drab canvas and was soon back at the fire.

"I'm glad to be out of there," he exclaimed as he filled the coffee pot full of snow. "It sagged so low it was like sleeping in a cave . . . nice fire."

"It will be," said Peter. "Let it burn down a bit before you put the pot on."

"I'm glad for a day of rest, Peter," said Jergen, stretching his arms then folding them tight about his chest. "I don't care if it is cold. The animals need rest, too."

"Especially the animals," agreed Peter. "But I'd like to continue until we get there. I don't care if it is Sunday."

"I don't think these people share your sentiments," said Madsen as he packed more snow into his pot to melt. "They aren't used to all this. They need time to get their clothes dry . . . prepare some decent food . . . besides we've covered lots of miles!"

Soon Claus Wangsgaard came to the fire, and then Trevor Wells joined them while all around camp people were stepping out of their tents and moving slowly about. Very shortly, axes were heard hacking away throughout the forest and fires began to crackle throughout camp. Men gathered wood for all the campfires; some liked to cook, but mostly women tended the blazes in preparation of breakfast.

The haste of a normal travel day was lost in the steady, methodical activity of cooking, eating, and arranging the camp. Laughter rippled here and there amid occasional calling for children to come to breakfast. Rope lines were strung near the fires for hanging wet clothing, snow was cleared and grass gathered for the animals, and more cut wood brought in.

Camp was bustling! The sun rose into a pale yellow ball and the day began to manifest itself under a high thin cloud cover that had moved in from the north. It would remain an iron cold and quiet Sabbath day, typical for January in Kansas.

As Peter's fire burned down, Jergen took his ax and using its head as a shovel, prepared a flat place on a bed of glowing coals. He then placed his coffee pot down while adding more snow as the contents melted down. He soon had a full pot of water.

"My mother always said the second snow is cleanest," commented Trevor Wells.

"This must be at least the tenth," said Jergen.

"At least," said Claus.

Shortly Peter's tent cracked open and Maren popped out. Her feet crunched the snow as she approached the fire.

"God Morgan, Maren," said Peter smiling broadly at her.

"God Morgan, Peter," she said, her breath floating gently about her mouth like puffs of steam. She kissed him lightly upon the cheek. "And Brother Madsen," she said, nodding his way. "How are you?"

"Cold but warmin' up," he answered, his eyes enviously glancing Peter's direction.

"I'm going to see how Elizabeth fared the night," Maren then said. "I'll be back to fix breakfast in a while." Peter thought he heard her humming quietly as she headed off.

"She didn't have much to say this morning, did she, Peter?" said Trevor. "Is she angry with you?"

Peter shrugged his shoulders. "I don't think so . . . at least she wasn't last night . . ."

"I know how that goes," said Claus.

"All women are the same," said bachelor Jergen Madsen. "Changeable as the weather."

Peter didn't comment. He didn't like the old cliché and watched as Maren made her way toward Elizabeth's tent. A sizzling sound turned his attention to the fire. The water had started to boil.

"There she goes," said Jergen Madsen cheerfully. "Time to add the grounds."

He removed his old tin pot, spooned in some coffee from a Mason jar then placed the pot back on the hot coals. It quickly returned to a boil and he let it roll for a few minutes before taking it from the fire.

"Now add just a little snow to sink the grounds," he said cupping a handful of clean white crystals from a place nobody had stepped. He sprinkled the snow over the brewed coffee where it quickly melted and most of the grounds did, in fact, sink. Except for a few which stubbornly floated around the edges of the pot, the coffee grounds sunk like tiny lead weights, straight to the bottom.

"And there you have it, gentlemen," said Madsen proudly, "perfection!"

The men held their cups out and Jergen poured. In the frosty morning the smell and taste of the hot coffee revived them. Nothing but a good washing could revive their clothing; Peter's rumpled trousers looked like he'd slept in them for a month and Jergen's were filthy. Both wore black woolen coats and English leather caps and had heavy beards.

All the men wore high-topped leather boots and in his pinstriped pants, trimmed beard and an old Prince Albert coat, only Trevor exhibited a faint look of civilization.

After sipping half a cup, Peter put his by the fire's edge. "I'll finish this later," he said. "I'm going to gather grass for my team. Anyone want to come along?"

"I'll be there in a minute," said Claus as Peter started away. "First let me get another cup of Jergen's brew." He squatted near the smoking coals to pour.

"Coffee will never replace good English tea, old chap," said Trevor.

"I don't know about that," beamed Claus. "This tastes pretty fine."

Jergen smiled; he was proud of his coffee. "Haven't you heard," he teased. "Americans have sworn off of tea. Something about a war with England ..."

"They don't know what they're missing," defended Trevor Wells curtly, neither man being aware that coffee *and* tea, were no longer approved of by Church leaders. They talked a bit longer, and then Trevor poured the last of his brown dark brew into the snow.

"I'm going to help Peter with the fodder," he said. "I want to have a talk with him."

In a knoll of the forest near his team, Peter was clearing away the snow to gather some dead grass. His gloves quickly soaked through and the cold hard work taxed him. Presently Trevor joined in and helped carry the grass to Peter's team.

"They're powerful animals, Brother Wells," Peter said patting a huge Clydesdale on the withers. A shudder rippled along and down the side of the magnificent animal and Peter placed a handful of grass under its steaming nostrils. "These are the kind used for plowing."

"I don't see how you dare get so near," Wells said respectfully. "And I don't see how you handle them so easily."

"There's really nothing to it; you approach them confidently and feed them plenty, especially when they're working."

"I taught school for ten years in Leeds before they made me Headmaster," said Wells. "The closest I ever got to a horse was when a rented carriage took me and my wife to the opera; wages being what they were, that wasn't too often."

The horse pawed the ground with a massive front hoof as if to acknowledge he was being discussed. "Cropped grass crusted in ice . . . quite a treat for old dobbin here," Peter said as he dropped grass within easy reach of the animal. "You know, Brother Wells, Maren has certainly been in Elizabeth's tent a long time. I thought I'd hear her calling me to breakfast by now. I wonder what they're talking about."

Trevor scrunched his mouth as they looked across the way at the tent in question. He shrugged his shoulders and opened his hands as if his pockets were empty.

"We had a hard talk last night, Brother Wells," Peter continued, "about what you told the men yesterday in meeting . . . you know, celestial marriage."

"Right," said Trevor. "And what did Maren have to say?"

"Let me ask you something, Brother Wells," Peter said pointedly. "Would you take an additional wife?"

The question wrinkled Trevor's forehead like a scrubbing board.

He looked at his feet and tamped a level spot in the snow with the toe of his left boot. "If it was God's will for me I would, Peter. And since you asked, plural marriage happens to be the reason my wife and I are separated at the present time. When I told her that I wanted us to immigrate to Zion she rebelled against me. She said once in Utah it wouldn't be long before I'd want a second wife and if that were ever the case she'd divorce me.

"I was only able to cool things off by leaving on this journey. I'm hoping when I return our situation will be improved, but I'm not counting on it. Plurality of wives may be ordained of God, but the first wife must agree . . . must have a testimony of it."

"Plural marriage is not practiced in England by church members, is it?" asked Peter.

"No," said Wells, "it isn't . . . although some missionaries I've met had more than one wife. Only apostles and a few select men can even perform the ordinance, and in my opinion a person needs to be in Zion for that to happen. Even there the principle must be an enormous sacrifice for people."

"I can't even imagine."

"Are you thinking of taking another wife, Peter?"

"No, Brother Wells, I'm not. I think I understand what the Lord is trying to accomplish, but that's where I draw the line. Maren would be heartbroken if I told her I wanted another wife. I love the church with all my soul, but plural marriage is not for me."

"It's a most difficult thing to be sure," said Trevor hesitantly. "My wife wouldn't speak to me for a week after I told her we should leave England . . . she told me the whole reason I wanted to go was to get another wife. Which is not the case, I might add."

"Having more than one wife means having more than one family of children; you know what I'm saying? I wonder how the leaders of the church manage," said Peter shaking his head. "President Young and the others."

"Some of them don't practice the principle of plural marriage," replied Trevor. "I've heard stories. Others thrive under it; I've heard that as well."

Peter stooped and picked up another handful of hay and fed it directly to the horse they were standing near. Like a warm stove, the heat the huge animal gave off seemed to take the edge off the weather.

It would be terribly uncomfortable having more than one wife, Peter thought to himself. *How would one wife feel if she saw her husband kissing the other?* He deeply felt the pain it would cause. *The brethren must be quite remarkable men . . . and the women who become their plural wives equally remarkable. Why would a woman willingly give her husband to another?*

Like Maren, all women are remarkable . . . he smiled as he thought of her. *Almost all women that is.* At that, Peter thought of Krista Holsen. *A dark little lady if ever there was one. Of all women, Ferdinand's lady is one I hope I never see again.*

America's Civil War cost hundreds of thousands of men to die, Peter's thoughts continued, *and created many thousands of widows, but the law of celestial marriage was given long before their war started . . . 1838 or so. It wasn't given because of an imbalance of men in the population then . . . I guess it does make some sense now . . . but we're hated because of it. Why would the Lord place such a burden upon this people?*

"Marriage in the new and everlasting covenant doesn't *require* all men to have more than one wife, Peter," Trevor interrupted his thoughts. "In fact it really involves just one. No man can enter into the fullness of glory being single.

"As it goes, I wouldn't trade my wife for any two others. She's a very fine woman and the mother of my children . . . I'm truly hoping to reconcile when I return to England."

They talked for another half hour.

By ten o'clock that morning everyone had finished breakfast and were gathered for Church services held in the center of camp. As they sang hymns and listened to the business of the past week, Maren stood hand in hand with Peter. He knew she was hurting and intended to talk with her further as soon as possible.

A pock-faced, skinny little Englishman named Jonathan Allmet was the first speaker His subject came from Matthew the twelfth chapter, wherein the Savior proclaimed himself the Lord of the Sabbath and where He'd incurred the wrath of the Pharisees for healing a man with a withered hand on the same.

"And he said unto them, *What man shall there be among you, that shall have one sheep, and if it fall into a pit on the Sabbath day, will he not lay hold on it, and lift it out?*

"You'll find that in the fourteenth chapter of Luke verse five." As usual, the English speakers, with their proper accents and rapid fire delivery, had Peter in linguistic mire. Normally Trevor Wells' labored Danish translation helped, but this day Peter's mind was elsewhere.

A Danish speaker named Hansen was speaking from the parables of Christ next, ". . . and blessed are the pure in heart for they shall see God," he was saying mildly when Peter's mind happened upon his words. "And blessed are the peace makers . . ."

Peter saw a tear trickle down his little wife's cheek. She loved the Lord more than life itself. So did Peter. Why indeed would He impose this difficult teaching called celestial marriage and spoil their peace? Why indeed. "Better to be obedient than to sacrifice," he could hear Trevor's words from the Old Testament as they had fed the horses.

We've given so much for this gospel; left our families, our country. And when my dear mother passes this life, Ferdinand gets the mill! I think we've given enough. I'm not going to live this polygamy thing and I need to convince Maren of that.

The meeting progressed, and people shifted from one foot to another tramping the snow underfoot until the area appeared as a huge room with a bumpy white rug covering the floor, but despite the chill of the morning hearts were warm and light.

In the business portion of the meeting, Trevor told them that according to the map they'd be in Winter Quarters in a week; that news plus words of Christ lifted everyone's spirits. After the closing prayer people clustered in small groups to talk for a while, but soon returned to their campfires.

The sun moved higher and softened the snow, and people kept warm by keeping busy. Fires were burning brightly everywhere as women and girls cooked extra food for the trail, hung clothing to dry, knitted and watched while children played in the snow. Cold and wet from snowballing, they went back and forth between camp fires while their fathers and older brothers repaired tents and wagons and cleared snow for prairie grass to gorge their livestock.

After the evening meal, the immigrant pioneers scrubbed their tin cookware with handfuls of dirt and snow, bedded their animals, gathered for evening prayer meeting and retired early. Ahead was another week of constant slogging. Tents and wagons glowed from the light of kerosene lanterns amid the sounds of children's giggles, then as night fell and temperatures dropped, one by one they became dark and silent.

Lying next to Maren, Peter gently placed his hand over her slightly protruding stomach. "How is the baby?" he asked tenderly.

Maren rubbed his knuckles and tears welled in her eyes. "I thought you'd completely forgotten."

"How could I?"

"You've not mentioned a thing . . ." He felt a tear trickle on his arm.

"You are the silliest girl . . ."

"Do you think I'm pretty, Peter?"

He kissed her tenderly. "Your cheeks taste salty . . . why would you wonder, Maren? Why would you ever wonder? Of course I think you're pretty. You're beautiful! When I first saw you in Norre Park I felt my heart jump. Shopkeeper's daughter, hard working and what conversation! I'd been so engrossed in my studies I could barely speak to people anymore; you opened my mind."

"Last night I couldn't sleep, Peter. All I could think of was plural marriage. I knew I couldn't stand it if you wanted another wife."

"I thought we covered this."

"Elizabeth and I discussed the *principle* somewhat. She has strong opinions... but she gets amused at my broken English; it gets worse when I'm emotional.

"Elizabeth is wise. Every talk with her brings something new. With the loss of her husband, her mother, and her daughter, she should be a very bitter person. Instead she has turned her life over to healing and helping people. Like me with English. I'm doing well, by the way. I understood much of Brother Allmet's talk today."

"I wish I could say the same... but there are so many Danish people where we're going I won't need English," replied Peter.

"You spend too much time with Claus Wangsgaard and Jergen Madsen. Of course you'll need English." Peter was surprised when Maren snuggled closer to him.

"There isn't enough Trevor Wells to go around. You're lucky to have Elizabeth."

"I am," she agreed.

They were warm and alone and awake. The tension of the night before had dissipated and Peter wondered why. It appeared they were finished with the painful subject of plural marriage. It felt so wonderful being in each other's arms, and shortly one thing led to another. They made love to each other that night; gentle, caring, long, full and sharing with a memorable crescendo to each. When it ended they kissed each other repeatedly and fell asleep in each other's arms. Just the two of them, their unborn child nestled safely in Maren's womb.

Chapter 4

Torkil

*T*orkil Olsen stepped out of his cabin and took a deep breath of crisp winter air. With a thumb in each loop he pulled his suspenders over his heavy woolen sweater and went back inside to put on his coat and gloves. All the animals but one had survived the brutal season so far, and unable to afford wasting an once of anything of substance the dead calf was butchered, wrapped in leaves and mud, then cooked buried under a huge bed of hot coals.

We haven't done so badly out here, Catherine Jensen's former employee mused as he walked briskly toward the barn with a milk pail swinging in his hand. *Uncle Sebastian and my sons, Emil and Paul, have worked very hard.*

He was still amazed by the whirl of events that led him into his current situation in the small village of Madison, Wisconsin (they'd never made it to Moorhead, Minnesota as originally planned). First the long trek, then the week after they had arrived in Wisconsin, he'd found an abandoned log cabin in which to live, and not only that but he'd secured a job at a small cheese-making facility in town. Considering the fact that winter was in full swing these accomplishments done in such short order were truly miraculous.

The smelly little cheese factory consisted of two cast iron vats, four cheese presses, a few bolts of cheese cloth, half a barrel of paraffin and a series of cheese molds. Its owner, an elderly man by the name of Abraham Swenson, ran the place with his wife Isabelle and a workman everyone called Steed, and eked out a comfortable living.

There were two other cheese factories—if you could call them that—nearby, but with new settlers coming in steadily, each business survived. A recent stroke left Abraham partially paralyzed, and he needed a man like Torkil Olsen badly; thus the former miller took the job with joy and humility. In the course of a month he understood the process of making common Farmer's Cheese—Abraham's main stay product—and he'd met several dairymen and farmers who supplied Swenson with milk.

Little money changed hands, as most often farmers took finished cheese in exchange for their excess milk production; however cash was also part of the operation, especially when dealing with larger dairymen.

In the middle of Torkil's second month at the tiny cheese making facility—a building consisting of one twelve-foot by ten-foot room and a tiny office—Isabelle Swenson showed up at work with the horrific news that husband Abraham had died in his sleep. She gave Torkil the details, hurriedly, almost like a eulogy in a newspaper; then surprised him with an offer to own the tiny operation. With dry mouth and reeling mind, the former miller stood and listened while his deceased employer's wife summarized with the following:

"I don't want much for the place; in fact you can work most of it out . . . Mister David Steed here doesn't have sense to run it, but I think it would be a shame to close the business down. Don't you, Mister Olsen?"

"I-it would be a shame, madam," said Torkil sadly. "But what are you saying?"

"I'll explain in a moment," Isabelle stated shakily. Steed hadn't flinched when she'd figuratively hit him in the stomach and doubled him over, but the next thing she said stood him back up again.

"Now, David knows the recipes around here, there are just two or three, but he knows how to make others. And he's a very good worker...one of the best. I wouldn't want to see him without a job..."

"Oh right," agreed Torkil, "he shouldn't have to lose his job; and yes he is very knowledgeable..."

"But he doesn't have any money, do you, David?"

"No, ma'm..."

"Or any place to get any..."

"No, ma'm, I don't," David Steed said, again with little emotion.

"So what I'm saying here, Mister Olsen is that if you can round up eight hundred dollars this business is yours."

It had all happened so fast Torkil's mind was still spinning. He had three hundred dollars to his name; a goodly sum, but determined to only use fifty of it (who knew what might come up), he drew up a contract to secure another four hundred and fifty from his uncles, two hundred twenty five from Sebastian, two hundred twenty five from Jonathan, and ended up giving the widow Swenson five hundred cash and a note for the balance.

Small operation though it was, four months into America Torkil Olsen and his uncles were in business for themselves. But being older than Torkil, Jonathan quickly found he couldn't abide taking orders from his nephew, especially knowing he'd put in nearly five times more money than Torkil, and after one particularly tense confrontation, Jonathan decided he wanted his money back.

It had come to blows, but Torkil being a powerful man twenty-two years younger than his uncle, could, if he'd have wanted to, killed him. As it was, the mighty Thor (a knick-name given him in Copenhagen) knocked Jonathan down before getting him in a painful bear hug around the chest, where suffocation and fear stopped Jon's struggling.

Torkil released his uncle, leaving him blue-faced in the snow, and what amazed him—the victor—was that Sebastian, Jonathan's brother, had not jumped to his aid.

"I'm done with you, Torkil!" Jonathan gasped as he got to his feet. Blood dripped red from his nose and only a trace of breath escaped his lungs. His chest burned from lack of oxygen and his hair was tangled in icy snow. "I'm done with the stinking cheese business, too! There'll be no more milk from my stock . . . and I will get my money back."

"Can't you understand," pleaded Torkil, "your money's all tied up!"

"Come on, Seb! Let's leave this place. Get away from here!"

"Not goin' with you, Jonathan," Sebastian said as he looked down and shuffled his feet. "Not goin'."

"You're not going?" Jon growled picking up his hat. "And why not?" He demanded.

"Because you're wrong on this one, Jon. I'm gonna be working here and I'll see you get your capital back . . . I'll see to it."

Jonathan's breathing was erratic. He glared at his brother momentarily then turned on his heel and walked toward his horse. "So you say, brother. But I'll never have anything more to do with him or anyone who does!" He stubbed his finger menacingly toward Torkil and had the finger been a gun the former miller would be dead.

"Hang on, Jon," Torkil pled. "We've been through a lot together. I'll get you the money, soon as I can. Don't let it be the cause of you two separating!"

"His choice," said Jon sourly as he mounted his horse.

"Hold on, Jon," Torkil said making one last plea. "I'll make you a deal. You said you wanted to own that section of land I claimed down by the creek for Hedelius' cows . . ."

"What about it?" The horse snorted as Jonathan drew back the reigns.

"Your two hundred an' twenty-five dollars left with the widow when she moved to St. Paul. Give up your portion of the business and you can take my claim."

Jonathan held the reigns back. He knew a bargain when he heard it, but pride and anger stole his clarity. "I've had my say. I want cash money and that's final. Keep your land, creek, pond and all. There's ten thousand little lakes around here. And run your cheese business any way you choose . . . I want nothing to do with it!"

At that Jonathan kicked his horse, cursed his brother and Torkil again, and started away.

"I think it's a generous offer, Jon," Sebastian called after him.

"There's plenty of land out here, Seb." Jonathan called over his shoulder.

Torkil hadn't seen his uncle for two weeks but knew the issue was *far from over*. He sighed heavily recalling that terrible day.

More trouble followed the next day when the owner of the building which housed the cheese factory came calling.

"All she sold you was the business, friend. This here building belongs to me, and I want you out of it. My agreement was with Abraham, and him bein' dead an' all, I've rented the place to someone else."

The man spoke Danish, and after a heated exchange finally agreed to let Torkil stay in the building until the end of the month; that being said and done Torkil came to a clear understanding that all he (and Sebastian) got for the eight hundred dollars (five hundred down and three on a note) were two iron vats, two bolts of cheese cloth, three cheese presses, several wooden molds, and a few yellowed cheese recipes. Also—if they could pay him—a worker named David Steed.

Jonathan wanted his money, the landlord wanted his building, and by month's end Torkil and Sebastian—along with their faithful employee, David Steed—loaded up the iron vats, the cheese molds and everything else and set up shop in Torkil's barn.

♥   ♥   ♥

It was now late February, and the muddy path leading into the barn was the only visible bare ground around Torkil's cabin. Surrounding fields still rolled in white-blanketed snow, keeping temperatures just below freezing, and conditions were ideal for fermenting cheese while avoiding spoilage.

A hay stack left by former residents kept Torkil's Holstein cows chewing their cud and producing milk and coupled with Sebastian's small herd, along with milk small farmers brought by, the fermentation vats would be perking until Spring.

Making cheese was to Torkil much the same as milling flour and satisfied an inner need he had to serve mankind. Cheese, like bread, was essential to life and he was proud to be in the business of making it. Like bread, everyone ate cheese. Milk spoiled quickly during hot summers, whereas cheese lasted for months—especially when kept in cool dry dirt-cellars.

Most settlers knew how to make cheese, but like soap, producing quality cheese took time and detail. Get too busy with the horses, other livestock or gardening, and all you had was spoiled milk. Leaving livestock duties to his sons, Emil and Paul, Torkil, along with Sebastian and Steed, spent their time making Farmers Cheese, a relatively easy product to produce.

Looking back on the fight with Jon, other than splitting the profits, Jonathan really had little interest in helping build a cheese business. His heart was in raising cattle; oxen too. More and more people were going west and Jonathan anticipated a brisk market for beasts of burden, but it took land and plenty of it.

The rift between Torkil and Jon Olsen would soon end. The land in question consisted of twenty acres with frontage on a tiny creek which fed a pond—one of hundreds in the surrounding area—and giving it to Jon in exchange for his investment in the cheese business truly was a good deal. But the mighty Thor didn't feel so mighty when he thought back on the fight with his uncle. Surely there were better ways to settle a disagreement. At last he shrugged his shoulders, stepped into the barn and began milking. "Uncle Jonathan will come around," he said assuredly. "His pride is just in the way."

Torkil still couldn't believe his uncle Sebastian had sided with him. The youngest of three brothers, the big patient man reminded Torkil of his own father both in resemblance and attention to detail. Making cheese took careful attention and fit Sebastian's temperament perfectly.

Seb's verbose and repeated words of others didn't bother Torkil. Having the big man around was like getting a second chance to hear something he might have missed. And Torkil liked Seb's wife, too. Lucille Olsen had Scandinavian written all over her substantial blonde frame. Fair skinned, tall, she'd been beautiful as a girl . . . now, like Seb, she stooped a bit, yet had a sharp mind and trusted Torkil's judgment more than her brother-in-law, Jonathan's.

Surely God led us here, thought Torkil. *We worked like dogs on the journey; but finding all these abandoned cabins was truly miraculous!*

The cabins had been owned by a lumber milling company gone bankrupt and abandoned by former employees; lumberjacks, pit workers, mechanics, cooks and the like had packed up and left. Pioneers trickling in to the abandoned community were grabbing up the best of them, leaving those with caved-in roofs and dilapidated dwellings such as lean-tos for late arrivals.

There hadn't been anyone here for at least a year, and how I got to this precious barn before anyone else on the wagon train is another miracle . . .

He remembered how a light snow storm had obscured the day, and driving his wagon while exploring the forest where ax and saw had felled hundreds of trees, Torkil instinctively followed a small creek and coming to a hillside, there it stood: Big, gray and beautiful, completely abandoned; only a broken old plow spoke of past activity. The large barn needed repairs and completely hid a cobwebbed cabin on the other side.

His adrenaline running like a faucet, Torkil parked his team, ran to the barn, then to the cabin and soon discovered a winding road leading up the small hill from the other direction. Why hadn't anyone else come that way? He didn't know, but first-come first-serve is what everyone agreed upon before they drove their wagons around the area looking for a place to live.

Now the barn was a cheese factory with six fine Holstein cows as residents. Torkil paused and looked heavenward. "Thank you Jesus," he said aloud.

♥   ♥   ♥

"The rift between Torkil and Jon was bound to have happened," Lucille was telling Sebastian that morning. "They fought all the way from New York to Wisconsin. One night I thought they would kill each other; it scared me. It was wisdom leaving the crowded tenements in New York, and wisdom when Torkil bought the cheese business. He'll be rich one day, watch and see. We all could be rich."

The childless couple were having hot tea in a cabin they were fixing up, located not half a mile from Torkil's, and having a rare discussion about their business partner. "We need better presses," Sebastian ventured. "Torkil came across a Sears & Roebuck catalog in town yesterday with all kinds of things in it. All kinds of things."

"Then you two should get what you need," said Lucille. "I've always said we've been blessed by Torkil's leadership. Finding this old settlement . . . we were out in the cold, Sebastian; we could'a spent the entire winter in our wagon. A miracle pure and simple!"

"And the barn on Thor's place," said her husband. "It's sizable. What a blessing! Where would we be without it? We got the vats set up there, and we're making cheese. Making cheese!"

Half a mile from Lucille and Sebastian's cabin, the object of their discussion was still outside his barn counting his blessings. Gently rolling hills amongst a vast and generally level landscape; he could only imagine what this country would look like in the spring. Even though everything was so frozen over, he had some idea that the land was dotted with thousands of lakes and ponds. Many of them were spring-fed, whereas most were the result of their close proximity to the behemoth, Lake Michigan!

A dairyman cattleman's and cheese maker's fondest dream, Wisconsin's rich topsoil, millions of acres of lush grasses and ample water to keep things green were like nowhere else on Earth!

♥   ♥   ♥

"Everybody knows how to make plain everyday Farmer's Cheese," Torkil confided to Sebastian, Emil, Paul and Steed the next day. "But starting Summer we'll be making another type of cheese—a rich, meaty, satisfying Danish blue cheese. In a month I'll show you an experiment I've had going. If everything turns out as I want, we'll have two types of cheese to sell people."

"We only have so many cows between us. How much of the yield do you plan to use on the blue cheese?" asked Steed, a cautious man.

"About half," said Torkil confidently.

"That's a big gamble," repeated Sebastian, "a big gamble."

"What ever it is, if you can make it," said Emil with enthusiasm, "I can sell it."

"*We* can sell it," corrected Paul.

"Now I want to fill you men in on my plans for the day," Torkil continued. "That is if I can trust you to keep working after I leave." He winked at that, but Sebastian could sense something serious in the wind.

"Where are you headed?" he asked.

"To see your brother . . . my uncle, Jonathan."

"Don't you think it's a little soon? It hasn't been that long since he stormed away from here. He was pretty mad at you, Torkil . . . pretty mad."

"That he was, but I can't help it. This thing is like a boil under my saddle and I'm finished worrying about it. The offer I made him is fair enough but I'm willing to sweeten the pot a little. What would you think about my offering him a portion of our profits for a year or two; at least until he's doubled the money we owe him? Say we go twenty five percent or so, just till he's paid off?"

"There may not be any profits the first two years," said Sebastian rolling his eyes over toward Steed. "No profits at all."

"Hey, keep me out of this, man," said Steed. "I don't even know your brother."

"Just watchin' your reaction, boy. Like I said, there may not be much profit, Torkil . . . then what?"

"If it takes us five years to turn a profit—but it won't—then so be it," said Torkil. "I'll just tell Jonathan we will split with him until he's got his money back twice over. What about that?"

"I like it," said Sebastian after a minute or so. "This community is too small to be havin' any bad blood in it. Especially in families. Too small."

"That's where all the bad blood is," offered Steed. "Families."

Both Torkil and Sebastian ignored him. "Tell him like you said, Thor . . . we'll split the profits until he doubles his stake in the business. That way you don't have to give up your land. Like Jon said, there's a bunch of land out here. He didn't have any respect for yours; either that or you'd be just too close a neighbor for him."

"That's what it was," said Torkil. "Jonathan's a funny duck. He likes to be in charge of things and when he can't be, he wants space from those he can't rule. I saw that on the way here. Him and me were like two cats in a bag. Scratchin', always tryin' to best one another and then not speaking for a day or so . . ."

"Lucille and me was talking about that just yesterday morning."

"Well then if you two men promise not to burn down the barn while I'm gone . . . I'll find Jon and give him the offer. Wish me luck."

♥   ♥   ♥

Torkil found Jonathan out near a rickety hay barn tending to a cow. His place consisted of four small square pens surrounded by a two-board fence, two pens being empty and two muddy ones with four black and white cows tramping about. Nearby was a pile of wild hay mixed with dead grasses dusted white with snow but hollowed out brown where his uncle had been at it.

Somehow Jonathan had acquired a few scraggly chickens which were at that time pecking about the hay stack, and just beyond that lay a log cabin with an open shed attached. A stack of cut wood and a smoking chimney announced there was life inside.

As Torkil rode up, his uncle had his back to a large Holstein's rump and had its hoof held fast between his legs while he examined it.

"Be careful there, that old girl will kick you into next week!" Torkil greeted him.

"If she does we'll all be having beef steak tonight," Jon said not turning to face the familiar voice. "Throwing out an olive leaf are you, Torkil?"

"Maybe a branch, Uncle."

"I'm too tired to fight with you, Torkil. I was up with this one all night."

"Sorry to hear that, Uncle Jon," said the former miller turned cheese-maker. "But about fighting, I feel the same way . . . and I got to thinking about what you said."

"About me not wanting anything to do with cheese?"

"No. About there being plenty of land out here . . ." He blew a cloud of steam as he surveyed the surrounding area. Leafless trees near a frozen pond promised shade in the Summer and Torkil sighed. They'd been cold ever since arriving in America.

"I just don't want to be your neighbor," said Jonathan letting the cow's hoof drop.

"She's heavy with calf and she's got a limp . . . but I don't see a thing in that hoof. No thorn . . . nothin.'"

"I got to thinking that you might not want land close to me," said Torkil appreciating Sebastian's observation, "so I've come to talk with you about another way to handle the money we owe you . . ." and without waiting for Jonathan to comment, Torkil launched into the offer of money instead. His steamy breath resembled a small train, puff, puff, puffing along as he told him he and Sebastian would split profits etc., and when he'd finished speaking he forced a smile towards his uncle. "Well . . . what do you think?"

"What do I think?" said Jonathan sarcastically. "I don't think you'll make much money is what I think, but that said let's put a time limit on the deal. Double my money as you can, but I won't give you more than five years . . . It would have taken that long anyway."

The bargain was struck, at least for the present, and cold as it was Torkil rode away with a warm heart. He hated contention. His mother had raised him knowing contention came from the Devil and he believed her. He simply didn't want to start life in this beautiful land owning a business with such promise and yet having a relative living so near who hated him.

Jonathan had seemed pacified, but something in the back of his mind told Torkil the issue was far from settled. His Aunt Meribaugh, Jonathan's wife, would have her say in the matter, too.

Chapter 5

Indians!

Six in the morning found the Mormon immigrants packing up to resume their journey. Tents, stiff with ice, were folded and laid on the wagons along with pots, pans and other bulky items. Animals reluctant to leave their fodder were forced into halters, and their bawling and snorting resounded off the snowy hillsides.

Men and women blew warm breath into cupped hands, wrapped them in strips of cloth to cover splitting fingers and sores and then held them under their armpits for warmth. Some boots and shoes were coming apart and were wound with thongs of rawhide or rags, and people grew taller with each step as the snow clung to the wrappings only to shrink when clumps broke off. Small children with cheeks rosy from chafing were loaded on the wagons and packed tightly together for warmth; their laughter cheered everyone.

After morning prayer, jerked beef and biscuits and they broke camp, leaving dozens of blackened pits where fires had burned down, flat rectangles (tent imprints), tens of thousands of foot prints, animal droppings, and yellow holes in the snow. It looked like there'd been a small war in the valley.

A north wind began to blow as the wagons trundled slowly away, and soon drifting snow hid evidence of any visitors at all. A miniature version of the children of Israel strung out for over a mile along with small clusters of pigs, sheep, cows, a few goats and a dog or two trailing behind the wagons. By noon, frost and powdered snow had dusted people, wagons, animals and leafless trees in glittering white.

Ice particles blasted their eyes until horses and oxen were pulling wagons blindly. "Thank heaven for the frozen river!" Trevor shouted to Peter.

"Amen," he called back.

Amid yells and cracks of whips, the animals grudgingly pulled their loads, and behind them came lines of people walking. Soon the tempest made conditions too severe to see at all and Trevor and Peter, who were leading the charge, dismounted to pull their teams by the reins.

This day Maren stayed in the wagon bundled up in blankets—Peter insisted—and seated around her were at least a dozen children. Andrew Coffey drove the third wagon, Terrin Forsgren the forth, Simensen Kjevelsrud the fifth, followed by Dewey Farnsworth, William Herzog and a man from Wales making eight spoke wheeled conveyances in the train. Everyone else walked.

At midday the weather beat them mercilessly, and Trevor wondered if they should simply "pack it in," as he was fond of saying. Snow on the ground was less than a foot deep but its blowing powder made it difficult to see more than ten yards in any direction. Horses began fighting their reigns, and oxen were snorting loudly, reluctant to continue.

No one was talking much, just struggling along watching the backs of those ahead of them when suddenly Trevor, Peter and those wagons leading out became aware of a strange dark presence, sinister, almost palpable.

Looking up and to the left, to their horror stood roughly fifty or sixty Indian warriors with bows and arrows and spears, standing alongside the way. *Cheyenne.* Several yards behind the feathered warriors was a sizable village of tepees, many with smoke wafting from their top openings, and most of a hundred Native American men and women were standing outside. Until this precise moment these dark skinned humans were nothing more than a myth to the Europeans; strange people in story books.

Now here they were, hairless unpainted faces grave and menacing, staring at the Mormon immigrants as if watching a passing troop of cavalry. Neither speaking nor making any movement, they resembled marble statues; icons from a lost age placed as territorial markers guarding the banks of the Missouri River.

Black menacing eyes, shaggy hair, feathers; wearing snowshoes, buckskin leggings and some in heavy buffalo robes, others were coming from the woods.

They wore no war paint but it was clear they weren't friendly and that they'd been totally surprised by the bearded-faced and oddly dressed travelers. Feathered spears, bows and arrows, and a few with old muskets lying across their arms; their weapons were clearly visible. Neither Peter, who was now ahead of Trevor, or those coming into the warriors' view knew what to do, so they simply lowered their heads, tightened their grip upon what ever they were holding and continued relentlessly forward.

"Come on, come on! Come on, come on!" Peter said between clenched teeth as his team struggled against him. The muscles of his legs were burning, yet feeling the danger, with aching arms he kept the reigns tight and drove on, cutting a trail through the snow.

Behind him Trevor's eyes were bulging as he fought to keep pace. "Carry on, Peter," he kept saying under his breath. "Carry on." He pushed ahead and incredibly so did everyone else. All five hundred thirty five people, their livestock, and wagons slowly passed the stone-faced Cheyenne.

In the snow shrouded weather, sentinels had sounded the alarm only minutes before, and the Indians were no more prepared for a fight than were the Mormons. Except for eight which were removed for inspection, loaded and placed one to a wagon, the old Maxwells purchased at Fort Leavenworth were still in crates, but the feigned purpose displayed by these immigrants—who appeared confident as to why they were out here in the first place—caused the Indians to leave their bows un-pulled and their spears and rifles laying across their arms.

Perhaps they pitied the unusual intruders, or maybe they were just sizing them up. Whatever the case nothing happened; not a shot was fired from either side. One hour later Peter could stand it no longer. He'd been pulling his team, not daring to look back except to check on Maren occasionally, but Maren hadn't seen anything. She was wrapped head to foot in a snow-covered blanket and sleeping while sitting up.

The wind was still making its presence known and Trevor, in a rasping voice, kept urging Peter to carry on . . . keep going! Behind them, English and Danish chatter emerged, subdued at first, then soon sounding like a small riot.

"Peter!" called Maren as her head came out of the blanket. "What ever is happening?"

"Whoa! Whoa!" he yelled to his horses. He tied a reign to a short bush as Andrew Coffey came running forward, slipping against his wagon and nearly falling under its wheels; then came Claus Wangsgaard, Jergen Madsen and many others until Trevor and Peter were surrounded. Everyone was talking at once.

"*Gjorde jo sig?!* Did you see them?!" Claus said as he caught his breath.

"*Hvor kunne vi hjælp men se efter sig?* How could we help but see them?" said Peter, helping Maren down from the wagon.

"Who did you see?" she asked.

Before Peter could answer, a deafening bellow assaulted her ears. "Brothers! EVERYONE! Listen to me!" shouted Trevor, pulling his long scarf from around his neck. "Everyone be calm!"

"We gotta git ta' muskets owta the crates!" Andrew Coffey interrupted, yelling as he came running to the wagons.

"Peter!" said Wells, turning to him. "You did exactly the right thing, old son. Exactly! If you'd have stopped . . . no telling what would have happened!" Trevor's face was crimson—red and swollen, his nose running, and his fluster demanded action.

He took off his cap and wiped his face. "What else was there to do, Brother Wells? They looked very dangerous!"

"Would someone please tell me what's going on?" pleaded Maren.

"Indians, Maren," Peter answered soberly. "You should have seen them!"

"We must get the muskets ready brethren," shouted Wells. "You men! Unload those muskets quickly!"

"Over here," yelled Andrew Coffey as he jumped to his wagon and pried at the lid of a crate he'd been sitting on. The lid squawked as he tore it from the long wooden box and threw it aside. "Few o' these men 'ave ever shot a musket, Brothair Wells."

"Only experienced men get one, Brother Coffey," Trevor said siding up to him. "But regardless we're going to fire off a round. We need to get comfortable with these muskets."

"We should have learned to shoot back at that military post," William Herzog barked into Trevor's face.

"Those of you who know what you're doing take a musket and get to the rear immediately," Trevor shouted, pushing past him.

"Those savages back there could have easily killed us, Wells," the wily little man persisted. "We were totally unprepared for them!"

Andrew Coffey abruptly stepped up to Herzog. "Evairr shoot one o' these, Hairrzog?" he asked sarcastically.

"Of course not. Few citizens of Great Britain even own a musket . . ."

"Well, yer about ta lairn then," interrupted Coffey who had served in Ireland's prestigious Reserve Guards, shoving a long rifle into his hands.

William Herzog's nose twitched, exaggerating the size of the hairy wart on its left side, and he felt a surge of excitement run through him. He held the rifle clumsily but smirked as his dark little eyes traced the rusty bluing of the barrel.

Trevor took position in front of the men. "You brethren!" he shouted, "Give Brother Coffey your attention!"

"We'd better 'ave a fast lesson 'ere brethren," Coffey said as he stepped to Trevor's side. "No time like ta present."

The wind weakened into a slight breeze as a line of men and one woman from Trent facing the frozen river was formed. Powder horns, flint, ball and firing caps passed along the line of volunteers. Those standing around gazed anxiously back at the empty country over which they had just traveled. A ragged trail cut through the stark landscape; not even the smoke from the tepees they'd passed roughly three miles back was visible.

It took several more minutes of shouting for Andrew Coffey to get the men in a position where he was comfortable they wouldn't shoot each other. Normally patient, Coffey became increasingly shaken, agitated and fearful as he watched their clumsiness.

"Ahll right na' let's 'av a go at it!" The Irishman held the muzzle of a musket in his left hand, its butt resting on the toe of his boot, while with his right he flicked the tethered cap off a curved steer's horn and poured black powder down the barrel.

"Measure just this much!" he bellowed, holding up his hand up with the finger and thumb less than half and inch apart, "Or ye'll blow yerself ta 'ell! Then git yer rod an tamp it on doun, like this!" Coffey pulled the ramrod out of its carriage and ran it down the rifle barrel to demonstrate. He jammed it firmly at first, then with the flip of his wrist two or three times more until the rod bounced. "Do ya see? When it bounces like mine is doin' then ya've got it right!"

Soon ramrods flew up and down like bowstrings in a rural orchestra. Experienced men were easily spotted; not only were they already loaded they had their muskets sighted in on a distant tree.

"Next goes wad," he continued, only satisfied once they'd finished that step. Coffey placed a square of cloth at the muzzle of his musket and rammed it down his barrel again, tamping it in place. "An' then ta shot behind that. If ta shot is small und falls down the barrel fast then put anothair wad behind it orr it'll roll right back out!"

"I've got one like that," called a young Welshman down the line. He lowered his barrel and a small lead ball rolled impotently into the snow.

"'E does 'ave one!" Coffee shouted, glad to have an example. "Put it back in, laddie, an' shove a wad behind it!" Trevor furiously translated Coffey's information in Danish and all along the line ramrods continued to wave like so many swords. Andrew shook his head painfully until he was satisfied everyone was loaded. "Ahlright now, before this last step mek sure yor musket is aiming at ta river!" When he was satisfied that all 48 muskets were pointed in the right direction, he shouted, "Last comes ta' firreing cap! Pull yer hammers back w' one click! Like this!" Coffey cocked his hammer back and carefully placed a firing cap on the strike. "You men that know what yer a doin' watch 'em!"

"Your weapons will now kill, brethren!" shouted Dewey Farnsworth after the last step was completed. "Keep them pointed down line!"

"Now yer all loaded . . . ah only want every other man ta shoot!" Coffey shouted. "That way half `r always loaded! Count off so half o' ya are ones and half 'er twos."

Trevor translated and soon one, two, . . . one, two, went down the firing-line.

"All right na' cock your 'ammers one more click and take aim. When ah holler fire, twos shoot first! Only twos first!" he repeated. "Then when they start ta reload, ones fire off a round.

"Spread yerselves . . ." There was some shuffling along the line as men moved even further away from each other. "Ahll right **twos**, snug ta rifle butt against yer shouldair! Pick out a bush or tree . . . take aim! Ready na' . . . aim . . . fire!!" .

One early explosion, then two or three, followed by a tumultuous roar accented by a late shot followed Coffey's command. Clouds of smoke engulfed the area as a cheer went up from the onlookers. "Na' the ones! Fire!!" The valley echoed as if the Civil War was still underway. More cheering was heard from the immigrants.

"Do you think they heard that?!" shouted an Englishman, voicing the sentiments of everyone.

"Hear! Hear!" shouted another Englishman standing next to him. At the mercy of Americans since they'd arrived, the immigrants suddenly felt a surge of raw power. Nobody was going to push them around again, not even Indians!

Maren, whose first and last experience with a musket was the night her father had scared off the intruders in the family warehouse, felt her heart racing. The report of so many weapons reverberating off the hillside was thrilling. People were clapping and cheering, and as the smoke cleared, a man from the second volley was on his back in the snow (the blast from his rifle had knocked him down) and down from him another unfortunate man whose musket had backfired (his firing cap had been crooked), was on his knees rubbing his blackened cheeks with snow.

"It's like thunder," Peter said to Claus. Both men's barrels were still smoking. Peter had shot a musket many times as a border guard during the war with Prussia, but to him the scene was impressive none the less.

"It is," agreed Claus.

"It must have been like this for my brother, Hans . . ." Peter's voice dissipated with the smoke. In his imagination he saw Flensberg under attack, and there in his dark blue uniform with its blood red trim, stood his brother. Deep emotion stirred in Peter's heart. He winced with pain.

"What is it?" asked Claus.

"It's nothing," answered Peter shaking his head. "Nothing at all."

Andrew Coffey called for everyone to load up. "Ever thing but ta cap." He turned to Trevor Wells. "Nobody hurt, but our ears will be ringin' fer days."

"At least we know we can defend ourselves; capital job Andrew. Capital. We'll place a guard tonight . . . take turns relieving each other every hour or two."

"Aye," said Andrew. "T'would be a wise thing. Na' sense lettin' 'em sneak op on us."

"The Indians won't be following us," Dewey Farnsworth offered. "You could have heard those muskets a hundred miles away."

The white countryside sprawled peacefully over the Saints like a cotton blanket again. No sign of anyone but themselves. "Let's put a few more miles behind us, shall we gentlemen?" Trevor, with adrenalin pumping through his veins was exuberant, renewed and confident. "I want to get as far along our journey as possible," he stated boldly.

As families returned to their positions along the march there was a certain swagger about those with a rifle; even the man with the blackened face seemed cocky. It was the first time in his life he'd shot a musket, and here he was still alive to tell about it!

Soon wagons, animals, and humanity were en route, and 48 men carried loaded muskets over their arms; muskets that became cold and heavy but as much a part of them as their boots.

Section Notes

1. Pendant reference—For safety's sake, Peter had never made reference to the necklace in public or in his journal and had he not been so exhausted, more than likely he would not have even mentioned a pendant in this late night, snow-bound prairie entry.

2. Book of Commandments—The Book of Commandments contained sixty-five of the original revelations of God given to the prophet Joseph Smith. The press which printed it, and most of the available copies, were destroyed by mobs in 1833. Fewer than thirty copies remain today, making the book one of the rarest in existence. During the time of this novel, even though the Doctrine and Covenants (which was printed in 1835) contained all sixty- five revelations—and more—many people of Peter's day still referred to the D&C as *The Book of Commandments*.

3. Sanctioned by God—In Old Testament times when the Lord commanded Abraham, Jacob and a many other righteous men to take more than one wife *from among righteous women,* the purpose of the law being to build up a righteous seed or posterity. The law prevailed for a certain period of time and the children of Israel were blessed; however wickedness and perversion eventually crept in. Men—especially the wealthy—were taking concubines and performing other atrocities, and the Lord withdrew His Spirit and the law from among them.

Plural marriage was again imposed upon the Lord's people through the Latter-day Prophet Joseph Smith and was likened to Old Testament times; to build up a righteous posterity. The law was sacred, difficult to live and would be embraced by less than five percent of the members of the Church of Jesus Christ of Latter-day Saints.

As recorded in the Book of Genesis, when childless Sarah gave her handmaiden to Abraham, and Rachael likewise gave Bilhah to Jacob, the choice of the plural wife often fell upon the first wife. Even so, God sanctioned these unions. Being human, jealousy, selfishness and loneliness naturally brought hardship; on the other hand when families served the Lord with all their might, mind and strength and also served one another, things generally worked out very well.

Although a people committed to God and to living righteously, for the Latter-day Saints plural marriage ignited cruelty and violence from their neighbors, whereas adultery and fornication were perfectly acceptable and widely tolerated. Then, as now, public lasciviousness was given a pass, where on the other hand, as in Old Testament times, a people claiming to be chosen of the Lord, obeying a difficult principle for a sacred purpose, incited the population at large to murder, rape and plunder.

Though legal (at the time) in the United States, the practice of plural marriage didn't escape the self-righteous eyes of ambitious politicians. The honorable John W. Throckmorton, a Democrat from Illinois, was a widely known philanderer who loudly decried polygamy and slavery as the "twin relics of barbarism", fancy wording however hypocritical, because not only was Throckmorton unfaithful to his wife, but he voted against everything President Abraham Lincoln did to crush slavery. That said, Throckmorton himself was up for re-election, and Mormons having been driven from his home state twenty-one years previously, his bombastic stance against plural marriage proved popular with voters and resulted in his re-election.

Jacob, Chapter 2 verse 30—Apparently at certain times in the history of man, and to establish a righteous people, God has commanded the law of plurality of wives to be established among his chosen people. "The hand that rocks the cradle rules the world" being more truth than poetry, mothers in Zion have a much greater influence upon the development and education of righteousness in their offspring than do the men.

Righteous living, selflessness and faith in God, being natural to and more common among women than among men—seemed to be at the root of the difficult marital arrangement. Scripturally sound and historically accurate, ancient Israel did in fact practice plural marriage as ordained by God. However, as earlier stated, gross disobedience in Israel resulted in bondage and a scattering of its people throughout the entire earth, also the loss of many blessings including this sacred order of marriage.

Restored to Latter-day Israel through the prophet Joseph Smith, and again for the establishment of a righteous people on the earth, the law of plural marriage proved just as difficult to live, and brought upon modern day Israel great persecution and severe trials of faith. Nevertheless, after the trial ended (members of the Church practiced the order for just over 50 years) tremendous good came from living the law and a righteous posterity and solid foundation was laid that continues to bless the Lord's Church and its people to this very day.

4. Fort Castle Garden—Called Castle Clinton today, the site began its existence as a fort built to defend New York Harbor from the British during the War of 1812. Twelve years after the war, the expansive red-stone building was ceded to New York City by the U.S. Army. In 1855, Castle Garden became America's first immigrant receiving station, (preceding Ellis Island) and before it officially closed on April 18, 1890 processed more than 8 million immigrants on their way to becoming citizens of the United States.

Section Two

Chapter 6

New York City

As if to warn the immigrants spilling out of Castle Garden that things could get tougher, like a thief, New York City put on a sinister face that Winter evening. Dimly lit gaslights shining on cobblestone streets cast tall and foreboding shadows. Along narrow streets these images resembled huge eerie candles with flickering flames. Beneath their dim halos, street vendors standing over their carts called, beckoning people to "come and see . . . come and see . . ." and near the sliced alleyways beggars stretched forth their skeletal hands, as did the filthy pick-pockets trying to squeeze the last drop out of the day.

It was almost six p.m. when Catherine Jensen and the large company of Saints from Denmark and England filed out of the old British fortress and moved slowly away from the docks to seek a place for the night. Ships with sails drooping, small colorful flags from around the world a flutter; the place resembled Copenhagen; nations of the world did business here.

Their first day in America proved exhausting, especially for the children. Clopping along in big brother's shoes (nicer than everyday wear, but didn't fit) and caps that drooped over the ears, the little fellows came to show America they had good breeding; and like their shy little sisters, clutching a rag doll or blankie, all were big eyed . . . expectant!

Buildings soared higher than anything they'd ever imagined, windowed and boasting above them in great number. They passed innumerable offices, warehouses, stores and shops and while gazing down their narrow streets, discovered that many simply ended at the water's edge. "A very narrow island," people said. "But so much commerce!"

At five o'clock the thermometer outside the immigration building sunk dangerously low; a snap in the air seemed to carry voices for blocks. As they headed into the city, people instinctively talked more quietly to one another, fear nipping at their heels.

"Did you see how many women were at Castle Garden by themselves?" Catherine exclaimed, avoiding any discussion of the attack.

"I did," observed Casten Pedersen sadly. "One poor lady, completely out of her head and crying, had six children clustered around. I went over and she kept saying, 'He promised to be here. He promised to be here.' My good heavens I wanted to take her in my arms! I would have done so if it weren't for all those children and trunks about. I think she was Italian; I couldn't understand her."

"It's a sad state of affairs," said Catherine. "I heard more languages today than I have in my entire life! And all those children and women alone . . ."

"I'm sure the woman you saw will be helped, Casten," said Evette. "I've never seen so many officials . . . remember the man told us if people couldn't find a place to stay, we could come back to Castle Garden. There are beds . . . I saw them all lined up in that big open room next to us."

"I felt uneasy with so many soldiers about," said Krista.

"I know," replied Casten. "But they were clean and impressive. I guess it was their new uniforms."

"All around the manifest tables, standing by the doors, blue coats with beards and muskets. They reminded me of Prussians," Evette injected distastefully. "I'm so tired," she added.

"It was a trying day," stated Catherine. "But where would we be without these warm accommodations? 'Til the day I die I'll praise the organization of church leaders here in New York City. Can you imagine securing a place to stay for three hundred and fifty people in this already overcrowded island?"

"Don't forget the volunteer guides who got us here," said Casten.

"Never!" exclaimed Evette.

"But we're scattered all over the place," worried Krista.

"How will we ever get back together?" agreed Evette. "This city is more crowded than Copenhagen and nothing but English rattling in my ears. Pushing, shoving . . ."

"We'll all meet in two days at the train station," said Catherine calmly. "Then we load our trunks and head for Chicago."

"It's all so unbelievable," said Casten. "I'm overwhelmed. Give me the farm. Give me Holbaek!" At that the heart of every woman in the room floated back across the ocean to the gently rolling hamlets outside their native town. Holbaek, Denmark; winding country roads, bright elm trees, a thatched roof here, a large barn there and near the small wandering stream stood the Jensen grist mill, its wind-wings turning slowly in the breeze.

"Thank the good Lord for men," interrupted Evette. The dark hotel room was quiet for a moment.

"And what do you mean by that, dear?" asked Catherine.

"It just feels good to know they're sleeping a level below us is all. Anybody trying to get up here must pass through them first."

Catherine grimaced at the scene one floor below them. Men lined up like so many chopped logs filled the rooms and hallways of the old building. As they made their way up the stairs and down the halls finally arriving in their own tight quarters, a sour pungency permeated throughout, and Catherine could only imagine the acrid smell of men after a night of this. Steam from woolen clothing worn for weeks aboard ship was offensive for some but after being in the steerage of the good ship *Carthage*, most barely noticed.

"It would be quite a chore for a bandit to get up here," she said.

"Still I'm glad my Otto is here," injected Casten. "He's a very strong man and more than once came between myself and the groping hands of street people."

"He makes his presence known," agreed Catherine.

"I have to go, Mommy," little Hans begged Evette. "I've held it so long."

"There's a chamber pot in the corner," said Casten, hoping the unfortunate urge didn't hit her in the middle of the night.

"I like President Wilkins," stated Krista as she tucked Anna Katrina under the covers, the beautiful curly-headed child already fast asleep. "He's very sure of himself, and certainly knows this city."

"I'll say," Evette agreed, looking around as women spread blankets, arranging little nooks so they and their children felt together. "If someone were to ask me to go back to Castle Garden, I'd never get there."

"At least this floor is level," sighed Catherine, her white bedclothes reflecting moonlight as she climbed between her blankets. No wardrobe in the room, but pegs along the wall provided hangers for long dresses and other clothing. "And it's dry . . ."

"And it's not moving," injected Krista irritably.

"I was about to say that, dear," Catherine snickered.

"The necessary room actually smells clean, and water isn't splashing on your backside . . ."

"So do you miss the water-closet aboard *The Wortham* dear?" Catherine snickered sarcastically.

"I never want to be on a ship again in my life!" Evette answered, taking little Hans carefully back to their bedroll and helping him in.

"Nor I," Casten yawned, "but as I look back on it we've done something quite remarkable by arriving safely . . ."

"We've only just begun this adventure," interrupted Catherine rolling on her side.

Not to be dissuaded, Casten said, "America. Doesn't it thrill you that we're actually here?"

♥ ♥ ♥

Later, Catherine sat quietly in the window of the crowded hotel room watching the billowing snow dancing around the gaslight below. Her mind raced in a thousand directions and not one of them towards getting some sleep. Every person she held dear was in that building; primarily in that very room. Except for her son Ferdinand, everyone she truly loved had immigrated to America. Far across the choppy ocean and half a world away Ferdinand still ran the mill; for his sake and because of his drinking, she hoped he hadn't run it into bankruptcy.

One way or the other, Catherine knew she'd never see a penny from the mill's operation and yet felt absolutely no remorse.

She looked over at her wayward son Ferdinand's little daughter, Anna Katrina, thumb in her mouth and fast asleep beside her mother, Krista Holsen. Monetarily rich, Ferdinand had given up life's most valuable treasure and for what? Worldly pleasures and alcohol. Catherine hurt for her son, but not for herself. Never had she felt so alive and excited. Land of the free home of the brave, and a religion that brought joy!

She had her worries; the heiress worried about the planned train trip to . . . Chicago was it? What an odd name. Tickets were yet to be purchased, but the immigrants were assured trains left twice a day and they would be on one. And what would she do with the rest of her life once settled in Zion in the Great Salt Lake valley? Start another milling business? Hardly. What Catherine saw herself doing was simply being mother-in-law to her two daughter's-in-law, Evette and Krista (three if she ever found Maren and Peter), grandmother to two fine grandchildren, little Hans and Anna Katrina, and perhaps mother/councilor to son, Peter.

She didn't need to work. Catherine had assets enough to sustain her for the rest of her life, but she would need something to keep her busy. What that might be did concern her, but she'd cross that road once they got settled in the Utah Territory. Catherine's life was transformed by finding the Gospel of Christ. To be led by inspired leaders under the direction of a prophet of God gave her inner purpose. Catherine had studied hard, prayed hard and lived the commandments to finally gain a testimony, to truly hear the Spirit of the Holy Ghost gently guiding her along, warning her; even helping her know what to say at times.

But as surely as she knew her own name, Catherine knew the Spirit had guided her to the Church and to America. Because of her community and financial stature, *to her face* old friends feigned sadness at her departure, but behind her back they called her deranged. She knew that too. *What do I care?* she thought as she sat quietly going over the days' events. *I don't.*

And how could the lady at Castle Garden be so hateful, she wondered. *She's in a land free of tyranny, and she wants to be tyrannical. America is supposed to be recovering from a terrible war and look at the prosperity. On every street corner were carts loaded with food and things to make life easier. Union soldiers wear crisp new uniforms; why even this hotel . . . it's old, and yet the chandeliers are crystal, the carpets a bit worn but contain interesting printed designs and the woodwork is dark mahogany . . . it isn't luxurious but certainly nothing to be ashamed of.*

I heard that President Wilkins had known the owner of this old Metropolitan Hotel and paid him extra to allow us to sleep in the hallways, and as many as ten to a room. That saved a lot of money. The walls are thick and everyone is dry and warm; there is even a restaurant on the first level.

♥ ♥ ♥

The Metropolitan Hotel where Catherine and company were staying was just off New York City's Park Avenue, one of the busiest boulevards on the island. It had known prosperous and busy times, but the bustling city had turned her back on the Met and in just a few years the place would be renovated into tenement apartments. For now it was as Catherine said—a comfortable shelter from the storm.

Without any knowledge of her arrival in America, or that she'd even been baptized, Peter—when she finally met up with him somewhere out West—would marvel; more than that he'd be absolutely astounded! Catherine almost giggled at the thought of his facial expressions once they met up with each other in Zion.

A darkening gloom eased its way across her mind as she tried to comprehend the immensity of this nation. It was over two thousand miles to the Great Salt Lake! When she thought of the endless journey, her mind reeled. Look where they'd been ... what lay ahead of them? She'd written to Peter that she'd been investigating the Church, but having no idea of his whereabouts, had addressed it to: General Delivery, Great Salt Lake City, Utah Territory. That seemed years ago.

Thinking about it, she almost hoped he wouldn't receive her letter before she arrived.

Her mind next shifted to Peter's deceased brother, Hans. Killed in battle in the war with Prussia, each time she remembered and thought of him she felt her heart would break; what a thrill this handsome and daring son had returned to her in the person of grandson Hans. Dark hair, dark brown eyes ... big Hans, her soldier son, had literally cloned himself, and Catherine received the boy's mother, Evette, as she might a daughter.

She smiled secretly as she saw little Hans curled up next to Evette; and there on the other side of him, thumb still in her mouth slept little Anna Katrina. Krista now had her front to them, snuggled in closely, protectively. Pretty Krista—how the Gospel had softened her! Formerly hard as all outdoors, she'd taken on the glow of youthful motherhood—soon to be seventeen, son Ferdinand's would-be-wife now appeared very womanly.

How rich I am! Catherine exclaimed in her mind.

The future high-rise tenement housed fully one hundred and fifty of the original Mormon company aboard *The Carthage,* their ship out of Liverpool. The rest of the members were scattered throughout New York City. Concerned though she might be, but secure among friends, Catherine finally undressed, slipped quietly between her blankets and switched off her mind.

♥   ♥   ♥

Breakfast next morning—truly an amazing feast—consisted of fried potatoes and salt pork, scrambled eggs and hot oatmeal complete with creamy milk and sugar! Not since Liverpool had the children tasted milk. No rushing around, downstairs with children and mothers seating themselves first while two muscled, glistening ebony cooks labored over the flaming gas griddles and their counterparts, former slaves themselves, brought mountains of steaming hash and cereal to the tables.

The restaurateur in grand form glided among his windfall clientele with all the grace of a French chef. "Welcome one and all," he said over and over as he passed between the bulging tables. "You will find our fair city a haven of opportunity."

"The bloke obviously doesn't know we'll be pushing along," one Englishman said to another at the table next to Catherine and her adopted daughters.

Little Hans had mush all over his fingers, sucking first one then the other free of the sweet sticky oatmeal. Patiently feeding the same to Anna Katrina, Krista appeared the picture of contentment. "I slept like a baby," she exclaimed.

"Like a rock would better describe my experience," Casten injected. "I felt knocked insensible, drugged is more like it . . . when my eyes finally peeked at the world. This being on land is difficult to get used to."

"Indeed," said Catherine. "Coming downstairs I had to grip the railing or lose my footing. It's truly strange. How about you, Evette? Did you sleep well?"

"Fru Jensen, I've never felt so rested. The hardwood floor was firm yet giving and little Hans slept the entire night through."

"That's because you took him to the chamber pot just before he fell asleep," said Krista.

"After President Wilkins gives us instructions for the day, what would you all think about a bit of shopping and some looking around?" asked Catherine.

Chapter 7

Wyoming City, Nebraska

The immigrants were camped near dense woods fifty yards from the frozen Missouri River and five miles from the spot where they'd had their shooting instruction. The night was clear, the moon shone boldly and stars lit the heavens like billions of tiny celestial lights. Campfires flickered their last; tents were quiet and the vast bluish-white landscape glittered like an ocean of diamond dust.

"Psst! It's your watch, Peter . . . Peter!"

"Peter, get up," said Maren. "Jergen is out there.

"Uh . . . oh . . . I'm awake, Jergen. Thanks."

Peter sat up and came out of his blankets, pulled on his pants and boots then unrolled his coat, put it on and crawled out of the tent, careful not to disturb Maren. In his groggy state of mind, Peter stumbled over the ropes of the next tent, causing a loud "Gruumph" from inside.

"Who's out there?" said the voice of Claus Wangsgaard.

"Sorry, Claus," said Peter as he bent down on one knee and tied his boots, "I tripped."

Having taken Andrew Coffey's place two hours before, Jergen was cold and tired but had to make sure of his relief before he could retire.

"I'll be grateful to hand you this musket, Peter. The thing feels like lead."

"Good night, my friend," he said as Peter stood. "Terrin's waiting for you up there. Try not to freeze to death."

Peter followed Jergen's tracks until he reached the hill. Once on top he found Terrin Forsgren leaning against a tree huddled in his greatcoat like an old man waiting on a train. "My ribs are killing me, Peter . . . I wasn't sleeping."

"You don't have to explain anything to me," said Peter, remembering leaving Arsenal Island and the horse that had kicked Terrin in the chest. It seemed a lifetime ago. From their elevated vantage point they could see every tent, wagon and animal in camp.

The snow was trampled into a well-worn path extending roughly ten meters in both directions along the crest of the hill. "You'll need to keep pacing to stay warm," said Terrin. "It's probably senseless . . . we made so much noise those Indians are still running."

"According to a book I read, they're not supposed to fight at night," said Peter.

"Umph," said Terrin.

Peter shivered as he looked around. There were few trees up here to break the wind and behind him the forests of Missouri rolled forever in the distance. "America's a huge place, Terrin."

"It is that,"

"You feel swallowed up in it," said Peter.

"I wish we could have a fire." Terrin said.

"Are you crazy? Only way to stay warm up here is to start pacing."

"Go ahead," said Terrin wearily. "I think I'll just close my eyes for a minute," he added, settling back against the tree. "Keep your eyes peeled for both of us."

"I'll do it," said Peter. "By the way, who's your relief?"

"That beady eyed little Englishman . . . Brother Herzog."

"You don't like him?"

Terrin shook his head slightly. "He acts very pious one minute and the next he's got his loud mouth open. Did you hear him yelling at Brother Wells?"

"I did," said Peter.

"I wanted to smack him down," Terrin said seriously.

"One day somebody will," Peter said then started pacing. The snow-covered landscape was too peaceful and beautiful to spend it talking about the noxious little Englishman. Lookout shifts overlapped and he'd be spending an hour with him anyway. A gust of wind blew powdered snow into his thick beard, soon melting down the corners of his mouth. Refreshing, quenching a slight thirst.

Peter, now very alert, stopped to scan the countryside. His eyes adjusted to the dim light of the moon, and he could see the trails of deer and rabbit criss-crossing the smooth whiteness. Considering the events of the day, the Indian warriors were nothing like he'd ever imagined. Their lean faces look carved from wood and completely hairless, but they were men, children of the most High, just as he. He prayed he would never be forced to kill any man.

The first hour passed and Terrin was relieved by William Herzog, who took to his duty with great enthusiasm. Musket propped straight up over his shoulder and one arm sweeping back and forth like the pendulum of a clock; the small Englishman resembled a little tin soldier.

Peter leaned wearily against the tree and watched with amusement as Brother Herzog stopped at each end of the trail and pivoted around on one foot abruptly changing directions. Once he slipped as the pivot point had turned to ice, but when he passed Peter he marched like a Prussian doing the goose step. Not much passed between the two men, and night passed without incident.

As did the next several. Forward scouts brought down an occasional deer providing fresh camp meat but the passing wilderness was void of human life; an abandoned farm here, a burned out cabin there, other than that just miles of nothingness.

♥   ♥   ♥

Eleven days from Atchison, Kansas the immigrants gathered on the slope of a large gentle hill to look down upon a village of log cabins a mile in the distance many with smoke rising from their chimneys. Lean twos, tents and wagons of many descriptions also studded the landscape, and surrounding the outskirts plowed ground, smooth and clear of obstruction lay dormant under the snow; potatoes, corn and other vegetables harvested long since and put in cellars for winter use.

Corrals throughout the town were crowded with oxen, horses, mules and milk cows; fenced areas for sheep, pigs and goats; rickety chicken coops, rabbit hutches, large weathered barns and covered wagons parked along snow-covered cross streets. The mile-square village resembled the slave quarters of a giant plantation and the distant sound of barking dogs, some tied to cabins and others roaming free, music to the weary travelers' ears. Mid-morning, there were even people moving about.

"Do you think that's it, Brother Wells?" asked Peter.

"I can't tell much from Osmond's map but it certainly has all the trappings," said Wells. "Let's hope so. The people have about had it."

"There's nothing else out here," Claus commented. "We haven't seen a soul for days."

"Let's go down, brethren," said Trevor decisively. "If this is Winter Quarters I'd like to be settled in before nightfall."

They walked back to their teams and soon the lead wagon trundled away followed by the next, and the next, as the ball of humanity and animals unwound and became a caterpillar-like procession. Stretched out, its long body surged and rippled along, finally bunching within forty yards of town. A welcoming party approached.

The travelers were spotted by those tending livestock, and a greeting party formed as people slowly emerged from log cabins and other dwellings. A buckboard leading a small group of townspeople was driven by a man dressed in buckskins and with a lady in a bonnet, long coat and dress seated beside him. Both bore a certain dignified but homespun air and were first to approach.

"Welcome!" the man said as he and she climbed down and walked through the snow to address the arrivals. He wore a side arm buckled high on his waist.

"I'm Jess Plowman, and this here's my wife, Samantha."

"Hello, and welcome," said the comely woman, smiling warmly.

"Trevor Wells here," said Trevor climbing down and removing his hat and gloves, relieved by the friendly greetings. "We hail from the ship *John Wortham*; mostly English and Danish immigrants . . ."

"Mormons, right?" said Plowman.

Trevor nodded.

"We knew you were out here somewhere, Brother Wells," said Plowman excitedly pumping his arm. "I'm the Bishop here."

"Thank God," exclaimed Wells.

"We got a letter from Chandler Shipping and Transfer from New York telling us the *Wortham* took the New Orleans route," Plowman went on. "Unusual, eh?"

"Quite," said Wells painfully.

"We knew you'd be comin' up the Missouri, Brother Wells, but didn't expect you 'til Spring."

"Bishop," said Wells remembering his manners, "This is Peter Jensen and his wife, Maren, Claus Wangsgaard, Terrin Forsgren . . ."

"Good ta meetcha one and all . . . young man . . . misses," said Plowman shaking as many hands that came his way. "Welcome to Wyoming City!"[1]

"Not Winter Quarters?" interrupted Wells, his face falling like lead weight. Plowman placed an arm around Trevor's shoulder and embraced him firmly a couple of times.

"No, good brother, no. Winter Quarters is about one hundred and fifty miles north. But you're among friends."

"Right," said Wells.

Standing beside him, Jesse Millard Plowman stood on stubby legs, but from any respectable distance he possessed a tall and commanding presence. Handsome with a farmer's reddish tanned face, he sported rich brown eyes, a mouth full of gleaming white teeth and sometimes—though he generally wore a serious expression—he'd produce a broad smile to display them.

Plowman fought under George G. Meade and though over sixty percent of his New York Regiment died at Gettysburg he miraculously survived. He limped and still carried the musket ball that caused it—in his pocket—as a good luck charm.

Converted to the Church of Jesus Christ through the lady he drove with, Plowman fully embraced the gospel. Thirty-five years young, his thick shoulders and arms pronounced him well able to take care of himself and lead a rough-shod, yet civilized, host of Latter-day Saints.

By now others were coming off the march, mixing in with townspeople like flour and salt; introductions took place amid snorting horses, baying oxen and nervous goats and cows. In spite of the fact there were almost as many new arrivals as there were residents, the people of Wyoming were glad to have company.

"Fine lookin' town ya've got hairre, Bishop," said Andrew Coffey watching the short man carefully. Andrew didn't trust anyone readily on first meeting; especially someone this friendly.

"Such as it is," said Plowman. "Biggest little place around these parts. Shrinks every Spring when the wagons leave, then grows slowly over Summer and Fall. I've watched the phenomenon for two years in a row. But this is it for me," he added. "I've spent my last Winter here. Come Spring I'm leading a wagon train west myself."

"You know the way then," Trevor said apologetically.

Plowman laughed heartily. His toothy grin was heartwarming to Trevor. "The way is well marked, Brother Wells," he said, "and we've got a few 'up and backers' amongst us besides."

What's an up and backer? Coffey wanted to know but he was afraid to ask. Troubled, Trevor had difficulty understanding the confident young man's eastern American accent and thought it best to stay quiet for a while.

The level of noise steadily escalated as more and more people came from their cabins to welcome the visitors; the scene took on the air of a political rally. Children at first gathered shyly but soon they were running around the wagons playing tag with each other. Mothers wanting to exhibit their children's good breeding held as many in check as possible but it was a losing battle with people struggling to understand the conglomeration of languages and getting their own points across.

Jess Plowman finally climbed on his buckboard and stood atop its wooden seat. "Brothers and sisters!" He called down the line. "We welcome you! One and all! As you are finding out, this is not Winter Quarters. I know some of you have relatives there who are expecting you! Don't be concerned!"

Everyone grew quiet; a few still whispered but most turned their attention toward Plowman. "I've recently returned from Winter Quarters and it's severely overcrowded. The people there are sleeping in wagon boxes and even caves! Anything they can find. There are no available cabins. Since the end of the Civil War many Americans are on the road west and Winter Quarters is on a main trail.

"You are lucky to be here. We have some empty cabins and we'll take as many of you into our own homes as possible . . . the rest will have to stay in tents!"

Trevor climbed up on the rear of the buckboard to translate the information in Danish. Bishop Plowman gave him time to do it but observed some troubled faces in the crowd.

"Apparently some of them don't believe you," Plowman said when Trevor stopped talking. "Tell them they can go visit Winter Quarters once they've rested up a few days."

Trevor translated then Plowman continued. "Let the best of our facilities go to the elderly, ladies in waiting and those of you who may be sick. The rest should pitch tents between cabins to be out of the wind some. While you're getting yourselves situated our folks are preparing hot stew and biscuits for tonight. We might even do some dancing!"

The cruel winter in Wyoming City left the people in frozen ruin; any prospect of relief was a wool blanket of hope. Teeth chattered in excitement and despite the cold day hearts were warm as summer.

"I'm through talkin'," said Plowman, helping his wife climb aboard their buckboard. Trevor had jumped down and came around to Plowman's side. "How can we ever thank you Bishop Plowman . . . Sister Plowman?" Trevor's eyes moistened. "You've been completely sincere and we're overwhelmed by this hospitality. You've no idea what we've been through thus far, brother, our boat was detained, many have died . . ."

Plowman placed his hand on Trevor's shoulder. "We'll have time to talk later, Brother Wells. You've had a long journey and for now what you probably need most is rest."

Samantha Plowman stepped in. "I'm sure you've all been through a lot. But you're safe now. No one will harm you here."

Jess squirmed with all of the emotion and changed the subject. "By the way, Brother Wells . . . where's your misses?"

"I had to leave her and the children in England," Trevor answered weighing his words.

"That so," said Plowman. "Then why don't you put up with us? We've got room haven't we, Samantha?"

His wife gave him a look of bewilderment.

"Thanks just the same, Bishop," said Trevor coming to her rescue, "but I'll stay in a tent for now. Freedom to come and go as I like, you know?"

"As you say," said Plowman enjoying Trevor's accent. "But the of-fer's open any time, isn't it, Samantha?"

"We're going to do everything in our power to make you comfort-able, Brother Wells." With her cabin as crowded as a closet, Samantha Plowman appreciated the Englishman's courtesy. She couldn't have taken in a cat, let alone a full-grown man.

"Thank you kindly, madam," said Wells.

Plowman then tapped his whip on the rump of his team, clicked his tongue and slowly turned the buckboard. Fifty yards later the Bishop of Wyoming City turned his head around and gave a look at the chaos.

"They'll all fit in somewhere, Samantha," he said with a twinkle in his eye. "Don'tcha think so?"

Life had been good to Jess Plowman. His rugged, cheerful face drew people to him; he had confidence, health, financial stability and a strong sense of direction in life. He knew there would be changes made among the English Leaders of Fifty among the new arrivals, but not with the Danish. With them, Claus Wangsgaard was considered a Bishop in his own right, but Trevor Wells was about to find great relief from the burden he'd been shouldering.

Chapter 8

Getting Settled

"You can put your things in here," said the lady who'd introduced herself as Sarah Bingham. Gunda Wangsgaard and Maren Jensen stood in the musty gray weathered cabin wringing their hands in front of them like school girls, concerned more about their trail-worn appearance than that of the ramshackle log dwelling they were moving in to. Elizabeth Anne Browne had come with them to translate and was comfortable with this "Women's President," as Sarah had been introduced.

Like Bishop Plowman, Sarah Bingham spoke with an eastern accent in impeccable English. Her role amongst the women of Wyoming City was as big a job as Plowman's, but she did it quietly and with little notoriety.

Sarah's clothes draped her tiny frame and hid her jutting ribs, hips and hollow stomach. Another person could almost get in them with her. Of medium height with warm intelligent eyes of clarity, fine brown hair and a soft quiet mannerism she was keenly alert, inoffensive and missed very little.

During her few minutes with the new arrivals she discerned that even though Gunda Wangsgaard suffered from illness she felt nurturing toward Maren Jensen and that Elizabeth Anne Browne was unattached.

"This will be just fine for them, Sister Bingham," the latter told her. "They're close friends and so are their husbands."

"You're not married then, Sister Browne?" said the efficient little lady.

"My husband died in England . . . of the pox."

"I'm so sorry," said Sarah apologetically. "Horrible thing. Many died of it I hear."

"Thousands, Sister Bingham."

Sarah looked genuinely forlorn. "There are several single ladies in town; you can stay with them . . . it's a ways from here, though." She turned her attention back to Maren and Gunda.

"Now here's the larder," she said taking two steps to a bin with a slanted lid. Raising the lid she looked in. "It's dusty but at least they're no mice in it. We'll get you some flour . . ."

"We have flour, Sister Bingham," said Elizabeth Anne. "The men were able to buy it at Fort Leavenworth."

"That's good," said Sarah. "Flour's the one thing that's always in short supply around here."

Maren and Gunda looked nervously at each other and then around the shadowy cabin. The cabin interior was a painful reminder of the huts on Arsenal Island. They understood a few of the words passing between Elizabeth Anne and Sister Bingham but "mice" came through clearly.

"I'll leave this lantern," she added, "and I'm going to lend you my broom for a while." She handed Gunda a thick handle straw broom and looked at her kindly. "I'll be back for it in half an hour."

"Thank you sister Bingham," said Maren making a slight curtsey. Gunda also thanked the Women's President, but just shook her hand. After all they were about the same age.

"Let's be on our way then, Sister Browne," said Sarah politely, efficiently.

Elizabeth gave Gunda a hug, then Maren too. "*Gud ske lov vi er her ovre!* Thank God we're here," she said in Danish, then followed the busy women's leader out the low doorway.

The log cabin town became an ant-bed of activity; people in and out of cabins, tents going up, trunks being dragged across the snow and men herding livestock into pens. Older boys and girls helped parents unload wagons and move into deserted cabins while younger children were darting between wagons shouting "you're it!" until grabbed by an ear and put to small tasks.

Out in the fields men were using horses to drag log pallets to clear snow so livestock could get at the dead grasses underneath:

The newcomers were settling in.

"*Mange feet nyde træde indeværende jorde.* Many feet have trampled this floor," said Gunda.

"But not those of prisoners, Fru Wangsgaard," Maren reminded her.

Gunda grimaced at the thought of Arsenal Island as her eyes surveyed the one-room cabin. It was dry inside, but it smelled of rancid grease and burnt wood. There were no beds and the walls looked like they had never been whitewashed. An iron tripod balanced in the center of a hearth full of ashes overlooked by a small split log table and one bench. Sarah Bingham's lantern sat in the center, a soft yellow glow flickering bravely.

"We're so fortunate not to be in a tent," exclaimed Gunda, "or do you prefer the damp, claustrophobic canvas?"

"For once being with child has blessed us," Maren agreed, remembering the rolling from side to side on the hard ground, trying to ease the baby crushing into her left side into a more comfortable position; painful cramping in her lower extremities; crying silently in the blackness of the tent, only finding relief as she walked along side Peter's wagon.

"You've felt sick the whole time we were traveling," said Gunda understandingly.

"Perhaps now things will settle down for you." She poked the handle of Sarah Bingham's broom in the fireplace. "We'll have to clean this out before we can build a fire."

The rock fireplace had a spacious hearth and a small built-in oven marked by an arch of inlaid stone and positioned to the top right of the mantle where heat stayed more or less even. The oven was the perfect size for one large loaf of bread. With everything in town so primitive, Gunda marveled at its modern construction. With one hand on her hip and the other to her chin she surveyed the rest of the one room interior.

"We must string a blanket across for privacy, Maren . . . Claus snores, you know."

"I think a blanket partition would be a good idea at night. What could we tie it to?" Wooden pegs for hanging salted meat, dried vegetables, herbs, pots, pans, and clothing studded the logs. "Those two will do," said Gunda, pointing up at two pegs anchored straight across from each other. "We'll need a length of rope, but if we string it from here to there we can both see the fireplace."

"But can you spare a blanket?" Maren hoped, embarrassed at her extended belly and the desire to remain modest.

I'll spare a blanket even if Claus has to sleep on the ground, thought Gunda. "We have an extra," she said aloud. "Like you, I intend to have privacy."

Maren removed the tripod from the hearth and stooped in to look up the chimney. "I can see light, Fru Wangsgaard. There are no bird's nests; someone has swept the chimney. The flue is wide; smoke will easily clear from the cabin."

Pushing the door wide open and taking the oilcloth off the windows (the cabin had two), the women started sweeping and scrubbing. While one swept cobwebs from the log walls and knocked old mud wasp nests from the rafters, the other cleaned out the hearth and dusted the table. Sister Bingham's precious broom barely scarred the hard earthen floor as they worked, and before long things were in order.

Before laying out their bedding, the women walked to the outskirts of town and gathered what prairie grass they could uncover to be used as bedding. Gunda's arms were numb with pain as she carried in load after load. So great was her fatigue her legs almost buckled. Her joints ached; she wanted to lie down and sleep for a lifetime, but knew Maren would overdo herself, so Gunda kept at it.

"Peter will bring us plenty of wood, Fru Wangsgaard," said Maren proudly. "He loves to chop."

"They'd better do something to carry their load."

By nightfall all tents were up, wagons unloaded, animals penned and the temporary citizens of Wyoming shared a hot meal of beef stew and homemade bread with the newcomers. A huge bonfire built near the center of town drew people like bees to honey. Jess Plowman was giving a welcome speech and a few instructions:

"What da' ye think a' this Bishop Plowman, Brothair Farnsworth?" asked Andrew Coffey in a low voice.

"He seems to have a good handle on the situation, Andrew," Dewey whispered. "I can say that for him." Dewey rubbed his eyes; the hot stew had made him sleepy.

"Shhhh," said Marjouri Coffey, her finger to her lips, frowning. Dewey's eyes watered and chills ran down his big frame; he folded his arms tightly around himself trapping any heat trying to dissipate. He leaned close to Andrew and whispered, "I'm about all in . . ."

"Ah'm a bit flagged meself," answered Coffey. "Ah wonder `ow muoch longer `e can talk?"

"Don't know," said Dewey shaking his head.

Peter and Maren stayed close to the Danish contingency and their section buzzed quietly as the information was being translated by Trevor Wells.

"There will be a meeting in Sarah Bingham's cabin tomorrow morning for the women leaders," Jess Plowman was saying at the moment, "Could I see by the show of hands just who you are?"

Newcomers and locals alike craned their necks to see who was who, and then Trevor told Gunda Wangsgaard to make herself known. After she gave a short but fiery speech, an audible tone of respect could be heard.

"Thank you, ladies," said Plowman. "Brother Wells, in the morning have your men meet with me and my counselors inside that barn over yonder. We've got a lot to cover."

"Right," said Wells touching two fingers to his brow.

"Both meetings," Plowman continued, "the men's and women's, begin sharply at ten in the morning; we all need extra sleep tonight."

Plowman instinctively knew his audience could endure no more. "We'll call this meeting to a close then," he said. "Brother Knippers, will you give us a closing prayer?"

A light snow dusted them as the crowd silently bowed their heads and a very large man moved next to Bishop Plowman. He prayed briefly, thanking God for the safety of the new arrivals and for a hopeful America free of slavery, and for the Lord Jesus Christ, Savior of mankind; then closed the prayer in his beloved and holy name. Afterward the exhausted people moved quietly and quickly to their various dwellings.

Chapter 9

Catherine

"This horrible smoke-belching monster," said Catherine as she leaned over to check on little Anna Katrina, nearly losing her balance and grabbing hold of the bench. The child in question lay writhing in Krista's arms, hot with fever, as the train surged and banged powerfully along the tracks, yet even covered with thick blankets the child shook uncontrollably. "Sip this broth, Anna," Catherine said softly. "It will strengthen you."

"Will she be all right, Fru Jensen?" Krista's eyes pleaded.

"She'll be fine, dear," said Catherine not knowing for sure and timing Anna's small sips of broth with the swaying of the train. The heiress closed her eyes momentarily and silently uttered a fervent prayer.

Anna's sickness came upon her sometime between the last two stops. As it took on water and wood they'd all departed the train, and the only unusual thing Catherine remembered happened when little Anna had insisted her grandma buy her a piece of fudge from a lady walking amongst passengers selling home-made treats. The candy looked clean (although the lady didn't) and Catherine was hesitant, but the child's pleading eyes and little hand reaching out softened her.

"How much," she'd asked.

"Five for a penny," the shabbily-dressed lady implored.

Neither understood the other and Catherine gave a nickel, the sight of which lighted the lady's eyes. She still remembered cringing as dirty fingers handed her granddaughter the fudge. She'd almost taken it and thrown it away.

Anna ate two pieces and Catherine did get rid of the rest, but now little Anna lie writhing around and her grandmother felt sick to her stomach. *I know it was the candy,* Catherine thought miserably.

♥ ♥ ♥

The mother, Krista Holsen Jensen, had only recently turned seventeen; a child with a child. A healthy olive-skinned girl, she had recently gained the benefit of two surrogate mothers: one Casten Pedersen and the other, of course, her daughter's grandmother, Catherine Jensen. These two experienced women sustained Krista during the voyage from Liverpool not only training her in the rudiments of motherhood, but because Krista had come from a large family and neglected by her own mother, they'd taught her much about being a woman.

Very recently gaining a testimony of the Gospel of Christ herself had given Krista the strength to break from the grips of an immoral past and also from Catherine's youngest son, Ferdinand Jensen, the alcoholic womanizing father of little Anna. The break was significant because having no formal schooling; Krista may have remained enslaved to a man like Ferdinand for the rest of her life. But the fact her own father had taught her to read—at the time rare for girls in Denmark—ended up saving her. In the depths of misery from Ferdinand's abuse Krista had turned to the Book of Mormon, and through it gained an understanding of who she was and also the hope of a better life.

It had all started at a fireside held in Casten Pedersen's beautiful home. Barely sixteen and already a mother, Krista had gone to the meeting mainly to get out of the house. Ferdinand's womanizing left her alone night after night, and responding to an invitation from missionaries, she'd cleaned up little Anna and sitting quietly in Casten's lovely front room heard the testimony of the young man from America who'd invited her. Nobody—not even Catherine who'd been shocked at Krista's attendance—noticed the halo that seemed to settle over Krista that night.

Morally unclean as a girl and later stunted from Ferdinand's brutality brought her to a point of almost being unable to cry; for a time she'd even contemplated suicide. But that night, hearing she had a Father in Heaven who loved her and that His Son Jesus Christ had paid for her sins, had liberated the guilt-ridden girl. Krista sat there quietly weeping, almost masking the light radiating from within her soul. The good news from the missionary from America came quite unexpectedly, made her yearn to read the book they'd testified of, and helped her covenant within to live a better life than she had in the past.

Young as she was, because of her sincere conversion, Krista possessed a child-like faith in God and in His Church. Struck with this sudden illness, her little daughter teetered between life and death but she'd be all right somehow. God would save her; wouldn't He? As the train rumbled along, its iron cold walls indicated otherwise, and although Krista was very frightened and felt like a child herself, she held to her new-found faith like a barnacle to a ship's hull.

From a family of ten children, and leery of men since her rough treatment by Ferdinand, Krista, actually Kristina, was savvy beyond her years; little Anna Katrina was her life and next time—if there was a next time—she introduced a husband and father into the child's life, she'd be sure he held the priesthood. Since meeting the missionaries and knowing the kind of men they were she'd also made that vow to herself.

Robust little Anna had crossed the Atlantic Ocean in the crowded steerage of the wind-ship *Carthage* without as much as a cough. Now the child seemed fragile as a flower. Frightened herself, not to mention the fact she was angry, Catherine felt like yelling at somebody. She also blamed herself. They'd spent sixty hours on the "belching, smoking monster" as she called it; the only time the train wasn't pitching from side to side was when it stopped to take on coal and water.

Casten had made her way from the women's necessary room with a cool washrag, and placing it on Anna's forehead said gently, "There, there, little one. You're going to be fine. Don't you fret now . . ."

"In this rolling chilly conveyance, it's a wonder we're not all sick," observed Catherine. "I can't seem to get warm myself!"

Indeed even with the very aisles of the passenger car crowded together with people, it still felt like an icebox. And everything was hard. Even though covered with button down leather, the benches were as unforgiving as boulders. The only relief those people without a berth had was to recline on the floor occasionally, and they did it in shifts. An hour on the floor, an hour on the bench, many except the corpulent few taking turns; others just gritted their teeth and held on.

The only saving grace—or curse, depending upon how one looked upon it—was this train happened to have a huge mail car responsible for delivering mail to many cities along the way, therefore stops were frequent. People got off often, taking short breaks from the roaring, swaying, powerful inferno while it dropped off or picked up mail.

♥   ♥   ♥

Tired and miserable though she might be, Catherine refused to sleep anywhere except her berth. Defiant of the train's discomfort, she stood or sat, but mostly stood.

A young mother herself, Evette seemed to be doing fine. Little Hans stayed right at her side (he didn't get any of the fudge) on their bench ever since leaving New York. They'd all been cautioned not to lean too hard on the brittle windows of the passenger car but during much of the daylight hours, little Hans kept his face pressed there anyway.

"Look at the factory, Mother, look at the soldiers!" Even miles and miles of open countryside kept his attention. Many times he sat on his mother's lap while she read to him, or laid his head there to sleep.

Pert, always in a long dress and normally very fastidious about her person, Evette sat erect wiping the soot from her face until her handkerchief looked like a blackened shoe rag.

Filthy train, she thought as she read "The Ugly Duckling" to Hans for the fifteenth time since they'd boarded train. *The constant bump, bump, bump of this clacking, chugging, smoke filled conveyance is driving me crazy!*

She wouldn't express these thoughts to her son. He was in the middle of a grand adventure and anything she said about it would be exciting and positive. "Look at that high mountain and the beautiful pine trees, Hans! Did you see the herd of deer in the meadow?"

Indeed, conditions were such to invoke endless nights for children and their parents, most of whom were Latter-day Saints; but besides mail stops, other less frequent and longer reprieves broke the monotony when the train took on fuel and water. Then, people piled off in droves, not minding at all standing about in the freezing weather. During night stops everyone, blacks, whites and Asians alike all looked as if they'd come from the coal mines. Dark shiny cheeks, white teeth ... brushing soot from the sleeves left hands black as charcoal.

Women kept their hair in tight bonnets and still it changed colors. Catherine's blonde tresses had gone gray. The fine soot penetrated everything.

"The food is what made Anna so sick," complained Krista. "Everything is soggy, moldy . . ."

"Or completely without flavor," agreed Catherine. "Barely edible."

"At least we're not on a wagon train like that miserable lot we saw clustered in . . . Cincinnati, was it?" Casten offered trying to cheer everyone. "What strange names in this country!"

"I'd prefer a wagon train," snapped Catherine. "Fresh air . . . that's what's killing . . . er making us all so sick. Fine soot hangs in the very atmosphere of these passenger cars. Just look around you."

"We have the worst of it behind us," said Evette. "I've counted thirty-five stops since we left Baltimore . . . another strange name . . . there are just a few hundred miles left."

At that moment Otto Pedersen came weaving down the aisle. Hand to bench, hand to bench, he made his way to little Anna and her young mother. Pausing, he gently brushed the child's bangs away from her eyes, looking gravely upon her. "You're going to be all right little one," he said kindly, then continued weaving toward the nearest men's necessary room.

"Men," said Evette. "When it comes to children they get the clean end of the stick. It's we who sit up with them when they cut teeth, we who teach them to use the potty, and we who anguish over their fevers . . ."

"We'll be stopping in an hour or two," Catherine said wearily. "I'm going to find some Calomel if I have to ask every passenger that gets off this train!" A person of action, her granddaughter was gravely ill, and she wasn't going to just sit and despair. Catherine's eyes followed Otto until he passed through the car on his way to a meeting with President Wilkins and she heaved a sigh.

"Did Otto seem somewhat indifferent to what's going on with our little Anna here, or am I just imagining things?"

"Don't be angry with him, Catherine," said Casten mildly. "He feels helpless with

Children's illnesses. Any time our son got sick, he always left his care entirely to me."

"Well I wish he would do something. Anything!"

Chapter 10

Tradesmen

Chill from the rock-hard dirt floor seeped up through the layers of prairie grass and bedroll Maren had earlier laid out. It had all looked so inviting; "We may as well be lying in a bed of snow," Peter complained.

"It's terrible," moaned Claus from the other side of the hanging blanket. "Gunda, you and Maren should have put down more grass . . ."

"There wasn't time," Gunda retorted sharply. "And there wasn't much to find anyway! These people have been feeding it to their animals."

Although just as cold as everyone else, Maren said, "We should count our blessings. This isn't Arsenal Island."

"She's right," stormed Gunda. "Nothing you men could say will make me unhappy tonight. We're here amongst our own, safe, and we're not sleeping in a wretched tent!"

Maren snickered quietly. She could almost see Claus cowering away from his fiery little wife. "It's strange to hear you both and not see you."

It did seem unusual to be sharing a cabin with the Wangsgaards, but to Maren who'd been afraid every night out on the plains, the added security felt wonderful!

"First thing tomorrow I will build a bed," yawned Peter as a shiver worked its way down his body. "It will take a week for the prairie grass to dry out."

"The bedding will be dry by morning," Claus said also yawning. "Our body heat will do the job."

"That and our fire," agreed Gunda, observing the glowing hearth. She had banked the hot coals just before crawling under her blankets.

"Odd how your face can be so warm yet your body so cold," said Peter, so tired he didn't really care one way or the other. "Tomorrow, I will build a bed," he added, repeating himself. "We need to get off . . . this . . . ground."

"I will help you," said Claus thickly. "I have a saw, rope and a brace and bit . . . cut a few boards, make joints and legs tight, drill a few holes here and there, tie the knots and presto we're off the ground."

"You make it sound so easy," said Gunda hopefully.

"It is," said Claus confidently. "Nothing to it . . . good night, everyone." Exhausted from putting up tents and feeding cattle, he snuggled against Gunda, putting a thick hairy arm around her waist and pulling her close. Miffed that her grass gathering efforts hadn't pleased him, Gunda stiffened but then slowly melted against him, smiling slightly.

On the other side of the hanging partition, as their bedding slowly warmed, Maren put her lips to Peter's ear. "I felt the baby move today."

"You did?" whispered Peter. He felt her nod, moved closer and kissed her gently. "He is glad to be here."

"And how do you know it's a he?" she whispered.

Peter reached around and rubbed Maren's back, warming it with each stroke. "I just know that's all," he whispered.

The banked coals began to darken and shortly the cabin became black as a cave. No one could see their hand in front of their face. In the not-so-far distance between cabins and the open prairie, the lonely howl of a coyote could soon be heard. As if in answer, a dog began to bark. Not excited barking, just an occasional yip, yap and horses began snorting here and there.

From the Wangsgaard's side of the cabin, Claus had begun to snore sporadically; Gunda didn't make a sound but her breathing had become steady and deep, exactly like Claus'.

"Not all that quiet on the prairie is it?" whispered Maren in Peter's ear and kissing him affectionately.

He smiled and returned her kiss followed by many more.

♥   ♥   ♥

The next morning the Wangsgaard-Jensen cabin awakened to the sound of Trevor Wells' voice outside. "Claus! Claus Wangsgaard!"

Peter stood and blinked, his eyes adjusting to the faint light in the cabin. Where were they? He looked down at Maren softly stirring under the covers and heard a rustle from the Wangsgaard's side of things.

"Who is it, Peter?" asked Claus.

Peter pulled up his pants and made it to the door just as Trevor called again, "Claus, Peter! Are you awake?"

Peter pushed open the door against several inches of new-fallen snow. A blue-sky morning, its brightness reflecting off the snow, blasted him square in the face partially blinding him.

"Good morning, Brother Peter," said Wells cheerfully. "Is Claus awake?"

"I am now," growled Wangsgaard from inside.

"It's a capital day out here," called Trevor. "We should all be up and at it."

"What's all the racket?" said a harsh voice from the Thayer tent pitched next to the Wangsgaard-Jensen cabin. Lyman Thayer and his wife, Annella, had a large family before Arsenal Island; now all they had were each other. The Englishman stuck his head out of the tent as Trevor eyed him mischievously. "There are people trying to sleep in here, Brother Wells!"

"Now, Lyman, you have a meeting to attend . . ."

"Count me out," said Thayre.

Trevor bent down, made a snowball and threw it at him, but Thayre pulled his head back inside the tent flaps just as it hit.

"You seem in fine spirits, Brother Wells," said Peter squinting.

"Having the time of me life," said Wells, bending down to form another white spherical projectile. "And Brother Jensen, could you and Brother Wangsgaard please hurry it along there . . ."

Peter closed the door and a thump followed. "Brother Wells is acting like a school boy out there. What time is it?" he asked Maren.

She was awake now and could barely see Peter as he sat on their bedroll to dress. "I'm not sure; does it matter? Perhaps eight o'clock. Did you sleep well, my husband?" she asked, reaching over and touching his arm softly.

"Like a dead man," he said turning his attention to his coat. After he'd pulled up his pants and suspenders, Peter habitually and carefully unrolled his coat. The necklace was still there of course; he could feel it, but checking was simply part of his morning ritual.

"You talk in your sleep, Peter," said Gunda Wangsgaard from her side of the blanket partition, her tone less than friendly. "You kept me up half the night . . . and will you men kindly get out of here? I'm not going to dress until you're both out of the cabin and the door is bolted!" Claus could see his wife's sharp little eyes cutting at him from just above the covers.

He groaned as he massaged his temples and tried to clear his head. "We're going to have to be tolerant of each other, Mother," he said rubbing his face. "Things like snoring. We may be roommates for quite a while."

"I'm going to put up a cabin for Maren and me first thing," corrected Peter from his side of things.

"Just like that, eh, Peter," said Claus wisely.

The blue sky and blanket of white enfolding the town was out of season. Normally gray this time of year, a southbound storm had dropped its load of snow sometime in the middle of the night and hastened along. "Just like that, Claus." Looking at what he faced, Peter didn't sound so sure.

As the men gathered inside a huge barn near the central campfire, it was as if they were seeing each other for the first time. All were rested; the hunted look absent from their faces, and all seemed to be talking at once.

The huge barn smelled of sweet hay and fresh manure and had its double doors thrown open for light. Cows still in their stalls were chewing their cud as the lower level of the barn quickly filled with people—so many some had to climb the loft to hear. With legs dangling over the ledge, they looked like young boys about to get some schooling. Latecomers gathered outside the open double doors as Jess Plowman climbed in a wagon's box to be seen above the crowd. Shortly he called for order.

"There is a great deal of work to accomplish here before wagons roll out in the Spring," he began authoritatively. "We're assembled together this morning to assess your abilities and to put each man in a place where he can do the most good. We've got wagons and handcarts[2] to build . . ." Jess Plowman spewed out a litany of things that needed to be accomplished; ox and horse shoes to forge, wheat to grind and so forth, and when he finished he looked to Trevor to summarize what he'd said in Danish.

The tall English leader stood ready to accommodate Bishop Plowman and he looked ten years younger than the day before. "*Vi har fik ox og hest skoene hen til lade ligge, kød hen til gold wheat hen til grimasse. vi har fik alle vi kunne sige nåde slut!* We've ox and horse shoes to forge, meat to dry, wheat to grind. We've got all we can say grace over!"

Claus Wangsgaard was steadily nodding in the affirmative, letting Trevor know that his Danish had become quite good on the ocean voyage.

"Harness, halters and saddles to make . . ." Jess went on, "for now Wyoming City operates on a sort of communal system. There's very little private enterprise, except for home production. We must work together for the common good if we're to leave in early Spring. All for one and one for all . . ."

Peter had momentarily quit listening. He'd felt a surge of electricity go through him like a bolt of lightening when Trevor translated 'wheat to grind' in Danish. Thoughts he'd repressed for months flooded his mind. He felt an urge to raise his hand and say something but looking around uncomfortably at the burly crowd decided against it. Plowman was still talking.

"The current demand for ox teams and a good span of mules drove prices so high that most of us can't afford 'em nor can we find many in these parts. Lucky there is timber to build handcarts[3] as well as wagons. We need qualified men . . . carpenters, wheelwrights and the like.

"So let's start there. First off . . . how many carpenters are here?"

No hands went up.

"What about wheelwrights?" Again no hands, and Plowman turned to Wells.

"We're off to a very bad start here, Brother Wells. What background do these people have anyway?"

"I'm afraid most of them are from the cities and ports, Brother Plowman," said Wells. "We've got fishermen, school teachers, shopkeepers, clerks . . ."

Plowman shook his head disgustedly. "Looks like we'll have plenty of help in the saw pits then. We can teach anybody to cut boards."

"We've a few farmers and miners," said Trevor Wells turning to the crowd of Danish men. "*De savn carpenters og wheelwrights.* They need carpenters and wheelwrights. *Har vi hvilken som helst imellem jer?* Have we any among you?"

At first no hands went up and Trevor quickly scanned the ship's manifest list.

"There are two Danes here who are coopers, Brother Plowman," he said as he came across the information. "Jergen Madsen and Simensen Kjevelsrud."

Plowman screwed up his face at the difficult sound of the last man's name. "We'll put them with Jud Glissmeyer over there. Jud raise your hand. You men go with this man." Trevor translated the instructions to Madsen and Kjevelsrud. "If they can make barrels they can certainly be taught to make wheels."

"*JEG skabe den bedst ler klods i alt i Danmark.*" offered Claus Wangsgaard, who was standing in the front.

"What did he say?" asked Plowman.

"He's a brick maker. Says he makes the best brick in all of Denmark," answered Wells.

"What I'm talking about here is wood!" said Plowman, exasperated. "Ask them who can work with wood?"

"I did a little furniture," said a slightly-built Englishman in the middle of the crowd. "As did I," said two others.

"Now we're getting somewhere," said Plowman.

"You men will work with Brother Hopkins here," he said holding a hand toward a tall, lithe man with long veins bulging distinctly in his large hands. "Let me warn you, Brother Hopkins is a perfectionist . . . he demands tight construction. Do what he tells you."

As Plowman spoke, Trevor furiously scanned the ship's manifest for any Danes who might be carpenters. There were many names with lines drawn through them, including Albert Larson, a skilled cabinet maker, and Ludvig Knudsen, a joiner. Both men were buried in St. Louis, Missouri.

"Broder Ingamar Christophersen. Broder Kjars, Broder Thorvaldsen, Holmstrop, Halversen, *der hvor er du mandskab?* Where are you men?" Wells said looking up at the crowd. A big blonde fellow leaning against the north wall chewing a straw of hay raised his hand, as did the other men whose names were called. All were standing more or less together.

"Birds of a feather," said Wells to Plowman.

"*Jer mandskab vil være i arbejde hos Broder Hopkins.* You men will also be working with Brother Hopkins." He said again pointing to Hopkins. "*Behage komme efter sig udenpå.* Please follow him outside."

"How about smithies?" Plowman called out to the loosening crowd. "We need all the horseshoes and rims we can make!" Two hands shot up. Both were English blacksmiths. Trevor looked relieved, and he translated Plowman's request in Danish. He got three additional husky men: Lars Olsen, Bent Gundersen and Mons Hansen.

"Now we're getting somewhere," beamed Plowman. "Brother Meeks," he said to a thick-shouldered man whose arms extended into hams who'd been waiting hopefully near the rear of the wagon. "Introduce yourself to these men."

"Bishop Plowman . . . Bishop Plowman . . ." Toward the front of the crowd the hand of William Herzog could be seen jutting upward like a weed in a wheat field. "I thought this was to be a business meeting!" Before Plowman could recognize him, Herzog went on. "Before everybody leaves on their assignments, I'd like to know when we're going to be paid back for monies we spent in getting here."

Plowman looked very perplexed. "What's he talking about, Brother Wells?"

"He's referring to pooling of money to buy our way off an island . . . a long story . . ." Trevor then turned to Herzog. "I told you, William," said Trevor, with a look of disbelief, "once we get to Zion the money issue will be taken to church authorities there . . ."

"And this sure ain't Zion!" someone called out.

The crowd sniggered but Herzog was deadly serious. "First things first, I've always said!" he shouted. "And I want to know about the money!"

Wells turned to Plowman, "He's been a trial to me ever since Liverpool," he said apologetically and in a low voice.

"We've got a few just like him around here, Brother Wells."

"I'll talk with you and Brother Wells right after I've made assignments for everyone else," said Plowman burning a hole in Herzog's eyes. "Brother . . . ?"

"The name is William Herzog."

"You and Brother Wells wait right here . . . we'll get this talked out. Fair enough?"

"But . . ." Herzog protested.

"I said after the meeting!!" Plowman looked like he was going to get down from the wagon. Herzog also began to feel the weight of the stares around him and so nodded slightly.

The meeting continued with the bishop of Wyoming City calling for men to hunt wild game and butchers to cut it up. He called for harness and shoemakers, tanners for cowhide, tinners for pots and pans and when he asked for gristmill workers, Peter Jensen raised his hand. Pride and embarrassment were written all over his bearded face because he was the only one there.

"Peter told me he was a longshoreman," Dewey Farnsworth said to Andrew Coffey as he watched him move through the thinning crowd.

"'E tol' me 'e did milling too," said Coffey. "Remember how 'e handled that sailor?"

"I'll never forget it," said Farnsworth.

"*JEG kunne lave alt i en grist mølle.* I can do anything in a grist mill," Peter said in Danish. "*Skærpelse den sten inkluderet.* Dressing the stones included."

Trevor gave a reverse translation to Plowman who said, "Brother Eugene Michalas here runs the mill, Peter." He indicated a tall, gaunt looking man to his left. "Your stones are never sharp are they, Eugene?" Laughter rippling through the crowd confused Peter.

"Not sharp enough," answered the gaunt, dark haired man. He reached out a hand to Peter. "*Goddag.*" he said smiling.

Michalas had been a lawyer in Illinois and learned what little he knew about making flour when he'd come to Wyoming City two years previously. A longstanding convert to the Church of Jesus Christ of Latter-day Saints, Michalas had served a three year mission to Denmark, not uncommon at the time because Denmark was one of the most fertile fields for Mormon proselyting in the mid-1800s. He spoke Danish fluently and knew the light-hearted yet industrious ways of its people very well. He and his older sons, along with anybody they could get, worked in the mill.

"*Vi skam savn jer.* We really need you," he said directly to Peter.

"*Jeg er hjælpsom hos alt.* I'm ready to help with anything," answered Peter, pumping Michalas' hand. Moments ago the heir to Catherine's necklace had wondered how he'd fit into this wilderness community; there was something predestined about this, and to think this man actually spoke Danish!

Shortly Peter found himself in a log building about three times the size of his cabin. One of the few in Wyoming with a wooden floor, in the center sat a set of millstones measuring two feet in diameter and eighteen inches high. The stones were married together and a triangle shaped *rynd* in the top center of the "runner stone" created an "eye" for the introduction of grains to be milled. The bottom stone (bed stone) was stationary, and coupled with its movable twin, comprised a single "run" of stone.

As the top millstone was turned, wheat, barley, or dried corn moved outwardly by centrifugal force to be pulverized between the close tolerance and groves (the dress) cut in the stones. Ground once, the grains became a gritty meal, or twice, a coarse flour. Processed three times they made flour fine enough for pastry, but there was seldom time for this luxury.

The stones were surrounded by a wooden trough for catching the flour or meal and hanging nearby were square bladed shovels, hand-tied brooms, balls of twine, hammers, chisels, and coarse burlap bags stacked on the floor. Manually operated by men walking in a circle pushing against wooden spokes dowelled into the outer rim of the runner stone, its capacity was at somewhere near a hundred and twenty five pounds of flour per day, plus another fifty pounds of corn meal and feed grain; not quite enough to feed the town and build stores for the trek West, still the grist mill was the pride of the town.

Peter belonged here! The mill was archaic and pitifully small, and he didn't see how it could possibly feed so many people much less their animals; but all the rich feelings were there. The clean slick wood, the sweet dusty taste and the powdery feel of everything; fond memories engulfed him.

Chapter 11

Cheese & Church

The large vats could hold up to one hundred gallons of cows' milk and served two purposes for Sebastian and Torkil's fledgling operation: first they were iron and dissipated heat evenly warming milk uniformly, and second after the rennet had thoroughly dissolved in the milk, the vats served to hold the mixture over a two day period while cooling to allow curds and whey to separate. Then it became a simple matter of shoveling the mixture into cheesecloth and presses to squeeze out the whey.

"Why doesn't blue cheese spoil as fast as Farmer's?" Sebastian asked David Steed one day. "The head man here is so set on making the stuff..."

"I am," said Torkil.

"I'm not exactly sure why it stays edible for so long," Steed told them. "But over centuries cheese makers discovered different inoculums such as Penicillium that complete the ageing process, stopping spoilage and also giving the cheese a strong flavor."

"Pennicil?"

"Penicillium Roqueforti is its real name, and you make it from moldy wheat," Steed said seriously. By himself, David Steed was worth the five hundred dollar investment into the cheese business. A man of fifty, he'd followed the cheese making trade most of his life. A steady drinker, he never had money, but came to work sober and knew the business well.

"So then, you think we can make Torkil's blue cheese?" Emil Olsen asked.

"I do. We've got a solid Farmer's Cheese recipe and that's the basic start for blue cheese. Once we have a good batch in molds, then we add the Penicillium to each and watch the magic."

"Penicillium is something I know about," Torkil took up. "It's a fungus and I **do** know one way to make it. I learned it by accident. One day in Catherine's mill I picked up an old saddle that had been sitting upside down in a damp corner of the mill on top of some wheat sweepings. Underneath that saddle grew a pile of the deepest blue green fungus you ever saw; it looked like a big moldy mop.

"The smell knocked me back and then Mons Krebbe comes over an' says 'don't touch that stuff. Let me shovel it in a sack . . .'

"What for? I asks him."

"'Blue cheese, friend. My Far makes Danish blue cheese out of mold like that.'"

"How about that," David Steed exclaimed.

"That Winter I had some of his Far's blue cheese," Torkil went on, "men, you never tasted anything so rich."

"You're making my mouth water," said Sebastian.

"We made many a batch of Penicillium Roqueforti using that old saddle . . . the thing finally got to stinking so bad we had to burn it. Anyway, that's how I learned."

"By accident . . ." said Steed.

"So what's the magic?" asked Sebastian.

At that David Steed took over. "Well, it takes time to grow a blue cheese mold properly . . . you've got to use just the right amount of wheat, time and water and seal it down under rubber, leather or impervious material. Wooden boards are also used. Torkil's saddle was an accident but leather grows a nice mold . . . quicker when you sprinkle on some malt first . . . rush the process and the stuff will make you sick . . . but whatever sealer you use, when you see these brush-like feathers growing out of the mass and it's all powdery dry, dark bluish green, it's perfect."

"That's exactly what we observed," amplified Torkil.

Sebastian didn't say anything. It all sounded complicated. Every day he became more grateful David Steed came with the business.

The three men were standing in Torkil's barn near one of the huge milk vats where cheese began its process. Smoke billowed from the rock chimney of the cabin and a light breeze blew across the snow-covered fields, giving clear indication that Winter wasn't about to loosen its iron grip.

Hot rocks wheel-barrowed from the house and shoveled beneath and around the iron vat gently warmed the milk inside, helping the rennet to dissolve and dissipate throughout the batch to begin the cheese making process. Open barn doors allowed light to stream in and a thick layer of clean hay strewn about had a friendly feel to it.

Wisconsin's limitless acres of luscious green wild hay and fresh water could support vast herds of Holstein and other dairy cows, and its cold damp winters created excellent conditions for making cheese. Like Denmark, Wisconsin had hundreds of lakes but unlike Torkil's tiny homeland, Wisconsin sported millions of acres of virtually rock-free land, and some days a sky so blue and clean, it hurt to look at it. Cheese making being as meaningful to mankind as milling grain, if Torkil hadn't been divorced he may well have been in heaven.

Emil and Paul and their families found cabins close to their father, as did Sebastian and his wife. All around, the formerly abandoned community was coming to life. There were friends and countrymen to drink beer with and talk of times gone by, so Torkil wasn't lonely, just somewhat empty.

An active role in Darold Stransen's growing, charismatic-type church also kept him from feeling sorry for himself; a sort of deacon he was there every Sunday, but the fact he'd lost his wife was a constant reminder of failure. An upbeat individual during his time at Catherine's mill, Torkil now possessed a somber, more serious attitude. "Someday I might remarry," he told friends, but at present he wasn't looking.

"I'll bet you're wondering how you know when blue cheese is safe to eat, aren't you, Sebastian," David Steed said squinting.

"Yeah, I guess I was . . ."

"The truth is there are stages. At one level it's good, at the next it's better, and at the third it's best. The best blue cheese is crumbly, sharp—definitely not bland—yet creamy like Farmer's Cheese; one day it'll be our mainstay. We'll make it as good as they do in France . . . or Denmark, for that matter."

Torkil looked pleased. "Somebody's got to taste our product before we try to sell it. That will be you Sebastian . . . if it doesn't kill you, then we'll sell it!" He laughed at that, but Sebastian didn't join in.

"I'll taste it after you do . . . only after you."

"As a batch ages," Steed continued, "what you do is test it by taking small bites, not enough to make a man sick, just on the tip of the tongue. Then we'll record everything—amount of inoculums, base cheese, dates, temperature and weather condition—when we get it right we'll just repeat the process."

"There's a big need for blue cheese in America, I can feel it," said Torkil. "We can even ship some to those big towns we came through."

"Now you mention it, a travelin' fellow I met in town was askin' for blue cheese," said Sebastian. "Said he could sell all we had." Seb then peered over the holding vat and with a wooden spoon took a small sip of the warm mixture. "It's about ready for the rennet . . ."

Just then a horse snorted, and winding up the road toward Torkil's barn came Darold Stransen's wagon.

"Here comes the preacher," said Torkil. "Don't say anything about our plans, he's got a way of movin' in on things. He's not making much from the church yet . . . come Spring he's gonna' be farmin.'"

Stransen looked dressed to make a sales pitch or to preach a sermon as he climbed from his rig and hitched his horse to the front railing. He'd lost fifty pounds on the difficult trek from New York to Wisconsin and could now button his great coat in front; wearing kid leather gloves, a tan banded derby all emphasized by his wide handlebar mustache he portrayed a prosperous and regal appearance.

♥   ♥   ♥

"Olsen Brothers' Cheese . . . people say it's the best in Wisconsin."

"How are ya, Preacher?" said Torkil ignoring his flowery mannerism. "You don't get up here that often. Is everything all right?"

"Ya is everything all right?" echoed Sebastian.

"Can't you at least offer me a place near that warm vat?" asked Stransen, feigning insult.

"Of course," Torkil said, motioning toward the warm iron vat with its feet and sides buried in hot rocks.

"Do I know this fellow?" asked Stransen, looking at Steed.

"Forgive my poor manners, Brother Stransen," said Torkil. "This is David Steed, he works with us here."

"Can't remember you at church," said Stransen pointedly.

"Don't go," said Steed.

"Um."

"We've had a fire roaring up Torkil's chimney all morning," explained Sebastian. "Heating rocks for the vat. Lots of rocks. Come over and warm yourself."

"Actually I'll get right down to it," said Stransen, taking off his gloves and shaking hands with all three men.

"I've got something to do," said Steed excusing himself and going over to inspect some cheese ripening in molds.

Stransen held his hands toward the cheese vat. "Ever since New York you two men have been my ministry's strongest supporters. There were most of a hundred people in our wagon train and I couldn't have got them here without you."

Because Stransen spoke English and knew his way around the re-United States, he'd come to believe it had been himself who'd organized the exodus from New York and found the abandoned area southeast of town, not Torkil Olsen.

Egos that needed feeding seemed attracted to Torkil, but he didn't care; settled into a cabin out of the harsh weather, an interesting way to earn a living staring him in the face . . . who got credit didn't concern him.

"You know I've appreciated all you've done . . . but a bad report concerning the two of you recently reached my ears."

"My brother's been to see you . . . ?" said Sebastian, surprisingly leading out.

"Well . . . yes, Brother Olsen," Stransen allowed. "Jonathan did come to me. He's very angry with you men."

"Still," expostulated Torkil. "I just had a talk with him . . ."

"He claims you cheated him out of his portion of the cheese business," Stransen went on, "and something about land near the creek . . . his wife was crying . . ."

"I knew Meribaugh would keep him stirred up," Torkil said exasperated. "I hope you came to hear *my* side of the story, Brother Stransen," he added irritably.

"I did. Jonathan and Meribaugh told me if I didn't fix things they'd quit the church. They want an apology and for you to restore what is rightfully theirs."

"Unbelievable," said Torkil becoming very formal. "This all started with a misunderstanding between Uncle Jonathan over how I capitalized the cheese business here. It also involves a section of land I claimed when we first got here. But the real reason for the trouble is that I'm the one that knows how to make cheese and Jonathan doesn't like taking direction from me."

"Go on," said Stransen.

"That's really about it, Preacher. But about the land . . . before we all got involved in the cheese business, Uncle Jon bought a small herd of cows from that man who decided to go back to Sweden. You remember, sold out cheap, got on a horse and headed back east?"

"Brother Hedelius, yes."

"Uncle Jon doesn't think he's got enough pasture to support those cows and come Spring wanted to have use of my claim that borders that creek down there." Torkil nodded in the direction of the meandering string of snow-covered trees five hundred yards in the distance.

"I had agreed to loan that piece to Jon for his herd but made it clear it would be a temporary arrangement. Now with him wanting the money he put in the cheese business back, I decided on another way to go about it. Did he tell you about us splitting the profits around here until he was paid in cash?"

"Well he and Meribaugh said so many things, I'm not really sure . . . the land is what stuck."

"I heard both deals, Preacher," said Sebastian. "First the land deal, but then Torkil comes up with the idea of payin' Jon cash until we double what he put in here."

"How much money are we talking about?" asked Stransen.

"Two hundred twenty five dollars is what he put in," said Torkil. "His part in buying out Mrs. Swenson when her husband died."

"Tragic event," injected Stransen, "but not unexpected . . ."

"It was not only taking orders from me," said Torkil. "Jonathan knew his investment in the cheese business was five times more than mine, yet I always have final say."

"We all agreed on that," said Sebastian, "and we signed our name to a paper with the widow. Somebody has to have the last word in making the cheese and we agreed that would be Torkil, it being his idea in the first place, then we all shook hands."

"That's right," said Torkil.

"And for good measure Torkil wasn't gonna charge my brother anything for grazing his cows on that land; he'd get to use it, that's all."

"When I offered him money instead of the land that all would have changed, Uncle Sebastian."

"If what you tell me is true, and I don't doubt it, then the four of us have got to get together and talk," said the preacher.

"Jonathan and his wife only show up to church cause it's good for their livestock business," interrupted Torkil irritably. "They meet folks that are sellin' cows and so on."

"Surely that's not the only reason they come," said Stransen.

"My brother and his wife tell people you're only in the gospel for money yourself, Preacher." said Sebastian pointedly.

"They've said that?"

"They have," said Sebastian. "They've been lookin' for a reason to quit the church. This money and land thing is just an excuse."

"We don't need all this name calling," said Stransen.

"Brother Stransen," said Torkil seriously, "once again . . . I don't have two hundred and twenty five dollars to give my uncle Jonathan right now. Like I told him, he can have my land for his interest in the cheese company or else wait a bit and we'll pay him double. I think our offer's been more than fair."

"It sounds like it, Torkil . . ."

Darold Stransen's congregation hovered somewhere between forty or fifty people each Sunday, and because they had a little money he hated to lose Jon Olsen and his wife, but he certainly couldn't afford to lose Torkil. Everyone in the congregation respected the former miller-turned-cheese maker.

"Let's all get together this coming Sunday," said Stransen. "We'll secure some kind of truce between you. The community is too small for this kind of conflict."

"Now that my aunt Meribaugh's muddied the water, I think we'd be wasting everybody's time," said Torkil.

"Wasting everyone's time," agreed Sebastian.

"But I agree, Preacher, the town's too small for this kind of trouble. Let's get everything out on the table, put it all behind us and carry on with our lives."

Section Notes

1. Wyoming City was one of 16 outfitting settlements organized by the Church of Jesus Christ of Latter-day Saints and used as a place to stay while converts either earned enough money or gathered enough food, livestock and equipment to make the trek West safely. Not only that but be useful and not a burden while en route and once settled in already hard pressed communities.

2. Handcarts—where handcarts in this novel are concerned, a few will be built travel along with our story. However where Church history is concerned, there were actually ten handcart companies organized under the direction of the Prophet Brigham Young between 1856 and 1860. Some of these companies had a supply wagon or two traveling in the mix, but consisted primarily of two wheeled vehicles drawn by human power.

Eight of the ten original handcart companies made the thousand plus mile trip across the plains successfully; however two companies met with extreme tragedy, they being the Willie and the Martin handcart companies. Hundreds of people died of exposure and starvation on those two ill-fated companies, while others were maimed or crippled for life and yet the true stories of sacrifice, faith in God and service to mankind are unprecedented throughout the annals of American history.

Latter-day Saints at large, including this author, revere the brave men and women pioneers of the Willie and Martin companies, because among survivors none ever apostatized from the Church, and all survivors left a legacy of hope, healing, sacrifice, and dedication to the Gospel of Jesus Christ that has uplifted and benefited millions. Many from the Willie and Martin handcart companies suffered terrible amputations due to frost bite; toes were removed, fingers and hands—even legs left in stumps. Their suffering and sacrifice often comes to the rescue of modern day Saints during times of trial. While Latter-day trials pale in comparison to those of the Willie and Martin companies, their examples of courage and fortitude bolster us in today's difficult times, like nothing else can.

3. Handcarts continued—During the 1850s and 1860s the great demand for horses, oxen, and mules caused prices to skyrocket. Even when

money was available animals were scarce, especially oxen. Between the years 1856 and 1860, ten pioneer companies unable to afford oxen at all comprising **five thousand** souls, pulled handcarts thirteen hundred miles from Winter Quarters, Nebraska to Salt Lake City, Utah. In the more affluent companies that followed, a few handcarts were still used, however not many.

A handcart was a vehicle approximately one-third the length of a covered wagon. It was made exclusively of wood (iron was used on some wheel rims) with its cargo box three to four feet long with side pieces eight inches high. The width of a handcart was the same as a standard wagon track. The carts weighed between two and three hundred pounds and carried five to six hundred pounds of flour, clothing, tents, bedding and other essential items.

Because they were inexpensive to build and needed no animals to pull them (handcarts could be moved faster than wagons), church president Brigham Young thought them an excellent idea. Pulled principally by men (oft times by women and children too), hundreds of Europe's poor who had joined the Church of Jesus Christ of Latter-day Saints and wanted to go West would have been unable to do so were it not for the humble but innovative handcart.

Section Three

Chapter 12

Milling Grain

Eugene Michalas' sons didn't speak Danish; one a gangly looking boy, often mistaken as fifteen or sixteen years of age with boyish features and hopeful eyes, turned out to be the mill's foreman. Looking to him for a signal, Peter, arms folded leaning against a shovel, waited to plunge it into an open sack of hard winter wheat and come up with the blade half full of golden-brown grain before feeding it into the center opening in the stones.

Each time, loose grains were brushed into the center opening by hand, and to make the half-ton runner stone operate, workers stood at one of four wooden pegs extruding like wagon spokes, and when all was ready began to push.

After pouring in the grain, Peter quickly stepped onto a well-worn path in the wooden floor and with the other three men began pushing. A rasping grating sound began as the men picked up speed.

"A new broom sweeps well," one laborer remarked to another.

"It won't last," said the eldest Michalas boy. "He'll be walking as slow as us by noon!"

"Our method is a little slow," Eugene Michalas called out loudly, "but it works!"

Peter kept pushing.

After several rounds the grinding sound abated slightly and the foreman shouted, "Fill it up again." At his signal, whoever was closest to the open sack with their place at the grindstones shoveled in the wheat and the process continued. Taking their turn at the stones—and with the shovel—soon found each man dripping with sweat, and although the outdoor temperature demanded a coat, Peter removed his and set it on a workbench.

"Here's a place to hang it," said Michalas taking the coat by the collar and walking to the front of the mill. Peter froze in his tracks watching him ever so carefully as he hung the coat on a peg. When satisfied his secret was still safe, the young miller turned his attention back to the millstones.

"*Igen hen til arbejde*! Back to work!" he said smiling faintly. The Michalas brothers—especially the young foreman—thought this over-enthusiastic Dane a little strange but were still grateful to have his help.

♥   ♥   ♥

February 3, 1866, we have been in this place just one day and already I am a miller! I work for a man named Michalas, a good man who speaks Danish. The mill is only one run of hand drawn marble in a building measuring four meters square. Stacked inside the building is a large harvest of grain and they've been slowly grinding away at it. Brother Michalas has little experience with flour and meal, but has a willingness to do the job. He learned what he knows from a miller who is already in Zion.

The people in this town have taken us in where they can, but Maren and I and the Wangsgaards are among the fortunate few who have a cabin. Most people pitched their tents between the cabins. Everyone has a job to do. Claus Wangsgaard, Brother Wells along with Terrin Forsgren, William Herzog and several others are helping build more cabins.

Maren is helping make soap and candles while Gunda is in charge of a group of women scraping hides for leather. Other women are churning butter, making cheese, spinning, and weaving on the looms. Wyoming City is a busy place.

Maren went to bed early, the Wangsgaards preceding her. She is curled up in our bedroll and I long to join her because the fire is dying. But we have candles and I have a project to do. At lunch today I told Brother Michalas I had an idea which would improve flour production; he didn't seem impressed but told me to put it on paper. Tomorrow I'll show him . . .

♥   ♥   ♥

Peter stopped writing and turned to an empty page in the back of his journal. Working by candlelight, he designed a simple yet effective way to mechanize the gristmill. Finally crawling between the covers, the last thing he remembered before Claus shook him at six a.m. was snuggling against Maren's delicious warmth.

When he arrived at work, stinging blood-shot eyes made him appear as if he'd been drunk the night before yet along with his fatigued vision Peter wore an expectant grin. The day was set against a grey backdrop with a heavy brooding sky that threatened snow. On the way through town he'd been thoughtful, but not so thoughtful that he didn't wave to Jergen Madsen at the wheel works or see Terrin Forsgren stepping over the barbed wire fence to the livestock pens, nor Lars Christensen going into a log building which housed the blacksmith's forge; how proud he was to be counted among the Danish tradesmen!

"*Broder Michalas Kunne Jer se pa indevaerende?* Brother Michalas could you look at this?" he asked as soon and he'd entered the low ceilinged log building. "*God Morgan*, Peter," Michalas said coolly as he took the sketch and moved to an open window for better light. Peter watched him like a schoolboy waiting for a grade. Shortly Michalas whistled. "*Due r en nok Så ambition fyr Peter.* You're a very ambitious fellow, aren't you, Peter?"

"We could do it easily," Peter said decisively.

"Probably," said Michalas. "But I'd have to get approval . . ."

"It could double, even triple production," said Peter pushing, but ever so slightly.

"Maybe," Michalas argued, "but we'd have to shut down the mill and I don't think Brother Plowman and his councilors will go along with this."

"We'd only have to shut down for a while . . . my family owns a gristmill in Denmark. I worked there all my life."

"I'll take it up with the brethren, Peter, but for now we'd better get to work."

A man of little open emotion, Michalas turned and walked away, making Peter feel like he'd just been doused with a bucket of ice water. He'd been brash and he knew it. Only a guest here, a new arrival, Peter was embarrassed by his ego and decided to redeem himself by diving into the work, shoveling, sacking, and taking his turn at the millstones with vigor. By day's end however, anger and frustration filled him more than redemption.

"At least your new employer didn't wad the drawing into a ball and throw it away," Maren told him later that night.

♥　♥　♥

By week's end Peter could stand it no longer. "This process is so slow that it's maddening, Brother Michalas. I'd rather work building wagons."

Michalas stopped in his tracks and glared at him, but Peter confidently stood his ground. "We'll never have the needed flour for the exodus from here!"

The millstones stopped grinding as Troy and Eric Michalas, who knew their father's temperament, thought they were about to witness a fight.

"Peter," said Michalas patiently, "*Jeg Kande due r langt fra plage producent*. I know you're not a troublemaker. But your idea is nothing new; something like it has been discussed many times." at that Michalas' shoulders sagged. He took a deep breath. "Are you sure we could do it?" he asked and watched Peter's eyes carefully.

"Yes," Peter said without blinking. "Definitely."

"And how long will it take us?"

"One week at most."

Michalas hesitated then let out a sigh. "Then let's get started."

Peter's eyes immediately widened. "Are you sure?"

"I'm sure," said Michalas decisively. Once he'd made up his mind on a thing the former attorney generally never looked back. "Maybe we can finish before Jess Plowman even knows what's going on."

Peter let out a whoop while the dust-covered workers standing around stared at him like he was crazy.

"You men," Michalas then said in English, "Come over here." Michalas took Peter's folded drawing out of his pocket and displayed it plainly. "Let's all go home and bring back hammers, saws, planers, wood chisels and boring tools. We're about to make some changes around here.

"Don't say anything to bring attention to yourselves, just get back here quick as you can."

Late in the day the mill looked destroyed; wood chips and sawdust were everywhere and Jess Plowman did catch them in the act. He and Michalas tossed a few hard words back and forth; things like, "You should have brought it to council meeting!" etc., but after reviewing Peter's sketch, Plowman finally relented. "The damage is done. What can I say but hurry every chance you get, brethren." With that the Bishop left, shaking his head at either feeling useless or speechless. It was hard to tell.

The proposed changes took five days, but by the middle of Peter's second week the mill was up and running again. The worn path around the stones would advance no deeper because outside the building a much larger circle would be cut and made by the hooves of mules!

Under Peter's direction, a hole was cut in the center of the mill's roof and the weakened place shored up by new beams. A log T-shaft was passed down through and positioned next to millstones. Outside, ropes dangled from either end of the "T" used for harnessing animals.

Smeared with grease, the wood bearings carved into the shaft held it in place, allowing the shaft to turn easily while geared to roof and floor. Another gear cut three feet from the floor engaged with a movable second gear, which was locked in place by a key bearing. The yokes from two ox teams were shortened and crisscrossed over the runner stone (leaving the center eye completely clear) and anchored where the turning pins once belonged.

Attached to the yokes was a fixed shaft with carved gear engaged with the movable second gear. Now, when the gears were all locked securely against each other, the main shaft turned with a four-to-one ratio instead of one-to-one, and by comparison the millstones literally spun while grinding grain into flour. A simple drive mechanism that worked with such efficiency astounded Michalas and company. No longer walking around in circles, workers heaved-to with new vigor. With mules turning the T-shaft, men shoveling grain and flour flowing from between the spinning stones, the lost production from the mill being shut down for a week had been totally regained.

♥　♥　♥

"*Enhever henne ved den mølle er glad hos mig.* Everyone at the mill is pleased with me," Peter said, proud but weary as he entered the cabin. Maren was standing at the log table peeling potatoes with a paring knife while Gunda, coiled next to her, sliced then chopped them vigorously into small squares. Peter closed the heavy door against the frigid night air and flour dust floated in the kerosene lamplight, settling like snow on the earthen floor.

"My husband the miller," said Maren, wiping her hands on her apron and going to him. To Peter her lips tasted sweet as a baby's.

"Another long day comes to a close, eh, Peter?" said Claus, strained and worn-out himself.

"A good day, Claus, but those marble stones dull fast now that they're mechanized. How goes the building of cabins?" Peter sat across from Gunda careful to keep away from her flashing knife. The agitated little Danish woman hadn't said a single word to him; she was chopping the potatoes in front of her as if they were alive and she wanted to kill them.

"Careful not to cut yourself there, Fru Wangsgaard."

Gunda stopped abruptly; her eyes darted at him then returned to her vigorous mincing.

"I wish we had some brick here," said Claus a bit louder than was necessary while stoking the fireplace with a poker.

"You'll get cinders in the frying pan, Hr Wangsgaard," said Maren.

Claus went right on stabbing at the glowing coals, moving logs so they'd burn better. "But building with logs goes fast. We should have a cabin for every family by month's end."

To Maren's relief he leaned the poker against the hearth and stood against the door. Deep in thought, his arms were folded tight as if to guard against any interruption. The flame in Sarah Bingham's kerosene lantern barely lighted the table and Claus seemed a shadow on the fringes.

Maren carefully scraped Gunda's diced potatoes into her apron, not dropping a single piece, and went to the fireplace to kneel near the iron skillet. Gingerly pouring potatoes into the hot grease, they splattered and sizzled, sending a cloud of heavy steam up the chimney.

"Having cabins for everyone is very ambitious, isn't it?" Peter asked.

"No," said Claus pushing off the wall. He walked over and sat next to Gunda. "When men work together much is accomplished."

"Humph," said Gunda, and immediately got up from the table, handing Maren a bowl of chopped salt pork stirred in with two fresh eggs she'd been given by a neighbor. Maren leaned back from the heat and smoke of the fire and wiped a few loose hairs away from her eyes, then leaned in again and began adding the meat and eggs to the potatoes. A rich aroma filled the room.

"And how goes your work, Gunda?" Peter asked conversationally.

Gunda looked at him as if seeing him for the first time that evening. "See my hands," she answered sharply and held them out for his inspection. "Red and cracked . . . they're absolutely raw from scraping those hides."

"You women have got the tanner busy," Claus commented.

"Men should do the hides," Gunda snapped.

"I thought some were . . ."

"There were none today," his fiery wife said angrily. "Not a single man!"

Claus looked cautiously across at Peter and for a while the only sound heard in the cabin was the crackling fire and Maren's hash sizzling in the pan.

Presently Gunda took the spatula from Maren and stirred the hash. "Men have the fun of hunting the animals so they should clean the hides," she said, covering her hand with her apron folded double and taking the frying pan from its place on the hot coals. She then placed it on the table right under Claus and Peter's hungry noses.

"I'll talk to Brother Plowman about it," Claus offered.

Gunda ignored him. "Let's go then, Maren," she said.

After filling a plate with half of the prepared hash, then leaving the rest in the steaming skillet, Maren and Gunda put on their wraps, grabbed a loaf of bread, and headed for the door. "It's for the Thayers," Maren answered her husband's inquiring eyes. "Sister Thayer is very sick."

"Something's really bothering Gunda," said Peter concerned.

"It's not the hides, little brother," Claus said after the door shut. "That's for certain."

The two sat in silence for a moment watching the fire in the hearth, Peter picking absently at slivers of steel filings imbedded in his wrists from sizing (sharpening) the millstones.

"Marks[1] of an experienced miller," commented Claus.

The women were back in a matter of minutes and set the table with what was left of the hash. "There's plenty of bread," said Maren. "Gunda baked four loaves today. Sister Thayer's had such a terrible time of it," she added. "First the deaths of her children on that horrible island and now this ague; Elizabeth Anne is there nursing her."

"Would you please say a blessing, Peter?" asked Claus glumly. The food had cooled noticeably, but neither man dared complain.

Chapter 13

Snowbound

An avalanche of snow and rock blocked the pass near Oxford, Ohio and while men worked in shifts shoveling to clear a path for the train, the day slowly waned. At first the stranded locomotive shot steam skyward in great angry clouds, but as night settled in and boilers cooled, the engine became as cold and immobile as the rails. Lanterns bobbed about as men moved up to take their turns at the shovels and wheelbarrows, clearing the way while in the passenger cars temperatures plummeted.

"We need to save the coal and wood," the conductor told Maurice Wilkins, Branch President, and Otto Pedersen—leaders of Catherine's group. "Once a path is cleared we'll need all we have to get up a full head of steam and take us in to Oxford."

"What could possibly have caused this?" President Wilkins almost demanded. "The mountains through here aren't that steep."

"I believe a Confederate raiding party blew this pass," the conductor stated angrily. "It's the only thing that could have brought down so much rock."

"But the war's over," Otto protested.

"Not to some, my good man. Not to some. More than likely this was Quantrill's Raiders[2] . . . but then, ever since the war ended he gets credit for every train robbery that happens."

"He's dead but some of his followers are still around," an American passenger threw in. "Jesse James is one of 'em. Carries a Bible and kills people. The Younger brothers, Jim and Cole, are out there too; last I heard they were operatin' in Kentucky and Indiana."

"Regardless of the culprit, or culprits, we're going to post guards. I'm not gonna sit here and have some bandits swoop down and rob the passengers. Mr. Chenoweth here will pass out muskets so volunteers can guard the train while we're working."

"All right!" a burly fellow in buckskin britches and wolf fur coat shouted at the men strung along the tracks. "Who can shoot?"

Commotion erupted for about ten minutes as men—Saints and

non-members alike—decided amongst themselves who would shoulder a weapon.

"This is no game," hollered Mr. Chenoweth. "We are in earnest here. I want two dozen experienced riflemen."

"Mr. Wilkins," said the conductor loudly. "We have plenty of kerosene and the chief engineer wants lanterns burning at both ends of these passenger cars all night long."

"So we can watch each other freeze to death," an English member was heard to say. "I thought by March it quit snowing in America."

"Schusss!" Otto Pedersen cautioned him. "He's concerned about temperatures in the cars tonight," he added in perfect English.

"We're not moving you know," the conductor said. "You'll be surprised how warm it gets in a car with folks all bundled up and breathin' in tight quarters. We might even have to crack a window or two before the night is over . . . let in some fresh air."

Satisfied, he waited while Otto translated the information into Danish

Stretched out for nearly half a mile the lighted passenger cars serpentined through the darkening night resembling an all night inn, or string of English pubs. Inside, shadows of women passing up and down the aisles could be seen and outside, men who weren't shoveling were stationed strategically in pairs from engine to caboose. Back-to-back, muskets in arms, their orders were to protect the train from roving bands of raiders.

Inside Catherine's car, little Anna's breathing continued rapid and wispy, her face scarlet with her bangs matted wet against her face. Her fever still raged, and as Krista gently rocked back and forth on a hard bench, tears streamed down her face, dropping on the child's forehead. Catherine had secured sleeping berths for herself, Evette, Krista and their children, but couldn't force anyone to retire. Krista feared little Anna wouldn't wake up if she tucked her away snug in such a heated state, and she wanted to be around friends as long as possible.

Catherine wanted to scream. Helplessness wasn't something she gave into easily; only Casten's presence calmed her. She couldn't sleep; every breath the child fought for kept her on edge, and at the very moment when she could no longer stand it, she turned, desperately searching for the face of Otto Pedersen, who as it went, somehow appeared right beside her.

Catherine wanted to stand up and grab him by the lapels of his coat and demand he do something, but his serene and kindly expression restrained her. He had just finished his shift outside shoveling and must have read Catherine's mind as he put a finger gently to her lips. Another man had come along with him, and taking a small bottle from his pocket he uncorked the top and poured a golden drop of consecrated olive oil on little Anna's crown.

"Anna Katrina Jensen," he began. "By the power and authority of the Holy Melchezedek Priesthood which I hold, I anoint your head with this oil . . ."

A radiant peace settled into the stranded passenger car as the man performed the sacred ordinance. All around people ceased talking and whispering; in fact, except for the priesthood holder's voice the car remained silent.

After the gravely ill child had been anointed Otto Pedersen—now Elder Otto Pedersen—placed his hands upon her burning forehead and began a blessing: "Anna Katrina, in the name of the Lord Jesus Christ, I seal this anointing and give you a blessing." With no hesitation he went right on, "The Lord has a work for you to perform on this earth, little Anna, and you will be healed of this malady which has struck you down . . . healed . . ."

Krista couldn't remember anything except the word "healed," but the light she *felt* surging into her child's frail body affected her as nothing ever had. Even before Otto finished the priesthood blessing, little Anna began to sweat profusely while her mother cried softly, in muffled uncontrollable gasps. Light filled her mind, her heart slowed and she truly felt the presence of the Lord. Prior to the blessing Krista had convinced herself that her daughter would die and was actually working on finding resolution.

Catherine, beside herself with joy, heard every word Otto pronounced and later that evening even wrote them down. The blessing had been a simple affair. No pomp and circumstance, just the sincerity of a once worldly and yet wealthy man who'd humbled himself to the dust before being baptized.

On that frigid night, while alone in the men's necessary room—as was his habit before giving a blessing—Otto had pled with God to help him know what to say; help him know His will. No memorized prayer; just a man of faith straining to hear the still small voice of the Holy Spirit.

A bit later with Krista and Anna Katrina along with little Hans, asleep in their berth, and Otto and his friend again taking their turn digging out the train, Catherine, Evette and Casten were talking quietly in the dining car. White tablecloths and kerosene lanterns gimbled on the chilly iron walls of the rail car would have made a cozy setting, were it not so cold. The ladies could see their breath.

"When Otto was standing there looking down on little Anna I had no idea what he was going to do, Casten; I know he is here to protect us, to lift heavy things and so forth . . . but I'm convinced his blessing saved my granddaughter's life." She bowed her head, shaking it slowly side to side then lifted her moist eyes. "Anna is going to be all right; I just know it, and I'm so grateful to your husband."

"Otto's a very deep person, dear friend," Casten volunteered. "Still wearing his ridiculous long bushy sideburns—a vestige of his days as a politician—when someone needs a blessing, he'll go off by himself . . . many times he's fasting. He's not the prideful person he used to be. I think our wayward son, Alof, broke him of all that. Anyway, he prays until he thinks he's ready to hear the will of God on a given situation; then and only then will he give a blessing."

A painful expression crept across her face, then she took a deep breath as the troubled look gently faded. "Three months ago, Alof came in late from a night of drinking. Badly bruised, he'd been beaten severely and his arm was dangling grotesquely in a serious fracture. I went for the doctor and between him and Otto they set the arm straight and plastered it. There were dark bruises all over my son's chest and stomach; he was passing blood and out of his mind with fever for the next several days."

Casten hung her head momentarily then lifted it and continued, "If only Alof would accept the Gospel..." tears streamed gently down her cheeks. "As you both know he's my only child. As it went, just like tonight, Otto disappeared for a while and then he came in and laid hands on our son's fevered head and pronounced a blessing..."

"What happened?" interrupted Evette.

"Well, let me put it like this... Alof waved goodbye to us with that arm. He's doing fine now and he's stopped drinking. He even promised to join us in America one day and I'm going to hold him to it."

"With children, there's always hope," stated Catherine sagely. She knew all about the rowdy Alof Pedersen and how many times he'd broken Casten's heart. She didn't exactly share Casten's faith that he'd stay away from drinking, but then she wasn't his mother. "I genuinely believe if you train up a child in the way they should go... you all know the scripture... when they are old, they'll return. If I didn't have faith, then what kind of person would I be? Perhaps even my youngest son, Ferdinand, will come around."

"He just might," said Evette brightly. "Just look at Krista."

"Going back to Otto's blessing of my granddaughter," said Catherine. "I was about to go out of my mind and start shouting at somebody when all of a sudden there stood Otto. I had no idea he'd even been thinking about little Anna!"

"As I said," Casten interrupted. "He goes about things concerning the priesthood slowly and in his own due time. He's given me blessings before. Not often mind you, but I believe my husband has the gift of healing."

"It's a priceless gift, this priesthood of God," said Catherine sincerely. "What is so astounding to me is that because of the faith and humility of a single fourteen-year-old boy who had the courage to call upon God, the true priesthood authority is actually here again upon the earth. Think about that for a moment. Just like the apostles of old, men of the church can be ordained to act in His holy name . . ."

"With true authority," added Casten. "But the priesthood is only a blessing if men will get out there and use it. Serve their fellow man. Otherwise they are no different than ordinary men."

"All I know is that my granddaughter is going to live and you'll never know how grateful I am!" said Catherine. "I feel like running up and down and shouting. I don't know what I'd have done if we'd lost her."

"I'll be even more grateful when they get this train moving," said Casten, beginning to feel the chill in the dining car. Looking around, she saw people leaning against each other, sleeping back-to-back or huddled on benches and even the floor. Lanterns glowed eerily outside the train's windows, revealing silhouettes of freezing men pushing wheelbarrows. The passenger cars were only slightly warmer, but at least people were out of the wind.

A porter came by with a tray of bowls full of hot corn chowder. Small bowls, but the promise of internal warmth cheered the three women. They thanked him and, surprised at how hungry they were, finished their small offerings before speaking again.

"I'll bet that revives you," Casten said looking at Evette's watering eyes.

"I don't know, Sister Pedersen. I'm about to drop in my tracks. I hope little Hans has saved me some room. He sprawls out like a crab. I haven't slept all that well, but it's been good getting to know Krista better. While our children struggle to get settled each night we talk a lot."

"The hot chowder is making me sleepy," admitted Catherine. "I think I'm finally ready to crawl into my berth."

"Before you go, Fru Jensen," asked Evette. "How far is it from here to Chicago? I mean in time."

"Two days," said her mother-in-law. "If they ever get this thing moving again. My dears," she added, "I never thought I'd say it but I'm just about finished with this whole business. Ships, trains . . . I'm going to bed before I get cranky."

"I'm right behind you," said Casten.

Chapter 14

Polygamy vs. Plural Marriage

"The Andersens are packed into their tent like pigs in a poke," said Maren, trying to make conversation. "Sister Andersen complained about it all the way home today."

"They'll be in a cabin by week's end," said Claus, looking up from his plate at Gunda. She wasn't smiling. "Families with children are first in line."

They ate in silence for a moment then a knock sounded at the door. "Claus, are you there? Claus, Peter, anybody home? Trevor Wells here."

"*Engelsk.* Englishmen," growled Gunda under her breath. She knew how awful she must have sounded, but couldn't stop herself. Her hands were raw, cracked, and almost bleeding from a day's work of scraping hides. Her legs throbbed with bulging varicosities from bearing her standing weight. Despite meager meals, Gunda somehow managed to maintain a few extra pounds, while everyone around her seemed somewhat gaunt and wasted. She knew what people must think; that she had a stash of rich food somewhere.

Lately a grumpy, pudgy woman, bitter at the world, Englishmen were Gunda's particular target. She keenly felt the burden of being a woman these days, especially with this polygamy thing rearing its ugly head. How could Maren remain so pleasant? To Gunda it was irritating.

"Come in, Brother Wells," Claus called getting up and opening the door.

"*Lad være arrangere*. Don't get up," said Wells, stooping as he entered and closed the door. "My it smells good in here, Sister Wangsgaard, Sister Jensen."

"Thank you," said Maren. "Can I get you a plate?"

"Not a thing," Trevor answered, wondering why Gunda didn't speak to him.

"Good evening, Brother Wells," said Peter, standing to shake hands.

"Good show at the mill, Peter," said Trevor going over to the fireplace and holding out his hands. "My word it's cold out there . . . transformed the place I hear."

"I had lots of help, Brother Wells."

"I've got to see it," said Wells rubbing his stiff hands together to remove the numbness.

"I hate to interrupt your fine supper, Gunda," he said changing course, "but Brother Plowman wants to see you, Claus."

"Has he taken over all your responsibilities?" asked Wangsgaard.

"Most of them," Wells said with a smile.

"Does he want me, too?" asked Peter.

"Just Claus," answered Trevor.

Claus was already putting on his coat, glad to be leaving the strained atmosphere.

"I won't be long, Mother," he said trying to kiss Gunda on the forehead. She leaned away from him.

"Don't eat everything, Peter."

"See you all tomorrow then," said Wells cheerily as he and Claus stepped into the black night, closing the heavy door of the cabin behind them.

"He's already seen enough of Brother Plowman today," said Gunda with repugnance.

"What's the matter with Brother Plowman?" Peter defended. He liked the Bishop of Wyoming City. "He has to see people when he can. He's a busy man, Fru Wangsgaard."

"I'll say he's busy!" said Gunda angrily as she went to the fireplace again and put the iron skillet back on the coals, pouring a little water in to clean it. "Did you know the man has three wives?"

Peter swallowed a half-chewed bite of bread, and quickly took another.

"Two are sisters if you can imagine!" Gunda went on. "And that's not all—our Brother Plowman has two of the best cabins here. Two large ones!"

"I've met his wives," said Maren almost apologetically. "We make soap together."

"So that's what's been bothering you, Fru Wangsgaard?" asked Peter.

"Any reason it shouldn't, Peter?" asked Gunda her eyes flashing. The water in the frying pan had started to boil, and with a wooden spoon Gunda began scraping the sides viciously.

"You should have used the spider pan, Maren, it's much cooler. These potatoes are burnt to the bottom; stuck like glue!"

She paused in her work and waved the wooden spoon threateningly in Peter's direction. "Do you know what happened today, Peter?" she asked, her face scrunched up like a wrinkled prune. Before he could answer she added, "Your Bishop Plowman told my Claus that he should take a second wife. He said Talitha Kjars would make an excellent choice and he might think about courting her!"

Dead silence prevailed in the one-room cabin. "You knew

something like that would happen before we got here, Fru Wangsgaard," Peter finally said. "Claus doesn't have to comply. Nobody is forced to live the order."

"That's not what I'm beginning to feel!" Gunda shot back. "Bishop Plowman told Claus he should talk it over with me first. The very idea! Every time I turn around . . . don't tell me they're not forcing us to comply! Today a lady was looking down her nose at me because she *does* share her husband and she said it's the *true* order of marriage!"

Maren went about slowly eating her dinner, not tasting a thing.

"Is your Brother Michalas a polygamist, Peter?" Gunda demanded as she moved away from the hearth.

"I believe he is. There have been two different ladies come by the mill to talk to him and several of his sons work there. What does it matter, Fru Wangsgaard? He's a good man. And it looks to me that he takes very good care of his family. Or families. They're all dressed comfortably and none appear unhappy."

"That may be so, Peter," said Gunda with acid in her tone. "But if I'd have known plural marriage was something the Church expected of *all* good women . . . I'd have never left Denmark!"

The cabin was deathly quiet for a moment then Gunda turned away from both Peter and Maren. "What's killing me," she said remorsefully, "is that Claus seems willing. He wants to be obedient to all Church teachings. Even this one." She started to weep quietly and wringing her hands and looking helplessly around, didn't seem to have her bearings.

Maren could sense that Gunda might be on the brink of a mental collapse. "*Jeg indtale hos jer udenpa pa egen hand Fru Wangsgaard?* May I speak with you alone, Fru Wangsgaard . . . outside?" Without waiting for an answer she again put on her heavy shawl and went to the door.

"Oh for heaven's sake, Maren, it's getting dark outside," Gunda said. Standing reluctantly from the table, she clumsily put on her shawl and followed the younger woman, leaving Peter alone with his food and troubled mind.

With squared shoulders and graceful stride (much lighter than Gunda's deliberate heavy pace behind her), Maren purposefully led the way to a cluster of trees. Just making its evening appearance, the moon lighted their way.

Just as with this little walk, lately it seemed to Gunda that every step in life slogged down with mud—or was it quicksand? The faith in Christ which had carried her before, prayer, the scriptures and the joy she received in serving others, all seemed to be absent these days. What was wrong? *Maybe I haven't progressed at all?* Gunda thought as she followed Maren. And all this time she'd believed she *was* moving forward, out of backward Europe, across the great deep, then touching down on American soil only to find her faith wavering if not absent. Because of this plural marriage issue, Gunda felt herself losing gravity.

And questions! Could one serve others *too* much? The deaths, the toil, the sickness, the bodily stench of humanity jammed together in a ship's steerage, the dreadful island, and now a drafty log cabin? Frozen ground like that beneath her feet, cracked and bleeding hands from scraping hides, the constant wailing of sick children! She wanted to wail herself! Did anything make sense anymore? Life had been pretty good back in old Denmark!

She'd come so far, sacrificed so much, but now her Claus taking another wife? No. No. No! Widely practiced in biblical times, was it that God wanted to test the faith of His true followers? Build their numbers? See how far they'd go to defend their beliefs? What was it?!

Gunda thought of poor Abraham. Childless, stricken in years and yes God promised that his seed would be as the sands of the seashore. Barren herself, Gunda could see why Sarah gave him Hagar. Then Hagar conceived and bore Ishmael; and though Abraham loved the boy with all his heart, Ishmael was not the true heir.

Time and events finally led to Sarah's conceiving (at ninety nine years of age!) and the bearing of Isaac. Scorned by her former handmaid Hagar, Sarah demanded that she and son Ishmael be sent away.

Abraham, the heavy-hearted father, patriarch, and legal husband, complied with Sarah's wishes.

Two nations sprang from Abraham's first two offspring—there were other children and wives as well: from one, the Twelve Tribes of Israel, from the other the boiling Middle Eastern nations. Abraham's numberless seed; God fulfilled His promise, but at what cost? The tearing to shreds and humbling to dust the pride and emotions of humankind. Obedience. Faith.

Am I willing to sacrifice my husband to another woman? His time and attention? Can I take this leap of faith? Gunda had to ask herself. *Haven't I already given enough? And what about the trek across the barren plains yet ahead? Can't God trust the depth of what I've already sacrificed?*

Beautiful Maren, thought Gunda as they slowly traversed the moonlit frozen path. *She grows more graceful with the days. Her courage continues to unfold like the petals of a rose; more than meets the eye is there as each day brings greater faith, surprise in a new opening layer.*

Maren stopped and turned to face Gunda, who was still lagging heavily behind. When they were face to face, Maren demanded, "What, Gunda? *Afgore mig.* Tell me."

"WHY??!!" exploded Gunda, rage firing her eyes and tongue. "Why this celestial marriage thing? You seem fine with it. Explain that to me! You obviously understand something I'm completely blinded by. Help me, Maren!" The rage that had simmered all evening flooded out in sobs, tears spilled down her face, her shoulders shook in violent spasms. A hostile stream then sputtered from her lips. "My God has betrayed me and my trust in Him has been broken. My soul is broken as well."

Gunda felt her knees buckle after the torrent of words and was reaching out for something to take hold of; Maren barely had the strength to stop her swooning friend but broke her fall, leaving both women sprawled face forward on the frozen ground.

"My goodness! Are you all right, Gunda?" Maren quickly untangled herself and sat up rubbing her cheeks free of icy snow, but left Gunda in a fetal position—pulling her stubby legs as tightly as she could towards her chest and pressing her cheek into the snow as if to be close to the earth, her Father in Heaven's divine creation.

Maren sat there gently rubbing Gunda's back, silently watching her tears drop one by one. Then all at once, the pinched face Gunda had worn all that day glistened with honesty. Peace overcame her. Maren greatly admired Gunda at this moment and almost breathed a sigh of relief. Finally the haunts that plagued every woman she knew were faced by this one, this dear soul whom she loved like a mother.

"It's a good thing one of us broke down before we both did together," she said quietly. "The two of us have been carrying a pool of sorrow within; now finally one of us lets it gush forth. From now on at least one of us has sturdy shoulders to lean on."

"You think those shoulders are mine?" said Gunda, sitting up and wiping her face. She let out a slight giggle, and before they knew it both women were laughing.

"Are we crazy?" asked Maren.

"Oh no," giggled Gunda. "Leaving comfortable homes in Holbaek, traveling through ridiculous hardships, enduring nature in its most hostile form, quarantined on a swampy island and now we are asked to share our husbands! No, we're not crazy . . . we're insane!"

At that Maren began laughing almost hysterically. "I'm sorry," she explained catching a breath. "But I just had a thought."

"A thought?" asked Gunda.

"Well, if you'll allow me to poke a little fun at Hr Wangsgaard; can you imagine his silly little walk and balding head prancing up to some lovely woman trying to woo her affections? And behind him Bishop Plowman saying, 'There's really nothing to it, Brother Wangsgaard. Just get up there and ask her to marry you!'"

Peals of laughter followed. If anyone had wandered by the woods they'd have had the two women committed.

"It's a hard existence, Gunda," stated Maren, both women completely rational now. "That poor little Andersen girl, kicked in the face by her father's horse last week . . . disfigured for life . . . I suppose she could have died. Might have been better off. And Brother Sandagar falls off his horse . . . run over by the wagon behind; he must have ruptured something; painful death. Another widow with children; what a load to bear."

The women's emotions had quieted and they found themselves silent for a moment.

"Please know," Maren continued, "there is despair in the fatherless child's face. Fear in their eyes. One of the savages out here could kidnap them, or they might even starve for lack of food . . . but not if a man who holds the priesthood is there to protect them, there to provide for them. There are women who stand alone and need help. Plural marriage is not always to serve the purpose of conception."

"BUT it sure is a part of it!" Gunda started up again.

"Only a righteous man and woman will be asked to serve in this calling," Maren continued. "It's difficult for women, but I do know it plagues and pains men as well. I can see it on their faces. After all, they are men and some are trapped in their inability to communicate the contents of their hearts. What their mouths say is never as intelligent as what their eyes tell. Sure it is easy for them to turn their head for a pretty woman. We turn ours for a handsome man. If a man is given this call, I think it's only natural for their first instinct to think of someone attractive. No matter how righteous they want to be, people still respond to beauty.

"But let it go, Gunda, or do go back to Denmark. But if you leave, if you abandon your testimony and walk the rest of your life without faith, you will never forgive yourself, being troubled by the question, 'what if.'"

Gunda felt humbled by the things Maren had said. She was thoughtful. She trusted the truth, and as much as she wanted to be angry she couldn't deny the spirit she felt in her heart. She could not deny it was the Spirit of the Holy Ghost whispering that Maren had spoken the truth. She took a deep breath and exhaled the last of her rage. Though she might have sat on the frozen earth talking with Maren forever, Gunda was ready to return to the cabin.

Upon entering, they found Peter staring absently into his untouched plate. He looked up and saw Gunda's swollen face and red eyes, and tears instantly came to his own. He also observed his wife's eyes and revealing courage.

"I'm sorry, Gunda. I'm sorry for all the trials we are going through. But I know we wouldn't keep pressing on through the mire if we doubted the words of our living Prophet. But . . ." and Peter's eyes assured her, "nothing permanent can happen until we get to Zion. There's nobody here with authority to perform the sealing ordinance. Why, half the men in town would marry Talitha, she's very attractive . . . regardless, it will be *her* choice, and nobody else's."

Maren stood, went to Gunda and put her arms around her whereupon Gunda began to cry—only briefly this time—then wiped her eyes with her apron.

"I'm all right," she said proudly, pushing away and taking a breath. Emotionally, Gunda was torn to shreds. Complex in nature, her anger stemmed from three main sources: First, for twenty-five years she'd been a devoted wife to Claus and naturally didn't want to share him. Secondly she loved the Church. She'd given up family and homeland for it and knew its teachings—except perhaps plural marriage, which she considered to be the work of the devil himself—were true.

Thirdly, Gunda felt terribly inferior to Talitha Kjars. The pretty widow was ten years younger than herself! But youth and Arian beauty weren't Talitha's only attributes. A kind and sensitive lady, a tragic life had humbled her and intensified her womanly compassion. She was truly a great person; Gunda even liked her!

Fifteen minutes later, the door opened and Claus blew back in. Powdered ice from the cabin roof followed him when he slammed the thick door. "Put another log on the fire, Peter. All of a sudden, temperatures seem to be dropping . . ."

"And what did the good bishop want?" asked Gunda sarcastically, putting a hand on Maren's shoulder.

"He wanted me to speak at Sunday meeting. What's going on around here?"

"Plural marriage," Peter answered simply.

"Still," said Claus. He looked into Gunda's face and realized her pain. He stepped over and took her gently in his arms; this time she allowed it. He held her a long time, rocking her slightly.

Regardless of the truce, the situation in the Wangsgaard's cabin remained akin to sitting on a powder keg for weeks. Gunda slept away from Claus. She'd never hear of a "celestial marriage" as some were calling it. "In your case, Norseman," she told him, "you're talking about polygamy, an unwilling wife . . . nothing celestial about it, and you might end up sacrificing one marriage to have another."

For his part, Claus sympathized with the widow, Talitha Kajars. He approached her once at a church meeting, just saying hello and felt foolish by her blank stare. Still, he felt compelled to get to know her. She did captivate him, and while he cherished Gunda and would love her until he passed this life, it remained difficult to be around her. Getting ready for the trek West plus making the city habitable for new convert immigrants had him and every man in Wyoming City pushed to the limit. Many times Claus looked around and felt overwhelmed by how much there was to do.

♥   ♥   ♥

Men and women—in fact, everyone—had reasons to be miserable in Wyoming City; not only was it hard being female in these sparse and emotional conditions but inept males such as store clerks, school teachers and accountants not accustomed to hard physical labor, found themselves failing. Axes, and shovels weren't so difficult to master, but they couldn't handle horses or oxen and worse yet, chickens and pigs. One city dweller, after trying to catch a chicken to kill for dinner, got so embarrassed that he quit the Church and left town without taking his family along.

Then there was Helen Slater, a convert from Pennsylvania who, after a wagon accident, dragged her injured husband for miles into town (all the while her baby screaming and exposure causing the loss of three fingers to frost bite) only later to watch both father and child die of pneumonia.

Illness and death being common in Wyoming City, few of the immigrant converts ever imagined that following a Prophet of God could be this difficult, but stakes were high, the adventure great, and adept or not, most were willing to try for the sake of freedom, religious and otherwise. Freezing weather, primitive dwellings, tough as things were, most everyone in town would rather die than renounce the Gospel of Christ, the Book of Mormon, living Prophets and everything associated with the restored Church.

And as outrageous as it sounded, men were being asked to take upon them another wife, and wives being asked to share their husbands. The complexities of marriage to one spouse being astounding, adding an additional adult human life, plus extra children in some cases, into an already impossible situation, could only work under the guidance and grace of God.[3]

Chapter 15

Millstones

*S*itting against a sack of wheat in the mill while eating his lunch, Peter absently listened to the Michalas brothers and three other workers in their Americanized-English banter. The situation between Claus and Gunda laid heavily on his mind, and as he rested from the morning's labor he wondered if plural marriage was really what God wanted for members of His Church. Couldn't there be a mistake somewhere?

Eugene Michalas, who'd been outside hitching a fresh mule to the T-shaft, came in and sat beside him. The double doors to the mill were open slightly and a bright snow-covered day made it easy to see.

"Jeg kunne ikke vent hen til nå til arbejade hver dag Peter. Jeg er taknemmelig hen til jer. "I can't wait to get to work each day, Peter. I'm very grateful to you . . . we're putting out a lot of flour. It's twice the accomplishment considering there's so little to work with out here."

"Tak for lån Hr Michalas. Thank you, Hr Michalas," said Peter.

A somber and righteous man, Michalas usually didn't have much to say, but this day Peter could tell he wanted to talk. He reached back into the open sack of wheat and picked up a small handful of kernels and tossed them into his mouth. "Good crop of wheat," Eugene said.

"You can make gum if you chew it long enough," said Peter.

"Everybody knows that," said Michalas. "You know, Peter," he added reflectively, "a gristmill is the key to civilized life. Flour and feed for man and beast. Since time began mills have been the center of a community. Mills and millstones are mentioned throughout the Bible. Millstones are often used in the parables of the Savior. One of my favorite stories of a mill is in the book of Ruth . . . Ruth and Boaz . . ."

"And the threshing floor," said Peter. He knew the story.

The workers settled themselves lower against the log wall and began to doze as the two men talked. The day had warmed slightly and the wind wasn't blowing. Inside the mill if you were wearing a coat conditions were perfect for a nap.

Peter decided the time was as good as any to satisfy Gunda's curiosity about Michalas' marital status. "*Du har flere sif kone lave jer ikke broder Michalas?* "You have more than one wife don't you, Brother Michalas?" he asked respectively.

Michalas looked Peter straight in the eye to determine any malicious intent then said clearly, "*Jeg har to wives og ti børn Peter.* I have two wives and ten children, Peter. Troy and Eric over there are from my first wife and," he indicated the opposite wall near the stack of flour sacks, "Feramorse is from my second. My other children come and go from the mill, bringing my lunch and so forth. You've seen them."

Peter nodded.

"What makes you ask? Is something troubling you?"

"Well . . ." Peter started. "Gunda Wangsgaard, Claus' wife, is extremely upset about plural marriage. She and Claus are not getting along at all just now."

"Have they been to see Bishop Plowman together?"

"I don't think so . . ."

"Claus may be putting the cart before the horse here. Gunda must be in on things from the very beginning. She has a right to be upset. Tell them to go see Bishop Plowman together or else tell them to come and talk with me."

"That's a very good idea. I'll do it," said Peter very relieved. "Claus has stirred up a hornet's nest in our cabin. I can't blame Gunda for how she feels; they've been married for many years. Perhaps she just doesn't understand *it*. What do you think?"

Michalas thought a moment before he answered. "Actually, women have a lot more understanding about plural marriage than do we."

"Really?" exclaimed Peter.

"That's a fact," said Michalas respectfully. "Women who accept this commandment make great sacrifice. Passions such as jealousy, selfishness and pride must be put aside. Others' wants and needs move way ahead of their own.

"It's the same for the men. Selfishness cannot exist. Only service. Both my families have tremendous needs. Food and shelter are only the beginning. Rearing children is the most arduous task. Spending ample time with everyone is the most difficult thing. My wives and children all need time to talk with me, counsel with each other and time to work together . . ."

"I see that," said Peter.

"Women are in control of what happens in a multiple marriage," Michalas went on. "It's they who should choose whom they would have come into the family unit. Or at least agree. Unequivocally. If women don't agree on the important things—children, work, who does what—a man's dead from the start. Even under the best circumstances there are petty grievances, jealousies. They simply can't be avoided, and must be worked out.

"The first thing worldly men see is the bedroom," Michalas went on. "If they only knew how unimportant that is. The workload of any two families is enough to kill a man. Can you imagine three and four?"

"I can't," said Peter shaking his head.

"There's got to be a great deal of organization in a multiple marriage or nothing works out," said Michalas. "In fact it only works as sanctioned by God. A man or woman can't just go out and propose marriage to whoever strikes their fancy. It's a calling directly from God."

"And some people don't get called?"

"That's exactly right," said Michalas. "Some people don't get the call. As for my families, things are working fairly well. Everyone is pulling in the same direction, we share each other's burdens, and much is being accomplished. My children are doing well; that was my main concern. More is taught at a woman's knee than in all the classrooms on earth and children benefit from having more than one woman around to love and to help them."

Peter thought Michalas was making things sound too easy but felt this man's conviction. "Do you ever fight and argue?" he asked.

"Naturally. We have our arguments," answered Michalas. "But not often, there just isn't time for it."

"How do the ladies get along with each other?"

"Maribah and Roxanna are their names, Peter, and they get along very well. They love each other; they're almost like sisters.

"What about other such marriages in this town?" asked Peter.

"Ha!" said Michalas. "I've seen a lot of people come through here. More people have left the Church over plural marriage than any other single issue, Peter. There's been plenty of bitterness. Property disputes, church courts, divorces . . . some people stay married even though they're miserable with each other. They think they've got some reward in Heaven coming. My own situation would be better if I had another house."

One of the workers stretched and stood up.

"But I just haven't had time to build one," said Michalas, winding down. "Looks like we'd better get back to work," he said standing. "We can talk later."

Peter nodded.

"Back to work," Michalas said, walking over to two of the dozing workers and nudging them with his foot. "Whose turn at the mules?"

The eldest of the lot raised his hand slightly, stood and stretched and went outside. The other workers got up and reluctantly went to their jobs of sorting weeds, dirt-clods, and other foreign objects from the wheat, and some went to sewing sacks. Peter took his place shoveling wheat into the center of the millstones; they'd soon be turning.

♥　♥　♥

Inside the mill and throughout the sprawling outfitting settlement, in the fields, barns, cabins, chandler's shop, tannery and throughout Wyoming City, while people performed their labors, pain found their backs; pain found their shoulders and played its cruel game of chase from one side of the body to the other, surging throughout the knees and elbows like fire feeding on dried kindling. If a man or woman's hands were not cracked, cut, swollen or bleeding, it was only because they somehow got out of working.

They'd joined the Church and immigrated to America for a better life, but knew if they were to have it, they'd earn it by the sweat of their faces.

♥　♥　♥

As the days passed, Peter Jensen and Eugene Michalas became trusted friends—confidants—and because of the quality of flour now produced at the mill also won greater confidence from members at large. The mechanized mill now made double and triple passes relatively easy, and the resulting finer flour had residents of Wyoming City, especially the women, overjoyed; their hot bread never had smoother texture nor tasted as good.

"We can't run the mill much longer with the stones wearing thin as they are," Michalas told Peter one morning. "They could break at any time."

"I've been worried about them as well," Peter agreed. "Granite is too soft, we're constantly sharpening them. We need to quarry another set. Quartz is best."

"There's no quarry anywhere close," said Michalas. "For instance, these stones came from Ohio. But I've advised the brethren of our problem and they've authorized the purchase of a new run of French Buhrs. The Church will need this grist mill for several years to come."

"French Buhr stones are expensive," said Peter, impressed Michalas knew about them. "They only need sizing once or twice a season; but where can you get such stones?"

"Chicago," said Michalas. "I'm going there to buy a set, and Bishop Plowman wants you to go with me."

"What? W-well I would certainly go with you, Brother Michalas!" Peter was astonished. "Where is it? How far from here?"

"Chicago is a city in the state of Illinois; it's over four hundred miles from here, but we'd travel most of the way by train."

"Are you sure we can get the French stones there?" asked Peter.

"I'm quite certain," said Michalas. "Chicago is the busiest milling center in America. French Buhrs are used as ballast in ships, that's how they get to the States, and although expensive they're commonly used. Cheaper millstones use sections of French quartz layered between Ohio marble and held together with iron bands. Plaster of Paris is then smeared on top to give extra weight."

"Hmm," said Peter. "I've never seen plaster on stones. At our family mill in Denmark the stones we used were a hundred percent quartz."

"Chicago is also where I used live, Peter." A certain longing came over Michalas. "My mother still lives there," he added. "You'll accompany me then?"

"Absolutely," said Peter, alive with excitement. Viking by birth the adventurous young miller wanted to see as much of this huge country as possible. "I will go! When are we leaving?" he added cautiously.

"Saturday."

"Whew; how long will we be?"

"A month, maybe a month and a half . . ."

"I'll have to discuss this with Maren . . . a milling center you say?"

"Largest in America."

♥　♥　♥

Even though it would only be a few weeks, Maren felt extremely insecure by Peter's wanting to go and leave her alone. And although he cared about her feelings and understood her worry, Peter could hardly contain himself. The opportunity of a great adventure had befallen him. He would see a modern American city, one undamaged by civil war and one in which he wouldn't be treated like a prisoner. His mind whirled with ideas.

February deepened its icy grip on Wyoming City; people had to travel farther each day to get wood and conditions in the cabin grew more and more tense. Peter felt his leaving might serve to ease things somewhat; perhaps the Wangsgaards would assume the role of parent over Maren, give her some attention and stop bickering with each other. When he broke the news to Maren the Wangsgaards were away visiting the Forsgrens, giving time to talk.

"I know milling equipment better than anyone in this town, that's why Bishop Plowman wants me to go with Brother Michalas."

"But if you don't return, if you're killed by accident or some other terrible thing . . ." Maren sniffled. "Then I'm going back to Denmark. What do I care about this place, this country? What would I have here?" They were sitting on the edge of a crude bed he and Claus constructed from split logs and strips of leather.

"You'd have the church . . . the Wangsgaards . . ." Peter put his arm around her and kissed her cheek. "I have to go," he implored. "Maren, there is something I must buy in this Chicago place. Something extremely important to the future."

"Where will you get money?" she demanded.

"I'll tell you all about it . . ." he said hesitantly. "Mother sent me away with more than I want people to know about. I've been thinking of building a mill once we get settled out West . . ."

Just then the cabin door flew open and Claus Wangsgaard came booming in with Gunda right on his tail. "What is this?" he demanded "Are you two fighting?" He went immediately to Maren; "Now, now little dame, don't cry. Gunda and I are right here . . ."

"We're not fighting, Hr Wangsgaard," said Maren, wiping her eyes.

"I think every man alive should have to bear a child," said Gunda sharply, "just once in their life. Maybe then they'd understand!"

Gunda had never been pregnant herself but had a way of making people think she'd had ten children, and done most anything else that needed doing.

"It's not the baby," said Peter, staring at his boots. "Brother Michalas wants me to go to the big city of Chicago with him."

"We just heard," said Claus. "Bishop Plowman and his wife, Samantha, stopped by the Forsgren's. He told us you might be going."

"We won't be away that long," Peter added unconvincingly.

"Ha!" said Gunda. "You won't be away long? It's five hundred miles . . . seven hundred kilometers. You'll be lucky to get back before the wagons leave for Zion!"

Everyone's vocal cords started escalating at once, Gunda's a high soprano, Claus booming at base, Peter a mellow tenor, and Maren a strong alto; each sound a different song. Loud songs! Presently Maren stood and went to the fireplace. "I want you to bring me something from the city, Peter . . ."

The verbal music stopped.

"Anything," he said relieved. "Just name it."

Gunda was all ears.

"Some material for a dress."

"I'll buy you a dress already made!" he exclaimed. "A factory dress and bring you a box of candy, too."

"What about me?" pouted Gunda.

Peter turned to her, then looked back at Maren and wrapped his arms around her. "You'll let me go then?" His hug nearly crushed her.

"I could stop you?" she said.

Peter spun her once while Claus stepped back to dodge her flying feet.

"Be careful, Peter," barked Gunda. "The baby . . . you'll make her sick."

"You won't be sorry, Maren," Peter said exuberantly as he put her down. "I'll buy you the finest dress in Chicago! And Gunda, if you promise to take good care of my bride I'll bring you something to make you smile . . . something very expensive!"

"You have so much money," she said sarcastically.

"What about money?" asked Maren.

Peter felt his face flush. "I told you I've kept a little back," he said offhandedly, defensively.

Gunda looked at Claus and scrunched up her mouth. "So the man has money does he? Where has it been all this time?"

Claus stood twiddling his thumbs. "He's paid his fair share all the way, Mother. You know that."

♥ ♥ ♥

By Friday evening the town's resident millers were ready to leave. Sharp weather greeted them at Jess Plowman's barn where a dance was being held. People with side dishes and a few with lists of things they wanted in Chicago crowded in.

Somebody had killed a steer, and outside on two glowing beds of hot coals, heavy chunks of it were turning on spits. The aroma of sizzling beef and brisk country music filled the air as Dewey Farnsworth and Keith Jones tried to outdo each other on their fiddles. In the lantern-lit barn, shadows danced across the rafters and conversations were lively. Word spread quickly that Peter Jensen and Eugene Michalas were heading for civilization, and money in tied handkerchiefs and small leather bags with notes attached were forthcoming.

Inside his cabin Jess Plowman had counted the money, sorted out the written notes, recorded names and placed everything in a wooden box. "You've already got a lot to keep track of," he was saying as he also handed Michalas a stack of bills. "There's enough here for a set of stones, and related machinery. Hopefully Peter has enough money to pick up a wagon and span of mules to haul it all."

"He tells me he does Bishop. I trust him." Michalas folded the paper money and shoved it deep in his pocket.

"It's tithing money," Bishop Plowman warned. "Everyone here and people yet to come will benefit from the mill. We're praying for your success!" Even in the smoky yellow light from the kerosene lantern hung above his head, Plowman's snow-burned face looked youthful. Worried wrinkles in his forehead were overcome by that flashing, confident, white-toothed smile. He'd given Michalas some personal money and a shopping list as well.

Jess Plowman's cabin in no way resembled the stark, bare-walled hut Peter Jensen shared with the Wangsgaards. An iron stove sat in a corner near a china cabinet, table, and six chairs. There were shelves on the walls, two large beds and two three-level bunk beds all covered with thick quilts; white washed walls, a braided rug on the floor, clean linen on a long table, glass windows and curtains; pots and pans, along with salted meat, dried vegetables and cheese, were hanging orderly from the rafters; and several big-eyed children, whose mothers were probably at the dance, were peering down from the sleeping loft, giggling.

The Plowmans had lived there three consecutive years, and with the obvious effect of a woman's skilled organization (two in this case), the surroundings were very homey and comfortable.

I'll have a place just like this one day, Peter thought to himself.

"Peter actually wants two wagons and teams," he heard Eugene Michalas saying.

"You're going to need them," said the Bishop of Wyoming City, and then laughed. "You might need three to haul the stuff on these lists.

"Are you certain your sons can run the mill while you're away, Brother Michalas?"

"It practically runs itself, Bishop," said Michalas, "but I've asked Lyman Thayer to oversee. I just hope the stones don't break before we get back. With quartz stones we won't have to worry about that next year. We'll also be able to set more acreage to wheat and corn."

Peter felt important listening to the exchange between the two men, proud to be in on things. Nervous if not excited about the trip, pangs of worry over Maren passed through his mind, and just then the Bishop handed Michalas a large black handled revolver.

"Use it if you have to," Plowman said seriously.

♥   ♥   ♥

Outside, near a cooking fire, Maren and Elizabeth Anne stood watching cooks turn the spits of roasting beef, talking quietly one to another. All in spirited moods, people were lining up for a juicy slice of meat.

"They're two strong men, Maren," Elizabeth was saying. "I'm sure they'll be all right."

"What about Indians?" Maren exclaimed.

Elizabeth reached around and wrapped Maren's shawl a little higher. "There's a military post along the way. I'm told the Indians on the way east are peaceful. You should be inside," she added. "You'll catch your death." Maren was beginning to keep a slower pace. She should be gaining more weight, but her cheekbones seemed hollow and her wrists frail and thin.

Snow was melting into a brown wet ring around the edge of the fire, while the glacial world that surrounded it seemed unaffected, suspended in time. A pale blue halo glowed above the fire, and except for the activity around Plowman's barn, the emptied streets of Wyoming City resembled a frontier ghost town.

"I'm doing fine, Elizabeth Anne," she answered in steadily improving English. "But I wish Peter would hurry. He's been in the Bishop's cabin a long time."

Trevor Wells came out of the barn with a plate of food in his hand. "Are you ladies being wallflowers?" he asked cheerily.

"Maren's already missing her husband," said Elizabeth.

"*Han vil være igen I nævaerelse af jo sig* Maren. He'll be back before you know it, Maren," said Wells in Danish. "What they're to do will benefit the community for years to come."

The comment wrinkled Maren's nose and brow and for the first time she could remember, she snapped at Trevor. "I don't care, Brother Wells! Peter is all I have and if he's killed by Indians or wolves or whatever else is out there, I don't know what I'd do."

Wells knew he'd stepped on her toes. He nodded as he bit into a piece of meat. His jaundiced skin and sallow face would benefit from the blessings of this protein.

"I might just go back to Denmark." Maren said hopelessly.

The fire popped, sending sparks into the dark sky and everyone stepped back a pace. A shiver rippled down Maren's back and she huddled inside her shawl. "I think I will go inside, Elizabeth," she said and just as she did Peter emerged from Plowman's cabin. He came directly over to the fire; Elizabeth spoke to him first. "You should be ashamed of yourself, leaving her out here like this."

He didn't completely understand what she'd just said, but he couldn't remember being this close to the widow Browne since their experience on the good ship *John Wortham*. Baffled by her comment—he could see in her face that she was unhappy with him—he nodded to Trevor.

"Are you doing all right, Maren?" he asked putting an arm around her and drawing her close.

"I'm a little cold is all."

"We should go home then."

"I wanted to dance."

"Did you eat while I was with the Bishop?"

"I said I wanted to dance, Peter," she stated once again, not answering Peter's question.

He stared at her for a moment. "Come on then, let's go inside the barn."

"A charming couple," said Wells as he and Elizabeth Anne watched them walk away.

"They are," Elizabeth agreed.

An outside observer might think there was a bit of distance growing between Peter and Maren—they'd be mistaken—but Elizabeth continued to watch them while feeling certain heartache, as her mind filled with memories of when her deceased husband used to place a protective arm around her.

Section Notes

1. Marks of an experienced miller: Using hammer and chisel to cut sharp curved or straight slots—called the *dress* of the stones—into the meshed sides of millstones allowed for a scissor like effect on dried corn, barley or wheat creating grist, or when millstones were set at close tolerance, fine flour. This chiseling or cutting of sharp edges in the *dress* of millstones made steel filings and sharp pieces of quartz (or granite as the case may be) to chip away and embed in the wrists of the worker, resulting in small discolored pock marks or tiny tattoos.

For an applicant at a mill, "Show me your mettle," (the extent of wrist tattoos) was the equivalent to showing the boss a résumé in the early days of milling.

2. William Clarke Quantrill was a teamster for the Federal Army dispatched to Utah during the Utah War. After leaving the U.S. Army, Quantrill tried his hand at gambling for a while but desiring to return to a military career—even though Maryland was his home state—denounced the Union altogether, securing the rank of Captain in the Confederate Army where he became expert in guerrilla warfare.

Harassing Union troops and pro-union citizens even after the Civil War, Quantrill, being a handsome and charismatic individual, attracted a gang of pro-rebel thugs including Jesse James and Cole Younger to his cause, and continued to operate using guerrilla tactics which included robbery and arson of Union loyalists and outrunning the law for several years.

Called murderers by some and heroes by others, during their checkered career, Quantrill's Raiders plundered towns and villages throughout the Midwest, with their most notable debauchery the killing of nearly 200 men and boys (ages 7 through 90) in Lawrence, Kansas.

Operating from the end of the Civil War to the Spring of 1865, at their peak Quantrill's Raiders boasted 400 plus members, but due to internal fighting and bickering were down to less than 12 men when Union troops finally ambushed them in Kentucky, killing Quantrill himself. It took a few years longer to finally catch up with Jesse James and his brother, not to mention Jim and Cole Younger, but that's another story.

3. Grace of God—Their surroundings being raw and abnormally lean at the time, Claus and Gunda Wangsgaard, not to mention pioneer men and women in general, should have easily grasped the understanding of mutual protection and team work that plural marriage offered. That said if a man or woman did not want to enter the order they were certainly *not* compelled to do so by Church leaders. In fact, less than five percent of the members of the Church of Jesus Christ of Latter-day Saints practiced plural marriage. Men, who *did* take more than one wife in plural holy matrimony, did so only at the consent of his other wife or wives not to mention Church leaders.

Adultery (and other serious infractions) in today's world and during the time of the novel, generally meant disfellowship or excommunication from The Church, but back then if a man had more than one wife, and multiple offspring, he *was* held strictly responsible by the Church for their care and well being, both spiritually and temporally. Plural marriage was a most sacred responsibility.

Section Four

Chapter 16

Religion on the Road

"Our cheese presses are contaminated, Torkil, Sebastian," David Steed was saying after shaking the putrid remains of some Farmer's Cheese from the cheese cloth that lined one of them. "We need new presses and not ones made of wood. Wood presses absorb water causing them to warp and they're impossible to sanitize; even washing them in vinegar doesn't seem to work. Poisonous mold grows quickly in them."

"For what we paid for all this equipment," said Torkil, "we sure have little to show. How long did you use these presses, Steed?"

"One season too many I guess," said David Steed. "This entire batch is bad. Come Spring we won't have anything to sell if we don't do something drastic. I wanted to get started on a large batch of blue cheese. The culture's just about ready, but at this rate we won't have the base product."

"What should we do?" asked Torkil, visibly upset.

"Well, we can sit here on our hands or one of us can go to Chicago and buy some o' them ceramic lined presses that drummer told us about last week. He let me tear the broadside off his wagon."

"Do you still have it?" asked Torkil.

"I've kept it folded in my pants pocket. A manufacturer named Borden[1] is shutting down its cheese division; all they're going to make is condensed milk. Cheese molds, slabs of wax, vats and ceramic presses . . . everything will be auctioned off in a series of sales in March."

"I'd like to have them ceramic molds," said Sebastian. "I hear the cheese slides right out of ceramic; they're easy to wash and don't give you a foreign taste like wood. No foreign taste."

At first, Sebastian's habit of repeating himself bothered David Steed but he'd gotten used to it. He liked the big man and looked forward to working with him for years to come. "It's only a little over two hundred miles to Chicago," Steed said lightly. "I could make the trip in time for the auction and be back in ten days."

"I'll be going," said Torkil.

"You'll never make it alone," scoffed Sebastian. "You'd get lost as a goose."

"I've been talking to Brother Stransen ever since that drummer came," said Torkil. "I showed him Steed's paper. He says he'd drive his wagon to Chicago and help haul whatever we buy . . . of course he'll want some money."

"I'll go with you for free," said David Steed.

Torkil shook his head. He'd already thought about that, but knowing how Sebastian might take it, and because not all the cheese ripening in molds had gone bad, he wanted Steed to monitor things.

"You're needed here, David," said Torkil flatly.

The company's only non-family employee considered arguing with his brand new employer, but wisely decided against it and resigned himself to seeing booming Chicago at some other time.

"You're right, of course."

It didn't take much persuading to get Stransen to go. Late February winds and sub- zero temperatures plummeted attendance at his full gospel assembly; therefore he had little to do to keep him occupied, and so for a price the preacher agreed to guide Torkil to Chicago.

"I wouldn't hear of you making the trip alone, Brother Olsen; I'll leave my dwindling pastoral duties to Greta. You're going to need an interpreter anyway."

"I'm grateful," said Torkil.

"You know, I've never seen Chicago; it will be worth the effort. All we have to do is drive east to Lake Michigan then turn the wagon south to Chicago, following the edge of the lake all the way down."

♥   ♥   ♥

For fifty dollars—half before they started and the rest after Spring cheese sales—the Danish cheese maker and the Pentecostal preacher soon found themselves on wagon and horseback heading toward Lake Michigan on their way to Chicago.

Freezing nights and cold grey days; sometimes they both rode in Stransen's wagon with Torkil's horse tied behind. Other times, to rest their backs, they took turns riding the horse, stopping occasionally any time a thick patch of prairie grass showed up in the thinning snow. They also took turns sleeping in the wagon box, but the promise of hot baths, soft warm beds and a little civilization kept them pushing on.

"Your broadside states that this Elgin Company is owned by a man named Gail Borden and is located forty miles northwest of Chicago, on the Fox River. Says here they've decided to make nothing but condensed milk and butter. I guess cheese hasn't been profitable for them. I hope for your sake we're not too late . . . also that it's not a scam."

"A what?" Peter spoke loudly so as to be heard above the constant whistling of the wind.

"A scam . . . you know a hoax, just getting people to come and buy things they really don't need."

"Oh . . . scam."

"It'll probably be like an auction. Gather a crowd and yell at them: What am I bid on this fine cheese press . . . ? Man I love a crowd. I really know how to work one. Get folks all stirred up, get 'em religion . . . an auction's no different; get people all excited and they'll buy anything."

"Even religion, 'eh preacher?"

Stransen raised his eyebrows at that. "Yep, Torkil, even religion. But that's a good thing. Gettin' people the Spirit is what counts. And I don't care how much it costs them; it's worth it. Saves their Damned souls, it does."

"I suppose so, Brother Stransen," said Torkil. "Me, I don't mind contributing to your church—*any* church—but salvation is a free gift available to all. It says so in the Bible."

"You are right, Brother Torkil, to a certain extent, but tithes is part and parcel of salvation. How else does the Lord know you've repented? Put up or shut up, I always say. Money on the plate . . . cash speaks louder than words brother, and the lord commands people to tithe. Why just look at Cain and Abel . . ."

Torkil let the hot air preacher entertain himself for hours. They passed through hilly regions, low mountain passes, evergreen forests and wide bushy plains—the last town being two days ago—and then this monstrous lake! Or was it an ocean? Lake Michigan: Like a gigantic magnet, the immense body of water had a pull all its own, seemingly drawing wagon, horses and riders off the trail and into its bowels.

I must have been crazy to listen to that Drummer. Chicago, Illin . . . I can't even say it. If we find the place what will be left? They've probably sold all the equipment already.

Torkil paused in his self-incrimination and looked up at Stransen hunched over; whip lying across his lap, bumping along in his wagon and still talking out of the Old Testament.

He's up to Noah now.

"Folks think the Lord sent 'em two by two, Torkil," said Stransen not caring if he heard or not. "But it's not so. The clean beasts came into the ark in sevens, and the fowls by sevens also . . . humm, clean and fowl . . . must be some symbolism there."

At times the preacher has way too much to say. The only time he lets off preaching is when he's talking about money, or when he sees a pretty long dress go by. Stransen loves to look at women. Greta better keep a watchful eye.

But he goes crazy over religion, like at that revival we found...

Torkil's mind then went back to the wagon train across the northern states. Forested near the town of Hamilton, Ohio, feeding their stock to fatten them up for the push across Indiana and Illinois, a camp meeting on the outskirts of town drew not only Stransen, but several people from the wagon train and half a dozen local preachers as well.

Torkil went out of curiosity. He didn't know it of course, but Ohio was a large part of the "Burned Over" region of the United States and still smoldered from the numberless revivals which assaulted there during the 1830s through the 1850s, taking a short breather during the Civil War. Circuit Riders[2] still found eager audiences there.

That night, with lanterns blazing near a big tent and lighting up the podium, a blasting discourse given by Darold Stransen—in which he threatened everyone if they didn't repent they were going to Hell—was followed by a sincere and unobtrusive bald headed little man with horn rimmed glasses and a big black Bible.

Stransen being out of wind so to speak, the smallish fellow with a kindly face took over the podium. The crowd had grown to well over a hundred souls, and opening his Bible the little man went straight to the twenty-seventh chapter of Matthew.

He spoke from his heart, not particularly eloquent but very informative—he knew his scriptures—never yelling, just talking, and the audience heard every word. But when the little man read verse forty-six where the Lord Jesus Christ, cried aloud, "My God, my God why hast thou forsaken me?" Torkil wept. Not sobbing, just a steady flow of tears as he truly felt the Spirit of God.

Afterward the preacher invited those who would accept salvation to line up and come forward. Torkil, his broad shoulders hunched over and thick reddish mane bowed so no one could see his face, made the trip.

Although fully accepting Christ as his personal Savior that winter night, in reality the mighty Thor had always lived a righteous life. He has always been loyal to his wife (she'd been the unfaithful one), and at the Jensen mill; "Honest labor, no stealing and no dirty talk on premises," were his instructions to all newly hired men, rules he lived by. Even as Torkil pushed his men to produce flour and grist, he led by fairness, virtuous example and hard work.

As his horse clopped steadily along behind Stransen's wagon on their way to Chicago, actually Elgin, Torkil's eyes welled remembering that night in the green forest. He believed in Christ and resigned himself to follow him.

♥ ♥ ♥

"I'll tell you somethin' amazing about American religion," Stransen said, bringing Torkil out of his reverie. "A man can start with nothing but lies and build himself one fine following o' people. I seen it happen many times but never like in the '30s. I was just nineteen or so when I heard about the excitement. A fella named Smith claimed he'd seen an angel and that he'd found a gold Bible buried under a rock in upstate New York."

"Uh . . ." said Torkil trying to interrupt.

"Told folks he'd seen God hisself."

"Is that so," commented Torkil.

"Did for a fact. Said he was out wandering around in the woods and there came this fire, bright enough to burn down the whole place and standin' there was Jesus Christ telling him he was called to preach." Stransen took a breath. His gaze seemed far away, remembering. "You know, Brother Olsen, I almost fell for it myself. I heard him all right, well no actually it were his brother Hyman Smith I heard. Think that was his name. Hi- somethin'. Anyway he came through town selling those gold Bibles and spoke at a church I went to one night."

"What did he have to say?" asked Torkil, genuinely interested.

"I'll never forget what he said," Stransen went on. "He said his brother was a Prophet of God. That God had spoke to him and helped him translate his gold Bible out of ancient language and that it was as true as the Bible. Said we should read it right along with our King James because one proved the other."

"What else did he say?"

"You know, I'm trying to remember, but it weren't so much what he said that night..." Stransen paused and looked heavenward. The skies were iron gray and the bite of the weather pronounced. Bare trees seemed to gather as if they too wanted to hear what he would say. "Not so much what he said, Torkil, it was what I felt. Lord let me tell you what I felt. When Smith said that God had again opened the heavens and spoke to man it was like a thunderbolt went through me."

A potent mix of emotion washed over Torkil; he felt like a good cry. Of a sudden he was back in Holbaek, sitting in Casten Pedersen's parlor listening to a young man in an old Prince Albert coat giving a similar report. He'd listened carefully that night, but was so upset over his wife's infidelity he'd absorbed little. Then the scene quickly shifted. Now he was out front of Casten's house standing next to Catherine's carriage, love struck and confused, telling the only person in the world who he truly respected that he'd be leaving Denmark.

Respected? Far more than respect passed between them that night...

"I went to my preacher the very next day and talked to him about Smith," said Stransen's voice, "an' you know what he told me?" Torkil blinked and the beautiful memory evaporated.

"What?" he asked shaking his head as the horses clopped along.

"He said now you know what the Devil feels like! He told me the Devil can even turn himself into a angel of light. Said that Smith was a liar and a deceiver and that Prophets already gave us their word in the Holy Bible and there'd be no more word. No more prophets."

"What about Smith telling everyone to read his book right along with their Bible?"

"Part of his tricks I suppose," said Stransen. "But like I was sayin', you never saw such an uproar over religion! Folks were stirred up I'll tell you, and Smith baptized a bunch of them. Next day he and a friend companion had a gatherin' at a pond in the woods and I'll bet he ducked fifteen maybe twenty people there. What I'm tryin' to tell you is that even with lies, a man can build a church."

"If with lies, what about with truth?"

"Well sure, that's what I do. You get it straight from the Bible at my church don'tcha?"

Torkil nodded slightly.

"Yes sir, Smith built up a large followin' in that town. Few years later I heard they all went west to Ohio or someplace."

"I heard about him," Torkil said quietly.

Stransen didn't hear. "Hmm," he said, "see that's what I'm tryin' to do, Brother Torkil. Get me a following of two or three hundred folks, build my income up to where I can do nothing but preach and teach; build us a big new chapel. Can you see it there on the hill? We'll turn the little old one into a classroom . . ."

"Get up there," Torkil called to his horse. "He's getting tired, Preacher. We ought to stop soon, let them graze."

"Yeh. Look for a good spot . . . Smith was a charlatan, Brother Olsen. Sad to say but it got him killed. Back in forty-four people grew tired of him stirrin' things up and somebody up and shot him. There are still a few of his followers in New York."

"I heard about him in Denmark," repeated Torkil about to add more but not having much to say, didn't.

"You're kidding! You heard about Smith all the way over in Denmark? Must have been some other Smith. Joseph Smith, Jr.? Gold Bible?"

Torkil nodded. "The same," he said.

"Man!" exclaimed Stransen. "Way over in Denmark. I guess his lies are goin' all over the world."

"I'm not sure that's what's going on there," said Torkil feeling a certain amount of respect. "A young, intelligent friend of mine joined Smith's church an' lies had nothing to do with it." He was about to explain what he knew when Stransen interrupted him. "Have you been saved, Brother Olsen?"

Torkil didn't answer for a moment. The steady clop, clop of the horses seemed to be slowing. "That's the first thing I ever heard out of your head, Brother Stransen. And when you first asked us all that question, my answer would have been no. But since that camp meeting we stopped at in Ohio, I think my answer is yes."

"That so?"

"Yes, I think I felt the Holy Ghost there. I felt *something* that's for sure. When that little preacher talked about our Lord Jesus Christ I had to go forward. I couldn't stop myself."

"Ain't it wonderful?" said Stransen. "Praisin' God an' all."

"Truthfully, Brother Stransen, I think there's more to it."

"More to what."

"Just more. Let's stop over there. There's plenty of grass . . ."

Chapter 17

Eugene and Peter

Other than being stopped by a group of Omahas begging for food, Peter and Eugene's trip had been uneventful; on horses borrowed from Jess Plowman they followed the frozen Missouri river two days straight without sleeping, stopping only to rest the horses occasionally, and arrived where the Platte River joins the Missouri amid a freezing March rain.

A large herd of horses and cattle were wintered in the area, feeding on the dead bulrushes that lined the frozen waters and hay left during harvest time by the owners. Herdsman living amongst the bawling animals told Michalas he and Peter were just five miles from their destination. Half an hour later their horses crested a hill where below lay Omaha, Nebraska.

At first the town looked like a dead ringer for Wyoming City, only much larger, and railroad tracks cutting a straight path into the eastern side gave it a far more established presence. "That's where we catch the train to Chicago," Michalas explained. "It's the stopping place for the Central Pacific Railroad," he added as they urged their horses down the gentle slope towards it.

A wood-burning locomotive and several cattle cars stood patiently waiting on a spur connected with the main track, and behind them, a water tower and huge mountain of logs. They rode up to a wood frame, shingled roof building with a freshly painted sign saying "Ticket Office"—the first modern building Peter had seen since leaving St. Louis, Missouri.

"Civilization," he exclaimed as they rode up.

"I guess you could call it that," said Michalas dryly. Omaha had the same thrown together, rutted street, log cabin appearance as Wyoming City, just a lot more of it. There were also a number of sod houses and even a frame home or two. A building that could very well be a gristmill stood prominent in the distance near the remnants of what had once been a spacious military stockade.[3]

Late as it was, there was life in the town. A beardless man with spectacles could be seen behind the window of the ticket office and a few wagons and horses traversed Main Street. Splitting firewood near a small barn, a young boy leaned on the criss-cross fence to stare at the strangers, whose horses shuddered and jerked, anxious for the hay and warm barns they smelled.

"Hold them while I check the train schedule," Michalas said as he dismounted. "I won't be long. They're getting mighty uneasy."

Peter took the reigns of Eugene's horse while he went inside the depot, coming back in less than five minutes.

"Were in luck, Peter my man," he said mounting up. "There'll be a train here day after tomorrow. Now where can we get a good night's sleep?"

♥   ♥   ♥

With no room in Omaha's eight-room hotel, they ended up sleeping in a hayloft adjoining the livery stable. The price was right, the loft warm, and both men were too exhausted to care.

Michalas awakened next morning, straw sticking in his hair, and stretching as he looked around to get his bearings found Peter missing. Putting on his hat he started down the ladder.

"*God Morgan*," said a voice below. Peter was sitting on a clump of hay leaning against a barn post, barely visible in the shadows.

JEG indfald I'd bortkommet jer. I thought I'd lost you," said Michalas.

"I got up early," said Peter, standing in the light and brushing hay off his pants. "Couldn't sleep." A winter sun shined over the snow-covered town and thin beams of light shot from cracks in the ceiling. "I had an idea come to me that kept me awake all night..."

"Is that right," said Eugene yawning. "It must'a been a powerful idea."

"Let me ask you something, Brother Michalas. Do you think they might need another grist mill in Zion?"

"Hmm, I know there are several mills out there already. President Young sent two millers along with the vanguard company in '47. Here it is nineteen years later; I've heard of two in Salt Lake City. I'm sure each community has at least one now... but Peter, the Church is growing rapidly, hundreds of people are heading to Zion; there'll be room for more mills."

"That's what I think," said Peter.

Encouraging him further Michalas went on, "There are settlements going up all over Utah. A new area just opened by the Brethren is a place called Cache Valley, about a hundred miles north of Salt Lake City. There's probably the need for a gristmill there. Other places too..."

"I was hoping you'd say something like that," said Peter with determination in his voice, "because somewhere out there I'm going to build one!"

Being so early in the morning his enthusiasm was entirely lost on Michalas.

"Sounds like a good idea," he said stretching. "Bad as they smell, horses keep a barn fairly warm, you know it?"

"It won't be a small grist mill," Peter continued. "I want two runs of stone, and the machinery to drive them. My mill will feed hundreds of people and thousands of livestock."

Michalas smiled sympathetically, "Sounds pretty ambitious, Peter. Just how are you going to do all this?"

Except for a dozen horses in their stalls, the barn was empty. "Do you think we could sell these in Chicago?" he asked in a low voice. Peter opened the palm of his hand and two huge diamonds from Catherine's necklace burst forth with power and glitter. Even in the dim barn, sharp flashes of light flashed from the gems!

Michalas whistled. "Where in the world did you get those?" he exclaimed. "You must have a fortune here!"

"Shhh," said Peter frowning. "Somebody may come by."

One of the horses snorted and pawed the dirt floor; otherwise the stable was quiet as a tomb. "They're family heirlooms. My mother gave them to me."

"Let me have a closer look," said Michalas, touching one of the gems with the tip of his finger. He picked it up and held it to the light.

"Absolutely stunning, Peter," he said very much astonished. Then he asked the obvious, "Are they genuine?"

"They are, Brother Michalas," Peter nodded.

"Whew. Well, we won't have any trouble selling them," said Michalas confidently. "People are starving for beauty like this. With the war over, the city is prosperous; factories and mills are running in full swing and people are working.

"But if you buy two sets of mill stones and everything it takes to run them, you're going to need something extremely stout to carry them. You'll need a freighter!"

"I've thought about that," said Peter. "We have some time. Why don't we look around town and see what's available."

By now Michalas was fully awake. He'd never seen the likes of the gems and watched bug-eyed as Peter, like they were merely a few loose coins, casually dropped them in his pocket. They ate breakfast at the over-booked hotel while Eugene looked nervously about as if they might be robbed at any moment. When he asked the hotel waiter if he knew where they could buy any wagons, he was sure the man could see right into Peter's pockets.

"None to be had that I know of," he said firmly. "Have you asked at the livery?"

"No we haven't, but we will. Mind if I make a little announcement here?"

"It's not my place . . . go ahead."

Michalas stood overlooking full tables hosting an interesting variety of people, most as rough shod as he and Peter—farmer types—and like two roses among the thorns, seated smack in the center of the wall-papered room were two ladies in bonnets.

"Gentlemen," Michalas announced. "And you lovely ladies," he added, looking directly at the two women seated near the center. "Would anyone here know of any wagons or teams for sale?" Blank stares, a few negative replies and heads shaking back and forth. "If any of you hear of anything, my friend and I are at the livery stables." That caused a little snicker here and there and Michalas thanked them and went to pay for the meal.

He and Peter left the hotel empty handed but optimistic. Their stomachs were full; the cook had served up heaping plates of bacon, eggs and hash-browned potatoes, and with a day and a half to kill, they started off.

The sun peeked at the streets of Omaha, turning them slightly muddy. Horses, mules, oxen and wagons, people too, of which there were now a considerable number, filled the street. Standing near the high square façade which made the general store appear twice as large as it was, stood a man who appeared preoccupied with his feet. He barely acknowledged Michalas' overly friendly greeting.

"New ta town, are ye?"

"We are," said Michalas. "We're looking to buy a couple of wagons."

"So's evr' n' else."

"Not much available?" pushed Eugene.

"Nope. Scarce 'es hens' teeth," the man said. still looking at his feet.

Struggling mightily with English, Peter quickly determined this man spoke a different language! A well worn, oily, floppy hat covered a thick mop of hair, his coat thin and his face so covered with blackish-gray hair it was hard to find his eyes. His high-topped boots went half way up his short legs, and with their curved instep he'd form a peak of mud and melting snow then smash it down between sentences. Squish.

"Folks wi' wagons hang on t' 'em like grim death t' a dyin' man." Squish, squish.

"We have cash," said Michalas.

The man's narrow slits opened wide and red veined eyes became plainly visible. They had a suspicious look about them. *A poor farmer,* thought Peter. He'd seen many in Wyoming City.

"Start at ta livery'd be my advice," he said tamping down his last mound of oozing earth and snow.

"We did that," said Michalas. "Met the proprietor last evening. He gave us two leads. A farmer named Eric Olafson and one named Judd something."

"Know 'em both," said the bearded man, still not looking up from his mud game. "East a here. Near t' slough." He pointed the way and went back to staring at his feet.

Peter hadn't understood a word, but as he and Eugene walked away he turned and tipped his hat. "*Tak for lån.* Thank you," he said.

"Poor fellow," Michalas said under his breath.

♥   ♥   ♥

After saddling up and riding out to check the two farms but having no luck, Michalas turned his horse northward. "Let's head up this way,

Peter," he said. "We should have started there anyway. We've got friends in this town we haven't met."

They rode the two miles to the northeast corner of the large frontier settlement, and on a hillside Peter reigned in his horse abruptly.

"*Lede Broder Michalas!* Look, Brother Michalas!" Peter said, astounded and greatly perplexed. "*Den begravelsesplads er større end den by!* That cemetery is almost as large as the town! There must be a thousand graves[4]."

"I know," said Michalas as he stopped his horse next to Peter's. "I know." They got off and tethered the animals to a low tree branch. The weather had quickly turned chilly and overcast. "Back in '45 and '46 when the Saints were driven from Nauvoo, Illinois Peter, hundreds of members of the Church perished out here, most of them children. That's why this cemetery is so large, lot's of little fella's buried here."

"I see," said Peter despondently. "I guess I hadn't heard much about that from the missionaries." The two men gazed reverently at the scene for a moment.

"Winter isn't whipped yet," Michalas said, bending as he walked under the low hanging tree. "Lets go have a look."

They entered the cemetery through a sagging gate and both men took off their hats.

"Over there is Winter Quarters," said Michalas, pointing toward a village-like cluster of cabins and barns a quarter of a mile in the distance. "You know the history here, don't you, Peter?"

"Not exactly . . . a little I guess. Tell me."

Michalas' eyes turned misty. The difficulty church members had just getting here, plus sending away a battalion of five hundred able bodied men to fight in the Mexican War, was one reason he'd been baptized. He knew the sacrificial history of Winter Quarters as if he'd been there himself.

"Church members left Nauvoo in the dead of winter, Peter, and many of them were ill equipped to travel. But freezing weather held the mobs at bay, and Brigham Young decided ready or not it was time to leave. February 1846, they left comfortable homes, farms, businesses . . . and just walked away. With more than a mile between the banks of the Mississippi River, they started to ferry across. It was slow, dangerous work, and a couple of wagons were lost in the icy waters, but nobody drowned that day . . . I don't think, anyway."

"What happened then?" Peter asked.

Michalas continued. "Only a few people got across that first day, Peter, but that night an arctic storm hit and the river began to freeze over. It was so cold and miserable people on both banks couldn't do anything for two days straight. By the third day the river had frozen thick enough that the bulk of the wagons remaining in Nauvoo were able to drive across."

"We traveled the wide Mississippi," said Peter astonished. "How could so much moving water freeze like that?"

"I don't know, but it did."

"They drove across the Mississippi River on the ice?" Peter asked unbelievably.

"They did."

"That was a miracle," said Peter reverently.

"It was," said Michalas, "but it didn't last. Not all the wagons and stock made it across on ice. By the fifth day it began to break up and they were back using log rafts. When everybody that could got out of Nauvoo, there was a string of wagons for miles out on the prairie. They sometimes traveled in blizzards so fierce you couldn't see your hand in front of your face, and finally crossed some two hundred and fifty miles of Iowa territory before being forced to winter in."

"Here?" asked Peter sadly.

"Right here," said Michalas. "Over six hundred people died from malnutrition, exposure and black leg (scurvy) that first year. They're buried in this cemetery." The former lawyer reached up and wiped his eyes.

"It looks like others have joined them since," said Peter shaking his head. "How many people in Winter Quarters that first year?" he wanted to know.

"I'd say about four thousand," said Michalas, still wiping his face with a leather glove. "The population of Nauvoo was somewhere around sixteen thousand, give or take, and roughly one forth of them left that first year."

"What about those who stayed behind?" Peter asked. "Didn't mobs get them?"

"They had their troubles, brother," Eugene assured him. "An event called the Nauvoo War killed several, but after they promised the mobs they'd leave as soon as they were able, the remaining people were finally left alone. Most of them were simply too poor to travel with the vanguard company in '46; they had to stay behind and try to sell their property. Give it away is what they did, conditions being as they were."

"I can only imagine," Peter said shaking his head.

"Time passed though, and most everybody who wanted to, got out. Some no doubt apostatized from the church so they could stay. Emma Smith, the prophet's wife stayed, but Nauvoo became somewhat of a ghost town. Twenty years ago," Michalas added, taking a last look at the small forest of grave tablets and stone markers. "Seems like it never happened. We'd better get going along, Peter. It'll be dark before you know it and we've still got a few doors to knock."

The two men left the cemetery, put on their hats, mounted their horses and rode away. By day's end, all they'd found was one man in the area willing to sell a pair of bony oxen. Word quickly spread throughout Omaha and tiny Winter Quarters that strangers were in the area and they had money to spend. They did find a Mormon family that fed them supper and let them stay the night in an empty cabin next door that they rented out.

"Something will turn up, Peter," Michalas said as they lay in their bedrolls on the dirt floor. "This is a big settlement and we haven't covered half of it."

"Maybe we'll have to get them in Chicago," said Peter discouraged.

The air grew cold and damp as the fire died. Eugene yawned widely and pulled his blankets under his chin. "We'll see," he said. "But don't worry. Tomorrow's another day." He leaned over on one arm and blew out the lantern on the floor beside him.

Chapter 18

Heinrich Christophersen

Early next morning a faint knock came to the door. Michalas heard it and quickly put his feet on the cold dirt floor. The floor was hard, damp, and very uninviting. "I'm coming," he called. He got up, took one step, had second thoughts, sat back on his bed, pulled on his pants and boots then went to the door. Daylight flooded the cabin as it opened.

"*JEG høre jer brethren er ser ud nemlig en wagon og hold i oxen.* I hear you brethren are looking for a wagon and team of oxen," said the strained voice of a lean and weathered looking Danish man in his late forties. He was wearing a hat with flaps which were tied to the top and a thick buffalo skin coat which made him look twice his normal size, and his salutation revealed he was not only from Denmark but also a Mormon.

"Yes, yes we are," Michaelis replied, pulling his suspenders up over his shoulders. "*Du er Dansk?* You're Danish?"

"Yes," said the man. "It's not uncommon around here. I'm from Copenhagen."

"Come in, sir. Do come in." said Michalas cordially.

"Peter, we have a guest."

A rumpled head poked its way from under a thick patchwork quilt. Peter, looking around like he was lost, had slept deeply, catching up from the night before. Michalas left the door open for light and indicated the visitor to take the lone chair by the fireplace.

"Let me put on a log. Brother Michalas is my name, by the way," he said shaking the man's hand. "Peter and I are up from Wyoming City."

"Heinrich Christophersen," said the man.

Peter reached over and also shook his hand. "I'm Peter Jensen, brother. I'm also from Denmark."

"I'd heard," said the dark-haired gentleman leaning toward Peter and shaking his hand but not rising from his chair. Peter's face showed offense, but the guest was either in deep thought or else troubled.

At the fireplace blowing on the coals from the night before, Michalas soon had the one room cabin filled with smoke drifting toward the open door, but shortly a feeble flame licked away at the fresh log and slowly the cabin began to clear.

"That ought to do it," said Eugene out of breath. He stood, dizzy, and leaned against the log wall to keep from falling. Peter had on his pants and boots and was working on shirt buttons while sitting cross-legged on his bedroll, still trying to wake up.

"The misses and I have changed our minds about going west." The Dane said with defeat and frustration; some anger, too. Not looking at either of his hosts he appeared to be talking to himself. "That is *she* changed our mind. Now I've got to sell my wagons and teams because we're going back to Denmark." With that he looked up.

"What part of the homeland are you from, young man?"

"Holmstrup Holbeck, but I've lived in Copenhagen."

"Lots of us square-heads—as Americans call us—are scattered around this area," said Christophersen unemotionally. "Over three hundred last count. Buncha' Germans, too. Americans call them square-heads as well."

The term offended Peter; there seemed to be a lack of Danish pride all over this man. He wanted to brag to Christophersen about the two hundred plus Danes in Wyoming City but just said, "That's a goodly number of our people, brother."

Eugene had finally mentally translated his thoughts. "That's a fine buffalo coat you've got there," he said. "Warm, is it?"

Christophersen turned to him. "You're not from Denmark, are you?"

"Obviously not," answered Eugene Michalas. "Originally I'm from Chicago, Illinois."

"Our train stopped there," said Christophersen. "Your Danish is fairly good," he added.

"I served two missions to your country."

"I see," said the visitor.

A seed of cordial conversation could have sprouted at that point, but Christophersen abruptly got down to business. "About my wagons . . ." he said.

"Did you say wagons?" Eugene interrupted.

"I've got two Conestogas, as you Americans call them," was the prideful answer. "Big, strongly built . . . I also own twelve excellent beasts!"

"Unbelievable," exclaimed Michalas.

"Nobody around here has what they're worth," continued Heinrich Christophersen, "Since making our decision to leave, I've been sitting on them for a week."

"How much are you asking?" asked Peter, still trying to figure the man's blunt, unfriendly attitude.

"Fifteen hundred dollars American, each outfit, oxen and wagons," said the Dane. He then looked at Peter. "That's forty one hundred Rigsdaler apiece, Brother Jensen. I only want what I paid."

Peter set his feelings aside. Adrenalin surged through his veins. "Let's go see them," he said pointedly.

"You'll be pleased," Christophersen said. Without further discussion he put his hands on his knees and pushed himself up. "My place isn't far from here."

Peter and Eugene quickly laced up their boots and put on their coats and hats, then all three men stooped below the cabin doorway. Christophersen had come on foot and said little as he led the way across a wide snowy field. Once in a while Peter glanced over at Eugene who only lifted his eyebrows as if to say, "I can't figure him either."

Less than a mile away they came to a large barn situated next to a log farmhouse. Between the two buildings a water well, complete with rope and bucket stood, and behind it a huge stack of hay. The house and barn sat on a plowed five acre field surrounded by a barbed wire fence and looked like a giant white wash board on the ground. An ambitious fellow, this man Christophersen; it was obvious that he'd accomplished a great deal during his short time in Winter Quarters.

Behind the barn, Christophersen yanked the canvas covering off two large prairie schooners which had been parked there nearly a year. Their massive steel rimmed, spoke wheels were sunk a foot, and its curved hickory ribs lay in the wagon box waiting until Spring when at last they'd be covered.

"Impressive!" Eugene said, as the fine construction of the Conestogas registered.

Peter whistled. "They're huge!"

"And stronger than any you'll find in Denmark," said Christophersen, grabbing a thick side board for emphasis.

"You must have a large family," Michalas ventured.

The owner smiled weakly and tilted his head to the side. "Come in and see my animals." The Dane looked like a bear in winter coat as he led the way into the barn; it may well have been his place of hibernation. Animal warmth rushed out as the double doors opened. The strong smell of urine, manure, and sweat, softened by the sweet smell of dry hay, enveloped the men.

"I love a barn in winter," Michalas commented.

Twelve Durham Oxen, reddish brown in color, six on each side of the barn in stalls, stopped chewing their cud for a moment, lifted their large dark eyes and stared inquisitively at the human intruders. Peter stooped to pick up a handful of hay; this Heinrich Christophersen was a very rich man. He put the hay under the steamy nostrils and slimy mouth of the first ox and patted the spin of hair (cowlick) on its flat rock-hard forehead.

Shiny long gray horns, veined with cracks like marble, extended into black tips which had been blunted by Heinrich's rasp, adorned the massive animal. As it munched the hay its proud owner said, "That's Bully, my lead ox. I yoke him with Stig (stee), the big one in the next stall."

Going from stall to stall, Peter said empathetically, "I've seldom seen larger. And worth what you're asking."

Heinrich smiled faintly. "I'm a fair and honest man," he said. "These powerful beasts were my pride and joy. I've also got these two horses."

"What do you call this one?" asked Eugene, moving near an Appaloosa in a corner pen.

"That's Pepper," answered Christophersen, walking under a fat iron hook hanging from a rope in the center of the barn.

"Good Pepper . . . good Pepper," the wealthy farmer said as he rubbed the animal's jaw with one hand and with the other rubbed its mane. Well marked and aptly named, the Appaloosa's large moist, dark brown eyes displayed a gentle manner. Peter appreciated good horseflesh and came over to inspect.

"What a fine animal," he said.

A melancholy look crossed the Danish farmer's face. "If you men buy my wagons and teams, I'll throw him in for a hundred dollars."

Michalas raised his eyebrows.

"Won't be needing him," Christophersen went on. "I was going to ride him all the way to Zion. We'd have had a good time, huh, boy." He patted the horse affectionately.

"Who was going to drive the wagons?" asked Eugene, unknowingly opening Pandora's Box.

Christophersen let go of the horse and leaned back against a square support post. He finally wanted to talk.

"I bought one wagon and team for each wife," he began.

"But I thought you said . . ."

"That's the reason I'm going back to Denmark, brother. Olga wouldn't tolerate plural marriage. I forced it upon her, you see. My wife had a strong testimony of the church and I thought she'd support me in anything God wants of me. I'd gone ahead and married another woman secretly, and when I brought her home . . . my life's been hell ever since."

"No doubt!" exclaimed Michalas.

"Do you have more than one wife?" Christophersen shot back.

"I'm sealed to three women," said Michalas humbly.

Peter was startled at Michalas' answer.

Christopher turned to Peter. "You?"

Peter held up a single finger.

"The Lord never meant us to trample over the tender emotions of our wives," Michalas chastised Christophersen. "If your association with the second lady wasn't sanctioned by the first and sealed by proper priesthood authority, then it was adultery, plain and simple!"

Peter feared a nasty confrontation between the two older men at that but Christophersen bowed his head and said, "What I did was very wrong and I'm paying, believe me."

"If it's a higher law we're supposed to live," Michalas continued, "then all parties to the marriage must agree and all must be willing."

"Let me stop you right there," said Christophersen. "If you want to turn the very devil loose in your home just do things as I did. Screaming and fighting . . . those two women nearly killed each other. Then my oldest son got involved and now everybody hates *me*.

"The second lady finally went back to her mother, and I've been sleeping in this barn here." The would-be polygamist indicated a hay-strewn corner with a pile of blankets stacked below a kerosene lamp hanging from a nail in a post.

"We left a beautiful farm in Denmark," he said, changing the distasteful subject. "I can probably get it back; the man still owes me. But the last thing I want is to go back. I wanted a new life . . . peace in the mountains of Zion, you know?"

"*JEG er klar over, at.* I understand that," Peter offered weakly.

"As it goes," Christophersen continued, "my wife gave me an ultimatum: The only way she'll stay married to me—and so keep my children—is to return to Denmark. I agreed, but I'd rather die than cross the Atlantic again!"

The three men just looked back and forth at each other. Michalas appeared angry, Christophersen beaten and Peter bewildered. None of them had the faintest idea what they were dealing with here.

Finally Christophersen said, "I'll bet you men would rather be on your way than stand here listening to my troubles. What do you think, then? Do you want the outfits or not?"

"I want them," said Peter without hesitation, "but I feel like I'm stealing your dream."

"The dream is over for me," said Heinrich, all business now, and if Michalas wanted to take him on in the area of making money, farming or physical prowess, guaranteed the former lawyer would come up lacking.

♥   ♥   ♥

"I think you were too hard on him concerning his . . . er . . . wives," said Peter when they stepped outside to talk things over. "You're not his Bishop . . ."

"Wealthy men like him sometimes think they're above the law, Peter. God's laws or the laws of the land. He knew from the beginning what he was doing to be wrong. He just thought he could get away with it. A doctor named John Bennett in old Nauvoo had a similar history, perverting the law of the 'new and everlasting covenant of marriage' to such a degree that his deviant actions caused his excommunication.

"Later his attacks upon the Church became so vehement, and stirred up so many Mormon haters, he possibly perpetuated the very death of the Prophet Joseph Smith and the expulsion of the saints of God from Illinois! No Peter, I wasn't too hard on him."

"Let's talk about the oxen and wagons," said Peter, changing the subject.

They did, but things were tense for a while; the major issue being what if they couldn't sell the jewels and counting up the actual money they had—which came to a little over two thousand dollars. It was finally agreed that nothing could prevent the purchase of the millstones, and the things church members requested. When they returned to the barn they offered Christophersen the following:

"Five hundred dollars to hold the wagons and teams and the balance when we return from Chicago," said Michalas. "We won't have the rest of the money until we do some bartering there."

"I'll wait a while," Christophersen said, then added lightly, "and if you don't come back I'll take your money and run."

A little humor eased any tension between the men, and the truth was Christophersen wouldn't be going anywhere without selling his possessions. "I believe you'll be back, brethren, and I believe you'll have good fortune in Chicago."

Christophersen spent the next two hours with Peter and Eugene, showing them how to yoke up the oxen and drive them. Two-by-two he led the huge beasts from his barn and hitched them six to a wagon. Whip in hand, he then stood on the left side of the huge rig with Bully and Stig at the lead, and prepared to demonstrate.

"Don't forget," he said, "you always walk to the left of the team. Now to move the oxen out you call, Get up!" The traces tightened as the oxen stepped out and the Conestoga moved heavily forward. A few feet later he said, "To turn them slightly to the left, call softly like this, Haw, Haw, sharper left call louder, HAW, HAW. Tone of voice controls the turn."

Christophersen coaxed his animals along gently, but firmly. "To turn them to the right—which is more difficult because they must move away from your side—the command is Gee, Gee." The huge animals reluctantly obeyed and the wagon began a slow turn to the right. "Remember, louder is a sharper turn. GEE, GEE," he called and the oxen obeyed.

His voice modulated between loud and soft as he walked alongside of the beasts, straightening their path or curving it as he desired. Peter and Eugene watched in rapt fascination as the oxen snorted and obeyed. Making a full circle now and returning to where he started, Christophersen called, "Whoa! Backing is much more difficult, brethren, and is not advised unless they're unhitched. Say like when you want a pair to back up to a log you want dragged, or to hitch them up to a harrow. Do it two oxen at a time . . . yoked. Stand in front of them, place your hands on their foreheads and say: Back, back. It will take you much practice.

"Now back to business."

After another demonstration, Peter and Eugene took their turn trying to make the oxen follow Christophersen's tracks, and soon wagon and ox tracks weaved crazily about the expansive field's smooth thin whiteness, slowly turning it to churned mud. Later, with hundreds of chunks of sod thrown by ox shoes, it actually looked plowed.

Oxen weren't new to either man, especially not to Peter, but these animals responded stubbornly to new voices. Chains jingled, leather popped and once Michalas cracked Christophersen's whip above their unwilling heads.

"Stop it," Heinrich shouted as his teams passed, bawling their protests at being out in the cold and driven by strangers. "You've got to treat them kindly. Talk to them gently, like you would to . . . a . . . woman! Or to a child."

Peter couldn't help but notice that the burly farmer's voice broke.

"They'll get used to you!" called Heinrich as Michalas passed him again." So exhilarated were Peter and Eugene at the sense of power in their hands, even chilled by the weather, neither man seemed to notice.

♥　♥　♥

Later with oxen and wagon parked close to the barn, Michalas gave Heinrich five hundred dollars cash to hold them until he and Peter got back from Chicago. "We've got a long shopping list, which includes some heavy millstones," Peter explained.

With blasts of steam shooting from their nostrils, the oxen resembled two locomotives just arrived in a rail yard. "I'm sure they can haul them easily."

"You'll have no trouble hauling them," said Christophersen confidently. Michalas didn't agree. To him oxen were stubborn as mules, more trouble than they were worth. He preferred horses. "My family won't be leaving for a month or better. We've got a few things to settle up around here." He looked at his ox teams as if looking at them for the last time.

"You men ought to be on your way then," he added, sadly observing what had once been his. "I'll put these fellows back in the barn and take care of them `til you get back. "Who knows, maybe I'll catch up with you out there in Zion one day."

"Who knows," agreed Peter.

Chapter 19

Study Time

Torkil Olsen and Darold Stransen arrived in Elgin Illinois two days before the auction at the Borden plant. The smell of spoiled milk hovered over the industrial town like a pale green cloud. The Borden plant itself reeked with rotting cheese and curdled cream. How anything edible came out of the place was a mystery, and yet two mornings straight while Torkil awaited the auction, horse-drawn carts lined up to load up cheese, butter and case after case of condensed milk to haul to Chicago's rail yards and scattered cities throughout Illinois and Indiana.

Stransen and Torkil were allowed a tour of the factory, and amid the loud *clak, clak, claking* of a production line and steam hissing from condensing vats, listened while their host explained the wonders of bringing milk gently down to the thick creamy condensed product, then having it canned off and labeled by a host of men—and a few women—in long white coats. The finished product needed no refrigeration (which didn't exist), ice or dark cellar to keep it fresh. Once a tin lid was pressed into place the small cans of milk wouldn't spoil for a year or more. Industrialization and assembly created to feed thousands of soldiers during the Civil War had arrived in the big cities of America, just in time to accommodate potentially millions of immigrants beginning to pour in from Europe and Asia.

The Civil War had demanded food for its troops in the field—things like canned sardines that didn't spoil—and the Borden Milk Company had patriotically responded to the call. Assembly lines for weapons spawned those for peacetime purpose. In the nearby Chicago Stock Yards, killing and packing enough beef for the ever-increasing demand also brought on assembly line production. Men with sledge hammers greeted the unfortunate beasts, and one by one, after sending them to the Promised Land, hooked them up by the hocks to moving overhead chains carrying carcasses inside to be butchered and, just like Borden's condensed milk, cooked and canned—the end result for human consumption.

Botulism, food poisoning, long hours, poor wages and curiosity over what exactly people were eating eventually spawned food riots, riots over poor wages, Unions, Health Departments and the FDA, but just as dirt roads preceded rails and rails preceded paving, all things came in their proper order during the Industrial Revolution in the United States of America. For now, all Torkil Olsen wanted to do was buy some equipment for making cheese, molds etc. and whatever else Borden Inc. no longer wanted or needed, and to get as far away from the stinking town of Elgin, Illinois as possible.

In their hotel room, so troubled by the stench that he couldn't sleep, Preacher Stransen took to downing full glasses of cheap whiskey to render him unconscious. The auction (it was more of a rummage sale), happened on schedule and two days later with very little money left in their pockets, Torkil and Stransen loaded their bounty into the wagon, carefully wrapping the ceramic cheese molds in burlap sacks, and with all their belongings roped, tied and covered with canvas, they looked exactly what they were—immigrants on the move.

Among a mere dozen buyers at the Borden auction, good fortune had smiled upon them; they'd bought a large assortment of cheese molds, two barrels of wax, several bolts of cheese cloth, a wooden press, an assortment of inoculums and even a file box full of recipes. They'd made some unbelievable bargains, and now with everything loaded they faced an interesting decision.

"It's only forty miles to Chicago, Torkil," Darold Stransen implored. "What a shame not to see it! Next to New York City it's the largest metropolis in America. We just have to go there."

"There's nothing for me there, Brother Stransen. I've got everything I could possibly want right here in this wagon and need to get back to my little factory. My men are waiting and the season is soon upon us."

"Humbug," scoffed Stransen. "There's still snow on the ground. Cows won't get at fresh grass for a month or better. They're still putting the taste of old hay in their milk. Come on, Torkil, it's just two day's ride. Three at most. Let's go."

Torkil eventually reluctantly agreed, and the two men started off, but twenty-one miles later, the right front wagon wheel hit a deep crevasse on a bad turn and broke an axel, leaving them stranded between cities. Loaded to the hilt, the front of the wagon stuck in a jagged rut and with no spare parts, both men were furious.

"We're nineteen miles from help," fumed Torkil. "I knew we should have headed home!"

"Better to have broken down here than twenty miles the other direction," Stransen spat. "We'd been weeks getting back on the road. As it is I'll have someone out here in two days."

"So you say," growled Torkil. "And how do I know you'll be back? You could get into that Chicago town and forget what you even went for!"

"May I remind you that this is my wagon? Not to mention you owe me money and how am I going to collect unless I get you back to making cheese? Besides, someone might happen by at any time. This road looks fairly well-traveled."

"And what are the odds they'll have an extra axel?" seethed Torkil.

After a warm contention, the latter settled into his fate. With a lonely campfire, an old Henry rifle lying across his lap, Torkil leaned his back against a rear wheel of the wagon and watched as the preacher rode off into the sunset, so to speak.

Glad to be away from the stink of Elgin, Illinois (and free of Darold Stransen's rhetoric for a day or two), Torkil gathered some wood, started a campfire, took out his Bible and determined to find out what God had to say about some of the things the preacher had been putting out. For instance, making money by building a church; it galled him when Stransen berated circuit riders because they made more money and worked less than a minister like himself with an established congregation to watch over.

"Same with Evangelists," Torkil remembered Stransen saying. "They've got a new crowd to fleece every night. And when crowds start gettin' thin, they're off to another city. They take their leisure, enjoy their craft, go into new towns for a little shoppin' for the family . . . a little eatin' and drinkin' (as he put it), then at night there's a brand new crowd and fresh new money!"

The money thing bothered Torkil immensely. Is that all religion was? That's not how it seemed with the little man who'd talked about being saved that night several months back. That man was dedicated, sincere. He didn't seem into it for the money. And Torkil couldn't remember any place in the Bible that talked about Jesus taking payment for His ministry. Actually it seemed that things were the other way around—didn't the Lord feed the multitudes? Where was that story of the fishes and the loaves?

Then again, money must have been involved in Christ's church somehow. What about that story of the widow's mite? And the rich man's plenty. Where did that money go? And the tale of a man and his wife in the Book of Acts, who were struck dead when they held back some of the money for a piece of land they had sold. What was that all about? Knowing where that story was located, he turned to chapter five of the Book of Acts and reread it.

Strange . . . at one time they owned the land, and when they sold it they gave most of the money to Paul the Apostle. That should have been fair, so why had their lives been forfeited for holding back a little of the selling price? Was Paul the Apostle making money from the followers of Christ? Was greed a factor here?

With plenty of time on his hands, and ample kindling for the fire, he wanted to find out exactly what Paul was going to do with the money that had cost the lives of those two unfortunate people. He read chapter five, then from there all the way through the book of Acts looking for the answer. Not finding it, he began at the beginning of Acts, and there in chapter four found that apparently everybody who joined the church of Jesus Christ gave it [the church] all their possessions, their land, money and so forth. Therefore, when Ananias and Sapphira withheld part of the price of their land, that money actually belonged to the Lord, and they'd withheld it from Him.

And what was the Lord going to do with the money? Torkil wondered. He didn't have far to read. Acts chapter 4 verse 32 reads: "And the multitude of them that believed were of one heart and of one soul: neither said any of them that ought of the things which he possessed was his own; but they <u>had all things common</u>." Torkil underlined it. Then verse 34: "Neither was there any among them that lacked: for as many as were possessors of lands or houses sold them, and brought the prices of the things that were sold," and verse 35: "And laid them down at the apostles' feet: and distribution was <u>made unto every man according as he had need</u>."

Amazing! Converts to Christ of the New Testament gave all their possessions, sold their land, etc. giving all the proceeds to the church [to Christ] and in turn the church gave back, according to each person's need, money and sustenance. And then in verse 37: "Having land, sold it, and brought the money, and laid it at the apostles' feet." So here it was again! Christ's true disciples didn't charge for what they did, they held everything in common and gave back to the members of the church what they needed to sustain life.

Circuit Riders, Evangelists, preachers and so forth—modern day men who called themselves disciples of Christ—preached the gospel just to make a living from their flocks, rather than assisting their flocks to live! Everything Torkil read was contrary to the system Darold Stransen had been talking about.

So where is such a church today? Torkil wondered. *Where is a church that gives back to its members as much as it requires? More maybe. And how about ministers who don't charge money?*

"There isn't one," he said aloud.

Satisfied he'd cleared up at least one item, he put his Bible back in his old leather valise and stood to stretch. The snowy road before and behind being empty of travelers, he shook his head in frustration. Not a particularly patient man, Torkil decided to do what he could to get the wagon ready for repairs once Stransen returned.

The remaining horses being rested, and plenty of dead trees around, he knew he could make a skid and at least pull the wagon out of the crevasse. It took a great part of the day, but cutting a long thin pine and using a log for a fulcrum he levered the front wheel out of the hole, secured his lever against a tree and fastened a skid under the broken axel. Then with everything in place he hitched up the horses, easily pulling the wagon forward.

That done, Torkil cooked up a mess of fried beans and salt pork. Nights come early in the northern states this time of year, so tying the horses to some nearby trees, putting a final armload of wood on the fire, and placing his bedroll under the wagon, he slept with his rifle at his side.

Day two Torkil decided to find out what the Bible had to say about being saved. For years he'd wondered if Heaven or Hell was the extent of it. It seemed to him that given a chance most people were fairly respectable. Most were truthful, hardworking, and loved their families, so they'd probably all go to Heaven. But the longer he stewed upon the subject, he realized that while most people didn't hurt anybody, that those folks didn't do much to help anybody, either. Earlier he'd underlined Matthew 7:14, "Straight is the gate, and narrow is the way, which leadeth unto life, and few there be that find it." Did that mean few people go to Heaven?

There were people like his uncle, Jonathan Olsen: Unreasonable, selfish and sometimes brutal. Back in Denmark, Torkil had once observed the man beating one of his sons nearly senseless. *He's bad I suppose,* thought Torkil, *but then he's done good things in his life, too. For instance the idea to immigrate to America started with him. And what about Otto Von Bismarck? Thousands of people died because of his invasion of Denmark. Thousands more having lost husbands, fathers and sons— like Catherine's son, Hans—in the war with Prussia, were still mourning. Orphans too. With the wage earner taken from a family, the suffering of children lasted decades.*

Hell? In Torkil's estimation, some people certainly deserved it. Heaven? Thinking about what he'd read earlier, it seemed few people actually went there. Then after reading Acts 16 verse 31: "And they said, Believe on the Lord Jesus Christ, and thou shalt be saved, and thy house," Torkil felt confirmation on what he believed. However, did being saved mean you were going to Heaven? More information seemed necessary.

Just as he was about to close his Bible, the words, "There are also celestial bodies, and bodies terrestrial," registered in his mind. "What's this? Bodies celestial?" he said aloud.

A horse snorted and Torkil looked up to see two riders approaching, one on a dapple gray mare the other a large blackish-brown stallion. The men were stopped alongside the broken wagon in moments and Torkil stood up to welcome them. Neither spoke Danish, and Torkil's English being poor, the only thing clearly communicated was that they couldn't fix his wagon. The men did get off to look around at his predicament, and with gestures and pointing indicated they'd send somebody back to help, but Torkil didn't understand them.

After a few minutes they mounted up and rode off waving, but Torkil didn't feel good about the way the man on the brown had looked under the canvas of his wagon. He made a mental note to remain awake long into the night. Now what was that about bodies celestial?

Chapter 20

Maren

March 1866 would be the longest of Maren Jensen's life. An epidemic of consumption had befallen the community and several people had died, including two from Denmark. Dressing the bodies being women's work, Maren assisted with the dreadful chore and prayed that whatever had taken her countrymen wouldn't hurt her unborn child. On the day of the funeral she'd spotted, but kept it to herself. With nausea burning her throat, she didn't want Elizabeth Anne swooping in on her with bitter tasting tonics.

Early in February, butterflies had softly fluttered over the lower part of her abdomen whispering it was a healthy baby. Now she could feel the impression of a human elbow slowly press itself across her ribs and then with one swift kick, a foot jolted her belly. She already felt she knew the baby's personality. She was certain it was a boy; he'd become a precious trusted companion.

Regardless, Maren was lonely for Peter. She longed to have him touch her stomach and feel the life they had created together. It seemed years had passed since he had ridden off with Eugene Michalas.

She'd waved and waved until their horses had disappeared over the horizon, and when drifting snow covered their tracks it was as though her man vanished with them. Her twentieth birthday came and went; now she began to wonder if she'd be alone the rest of her life.

"Ridiculous!" Gunda kept telling her. "He'll be back bothering you any day now. He and Brother Michalas are smart men, well able to take care of themselves. I wish Claus was out there on some adventure!"

"Out there." An immense void in which her husband was swallowed up. After work each day, Maren would lean against the outside of the Wangsgaard cabin, watching the snowy hillsides for any sign of riders. She lay awake at night, tears silently coursing down her cheeks and still he didn't come. Although aware of her anguish, Gunda and Claus did little to help. "Chin up," they'd say.

Mercifully there was plenty of work to do. Regardless of weather or illness, the people of Wyoming City struggled in preparation for their approaching exodus. Billows blew and forges roared into blazing infernos in blacksmith shops, as shoes for the ox and horse and iron rims for wheels were pounded into shape on ringing anvils. At the wheel works, huge vats of salt water were kept boiling to cure wooden hubs and spokes. Before this process was discovered, a hub took two years to properly cure.

Boards cut from logs at the saw pits, then cured slightly in kilns, were stacked flat to keep them from warping and later used in the construction of wagon boxes. Building wagons and handcarts superseded all other male activities. Oak and hickory just a few miles away were still abundant, and behind every barn and shed men worked feverishly building crude vehicles to carry families and possessions West. Even cobblers set aside their punch and awl to build conveyance.

Clothes and bedding second only to food, women worked unceasingly at spinning wheels and looms. Needles and shuttles flew. Color was not sacrificed: Boiled Indigo, Madder Plant and Rabbit Brush dyed the cloth before it was dried and cut into patterns. Many women suffered from accidents with needles, as they were unable to move their fingers fast enough to escape their own stitching. Besides cotton and Lindsey Woolsey for clothing, scutching, winnowing and hickling flax made heavy fiber for tents and men's work pants.

Soap molds were filled and emptied; candle sticks dipped in sheep tallow; butter churns sloshed; curds separated from whey in cheese presses, then cut and waxed; strips of cut meat were dried in ovens or else in the sun then packed in salt. Every woman's hands cramped at night.

The tannery operated 'round the clock. Hides submersed in acrid-smelling boiled wood bark prepared leather for the cobbler and the harness maker, and in spite of Peter and Eugene being away, the mule-driven gristmill continued to operate full tilt, relentlessly grinding itself into dust along with the flour and grist produced.

Every corner saw intense activity and the frontier town strengthened like a plant rooting deeply in winter—maturing internally, preparing to burst forth with life in the spring. Travelers occasionally drifted through town, and Maren's heart fluttered each time anyone crested the horizon, but none were Peter Jensen. At worst they brought new mouths to feed, at best they brought news from the outside world.

Reconstruction of the South being underway, pages of aging newsprint told tales of suffering, want and violence. One stained and yellowed newspaper, dated January 1866 and passed from cabin to cabin, told of the South's stubborn resistance to comply with post-war law and newly "elected" government officials, many of whom were black.

"*Der står, at her over at carpetbaggers nyde rigged stemmeafgivning i den grad at Neger –er løbe ind i kontor.* It says here that carpetbaggers have rigged elections so that Negroes are put into office," Trevor Wells read aloud in the Wangsgaard cabin, translating into Danish. "And that whites have formed a secret society called the Klu Klux Klan[5] to terrorize them."

"It's people like that General Sherman[6] who caused all the hate," interrupted Elizabeth Anne Browne. "All the fine homes and priceless treasures his men burned. The hospitals and museums lost . . ."

"Such things do cause the blood to boil," Trevor agreed. "But the issue that started the war and the one that remains is prejudice, plain and simple."

"I don't care what the South's problems are," Gunda said coldly. "We've got enough of our own right here. We're no more ready for a thousand-mile journey into the wilderness than a trip to the moon! We don't have enough wagons, nor food prepared . . ."

"Now, Mother," said Claus reassuringly. "We'll be ready. There's still time to get everything done."

Gunda barely looked his way. The tension caused by Jess Plowman's recommendation concerning Talitha Kjars was still unresolved. "And there's no telling what Peter will bring back from the big city," Claus said.

"No telling," said Kathrin Forsgren.

Inviting friends to their cabin to hear Trevor read the newspaper at first cheered Maren, but at the sound of Peter's name her countenance dropped visibly. "If he ever does get back," she said despondently.

Seeing nobody wanted to hear any more from the newspaper, Trevor folded it up. "I must be off," he said as he stood from the table. "I'd like to share this with a few other people before it gets much later." He put on his muffler, and tucking the paper under his arm, started for the door.

"I'll go with you," said Claus. "Give the ladies some privacy."

"I'm glad you stayed, Elizabeth Anne," said Gunda, as the two men closed the door behind them. "Someone besides me needs to talk to Maren. She's listless as a cat and I can't seem to get much work out of her."

"I do my share," said Maren defensively.

"You burned the bread just yesterday Maren," countered Gunda. "You stare into space . . . go outside every five minutes." Gunda was just talking. She had a touchy question she wanted to ask the comely young widow and was cautiously inching her way toward it. Pouring a hot cup of broth for herself and one for Maren, Kathrin and Elizabeth she took a seat.

Working at the tannery, Gunda was up on the people and events of Wyoming City, and of late Elizabeth Anne was the target of vicious gossip. "Sister Browne," she said somewhat nervously, "there's been a rumor going around town about you lately . . ."

"A rumor?" asked Elizabeth Anne.

"Yes," said Gunda pointedly. "Something about you and our Brother William Herzog."

Elizabeth's face went as red as the glowing coals in the hearth. She bent to sip her broth to hide the embarrassment, whereupon Kathrin Forsgren, who couldn't imagine anything so explosive, looked at Gunda as if she'd gone crazy. Likewise, Maren's eyes were wide open.

"What is it you have heard, Sister Wangsgaard?" Elizabeth Anne asked, calmly looking up.

Gunda chose her words carefully. She had her own situation with Claus and Talitha Kjars to deal with. "I heard," she began carefully, "that the good Brother William Herzog has come calling on you."

Elizabeth didn't answer, and the other ladies didn't breathe.

"And," continued Gunda, "I heard you didn't send him away."

"Is that true, Elizabeth Anne?" gasped Maren.

"Where did you hear this, Sister Wangsgaard?"

"At the tannery," said Gunda pointedly.

Elizabeth shook her head sorrowfully.

Maren was dumbfounded. "He's married to Hilda . . . H-he's older . . ." she stammered.

"Since when did that matter around here," stated Gunda angrily. Elizabeth stood from the table and took a few steps toward the fireplace then turned back to the table. Tears softly rolled down Elizabeth's cheeks. "What should I do, Sister Wangsgaard?"

"Tell him to go away," said Gunda pungently. "If, like myself, you don't want any part of this polygamy business, tell the dirty little man to leave you alone!" Gunda hit the table with her fist and stood up.

"You're right, of course, Sister Wangsgaard," Elizabeth began weakly. "But the brethren are teaching the doctrine." Usually so sure of herself, the lady of herbs seemed helpless in this. Her beauty normally made her appear the picture of confidence and strength, but this thing with William Herzog had her reeling. She appeared physically sick.

Gunda put her arms around her for a moment. "I understand what you're going through, Elizabeth. You're lonely, there's a lot of pressure coming down from church leaders and all, but I'd hate to see you ruin your life."

"Don't you want a man who will treat you like a princess," Kathrin Forsgren took over, "a man who regards you as . . . ?"

"His equal," Maren injected.

"Yes," said Elizabeth firmly.

"Well then," Gunda went on, "if you marry the likes of Brother Herzog, you'll become property, not a wife, not an eternal companion!"

Tears were streaming quietly down Elizabeth's face and Gunda left her to tend the pot of beef broth still warming on the hearth. As she thought of Herzog and his cunning ways, her grip on the ladle became as tight as the braided bun on the back of her head.

"What God expects from a woman!" she said bitterly.

"I do love Hilda," Elizabeth Anne ventured as she wiped her eyes. "She's not healthy and so overburdened with those five young children . . . she could use my help . . ."

"For the love of might," snapped Gunda, "that is no reason to marry a man!"

"I should say not," agreed Maren.

Gunda stepped back from the fire, leaving the wooden ladle swirling by itself in the broth, and went to Elizabeth, taking her by both hands. Her anger subsided as fast as it had erupted. She spoke surprisingly softly. "Tell Brother Herzog no, Elizabeth Anne. Tell him you're flattered if you think you owe him that, but tell him you're not interested."

"What about the Lord's commandment to us?" Elizabeth almost pleaded.

Gunda threw her hands in the air. "The Lord doesn't expect you to go into slavery, young lady," she said sharply.

"There must be love present," said Maren as she, too, got up from the table. "Everyone involved must care about each other. Like they do in the Plowman home. I've seen how his wives treat each other."

"Have you talked to Hilda, Elizabeth?" demanded Gunda. "Has she talked to you?"

"No," said Elizabeth honestly. "I'm not sure she even knows about it yet."

"This request from Brother Herzog is lust not love, can't you see that, Elizabeth?" pleaded Kathrin Forsgren. "We all know Brother Herzog."

Elizabeth should have felt ganged-up-on, but she didn't. These women were her friends. Except for the popping of wood in the hearth the cabin was still for a moment.

"It's hard being a woman alone," Elizabeth said defensively. "Very hard."

"Oh, I don't believe you're so alone," chided Gunda. "There are plenty of men around to help with the heavy things. Do you love him, Elizabeth?"

The door of the cabin burst open and Claus came in. Gunda glared at him. "Can't you knock!?" she demanded.

"I-I live here," answered Claus timidly.

"You weren't very long, Brother Wangsgaard," said Maren respectfully.

"I'm sorry," said Claus off balance. "I could go visit someone else."

"Don't be silly," said Maren.

"I'd better be leaving," said Elizabeth Anne, taking her wrap from a peg.

"Terrin will be wondering about me," Kathrin added.

Claus felt terrible. Elizabeth gave everyone a hug, but Gunda, with her arms stubbornly folded, barely responded to the sentiment. Goodbyes went around and when the door closed Gunda said, "She's not convinced, is she."

"Convinced of what?" asked Claus.

Neither woman answered him.

"I'm afraid not, Fru Wangsgaard," said Maren.

♥   ♥   ♥

A total of five children had died since Peter and Eugene had left Wyoming City. Due to the continuous cold, damp conditions, pneumonia became more or less rampant; there were also two cases of cholera reported in town and Therold Johnson, an English convert, died of consumption. Two cabins away from the Wangsgaards and Jensens, Brigett Hansen delivered a perfect little girl into the world that took a few tiny breaths, smiled faintly at her mother then closed her eyes forever.

Despite all the heartache, the grist mill was still producing flour, the tannery leather for saddles and harnesses, blacksmith shops shoes for ox and horse, the chandler tallow candles, and the wheel works round, heavy iron-rimmed miracles which conveyed the loads West. Milking cows, shoeing horses, skinning and butchering wild game and cattle, and splitting logs, men labored. Jess Plowman had proven to be an effective leader. Newcomers and old timers were working smoothly together.

In spite of blizzards and cold weather, the men continued cutting and drying meat in brick ovens and building wagons and handcarts in barns. They were forced to travel farther each day to find trees for logs, but saw pits remained busy and board production kept up with demand. Claus Wangsgaard, Andrew Coffey, Dewey Farnsworth, Jergen Madsen and others—including Trevor Wells himself—worked sixteen hour days, and long after they were knocked senseless with fatigue and had crawled under the blankets, wives and daughters labored under kerosene lamp and candle light sewing patches, darning socks, preparing food and caring for their children.

When they had time after churning butter, scraping hides, cooking, or making soap, Sarah Bingham, Gunda Wangsgaard, Maren Jensen and Kathrin Forsgren—under the expert direction of Elizabeth Anne Browne—pounded roots, steeped tea and administered herbs to the sick and afflicted. No person, especially women, was ever idle. When they weren't spinning wool, working the looms or scrubbing men's dirty work clothes, there was always a snotty nose to clean or feverish child to rock. Six days a week everyone labored, but on the blessed Sabbath Day, except for dire necessities, the entire town rested.

For her part, Maren had a new pursuit on Sunday afternoons. When church meetings were over and there was little to do except sit in the cabin and suffer the tension between Gunda and Claus, Maren would don a heavy coat and boots and take quiet walks along the frozen Missouri River north of town. Trees grew thick in some places, and finding a secluded nook that reminded her of a small Winter park, complete with a fallen tree for a bench, Maren found peace.

Sheltered by a lattice work of frosted cottonwood branches overhead, her secret place had a thin layer of snow over a carpet of twigs and decaying leaves. As was the Danish custom, Maren brought bread crumbs and small pieces of dried meat for the winter birds, and during her visits to the peaceful yet frosty glade she eventually had a few regular customers: Most were sparrows, Starlings or an occasional Cardinal—bright red against the white background—but one day a graceful doe came carelessly out of the bush.

Just as startled as Maren, the doe paused curiously, her liquid brown eyes met Maren's, then quickly as she came, vanished. Had it not been for the snow she'd knocked off the branches, Maren might have doubted the deer had been there at all.

Fairly strong physically, emotionally Maren felt she might be coming undone. She worried incessantly about Peter. What if he'd been killed? Or lost? Or what if he simply weren't coming back? Who could blame him; Wyoming City was such a depressing hole. A young father (the second she'd heard about) abandoned his wife and children; just a week ago he got up early, saddled his horse, rode away and so far hadn't returned.

Nearly six months pregnant with her very first child, wives' tales swirled around Maren's ears like Autumn leaves; Karen Hansen told her to avoid anybody with a fever or the baby would surely be born deaf, and a woman she'd never met mentioned there wasn't a Torch[4] in Wyoming City to tell whether or not the child would be breech.

More than anything Maren wished her mother could be there for the baby. Homesick for Denmark and worried sick over Peter, surprisingly what troubled Maren most of late was Elizabeth Anne Browne's infatuation with William Herzog. The thought of a plural marriage between her dear friend and the manipulating little man had her heartsick. As she sat reasoning in her small forest sanctuary early one Sunday afternoon, she momentarily found herself understanding Elizabeth Anne's thinking.

Brother Herzog is a hard working man and financially well-off . . . no wonder she is attracted to him. Except for that wart on his nose he's not bad looking . . .

Startled, her mind came back to reality. *Doesn't she see what a severe and rigid person he is? Prone to overt control of Hilda and the children. How could a lady of such compassion and tenderness as Elizabeth Anne be attracted to him?*

"*He's very nice to me,*" *is what she keeps saying. As if no man ever had been . . . wait, that has to be the reason; no man has ever treated her properly!*

Maren then heard Gunda's voice in her thoughts: "*He's just a smooth talker Elizabeth! Why do you think you need him? You've always been quite able to take care of yourself.*"

"*He says if I'm obedient to the 'the law', God will bless me.*"

"Rubbish!" is what Gunda told her.

"You don't love him, Elizabeth Anne," Maren heard herself saying over and over. *"What's more he doesn't love you. It would only be a marriage of convenience. His!"*

"Maybe I just don't understand English people," she said aloud.

♥   ♥   ♥

Alone among the snowy trees one day, Maren debated the question: What if it were she? Widowed, no family other than my church family, no children? She lowered her head and prayed. *Dear Heavenly Father . . .*

She prayed silently to God for Elizabeth Anne, telling Him where men like William Herzog were concerned, celestial marriage was wrong; as she'd done that night in the freezing tent, she poured her heart out to Him. She wept; she expressed anger, and quickly apologized. She counseled Him: *Where bad men are concerned, for what purpose is this commandment, dear Father?*

Maren had no idea how long she wrestled with Deity; oddly she wasn't cold and when she finally stood and retraced her footprints in the snow, her mind had cleared of all anxiety concerning Elizabeth Anne. She'd received an answer, one of those deeply personal kinds. An answer not to be shared with anyone but her husband for fear it would be trampled upon; certainly not understood by anyone else except herself. She vowed not to speak of it until Peter returned.

And she knew he would return. With that clear and distinct knowledge in her possession, thousands of miles from home, the young mother-to-be left the woods light of foot, with gratitude in her heart and a mighty understanding of God's love.

Section Notes

1. Borden: Production started at Gail Borden's Elgin Milk Condensing Company in May 1865 and quickly became a major consumer of the local milk supply. In 1866, the plant used 303,560 gallons, leaving only 150,976 for shipment to other purchasers.

The factory's thirty cheese presses also turned out 240,079 pounds of cheese. But the cheese venture and other experiments proved unprofitable, and selling its cheese making equipment, the firm was later reorganized as the Illinois Condensed Milk Company. This nugget of history gold spawned the creation of Torkil's winter expedition to Elgin, Illinois to buy used cheese equipment.

As mentioned in the novel, condensed milk arrived at an opportune time in the nation's history. As postwar industrialization began to crowd families into cities, few tenement dwellers had access to fresh, pure milk or the means of keeping it safe to use. Borden's condensed milk was especially valuable for feeding city children, and the firm's ads tried to influence mothers to abandon nursing their babies. (See Wikipedia 2008)

2. Circuit Riders were a religious and moral force along the American frontier and in rural areas of the South. Originating in the 1700s with John Wesley in England, they were largely responsible for the propagation of Methodism throughout the United States. The practice was soon adopted by other preachers and the term Circuit Rider was used to describe revivalists and others holding tent meetings to push their particular brand of religion.

3. The military outpost mentioned was Fort Atkinson, Kansas, established 1819.

4. A Torch was usually a young girl between the ages of 8 and 12 years old. In a time when medicine (and doctors in general) was still in the dark ages so to speak, people had great faith in folk remedies, berries, bark and herbs etc. and *even* special people or objects that they believed had certain powers. For example divining rods, a stick shaped like a 'Y', could be carried by a child or someone else who believed they could feel water below the earth's surface.

Similarly, a Torch was able to place her hand on the stomach of a pregnant woman and "feel" in her mind and hand which direction a baby's head was pointing. When people were worried whether the birth of a baby would be "breech" or not, they called in a Torch—if such a special child lived within the community. (See "The Seventh Son" by Orson Scott Card)

5. Klu Klux Klan: The first Klan was founded in 1866 by veterans of the Confederate Army, its purpose being to restore white supremacy in the aftermath of the American Civil War. The Klan resisted Reconstruction by intimidating Carpetbaggers, Scalawags and freedmen. The KKK quickly adopted violent methods. Increase in murders among blacks finally resulted in a backlash among Southern elites who viewed the Klan's excesses as an excuse for federal troops to continue occupation. The organization declined from 1868 to 1870 and was destroyed by President Ulysses S. Grant's prosecution and enforcement under the Civil rights Act of 1871. (See Wikipedia 2008)

6. Sherman: William Tecumseh Sherman (February 8, 1820–February 14, 1891) was an American soldier, businessman, educator and author. He served as a general in the Union Army during the American Civil War (1861–65), for which he received recognition for his outstanding command of military strategy but also heavy criticism for the harshness of "scorched earth" policies he implemented in conducting total war against the Confederate States. Military historian Basil Liddell Hart famously declared that Sherman was "the first modern general". (See Wikipedia 2008)

Section Five

Chapter 21

Looking for a Buyer

On an east-bound train to Chicago, Illinois Peter pulled out his journal and recorded:

We arrived in Omaha Nebraska and Winter Quarters two days ago. Not much different than Wyoming City but larger, more scattered. There were a few frame homes going up, businesses too, but conditions were still primitive.

God has blessed this trip so far. Brother Michalas and I were able to buy wagons and oxen in Winter Quarters and we left them in the care of their former owner. We used some of the church's money for a deposit but still have enough to buy millstones.

Peter paused at this point. The constant thump, thump, thump, of the rolling steel under his feet and the swaying of the smoky train had made his writing appear to have come from the hand of an old man; uneven and shaky. Smudged. A flutter of anxiety rippled across his mind and his stomach knotted.

What if we're not able to sell the diamonds?

On the tucked and rolled red velvet bench across from him, Eugene Michalas had his hands folded over his chest, his head back and swaying side to side, mouth wide open, legs stretched out as far as possible. Sound asleep, he looked as if he hadn't a care in the world.

Michalas didn't hesitate to give Henrich Christophersen the money, Peter thought. *And he doesn't seem the least bit worried about selling the jewels. Everything will work out; we've been lucky so far, I must not worry.* But he did worry, and to cool his anxiety Peter picked up his journal again:

Through my window the passing countryside is flat as a pond, a patchwork of white snow and large sections of brown dead grasses and leafless trees. There are some evergreens but the wilderness is endless. I am filled with wonder at the sheer size of it. We've stopped at two small towns to take on coal and water; there couldn't have been a hundred people in either place. Brother Michalas said we'd soon be traveling through a mountainous region. So far all I've seen is winter in America; will it ever turn green?

Peter wiped his eyes and face then looked at his soot-smeared hand. He didn't want to look like a lowly immigrant, so with the sleeve of his coat, he again wiped his face until he supposed it was clean.

"Would you like to buy anything?" asked a young boy dressed in a porter's uniform who'd made his way expertly down the swaying aisle. Peter didn't understand him, but the tray of candies and other confections looked tempting, self explanatory. He shook his head and gave his English a try. "Thank you, no."

Across from him, Michalas sat up with a start, looking around as if he was lost.

"The landscape hasn't changed much then, has it, Peter," he said groggily.

"Not much," said the latter closing his journal. The constant thudding of the train assaulted Michalas' ears, sending chills through his body. "Do you feel cold?"

"Somewhat," said Peter.

Michalas yawned widely. "Someday this will be the only way people will travel," he said, eyes wet and bloodshot; shuddering he folded his arms. "All the way to Salt Lake City and no ox teams!"

"Ya," said Peter doubtfully. He placed his journal aside and stretching his arms added, "Too bad it won't be us. How much longer before we reach Chicago?"

"The whole trip is fourteen hours. We've got half of it under our belts."

They sat without speaking for a moment and Peter had a feeling of emptiness come over him. "I wish my Maren could experience all this, Brother Michalas."

"Missing her?"

"I am," said Peter.

♥ ♥ ♥

The population of Chicago, Illinois in 1866 stood at approximately 100,000 souls—about the same as Copenhagen, Denmark, but its geography covered a much larger area. Located on the eastern shores of Lake Michigan, the city had room to stretch westward, so buildings weren't the jammed-together moss covered marble, stone and ancient thatched roof, bindlingsvaerk[1] conglomeration Peter had known. Most buildings consisted of fired brick and wood frame construction. Commercial buildings stood close together, a few were four and five stories tall and, like Copenhagen, narrow side streets cut in between. The wind being just right, potent smells from hundreds of bawling cattle jammed in the Union Stock Yards sometimes assaulted the nostrils.

Situated right on an ocean-like lake, Peter expected bustling fish markets just like Copenhagen's, but instead he observed steam boats, passenger skiffs and many barges filled with iron ore lining the shores. The city's busy factories spewed smoke into the sky, and railroads approached from ten different directions carrying men in top hats and business suits, evidencing a raw and aggressive financial center. Over a hundred trains arrived or departed Chicago on a daily basis making it the country's busiest rail center.

In addition to trains, the Chicago River flowed through the heart of the city, and the Illinois and Michigan Canal[2] cut a ninety seven mile path from the Mississippi River, where shipping of grain and other heavy cargo had the city exploding with growth. Bridgeworks of criss-crossed steel spanned the Chicago River, and during the Civil War also helped it become a major supply center for Union forces.

Grey and wet the day Peter Jensen and Eugene Michalas' train arrived, a mist of rain and fog swept in, turning the streets into a slurry of mud and manure. A constant flow of horses, wagons and buggies cut ruts that quickly filled with water, giving a glistening pin-striped effect.

Businessmen in top hats and round black derbies swarmed like beetles amid office buildings, banks, hotels, clothing stores, crowded cafes and stuffy insurance and real estate agencies. The business district also boasted hardware and jewelry stores, barber shops, pawn brokers, and shoe shops—all somewhat entwined with lawyer's dens.

On the fringes of the business district were quaint little shops; well-stocked general stores; milliners with bells tinkling in the door-ways where women in hooped dresses, and high buttoned shoes hurried in and out with baskets under their arms, proud bustles bouncing and ringlets bobbing (with children in tow); giving the uncivilized city a very civilized flavor.

Union soldiers swaggered on the boardwalks but not near so many as were in St. Louis; but even more ominous were bullet-hat police-men, night sticks swinging and handcuffs at ready. Freed blacks cleaned boots and portered in hotels, waited tables and bused dishes, while out-side panhandlers and waifs shouted from their posts near the alleys and men in black carriages, enclosed with opaque windows, crawled along the streets with an aura of power and wealth.

Chicago was rich, but all the hustle and confusion made Eugene Michalas long for the stone-age and relative quiet of Wyoming City. Formerly a prominent downtown lawyer, he'd had all he wanted of big city life before converting to the Mormon Church. In a hired buggy, he and Peter were conveyed through the din in the streets, watching as lamplighters wiped the soot from the gas lights and with flint strikes lit them for the evening.

"What do you think of it, Peter?" Michalas asked as he and Peter, valises in hand, headed into the city center.

"It's too crowded," answered Peter uneasily. "It reminds me of St. Louis . . . all the uniforms . . ."

"Chicago's a big place," said Eugene. "A crossroads; anything new in the East quickly finds its way here. Take gas lights for instance. The city was just behind New York in getting them." Peter stuck to Michalas like glue; the energetic way he moved through the crowd showed he definitely knew his way around. "It's grown since I was last here, Peter. Winning a war does that to a city . . ."

"Is it far to your mother's house?"

"Only a few miles from here, on the north side of town. But I think we should take care of our business first. Mother's getting old and I'd like an unhurried visit."

They walked several blocks, finally dropping their grips in front of a two-story building with a wrought iron sign reading:

CLEAN ROOMS
50 cents

♥   ♥   ♥

"This will do for tonight," said Eugene. "A bit rundown perhaps, but a good location. There are several pawn shops and jewelry stores in this district. At least there were a few years ago."

A grandmotherly-looking woman with thinning hair, plump arms and hands clutched together stared at them from behind the desk as they entered the lobby. She had a mending basket near her side and the flowered wallpaper and musty curtains hanging in the small room behind her indicated residence.

"We want a room with two beds," said Michalas.

"How long will you gentlemen be staying?"

"We're not sure," said Michalas. "A night, maybe two. How's the food?"

"You'll have to judge that for yourself," said the woman confidently. "Meals are two bits each . . . in advance."

"Fine," said Michalas, handing her two silver dollars and signing the register. "This ought to cover it."

A square, high ceiling room with plain yellowed paper on boarded walls, porcelain bowl, a pitcher of water, a three drawer wood dresser and braided rug greeted them as they flopped on their squeaky beds and stretched out.

"The milling center isn't far from here either," said Michalas, following his comment at the front desk. "They haul the grain in by rail car and store it in tall silos near the tracks. Wholesalers in the district have milling equipment galore; buying millstones will be a simple matter. They have scads of them in the district; they come to the States as ballast in European ships."

"Ballast . . . that's good to know," said Peter. "A surplus of anything keeps the price down."

"You're right there, Peter. We should be able to buy millstones at a fairly decent price. Our real challenge will be selling your jewels . . . without being cheated that is. I'm no expert, Peter, but if they're genuine diamonds, and they obviously are, the trick won't be selling them, but getting a fair price."

"*De er gedigen*. They are genuine," Peter stated confidently.

"Well then, we're in the heart of commerce, everything we need is within a mile or two. With a little luck we can accomplish both of our main tasks without wearing out much shoe leather."

"I'm very interested to see the milling center," Peter commented, yawning. "To see everything in daylight."

♥ ♥ ♥

The next day, after canvassing Chicago a full ten hours, except for sore feet Peter and Eugene had little to show for their labors. Selling the diamonds had proven extremely difficult and perhaps even dangerous. Every pawn shop owner's eyes had bulged, one even offered fifteen hundred dollars for each stone, but to a man couldn't pay much more; either they didn't have the money, the right clientele to sell them to, or thought the diamonds stolen. One man they spoke to didn't intend to, but vocalized a ray of hope:

"They obviously came offa something fancy like Sterling Marks would make," he said suspiciously. "How'd you come by 'em?"

"They're not stolen, if that's what you're inferring," said Michalas firmly. "My friend here brought them over from Denmark."

The low end jewelry store owner, a heavy and abrupt man with jet black hair hanging limply over his forehead forcing him to occasionally brush it from his eyes, sported a sunless pale face indicating long hours in-doors, and soft fleshy fingers upon which flashed diamond rings he could ill afford. His woolen coat and blousy shirt cost him dearly at one time, and he smelled of stale cologne. Standing at a wooden counter, arms folded and magnifying glass in hand, he scanned Peter head to foot, then also the seven-carat diamonds brilliantly glittering on Peter's unfolded handkerchief.

"They look hot to me," he said at last. "I'll give ya a thousand apiece for the stones . . . and count yourself lucky."

Michalas stared at him numbly for a moment, then speaking Danish said to Peter, "*He's offer to tusind dollars. og vi savn hen til slippe ud af her ovre.* He's offering two thousand dollars total . . . and we need to get out of here."

Peter felt sick inside but noticed a steeled glimmer in Michalas' eyes.

"We'll go elsewhere, my friend," said Michalas, calmly picking up the diamonds, wrapping them in his handkerchief and shoving them in his pocket. "By the way, who is this Sterling Marks?"

"You don't know 'im?" the surprised jeweler asked, then added a few anti-Semitic remarks, including rich Jew etc. "Mark's Jewelers, State Street and Melrose, most exclusive store in all Chicago. Makes his own stuff..."

"What does that mean?"

"He's a manufacturing jeweler, man. We're all forced to buy from him; he's got connections in Europe... South Africa."

Chapter 22

The Chicago Branch

Catherine awakened with a jolt. Outside, darkened trees were slowly passing the windows. The train was struggling to build up a head of steam, and it bucked and snorted violently, like a wild horse. Albeit slowly, it *was* moving, and a broad smile crossed her face. Warm beneath the covers, Catherine reached out and found little Hans curled up beside her.

Because she could afford a private berth, most nights Catherine slept alone. Only twice on the trip had her grandson joined her. Tonight would make three. The boy adored Cousin Anna Katrina and had become her miniature body guard. But there he lay sleeping . . . and the boy did sprawl out like a crab! It didn't bother his grandmother. To give him room, she slept on the edge near the walkway and the impression of her back was obvious to a person passing down the aisle; in fact she'd been brushed more than once.

But compared to the good ship *Carthage*, this train was paradise. It rocked and swayed, but never, never gave the feeling its entire mass was being swallowed whole, or falling over a cliff! And although cold, the train wasn't damp. It didn't leave a person clammy or feeling like something had been crawling up a pant leg or skirt.

What a wonder little Hans was! A miniature replica of her brave, but long-lost son. This child would never know the joy and comfort he gave her. Catherine tried not to let it show, especially to Evette, but she remained on guard like an eagle; her talons remained at ready any time the boy was entrusted to her, or any time she happened to be in his and Evette's presence.

And now they were heading for Chicago. Catherine scanned the newspapers, trying to pick out the few English words she knew. Prior to coming to America she'd read everything she could get her hands on concerning New York, Cincinnati, and other large cities in the states, including the sprawling, blustery city by Lake Michigan. Chicago had been wide open during America's civil war. More troops and supplies for transportation eastward on the Mississippi had been shipped into the city than it could possibly handle during the war. Warehouses were still bulging with overstock. There were many panhandlers and displaced citizens in town, and Catherine would watch every move little Hans *and* his mother made there.

After digging themselves out of the avalanche near Oxford, Ohio and bumping tediously along for another two full days and nights, Catherine's train finally steamed into in the *Windy City*, ten minutes after midnight of March 28, 1866.

Numb from the noise and feeling as if they'd been whipped, the passengers spilled out of the train and crowded the boarded-floor, arched depot like rabbits. Trunks and hat boxes, leather grips and bags were collected from luggage cars, then like a convention of street people, the three hundred plus immigrants gathered their trunks, their children and all they possessed and made their way down State Street to an old rented church and spent the night.

Blankets spread on pews, in classrooms and down in hallways— even near the podium—the immigrant Saints made themselves at home. There being a kitchen in the church complete with fireplace and built-in ovens the size of a loaf of bread, one might think cooking utensils and a full larder would come with the package, but alas—other than two outdoor privies located in the rear of the building, the church was bare of creature comforts.

Their quarters—secured by the local Branch President—happened to be a two story Victorian building housing an elderly Anglican congregation who only used the building on Sundays. Worn benches splitting from lack of oiling, musty-smelling wood paneling, and not insulated, the chilling wind off Lake Michigan cut through the old brick structure like a knife. But to the exhausted Saints, thrilled to be out of the rocking, bumping train and out of the wind, the old church may well have been a mansion.

Next morning, a Thursday, President Wilkins held a special Fast meeting, and Latter-day Saints from all over the city crowded in. For the first time since their feet touched American soil, immigrant members actually felt wanted. An instant church family had gathered, bringing, beef stew, boiled potatoes, new bread for a lunch to be held right after the meeting concluded.

Wilkins had a difficult time bringing his sheep to order. Choppy conversations peaked and ebbed like the waves on Lake Michigan throughout the chapel. English, Danish, Norwegian, Swiss and German Saints sought out countrymen with generosity and warmth. English speaking Saints dominated the crowd, but most everyone found somebody to talk to in their own language.

"*Du er af Holbaek? Hvor kan det være at JEG kende adskillige folk af der. Holbaek er placeret oven på oven på en fjord, berigtige?* You are from Holbaek? Why I know several people from there. Holbaek is on a fjord, right?"

"Liverpool is it? Let me tell you what mate, the fish here don't hold a candle to those at home."

"Ah Lassie, ya've coom far ya have. Far from home . . . how ah' miss it."

Home. The Church crowd felt like home and family to the immigrants. Loving people, they also missed family and friends from back East, from Scandinavia and Europe too, but the warm familiar spirit among the Saints felt like Heaven, like they'd known one another for ages, perhaps before they were born. Even though they'd come from hinter and yon, they'd all heard the voice of the Savior; that they were His family, His sheep was very apparent.

"All right, all right," said President Wilkins taking the stand, "there will be time for socializing after the meeting. We've much to cover before the day is out, so let's get started."

People reluctantly took their seats; children were difficult to settle but eventually a hush fell over the instant congregation. "A Poor Wayfaring Man[3] of Grief," wafted solemnly across the audience. All eight verses were followed by a long and poignant prayer.

There followed a lengthy list of business (the people would be housed here for two days), and then the administration of the Lord's Supper. A pure white linen cloth was spread over a table, two humble brethren knelt to bless the bread, and after eight deacons passed the emblems to the congregation, what became a four hour testimony meeting —relatively short for the time—began in earnest.

"I heard the Prophet Joseph Smith speak just weeks before his martyrdom," said an elderly man as he stood up toward the meeting's lengthy conclusion and testified boldly. "A more intelligent individual I never had the privilege of hearing." The chilly paneling of the church itself seemed to warm up and listen.

"The occasion being April Conference of 1844, and over twenty thousand Saints were gathered . . . we covered the hillside surrounding the temple like so many ants. The Prophet Joseph approached an outdoor podium we built for the occasion, and gave a sermon I shall never forget. He wore blue pants and a tan coat with tails that morning, and above his bloused shirt a brown bow tie. What a handsome individual, rugged . . . but his face as innocent as that of a boy. He presented a talk he'd given at the funeral of Elder King Follett and repeated that day for the benefit of all who'd lost a loved one."

The shaky old man seemed to gather strength at that moment. With grit in his eye, he leaned over the pulpit and spoke to the audience as if they were in his home.

"I knew King Follett personally," he said so all could hear. "He was a great man and faithful Latter-day Saint; I worked with him the day a large tub of rocks broke its rope and went crashing to the bottom of the well we were digging, killing him almost instantly. A terrible loss; an honorable holder of the Lord's priesthood taken from the earth.

"But in the middle of his discourse on King Follett, the Prophet Joseph Smith electrified the gathered Saints declaring that the greatest responsibility God has laid upon us in this life is *to seek after our dead!*

"He quoted from Malachi, the forth chapter verses five and six without opening his Bible: 'Behold, I will send you Elijah the prophet before the coming of the great and dreadful day of the Lord: And he shall turn the heart of the fathers to the children, and the heart of the children to their fathers, lest I come and smite the earth with a curse.'

"The audience was astounded as he fully explained the scripture, brothers and sisters! I still am today. There we were, gathered in the shadow of the temple where that sacred work culminates, and the impact of the Prophet Joseph's teachings ignited our souls!"

The elderly gentleman, white haired and humble as his years, paused and removed a handkerchief from his coat pocket and wiped his eyes. He then lifted his head and solemnly concluded, "Alas, after we were driven out of Nauvoo by mobs, that sacred edifice was razed, and in its burned and insulted condition, mercifully removed from the earth by God through nature's powerful forces. But other temples are underway in Zion, brothers and sisters. In Great Salt Lake City, in St. George, Manti and Logan; temples are going up. One day they will dot the earth . . .

"I testify that this great redeeming work for the dead is true my friends and that it will continue throughout the Millennium. This I declare in the name of Jesus Christ, amen!"

Catherine found her mouth gaping as the audience filling the old church repeated the silver haired man's amen. Not necessarily new doctrine to her because the Elders had touched upon sacred ordinances for the dead back in Denmark, but here among several hundred people sharing the same belief, the doctrine's impact felt so sweet, so right, that her soul glowed brightly from within. What a wonderful work! Despite hardship, Catherine's excitement for the gospel grew with each passing day.

These Chicagoans consisted of many old timers from Nauvoo and their testimonies rang off the walls of the Anglican Church like so many bells. Immigrants, too, stood to speak; sharing heartfelt experiences that strengthened the soul, as the spirit of God filled the meeting.

Afterward, while experienced members lit the stove to warm the food, most of the immigrants stepped outside the church for a fresh breath of air and to watch horses pulling sleds full of people. Chicago was busy and what a pity Catherine wasn't among those enjoying winter scene, because there amid the throng passing the church were two nicely dressed gentlemen carrying a trunk between them. They paused to look over the church crowd, and if the heiress had been outside she'd have seen that one of the men happened to be Peter Jensen, her son.

"I don't know what's the matter with me just now, Casten," Catherine, was saying, "All of a sudden I feel so emotional; even like crying for heaven's sake. I'm feeling very anxious, too, and for the life of me don't know why." They were still inside the church but moving slowly with those heading for the open double doors.

"Maybe someone you love is praying for you just now."

♥ ♥ ♥

As Casten and Catherine finally emerged and stood under the arch of the church, Peter and Eugene had moved through the crowd and were almost a block away.

"We're here in America, Casten, we're safe, only have one leg of our journey to go and we're in Omaha. Why this sudden tingling under my skin?"

"Nerves," said Evette, now joining them.

"Perhaps," said Catherine, as Peter and Eugene rounded the corner heading for the train station. "Yes, I suppose that's it."

"Have you ever seen so many people coming from church on a weekday?" Peter asked Eugene as they spied the train station.

"Could have been a wedding," said Eugene, forgetting that Fast Days were held on Thursday.

Chapter 23

Sterling W. Marks

"We need to change our address, Peter," Michalas said seriously as the two left the sleazy jewelers. "Places like his are short on cash and long on suspicion. Another encounter like that, we're liable to get ourselves arrested."

"What?"

"He accused us of stealing them," said Michalas. "All we'd need is for a fellow like that to call a policeman."

"What are we going to do?" asked Peter alarmed.

"First thing is to get away from this side of town," said Michalas pointedly. "The jeweler he mentioned is on the other side of the river, near the banking district. A very exclusive area."

They stopped in one last place, a large pawn shop, but had no better luck, and later, after checking out of their cheap hotel and crossing the bridge to State Street, Peter and Eugene found themselves in the very heart of the city. Outside a five story brick building located on the corner of a cobbled stone street that intersected with State, the sign read Mason Hotel.

"A room will cost a pretty penny," Michalas was saying. "On the other hand, we should have come over here in the first place."

Peter felt like rag doll. All day he'd watched his dreams of owning a grist mill out West evaporate, listening to lengthy unintelligible conversations and watching the eyes of pawnbrokers and jewelers. "Not interested . . . Too fancy . . . or quotes like the last they'd received.

"Sell them for whatever you can get, Brother Michalas," he said, discouraged.

"Peter, if we don't get at least five thousand dollars for *each* gem your mother will have been robbed," the former Chicagoan replied. "Don't be so worried. Things are looking up."

Peter shook his head as Michalas' demeanor took on a competitive look. This was his town and the big city lawyer in him finally came out. "Let's go inside."

The next thing Peter knew, he was in the lobby of a fancy hotel sitting high on a tuft and buttoned, leather upholstery chair, having his high-buttoned shoes shined. Michalas sat next to him waiting his turn, casually reading a newspaper; his thin and handsomely wrinkled face showing anything but alarm.

I guess he knows what he's doing, Peter thought to himself.

♥   ♥   ♥

After a while they made their way to their room, and next morning, after again dressing in Sunday best, the twosome enjoyed a leisurely breakfast in the hotel restaurant while waiting for stores in the area to open their doors. Ten o'clock finally rolled around and with shiny shoes and a prayer in their hearts, Peter and Eugene made their way toward an establishment with a gilded, old block lettered sign painted on the glass saying: Sterling W. Marks Jewelry - Chicago, Illinois.

Besides being a wholesaler, Marks dealt almost exclusively with Chicago's upper class, and did in fact produce gaudy, dazzling Victorian jewelry such as the suspicious pawn shop owner mentioned the day before. Like Gustav Hanse in Copenhagen, Sterling Marks fabricated delicate leaves, vines and berries as well as tiny cherubs, etc. in wax and plaster relief for necklaces and earrings, then in his own small foundry melted and poured gold and silver alloy. He also imported uncut jewels and fine china, and kept two jewelers busy embossing, sizing and polishing.

An icy and damp north wind whipped across Lake Michigan and sliced through their coats as Peter and Eugene approached Marks' ornate door.

"Chicago's a miserable place," shivered Peter.

"One reason I left," agreed the former resident. "Remember, Peter, friendly but not overly," Michalas cautioned. "Keep the diamonds wrapped until I give you the nod."

"I will," said Peter obediently.

Leaving the jewelry store, a man holding his top hat down with one hand and Marks' door open with the other, nodded at them.

"Thank you sir," Eugene Michalas acknowledged.

The two entered what could be described as Catherine Jensen's parlor in faraway Holbeck, Denmark. Warm and inviting, no common tinkling bell announced them. Under a cut glass chandelier glistening above the center of the store window a tiffany lamp, china plates, crystal goblets and place settings of fine silver on white napkins were displayed on a cherry-wood table adorned with a large, yet delicately crocheted doily.

Centering Marks' polished hardwood floor was a large, costly mosaic-patterned Persian rug and around its perimeter displays of porcelain vases, antique dishes, polished brass and glassware greeted the eye. Gustav Hanse's humble shop in Copenhagen paled in comparison, and except for its foundry could be tucked into a corner of the place.

"What a charming place, Peter," said Michalas sounding a bit like an English gentleman. His slight accent would have made Trevor Wells proud.

"Good morning, gentlemen," Marks greeted them from behind his glass. "Feel free to browse around." He seemed preoccupied with an array of diamond rings, diamond stick pins, earrings, bracelets, gold rings and watch chains underneath the long glass counter, but seeing his two new customers approaching directly looked up and said, "And what can I do for you today?"

"Eugene Michalas is my name, Mister Marks, and this is Peter Jensen."

Bending over a watch with a pair of tweezers and a magnifying glass, Marks' grey haired assistant peeped over his spectacles then returned to his work.

"My friend here," Michalas held his hand out toward Peter, "Mr. Peter Jensen, recently arrived in Chicago from Copenhagen, Denmark with something to show that only a man of your stature in this community could possibly appreciate."

At first put off by the Barnum and Bailey announcement, Marks maintained composure. At sixty years old he'd seen a little of everything. Six foot four, hands like a farmer's—unusual for the delicate profession he'd chosen—Marks was nonetheless a fine craftsman. Like the ageing jeweler working on the watch, he also knew fine jewelry and could spot fake gems a mile away.

Denmark fit the tall raw boned man in the European coat standing next to Michalas, and after smiling briefly at Peter he looked back at Michalas and said sarcastically, "All the way from Denmark just to see me..."

Michalas blushed.

"My name h's Peter Yensen," is how Peter's self-introduction tumbled out. Venturing out with as much English as possible these days, Peter hoped he'd made a favorable impression but with a number of Scandinavians in and out of his place Marks only nodded.

Impressed with the big Dane's sincerity however, Marks reached out and shook hands. "Peter," he said, "it's good to meet you." Known for congenial mannerisms and tact, behind the scenes Marks also supported a hospital for recovering soldiers, Union and Rebel. Also very shrewd in business, customers generally left his store feeling they'd received their money's worth.

"Now what is it you have to show me?" He asked. "I'm a very busy man."

Peter reached in his coat pocket, retrieved the knotted handkerchief, untied it and placed the two diamonds carefully on a black velvet cloth lying on the counter. Trying not to show any emotion as he put a jeweler's glass against his right eye and squinched it firmly in place, Marks fumbled slightly, nearly dropping it. He seemed in a hurry at first, but his inspection slowed noticeably. The soft bluish tint of the 'brilliant' cut diamonds literally took his wind. He paused, and with a cloth polished the jeweler's lens vigorously, took a deep breath and again his practiced eye scanned each stone carefully. Marks seemed in a trance.

Michalas began to feel his shirt collar sticking to the back of his neck and beads of sweat dotted Peter's forehead. Radiating heat from its cast iron skin, stovepipe, and decorative nickel plating, the potbellied stove in the center of the back wall began to feel like a furnace!

Finally Marks took the jeweler's lens from his eye and took a few steps to his right. "Come around the display case, gentlemen," he invited, holding open a curtain leading to a back room. "Bring the gems, will you . . . and mister Berman, would you please watch the register? We may be a while."

Berman's spectacles rode up and down with the tip of his nose, but he didn't say anything. Little traffic so far that morning.

From the curtain, Marks led Peter and Eugene through the manufacturing room where another grey haired fellow was working and from there into a back office. A window lighted the small room; nevertheless he lit two large kerosene lamps—one on each side of the wall—turning their wicks high as they would go. Tin reflectors accentuated the light. Next Marks turned up the wick up on a third overhead lamp, then sat behind a rectangular desk upon which were various loose diamonds and small wooden boxes containing settings, and also a tiny scale.

Peter and Eugene sat opposite the big man, each knowing *few* visitors ever saw this office. Marks next positioned a mirror on his desk so it reflected and intensified light from the lamps. He now had controlled light of a small operating table. As invited, Peter placed the diamonds under the reflected light and Marks once again put the jeweler's lens to his eye. Except for the soft hiss of the burning lamps and breathing of three men, the room was silent.

"What do you think," Michalas ventured.

"Extraordinary," the manufacturing jeweler said finally. "Absolutely extraordinary!"

Marks showed a twinge of regret at such enthusiasm, but being an honest man, he couldn't help it. The cut, color and clarity of the diamonds were like none he'd ever seen. Normally he was far more cautious in business, but Sid Binder's Fine Jewelry being just two blocks away, if these men hadn't already shown Binder the stones, Marks would see to it they never did.

As he placed the precious gems on his tiny scales and carefully moved the weights, he seemed to be humming slightly. Next he picked up a set of tweezer-like calipers and turned the dial. "Slightly over seven carets," he pronounced at last. "How much do you want for them?" He'd started the bidding and for emphasis, Marks replaced his jeweler's lens to its velvet lined case and snapped the lid. He focused on Michalas.

Hoping the prosperous jeweler wouldn't notice his tenseness, Eugene rubbed his eyes, looked up and answered weakly, "How much can you offer?"

"They're worth a lot of money to your friend there, I'm sure, but I can't sell them as they are. I'll have to attach them to something or else cut them down entirely. Make several pieces of jewelry from them. What did they come from? Where's the rest of it?"

The jeweler's careful eyes rested upon Peter, whereupon Michalas began a hasty translation. "*Han virker nok så interesserede men ønsker hen til kende der hvor de kom af.* He acts very interested but wants to know where they came from."

Peter had to suppress a strong urge to bring his arm against the necklace sewn in his coat. "*De er af en forhenværende slægt arvestykke Broder Michalas.* They're from an old family heirloom, Brother Michalas," he answered candidly.

"They came from an old family heirloom," parroted Eugene.

Watching Marks with intrepid fascination, Peter could tell the man knew more than he'd ever show, and that he'd like to ask more questions. But being purposely abrupt, Peter showed that he'd said all he would.

"Hmm . . . well, tell Peter I might give him seven thousand dollars apiece for them," said Marks as if he were buying a couple of race horses.

Michalas felt a little faint. "What did you say?"

"I wouldn't go any higher than that, Mister Michalas," said Marks evenly. "Seven thousand is what I'm thinking . . ."

Like in a courtroom, Michalas showed as little emotion as possible, and secretly placing a hand on Peter's knee to restrain him relayed the following in Danish, "*Han er offer en ringe skæbnen her ovre Peter; netop hilsen jeres leder og vi vil samtale senere.* He is offering a small fortune here, Peter; just nod your head. We'll talk about it later."

"*At vil være nobel.* That will be fine," said Peter nodding slightly and suppressing a rush of sheer joy. He wanted to stand up and shout, but the weight of Michalas' hand remained.

"Peter says he thinks you're being fair, Mister Marks. Seven thousand each is workable . . ."

Inside, Marks was overjoyed, but this time showed little outward emotion. "Well then," he said candidly. "We may have a deal, but of course I don't keep that kind of money around here," he added. "You'll have to come back tomorrow . . . give us both a little time to think on it."

"I guess we can do that," said Michalas trying not to sound disappointed.

"If I lay out a security deposit . . . could you, ah . . . leave one of the stones with me?" asked Marks cautiously. "Er, for further study."

"I'm sure we can do that," said Michalas, still in legal posture but brightening slightly. "But how much do you propose?"

Marks opened his desk drawer, pulled out a small stack of bills, and counted out twenty-hundred dollar bills as if they were ones. "Will that do it?"

"I suppose so," said Michalas his emotions still guarded. "Yes, that will be all right." He casually picked up the money and speaking Danish to Peter who, of course agreed, Michalas added, "my associated says to pick the one you want; apparently they're nearly the same."

"They're identical," said Marks without hesitation.

Smiling somewhat, Peter tied the other diamond in the handkerchief and put it in his pocket. The two men shook hands with Marks but neither remembered exactly how they left the store. Later, as they walked against the wind looking for a restaurant, both their heads were spinning.

"Unbelievable," said Michalas, suddenly feeling faint. "The jewels literally sold themselves."

"What if he reneges tomorrow?" asked Peter, voicing Michalas' identical fears.

"We'll be back on the streets talking to other jewelers, I suppose. But time is precious; we've got to be about our business. The wagon train will be forming up soon. We've got to have a little faith here Peter."

"But he does want them, right, Brother Michalas?"

"Oh, he wants them. The man knows what he doing, but it's a long time till morning. It's down right maddening, you know it Peter? Every conceivable thing we need at our fingertips here in Chicago . . . and Marks holds the key."

"And what if Heinrich Christophersen runs off with the money we left *him*?" worried Peter.

"It seems unlikely," said Michalas. "But worse things have happened, I guess."

♥   ♥   ♥

Neither man had the stomach to stop at another jewelry store, not even for insurance so to speak; and later with two thousand dollars in their room and the promise of another twelve, nor did either man sleep well that night. But next morning, nervously entering Marks' doorway, a cheerful greeting dispelled all doubts.

"Gentlemen, gentlemen," the big man boomed. "Do come in. I'll be right with you." Chicago's most notable jeweler would take his time with the portly woman at the glass counter. Putting one ring after another to try on pudgy, already bobbled fingers, on the same velvet cloth he'd used for the diamonds, Marks was in no hurry.

As they waited for the woman to leave, Peter was looking around, trying not to act nervous, feigning disinterest in the porcelain and china, silently whistling while Michalas stood near the decorative stove— again sweating around the collar—talking quietly to the elderly man Marks called Berman. Occasionally they'd each look over at Marks—a picture of grace and charm, still as if he had all day, showing the well-fed lady one trinket after another.

At last she waddled out of the shop, and Marks again invited Peter and Eugene to the back room, where he turned his kerosene lamps to full brightness for a final inspection. Twelve thousand dollars in hundred dollar bills awaited them, but the stack of money remained untouched until Marks again examined both stones. It wasn't all that long before the deal was done, and later in their hotel room, both men fell ecstatically upon their beds. "Fourteen thousand dollars; can you believe it! I've never seen so much money!"

Michalas put a finger to his lips. "Shhh . . . walls have ears."

Peter sat straight up, also putting a finger to his lips then spread the money all over his quilt, gazing upon it like a small boy on Christmas morning.

"It's truly amazing," Michalas said with a twinge of jealousy. "I've never seen so much money in one place."

Peter counted out ten hundred dollar bills and placed them on Michalas' bed. "Five hundred for the deposit with Brother, Christophersen and five hundred for helping me," he said.

"I won't take your money, Peter," said Eugene, trying to hand five hundred dollars back. "It's far too much for the little I've done."

"I refuse it back," Peter said in English. "*JEG kunne ikke eventuelt nyde lykkedes uden jer . . . Behage formoder.* I couldn't have succeeded without you . . . please take it."

With his large family to support, Eugene really needed the money. "I'm very grateful to you, Peter. Very grateful. Providence brought us together."

"For me that is true," Peter agreed.

♥ ♥ ♥

The rest of their trip to Chicago went without much of a hitch. The two visitors hired a shipping agent, and then made their way back to the industrial district where they called on Gold Crown Milling Supply. There they bought three sets of mill stones—two runs for the mill in the West and one run for Wyoming City—for eighteen hundred dollars, including freight to Omaha. They also bought gear and shaft works, an Empire Smutter[4a] and iron gateing for water control.

"Grist mills in Zion are all built on rivers or streams," Michalas had explained earlier. At hardware stores they bought chisels and files to size their new French Buhrs, augers, mauls, axes, saws, punches, hammers, planes, factory-made nails and a box of modern window panes. At milliners they purchased several bolts of coarse silk used for sifting flour, and, for the ladies of Wyoming City, bolts of calico, linen, cotton-weave, linsey-woolsey and several precious yards of lace. Wool being cheap and in good supply, the church money bought enough for the Bishop's storehouse.

They went from shop to shop buying crockery, pots and pans, tins of herbs and fancy spices, not to mention scissors, thread, yarn and needles—darning and regular! *Nothing as important as needles!* Gunda had threatened Peter that he'd better not return without several, and meant every word. For women who dared to have it on their lists, they bought powder, perfume and cologne. Additional purchases included barrels of sugar, canned oysters, dried fruit, salt, molasses, salt pork, tea, coffee and Watkins salve!

Next on the list were knives, shovels, saws, picks, sledge hammers, and for the impossible situation awaiting them in the wilderness constantly on their minds, twelve [4b]Colt 1860 Army revolvers. They tried to anticipate every need. The goods were delivered to their shipping agent then taken to the railroad station and crated for shipment.

Taking time out of their shopping spree, Eugene finally visited his tiny, ageing mother. Eighty six, hard of hearing, brown age-spots on her temples and forehead, near blind with cataracts, she barely recognized him. Her conversion to the church the reason Michalas investigated in the first place—still she had no desire to go west and was angry with her son for giving up a law practice to do so. Having lost her husband while Eugene served his mission to Denmark, she still lived in a small white framed home with a sister far younger and physically able to care for her. After an extended yet awkward visit, Eugene left her some money and for the last time in this life, kissed her soft wrinkled cheeks.

He and Peter made one last pass through Chicago proper where Peter bought the dresses he'd promised Maren and Gunda, and then it was back to Sterling Marks' jewelry store for a set of china and another hearty handshake!

At a gunsmith, Peter bought Claus Wangsgaard a Sharps repeating rifle and one for himself. Then, before leaving the elegant Mason Hotel, lay totally shocked at the eight thousand dollars still available! He could only wonder at the power left in his mother's necklace.

Eugene spent nearly all the money sent with them by church members and most of the five hundred from Peter, but with little regret. They checked out, hired a buckboard to take them to the train depot, and on their way passed the same old church they'd seen before. Again, there were about three hundred people milling around in front.

"Lots of activity at that place," commented Michalas.

"Probably a funeral," Peter speculated.

"Sure a big one," agreed Michalas. "It's not the Sabbath, that's for sure." They stared at the people as they quickly passed but didn't recognize a soul. "It's an Anglican church, probably why they dress so European," he added.

♥　♥　♥

Peter and Eugene found all their goods loaded in a boxcar, clearly marked with stencil. The white granite millstones were stored separately, banded and nailed to the wooden floor to keep them from shifting and throwing the boxcar off its tracks.

"The shipping agent earned his money," said Michalas, as they stood inside the boxcar out of Chicago's incessant wind. "Now if Heinrich Christophersen hasn't skipped out on us. Like Jess Plowman said, we're going to need two wagons to carry everything."

Even if Christophersen had, Peter wasn't concerned. His newly acquired wealth gave him confidence. Not having earned it himself, he often reminded himself to shun pride. He patted the sides of a set of millstones fondly. "French Buhr stones . . . beautiful aren't they, Brother Michalas? I can't wait till Maren sees them."

Michalas looked at the huge, ugly, rounded chunks of laminated quartz. "I don't think she'll share your sentiments, Peter. She'll probably be grateful to see you, though," he added.

Leaving the boxcars, they climbed aboard the train, put their suitcases in their sleeping berth, and found an empty seat, the very popular Rock Island Run being the first leg of their return journey.

Hours later, their westbound train then crossed the state of Illinois, the wide Mississippi River, and was now steaming across the desolate plains of Iowa. Peter was again staring out the window. The passing countryside was still covered with snow and patches of brown prairie, flat and empty as before. The train was the same thundering, rocking, jerking, jangling predicament as before, but with the experiences in Chicago filling his mind the trip would pass quickly. An incredible dream; had it actually happened?

The proud owner of two brand-new runs of French mill-stones tucked his elbow against his side, feeling his mother's necklace; now with two of the four large diamonds missing, it still remained a treasury. And near his right foot, a valise holding a thick lump of greenbacks; glancing at two tough-looking characters seated across from him Peter felt like an unprotected bank.

He shrugged off the unsettling feeling, folded his arms tightly and as the train gathered steam, closed his eyes and let his mind wander pleasant fields of thought. Maren was there, and a smile crossed his haggard face.

Chapter 24

Heart's Desire

*T*orkil Olsen remained by the side of the road a full four days waiting for Darold Stransen's return from Chicago. The two riders who'd promised to send help never ventured back his way, nor did anyone sent by them. A few other wagons and people stopped to share a drink of water, some a bite of food, some even offered whiskey, but nobody brought the ability to help repair a broken axel. And Torkil couldn't leave the prized equipment loaded on the wagon for fear of looting!

On day five, he'd eaten the last strip of beef jerky, burned every sizable piece of wood in close proximity to the wagon, and couldn't remember ever feeling so angry and frustrated in his life. At times he was almost in a blind rage and couldn't think clearly. The only time he felt rational was when reading the Bible; and he'd nearly read it all. The morning of day six he finally decided to leave his bounty tied under the canvas and ride one of the horses into Chicago. If he bumped into Stransen he'd determined to kill the man, but just as he mounted his horse a wagon appeared coming from the south.

The preacher had another man with him, a new axel, a small sack of potatoes, cheese, bread and a slab of salt pork, so swallowing his anger

Torkil allowed him to explain his long absence. Tales of refusal to help, not finding the right part or being able to find anyone willing to drive the distance ran thin, but as Stransen rambled, Torkil was placated because the man Stransen brought had rolled up his sleeves and gone to work with a wagon jack.

After breakfast their wagon was finally on the road, and that evening Torkil got his first look at the vibrant, growing metropolis of Chicago, Illinois. Stransen had taken them to an older part of town where a few brick buildings lined the streets; however bars and brothels seemed to outnumber legitimate business. Led by Stransen, the maker of cheese quickly got into the spirit of things. There was a hot bath and a shave, beer flowing freely, bar maids flirting and food was cheap. But on the morning of April 7th, with a heavy, late year snowfall blanketing the streets with white, Catherine Jensen's former foreman had had all he wanted of the big city.

They'd taken a cheap hotel near the rail center and Stransen was still knocked senseless from drinking the night before. Disgusted, Torkil cleaned up, combed his thick, reddish-blonde beard and mane, put on his coat and decided to take a walk to cool his mounting anger. They had talked about leaving Chicago early that morning. *We could have five miles on the road away from this city behind us by now*, he muttered as he went along.

Passing stores and shops, he'd wandered near the train station—a better area of Chicago—and observed men in dress coats and toppers with ladies in long dresses and mufflers on their arm. Being alone and walking having cleared his mind, Torkil began to catch a more civilized flavor of the city. Of course, Chicago had a long way to go to match Copenhagen, but it seemed to be well on its way.

Ten o'clock found Torkil standing outside the main station counting the few coins left to his name and wondering if there was a restaurant inside. His head ached and he wanted to sit down and have a cup of coffee. A menacing black engine pulling a long line of cars blasted hot jets of steam on either side of the tracks and nearly deafened them as passengers loaded up. Torkil stepped through the mist it created and entered the station's expansive foyer with a flourish. He loved watching the mighty trains pulling in and out of the station. Brakes squealing, passengers spilling out or loading up . . . here was excitement. A country on the move! Commerce in the raw, steam pistons thrusting, rail cars rumbling, passengers waving and every person with a purpose!

Torkil envied them. Oh, he had a purpose in life—that of surviving. Being there for his sons Emil and Paul and their families, making money and building a business, yet the ache in his heart for a companion to share it with remained painfully on his mind. He thought he had a friend in Stransen, but now having first hand experience with the so-called preacher had put great distance between them. Once they were back in Wisconsin, he determined to have little to do with the man. Or his church.

His deep concerns must have absorbed his entire attention because when Catherine Jensen stepped directly in front of him, at first Torkil excused himself and looked for a way around her. To the left or to the right, whichever . . . because as it was, she had to insist he *look* at her.

"Don't you speak to friends?" Catherine's husky, melodious voice demanded.

Eyes wide, Casten was the first lady in the group Torkil truly recognized, and then Evette—the children in the throng scarcely received his glance—but finally his eyes rested upon Catherine, actually standing just two feet in front of him and he immediately went to her, wrapped his massive arms around her and nearly smothered the dear lady!

"For the love of might it really is you!" he exclaimed. "I can't believe it! I just can't believe it!" He kissed her cheeks then put a big hand on each side of her shoulders. "Let me look at you . . . what in the world are you doing here?" He'd never been so familiar and she absolutely loved it!

"I should ask you the same thing, Hr Olsen," she quickly came back. The heiress felt somewhat flummoxed. Her eyes were alive and her face glowed with excitement!

"This is Chicago, and not Copenhagen, am I right?" blurted Torkil.

"You are right," Catherine exclaimed. "Torkil Olsen, this is the happiest day of my life! Well, the second happiest; the first was when this little fellow showed up at my doorstep." Catherine bent down and came up holding her grandson, Hans. Brown tweed cap, expensive coat and shoes the shy little fellow didn't know what to do and so simply said, "*Artig dag hr.* Good day sir."

"Look at him now . . . if he doesn't resemble his Far I'd eat my hat. If I wore one," Torkil quipped.

Catherine next introduced him to Otto Pedersen, Krista Holsen and granddaughter Anna Katrina. He knew everyone else and shook their hands briskly. "This is amazing. Truly amazing! I was feeling so lonely . . . I don't know a single person in this huge city. Not a one except the man who brought me here that is." (At very that instant, Stransen was forgiven of all).

"You need to tell us about it," said Catherine, taking his arm. Everyone eventually filed into the train station's large restaurant, took a table and started talking at once. They were so caught up in this incredible reunion there simply weren't words or time to sort it all out! But they tried. They ordered breakfast, and fortunately it was a long time coming. The place was teeming with people. Talk flowed like a river among the Danes. They covered significant topics, including Torkil's cheese business, Peter's possible whereabouts, Catherine's baptism and her quick decision to leave Denmark, and of course the Mormon Church, as Torkil kept calling it.

He wasn't negative when the subject of the Church came up, but Catherine could tell had bad feelings toward Mormons; or was it religion in general? She couldn't tell.

As things were, there wouldn't be another train to Omaha, Nebraska until five o'clock that afternoon and just as the clock struck ten a.m. breakfast came around—eggs over easy, hot cakes, oatmeal, molasses, cream and something new: canned peaches.

Conversations and laughter ricocheted delightfully around and during the meal; later, as the waiter cleared the dishes, the seated group came to understand that Catherine wanted time alone to speak with her long-time friend and former employee. It was actually Torkil who made it happen, and not shyly.

"You know, Catherine," he said sincerely as he wiped his mouth with a napkin, "this might be the last time we see each other for years to come. You all are heading into the wild-west of America; I'm off to the North . . . could we take a short walk?"

Although extremely pleased, Catherine nodded discretely. "Why, of course, Hr Olsen. I'd really enjoy that. There is so much to see around this area of the city and we've plenty of time to waste. Everyone please let President Wilkins know not to worry about me. We won't be long."

"Let me leave some money for my breakfast," Torkil said, reaching for his purse.

"I won't hear of it," said Otto Pedersen staying his hand. "This exciting event is entirely on me."

"We're so glad to have seen you," added his wife, Casten. "It is truly a miracle!'

"It is," Torkil quickly agreed.

"I only wish we could talk you into going with us on the train," Evette jumped in.

♥　♥　♥

Catherine had seen a city park not six blocks away from the depot only the day before, and even though winter hadn't given up its grip, she was thrilled to see pigeons winging about, perching on surrounding buildings and strutting near park benches; it reminded of the promise of Spring. She thought the place perfect for a long discussion, and like a magnet to iron drew Torkil in that direction.

"I feel like a school girl," she confessed when they finally took a seat on a wooden bench. "The park is almost empty." Trees still bare from the season's wintry blast, thick branches hovered above them in a most protective manner, the air crisp yet slightly damp.

"You feel like a school girl? I-I can't put two words together." His face blushed almost as red as his hair.

"We're on equal footing here, my dear friend. You're not working for me anymore. In fact, this cheese endeavor you told us about may have the likes of me working for you!"

"I doubt that would ever happen," said he.

"How in the world did you ever come to be there?" Catherine wanted to know.

"I had told you that settling in Minnesota was our original plan, but things had a way of changing."

"Do they ever."

"Money ran short..." Torkil then told her how their cows and other livestock were suffering in the crowded pens in New York's stockyards. How even though it was Winter, son Emil came up with the idea of leaving New York, and nobody supported him; then how the fire in Stransen's apartments had forced their departure. He talked for an hour straight, telling her of their trip west. "We caught a stock train all the way to Ohio then drove wagons from there. We found a half abandoned town and had no sooner unloaded our wagons than I got a job in a small cheese factory.

"Even in heavy snow, things moved fairly fast for us."

He then told her of his close association with preacher Darold Stransen and that he was a deacon in his growing Spirit-filled church. Then he told her of their trip to Elgin, Illinois, and how Stransen was invaluable in buying the press and molds and other equipment during the auction at Borden and Company. But then he told her about waiting for the preacher for five days out on the prairie after breaking an axel.

"On the one hand he's been very helpful, and yet on the other he's been a big disappointment to me..."

"I see," said Catherine.

"It's like this, Fru Jensen . . ."

"If you don't start calling me Catherine, I'm going back to the train station," she teased, but pointedly.

"Catherine . . . I'm sorry . . . Lately I've had hard feelings toward the man. For instance, I've always enjoyed a friendly beer or two, for refreshment like we do in Denmark, you know. And here this Stransen is supposed to be a spiritual leader and the first time he gets away from his wife he gets stone faced, repeatedly. He's hung over this very morning. I think drinking is why he left me sitting out there with a broken axel for five nights running."

"Probably," she said frowning.

"But enough of this," said Torkil. "I've told you my history, now it's your turn. You left your mill and a fortune in property, in the hands of Ferdinand, I suppose?!"

"Yes," she said hesitantly. "I did."

He looked at her ruefully "And not long after I left. Mere weeks! All those loyal customers . . . you were years building that business! What happened?"

Catherine touched his arm to slow him down, and show him that she knew the choices she'd made were extreme. "What indeed, Hr Olsen? That is, Torkil. What indeed?" She reflected on events, her choices and why she'd made them. She explained how she'd hastily arranged her affairs at the bank, signing her home and mill over to Ferdinand, then saying goodbye to friends and country. "I did it for the Gospel of Christ, Torkil," she said with deep sincerity. "A flame kindled within me when I first heard it, a flame that at first I tried to extinguish. But it slowly grew into a fire and here I am."

"I knew you had feelings for the Church that night we met outside Casten's . . ."

"You were very perceptive, Torkil. I wanted you to come in that night so you might understand why, but could see that your mind was so complex . . . you were so torn by your wife's . . ." she stopped at his painful expression. "I did have a testimony of Christ at that time, Torkil, but not a clear understanding of His gospel. That came shortly after you left Holbaek. Don't think I didn't want to follow ... Peter, that is."

"It seems like years ago," he said shaking his head.

"I suppose my wanderlust increased with the death of Elias ..."

"Your husband died?" A faint light opened in his mind.

"That's right ... you couldn't have known ..."

"I'm sorry ..."

"Don't be," she said taking a deep breath, her eyes closed and her head shaking side to side slowly.

"How did it happen?"

"It's a very long story ... Here's a short version. You speak of your preacher friend getting drunk ... well, alcohol is what killed Elias. He fell down our stairs and hit his head on something, a corner of the stone foyer more than likely. A terrible thing ... I don't want to elaborate."

"I understand. My word! A lot has transpired since I left."

"Yes ... a great deal. Anyway, Torkil, what really happened to make such a profound change in my life actually began with Peter's conversion to the church."

"That really was something," Torkil agreed.

"I was very angry with him at first ... I'd disowned him in fact. But gathering his things from his apartment in Copenhagen I happened upon a Danish Book of Mormon. I kept it near my bedside for weeks, then one quiet day as I sat near my window I picked it up and started turning the pages. I don't know how long I read, but the sweetest feelings came over me. My mind cleared of sadness, anger and any feelings of malice I'd been carrying. I came away alive to the book's message of our Lord."

"Is that so?" offered Torkil.

"Yes. The book is true, my dear friend. And in reality it is the very reason I'm here. Certainly the things the Elders taught me before baptism strengthened my foundation, and my association with Casten and

Otto Pedersen had a lot to do with my decision to leave Denmark so quickly, but our dear Lord is really why I'm here, Torkil. Jesus Christ and serving Him."

"That I can understand Fru . . . Catherine. That, I can easily understand." He then leaned forward and calmly told her how he'd found faith in Christ at a revival meeting one night in Ohio. He explained how he'd truly felt the Spirit of God at that tent meeting and how it had softened him.

"You speak of anger," he said. "When I caught my wife in her adulterous lies . . . caught her and she didn't deny it—instead she belittled me—belittled all my years of hard work and providing for her. But when she told me that our daughter really belonged to another man . . . now there is anger! There is rage."

"Oh, I'm so sorry, Thor."

"I'd suspected it, Catherine. Emil and Paul are mine, which is obvious; they look exactly like me. But when Sigrid confessed that our girl belonged to another man it cleared up doubts I'd had for years. If you think you were angry at Peter . . . you know nothing of the bitterness that drove me from Denmark."

"I knew it had taken a lot to uproot you, Torkil. I'm not blind."

♥ ♥ ♥

By now they were the only people in the chilly park, and feelings so tender passed between them that neither Catherine nor Torkil were aware of anything else, including the weather. Occasionally a person or two wandered by, but they may as well been ghosts. Neither Catherine nor Torkil saw them. Shortly he slid closer to Catherine and took her hand. At first he patted it gently, and then he engulfed it in his.

"I guess it did take a lot to uproot me from Denmark as you say, Catherine, and the night we spoke outside Casten's home I wanted to tell you about it. Tell you everything; but you are right—my mind was so scrambled that evening, nothing would have come out right."

He paused and looked into her soft, languid eyes. "Your conversion to Christ makes me proud, Catherine." He thought of his own confession of faith; remembered the emotion of that night at the revival and suddenly, abruptly took a difficult path—one he hoped might eventually persuade her to join him on his. "But where does Joseph Smith come into the picture? Why must you narrow your faith to a single group of people when you could share what you have with so many?"

"I'm not following you, Torkil."

"What I'm saying is, it seems to me you are going out west to be isolated from the rest of the world."

"The Church isn't isolated," she said kindly. "You know there are branches in Denmark, and I know of some in England, not to mention several other countries. Why just yesterday I even attended a branch of the Church here in Chicago!"

Torkil wasn't impressed. "So why this emphasis to gather to the Utah Territory?"

"Again, we are led by a Prophet of God and he is encouraging a gathering to Zion at this time. We've been so persecuted . . . it's not popular being a so-called Mormon, Torkil. I'm sure part of the reason for the gathering is for mutual protection. Strength in numbers, sharing things in common . . . that sort of thing."

"Sharing things in common?" That shook him slightly. "If there's a church in Chicago, you might consider staying around here . . . or perhaps . . . well . . . maybe you could even come to Wisconsin . . ."

Catherine's eyes widened. "Are you proposing to me, Hr Olsen?"

"Well no, yes . . . I mean . . . Catherine, your train is leaving shortly. There's so much to talk about. So much I'd like to say. This is killing me. There are some things I'd really like *you* to understand."

"You've said a great deal, Torkil. And I'm flattered . . . but let me clear the air here . . ."

"Catherine," Torkil interrupted. "My experience at that revival was real! I was saved that night. I accepted Jesus Christ as my personal savior and I'm going to follow Him! Not some fallen preacher . . . Stransen isn't my religion!"

"Neither is Joseph Smith mine."

"Then why are you going to a place where most everyone is of *his* church?"

"It is not his church. That's what you don't understand . . ."

Miserable he'd taken a road so far away from the one they'd been on; nevertheless Torkil had felt it time to throw down a glove and sat there waiting for her to pick it up. But she didn't. Catherine knew how he looked at her decision to gather to Zion. She knew he thought she was crazy, a sheep led by a fallen prophet; she'd heard it all before. But knowing the Gospel of Jesus Christ had a much broader scope than he could imagine; she simply chose not to argue.

It would take hours, even days, for him to understand how far-reaching her faith went, but this surely wasn't the time or place to explain. Just as lonely and just as committed as he to his chosen path, and her raw emotions rising to the surface, Catherine closed her eyes and said a silent prayer.

"Torkil," she began slowly. "I'm not questioning your new-found faith in our Savior. I'm absolutely thrilled about it. Truly. I also see where you think I may have made a narrow choice. And where it is all right for you to think that, I assure you it's not the case. Not the case at all. But in our limited time just now, I'd like to choose a higher road."

She took both his hands. "And don't be surprised at what I'm about to tell you." She paused and looked softly into his eyes. Her gentle smile took his breath. "I have feelings for you, Thor, and I have for a long time. You were the father my sons never had. You are a man I can truly respect."

"I-I feel the same toward you," he stammered, ecstatic to be on track again. "I mean . . . but I feel a strong hesitation."

"Just know my mind is fixed concerning my destiny. Judge me how you will, but for now I'm going to Zion. I have things to do, Peter is out there. There are other situations I can't easily explain; you wouldn't understand unless you investigate the Church as I did."

"Investigate?"

"You can start with the Book of Mormon," she said softly. "I'll get you a Danish copy. No one can possibly know what's between the covers unless they've read it."

"Wasn't it written by Joseph Smith?" Now he wanted to argue again.

"No."

"I'm told you worship him . . ."

"We worship God and His Son, Jesus Christ; we do not worship Joseph Smith. We revere him as a Prophet of God, just as we now revere Brigham Young as a Prophet of God."

"They are men, Catherine. No different than Stransen."

"True they are, and were mortal men, Torkil . . . but nevertheless true Prophets also. This I know."

"But . . ." Torkil stopped himself. He would not let this monumental moment end in further turmoil. Turmoil he'd caused. He desperately needed more time with her, but where would he get it? "Can I write you?" he blurted.

"If you don't, I'll never forgive you."

"You mean it?"

"I do," she said, standing. Torkil almost leaped to his feet. Taking her into his arms he held her as one would a beautiful bird, gently but firmly; she wrapped her arms around his neck and put her cheek to his.

A long, full, beautiful embrace; two love starved individuals in the epicenter of America, both on a course through life neither was presently willing to alter. They kissed, hungrily, warmly, knowingly, slightly awkwardly, but such a moist, sweet kisses. Another, and another. And such embracing!

Fire in the hearth of love, and memories to sustain it, emotions to linger for months.

Chapter 25

Oxen and Wagons

Whistle screaming, steam shooting from the sides of the engine, the train arrived in Omaha, Nebraska Territory where a slight touch of Spring greeted Peter and Eugene. Still extremely chilly, nevertheless occasional soft warm breezes brushed across the snow, expanding patches of clear ground and creating islands of mud. It would be hours before their heavy freight would be unloaded, so Peter and Eugene went straight to the livery stable to pick up their horses. From there they rode out to Heinreich Christophersen's farm.

Refreshing air caressed their faces as they rode along, and although the horses jostled them more than the train, both men were glad to be alive and away from the continuous nerve-shattering noise and soot. Wonderful to breathe again!

No smoke rising from the chimney, the barnyard empty, Christophersen's place looked deserted from a distance, and Peter and Eugene were alarmed at first. But as they rode into the quiet farmyard and saw the Conestogas (still covered and under canvas) parked by the barn, both men breathed a sigh of relief. At that instant Christophersen came out the side door.

"I was worried you weren't coming back!" he called.

"Good day to you, brother," shouted Michalas, very much relieved.

"Likewise," muttered Christophersen irritably. He walked over toward them. "My own train leaves in two weeks or so. What took you so long?" Christophersen was only talking to hear himself. He was in no hurry.

Peter and Eugene dismounted and let their horses' reigns drop near a scattering of hay which lay near the wagons. "I knew I could trust you, my friend," Peter said as he shook his would-be benefactor's hand.

"Thought I'd be gone, did you?" Christophersen said bluntly. He eyed both his visitors to see their reaction. "My wife and children are away in town; I've been feeding the oxen. I did get another offer while you two were away. A higher offer."

It was true, he had. Immigrant traffic was picking up throughout the territory. As soon as grass on the plains fuzzed with green long enough to support the ravenous appetites of laboring animals, the trails west would be dotted with wagon trains.

Neither Peter nor Eugene said anything.

"But a deal is a deal I guess; I'm no con-artist." Christophersen sighed. "I'll even throw in my dog . . . if you want him." He swished around the remnants of some water in a wooden bucket and threw it out in the snow. "Last time I'll be doing this . . . wheeeet! Come here, Pug!"

A brown and white Springer Spaniel, shaggy in Winter coat with a broad, flat freckled nose, sauntered up to him. Tongue hanging, the dog's rear legs almost overran his front paws, making him appear to be running slightly sideways. Rather than wag, his long thick tail swished side to side like a feather duster as the broken man reached down and patted his head.

"We'll be glad to take the dog," said Michalas sincerely.

"We will," agreed Peter.

"My animals are like family to me, brethren. Please take good care of them."

♥　♥　♥

They talked a while, catching up on news of the heavily Mormon settlement, then Peter finally settled up with Christophersen; two thousand six hundred dollars, which included the price of the Appaloosa. Taking its former owner at his word, not wanting to offend, Peter offered no money for the dog. Bill by bill, as he counted the money into Christophersen's hands, he sadly noted the man's pained expression. He really didn't want to take the money.

They went into the snug barn and one by one Christophersen led each ox out and yoked it to the wagons. "Better to do it from the barn than coaxing them out of a field . . . takes hours. Each evening after grazing, I always lure them into their stall with a bucket of oats." Peter and Eugene recorded everything he said and watched each move he made; they'd soon be left to their own devices.

With everything accomplished, Christophersen turned and shook hands with each man. "Good luck to you, brethren. And God bless you." He and Peter embraced.

"Thank you," Peter and Michalas seemed to say in unison.

The devastated man strolled the length of his ox teams, pausing to rub Pepper's neck; the he shook his head sadly, and headed toward his cabin, never looking back. His barn now as empty as his dreams, soon he and his family would board an eastbound train for New York City.

♥　♥　♥

Each ox weighed over 2,500 pounds and yet was reluctant to pull the empty Conestogas five miles to the rail yard under the voices of their new masters. Regardless, Peter and Eugene 'geed' and 'hawed' the brutes across the semi-frozen landscape, finally making it to the train station to pick up their booty. Muddy and well-used, the ground near the loading dock resembled dark quick-sand as Peter gingerly coaxed the oxen along.

When he finally moved his wagon alongside the freight car which held the millstones, the spokes of its wheels sunk nearly a foot into the mud. Peter laid his whip on the wagon seat and pulling down on a long handle, set the brake. Dock workers moved a block and tackle into place, and its chain rattled loudly as they lowered its hook and fastened it to the first set of millstones. Clicking heavily, soon eighteen hundred pounds of layered quartz hung dangerously in mid-air; awkward to handle, and potentially dangerous, yet a thing of beauty to Peter, he moved in closer thinking to supervise their loading into his wagon.

"Idiot!" yelled the loading foreman. "Do you want to get yourself killed?" He swore an oath at Peter then added, "Step back and steady your oxen . . . I got this!"

"*Lad være henlægge sig! Jer vil slå itu mig wagon!* Don't drop them, you'll smash my wagon!" Peter exclaimed when the chain jerked and the stones quickly dropped a few inches.

"I said get back, and I mean it!! Wearing a beat-up engineer's hat, heavy coat, and leather gloves with holes in the fingers, the man wanted everybody to know who was in charge. His stinging tone deeply offended Peter, but suppressing his feelings the young miller walked to the lead ox, never taking his eyes off the prize millstones as they were brought slowly into place above the Conestoga.

"Blasted foreigner," muttered the foreman as a dockworker began lowering the stones again. The chains rattled dangerously and Peter stubbornly called out again, "*Ligeledes holdbar, det var da kedeligt holdbar!* Too fast, that's too fast!"

Eugene quickly came up to his side, and putting a hand on his shoulder said soothingly, "It's all right Peter, it's all right. We've come too far and been too fortunate to have any trouble at this point. Don't let his stupidity upset you. He's just trying to show his authority."

"As long as he doesn't drop my millstones he can talk to me any way he likes," exclaimed Peter angrily. At the sight of Michalas, the dock workers instantly took more care and the rattle of chains slowed. The foreman likewise changed his attitude and turned his back to check a Bill of Lading.

Half an hour later all the millstones were safely loaded, taking up eighty percent of Peter's wagon box and causing the iron-rimmed wagon's wheels to sink even deeper into the mud. Their other merchandise easily fit in at the sides and on top of the millstones, and the dock foreman finally gave the nod.

"A man could sure get stuck here," Michalas said as Peter climbed aboard the wagon and took up his whip. "Here goes . . . hey Bully! Hey Stig . . ." he called. "Get up! Get up! Gee, gee!" The mighty animals stepped forward, pulling the prodigious load from its muddy ruts as smoothly and effortlessly as a boy would a toy wagon.

"Guess not," Michalas corrected himself. Going back to his team, he shortly had the second Conestoga under the loading hook. The smaller run of stones, plus the rest of the wooden crates and barrels marked Jensen-Michalas were loaded, and finally the wagon's curved hickory ribs were put into place and the heavy canvas coverings drawn over them. The two horses they'd ridden from Wyoming City were tied behind one wagon, Heinrich's prized Appaloosa the other, and with Pug trotting sideways and following behind, Peter and Eugene drove their prairie schooners proudly through the frontier town and then started for home.

To ward off predators, they built a fire at either edge of their first camp, parking their wagons between, and then roped off an area where snow had thinned and the horses and oxen could nose through to get at the dead prairie grass. Both men kept a loaded rifle near the wagons but were too exhausted to maintain a watch.

"If there's any trouble, the dog will bark," Michalas rationalized as he fried up a hash of potatoes and salt pork. He threw a few strips of meat to the dog that, though still wary of him, lay a few feet from the fire and fairly close to Peter.

"I think he likes me," Peter said, holding out a thick piece of pork. He clicked his teeth, "Here boy . . . come get it." He clicked his teeth again and Pug, still down on all fours, inched closer. Giving him the meat, Peter stood up and retrieved his journal from the wagon. Returning to his bedroll he took off his boots and pants and crawled in. "I'm not ready to sleep yet, Brother Michalas," he said sitting there. "I think I'll catch up on my journal."

"I need to start one of those," said Michalas, putting another log on an already bright fire.

The dog crawled closer to Peter and finally lay at the foot of the bedroll. "I told you he liked me."

A lone campfire on the prairie and overhead the clear night sky a shower of stars, Peter felt the Spirit of God watching over them. His eyes filled with tears. Everything had gone so well . . . "*Thank you dear Father,*" he said so Michalas couldn't hear. "*Thank you.*"

A popping fire to warm them and the dog at his feet, Peter started writing. The date was April 14, 1866, exactly one year from the night Abraham Lincoln[5] was shot in Ford's theater in Washington, D.C.

The ox teams handled much easier under load, he began. *They move like a slow freight train, powerful and steady. Our journey to Wyoming will last five days because oxen need much food and rest. God has blessed us. We have procured every needful thing, as the scriptures say, including the millstones. They're the finest I've ever seen and I'll get them to Zion if it takes all my strength and resources.*

While buying merchandise in Chicago, Brother Michalas refused to speak to me in Danish. Frustrating at first, an unusual thing began to happen. I soon found myself understanding conversations he was having with merchants. I missed much but still understood main points! I can not wait to share with Maren.

My heart is broken for the man Heinrich Christophersen, but from him I learned, too. He made a terrible mistake with his family and it cost him dearly.

Peter put his quill into the bottle of ink and gazed across the campfire. Now also in his bedroll, Eugene's long silhouette appeared to be motionless. Fifty feet away the oxen were standing in a tight cluster, roped in and fog bound in their own breath. Staked out and apart from them, the horses looked like park statues.

Pug resembled a small sphinx; front legs stretched forward, tongue panting, the dog watched over his charge. Other than the crackling fire the night was perfectly still.

Gazing at the dark and peaceful surroundings, from somewhere in the back of Peter's mind a lovely full-length portrait of Maren seemed to form. So soft and real he almost reached for her; then oddly the image of Elizabeth Anne Browne stood there beside her. How lovely they were ... "Like sisters," he said aloud.

"Wha' ... ?" mumbled Eugene, rolling over.

Peter blinked his eyes, shook his head, and felt his cheeks burn. Was it the campfire? He quickly stole a glance at Eugene. *He must be fast asleep,* thought Peter, relieved.

What was I thinking there? His mind chastised harshly. *What is this coming from the thoughts of a married man?*

He lifted his quill, tapping off the excess ink, but failed to conclude his brief entry. Instead he reminisced about the night aboard the *Wortham* when he'd rescued Elizabeth Anne from the sailor. He could still feel her hot breath against his neck as he'd held her, comforted her. And the times he and Maren had sat at Elizabeth's knee as she tried to teach them to speak English. How kind she was!

He could see her doctoring the sick aboard ship, going from one crying child to another, from one vomiting adult to the next, administering herbal tea and tonics. What wonders came from her medicinal treasury, like the painkillers she used the night he'd wrenched his already-broken arm. The relief! And her friendship to Maren; only Elizabeth would have taken the time to console her as she did.

Peter loved the widow, there was no doubting, but then didn't half the men in Wyoming City? He thought about that; certainly everyone loved her . . . but somehow Peter felt a connection far beyond that. His feelings seemed sacred.

Peter abruptly stopped. Disgusted with himself, he wouldn't allow the continuation of this thought pattern. He got up, put his journal away, and then after wiping his feet slipped into the thick bedroll. Lying on his back with hands behind his head, he gazed far into the heavens. A full bright moon, the cooling breeze blowing an occasional wisp of cloud across; soon the warm sun would greet colorful wildflowers poking their heads through the snow. He, Maren, the Wangsgaards, Elizabeth Anne and everyone else would soon be heading west; what lay ahead God only knew.

Section Notes

1. Bindlingsvaerk: The word used to identify criss-crossed brown painted wood over white stucco exterior walls in Denmark. Thickly thatched gabled roofs and substantial rock chimneys are other common features of Danish homes at the time in question and even today. Combined with bindlings-vaerk, these city and country homes provide a charming feature specific to Scandinavia.

2. The Illinois and Michigan Canal:

Upon its completion in 1848, the Illinois & Michigan Canal joined the Chicago River at Bridgeport near Chicago with the Illinois River at LaSalle, 96 miles distant. The canal provided a direct water link between the Great Lakes and the Mississippi River, and helped to shift the center of Midwestern trade from St. Louis to Chicago.

Louis Jolliet first suggested the possibility of such a link in 1673 when he encountered the Chicago Portage. (See: The Encyclopedia of Chicago)

3. Poor Wayfaring Man of Grief:—Hymns # 153

Written by James Montgomery (4 November 1771) British poet, editor and sometimes political activist, his outspoken views got him imprisoned on two occasions. Otherwise a mild man and author of over 400 hymns, a statue in his honor stands at Sheffield Cathedral in England.

His hymn, sung by John Taylor (third President of the Church) just minutes before the murder of the Prophet Joseph Smith and his brother Hyrum, had recently become popular in the United States but had been on the lips of thousand of Englishmen for decades.

Preceding the trip to the Carthage jail, this tender scene has been reported: "Emma's eyes filled with tears. 'Oh Joseph,' she said . . . 'you are coming back!'" Joseph returned twice more before saying his final good-bye.

On 27 June 1844 inside the Carthage jail, Joseph and his companions languished in the sultry afternoon heat. John Taylor later recorded: "All of us felt . . . a remarkable depression of spirits. In consonance with those feelings, I sang a song that had lately been introduced into Nauvoo, entitled A

Poor Wayfaring Man of Grief . . . after a lapse of some time, Brother Hyrum requested me again to sing that song. I replied, 'Brother Hyrum, I do not feel like singing,' when he remarked, 'Oh, never mind; commence singing, and you will get the spirit of it.' At his request I did so."

4a. Empire Smutter: The brand name of a belt driven, metal circular basket-like cage used for removing the black spots of smut, a fungus like disease which may grow on wheat grains if they get damp.

4b. Colt 1860 Army revolver: Around 200,000 were made by Colt between 1860 and 1873. Nearly all were made during the War. It had a six shot cylinder and a 7½" or (more common) an 8" barrel.

Source: Hackman—Adams 2008

5. The assassination of Abraham Lincoln was the most tragic waste of human life in the history of our nation. That one such insignificant coward could extinguish the life of the most significant man to come along since George Washington himself was a travesty of colossal impact upon the United States. Indeed the nation's healing, especially in the South, was set back decades.

Lincoln never would have been as brutal to the people of the Southern States as were his predecessors, and unifying our country would have gone much smoother, faster and with less emotional and financial impact had he lived. Furthermore, the bitterness and hatred between the peoples of the North and the South would have been set aside quickly, whereas the blind stupidity and an ego run wild at Ford's Theater caused our nation such deep scars, many still painfully remain to this very day.

Section Six

Chapter 26

Reunited

April 19, 1866 found Maren leaning against the Jensen-Wangsgaard cabin feeling the cooling wind as it gently brushed her face and dried her tears. Her cabin on the outskirts of town gave a full view of the open prairie, but clearing ground greening and accented with clusters of early wild flowers went unnoticed. Spring being just around the corner, the vast area wasn't completely thawed and still threatened by occasional frost.

Reluctant to work in the tannery that day, still Maren waited for Gunda to emerge from their cabin to drag her away. The Wangsgaards had been arguing ever since Peter's departure and by now she paid little attention to it. Still, a nagging tenseness pestered that morning; it wasn't the Wangsgaards, but she felt irritable. People were friendly enough as they passed—Frieda Olsen had even stopped a moment to chat—but Maren barely remembered the one-way conversation.

A biting voice suddenly cut through the log walls of the cabin. "God himself will have to come down and tell me it's the way he'd have it, Claus Wangsgaard . . . and if you try and go through with a marriage to Talitha Kjars, I'll be on a boat to Denmark so fast it will make your head swim!"

"Lower your voice, Gunda," Claus' deep brassy voice said, "We've got neighbors."

"I don't care who hears me! Celestial marriage my foot! It's the devil at work, that's what it is!"

"You know better than that, Gunda," Claus came back, his voice steady with conviction. "God has called the leaders of this church and through revelation given them this law. Talitha Kjars is as good a woman as ever walked the earth and she needs our help. You should see her..."

"I see her every day," Gunda interrupted.

"She doesn't seem to know what to do with herself," Claus went on regardless. "She needs the support of a family."

Gunda stood her ground. "It's just her charms you're after, Claus Wangsgaard! I know where your head is!"

"For the last time," Claus said, trying to control his emotions, "you need to get that silly notion out of your mind. The Lord knows my heart, Gunda; my only desire is to comply with the laws of the Church. Lust is not my motivation. I believe Brigham Young is inspired and that plural marriage is a law revealed directly from God."

"Humph," snorted Gunda.

No man could deny the beauty of Talitha. Her milky white complexion, soft features and pleasant attitude were enough to set any man's heart aflame, but Claus genuinely held a protective and wholesome attitude toward the widow; a deep and genuine friendship. It could also be love, though he dared not utter the word. Talitha Kjars represented compliance with what God expected of him, and Claus believed himself ready to take on the responsibility and difficulties associated with [1]plural marriage.

Talitha was willing. Gunda wasn't.

Claus wasn't blind. Men like Jess Plowman never sat down. All they ever did was work. No doubt about it—peer pressure being part of the uncomfortable situation Claus found himself in, he believed faith the main driving force. Claus sincerely believed God was behind it all.

Even though he'd pled his case to Gunda with love and forbearance that morning, she remained totally unconvinced. "You'll just have to be content to chop Talitha's firewood and do other minor chores; I'll not share my bed with another woman . . ."

Gunda's voice fell off with that. Her bed had been cold for the past few years and she knew it. Since before her fiftieth birthday, the fires of youth seemed extinguished and though overlooked by Claus, sometimes caused sharp contention.

"I'm getting too old for that nonsense," she had told Maren recently. "Claus will just have to live with it. We hold each other and share an occasional kiss, but I want nothing to do with intimacy." Gunda started to cry at that; she lowered her head, shook it sadly and cried as though her heart would break. Her tears lightly wetted her flowered apron. "I couldn't stand it if another woman gave him a child, Maren. I just couldn't. On life's painful trail, it's the greatest burden my soul has born."

When Gunda confided this to Maren, that day heartbreak and certain longing were written all over her countenance. She loved Claus, and true it was she'd never given him children; perhaps the very reason behind her coolness. Maren tried to understand and comfort her during that conversation, but failed. Nothing ever would comfort Gunda Wangsgaard where a childless marriage was concerned, and she planned to take it up with God soon as she saw Him!

Would things one day be the same where she and Peter were concerned? Even though she was expecting a child, she'd never felt cold toward her missing husband. She hoped she never would. She longed for him, could not wait to see him again! Except for the muted sound of Gunda's sobs that morning, silence hovered around the cabin.

Nine thirty in the morning a late rooster crowed his presence amid cows bawling to be milked. Normally the sounds and smells of morning cheered Maren, but nothing would today. The situation with the Wangsgaards kept her just plain fidgety.

Would Peter *ever* come? She felt like screaming at the giant deserted plains to give him up! Then again, she wasn't sure what she'd to him when (or if) she ever saw him again. Anger, that's what it was; Claus and Gunda's continuing battle didn't help matters one bit.

At first she thought the dark spots crawling down the distant incline were her imagination. A herd of deer perhaps—there'd been many seen that direction—but the spots grew into a long train consisting of two covered wagons pulled by two teams of massive oxen, with two lanky, bearded drivers, whips in hand, walking alongside. "Wheeeet, hah!" She knew that voice anywhere, and the beard and leather cap of its owner were unmistakable!

Maren pushed off the cabin and began running through the thinning snow. She wasn't the only one who'd heard the crack of Peter's whip and seen the wagons approaching. Anyone doing outside chores heard and word spread quickly.

Twelve oxen pulling two huge prairie schooners loaded to the hilt with goods and supplies appeared, followed by two Bay horses, a fine Appaloosa and a brown spotted Springer Spaniel trotting proudly, sideways—as if it were the owner surveying the goods—alongside. The entourage resembled a sheik's caravan. If Peter Jensen had tried to go unnoticed in the past, tried to blend into the background so to speak, the facade was forever erased.

Hearing the faint but rapidly growing clamor, Claus Wangsgaard stepped outside the cabin. "Gunda," he called. "Come out and see! I think it's Peter!"

"Go to blazes!" she shouted.

Fifty yards away, Peter and Eugene brought their oxen to a halt. By now the oxen knew their voices and both men drove them without reigns. Peter reached in and set the brake to his wagon and ran to meet Maren. He only had a few steps to go. Picking her up, he swung her once around then embraced and kissed her. Lovingly and unashamed, he kissed her soft moist mouth repeatedly, drinking her in like sweet nectar! He held her tightly; perhaps a little too tightly.

Laughing and crying all at once, Maren hugged his neck for dear life then kissed him. "You'd better be careful with me, sir," she whispered breathlessly.

"I'd almost forgot," he exclaimed instantly relaxing his arms. "The baby!"

"Oh you didn't hurt me . . . I've missed you terribly! I began to think you were never coming home!" Kisses wet with tears, she kissed him again and again then buried her head against his chest. He held her gently. "Thank God you're all right . . . I worried so."

Gradually the young couple became aware of Brother Michalas— who'd also brought his team to a halt—and a few others gathering around them.

"Oooos and aaahs," salted the air. "Can we never be alone?" Maren whispered. "Excellent stock here, Brother Michalas," Lyman Thayer said to Eugene as he boldly walked up to the lead ox and petted its flank. "Gentle, too."

"Yes they are," said Eugene above the growing noise. "They all belong to Peter . . ."

"That so?" said Thayer.

"Old 'diamond Jensen' himself," someone else said; Peter wasn't sure who. Four men stood between him and Eugene. Even so, the term stuck. He'd hear it again. Two of Michalas' wives were soon there, but their greeting to their husband far more discrete than Peter's; more like two sisters reuniting with a brother. They were happy to see Eugene, and both women kissed him, but on the cheeks.

Soon the growing crowd included Trevor Wells and Jess Plowman.

"There won't be much accomplished today," lamented Jess as he shook Eugene Michalas' hand. "Welcome back, Brother Michalas."

"It's good to be here, Bishop," said Eugene.

"And Peter! We thought we'd lost you both to the lure of the big city."

Peter shook Jess' hand. "Thank you," he said in English. "It . . . is . . . good to be . . . back."

"They can have city life," said Eugene. "Right, Peter? We couldn't wait to get home."

"We pushed . . . hard," Peter answered.

Jess went behind the wagons to inspect the millstones and Trevor Wells walked over to shake Peter's hand. "Your English is coming right along, old son."

"It is," agreed Claus.

"Six . . . weeks . . . he . . . made me speak . . . English of the King," Peter said with a grin. The two Danish men embraced and beat upon each other's backs.

"You rascal," exclaimed Claus, trying to get past his argument with Gunda by putting on an act. "We missed you!"

"We did," said Trevor, but solemnly.

"What is wrong, Brother Wells?" asked Peter earnestly.

Trevor's already sober face deepened into a grimace. "We've had several deaths while you were away, Peter. Cholera. We buried the little Forsgren girl just yesterday . . ."

"I'm very sorry to hear that."

"Gunda and I dressed her little body," injected Maren.

"The parents are taking it pretty well, all things considered," said Claus.

"Sorry to spoil your welcome, Peter," continued Trevor. "I know how close you and Terrin are."

"You didn't spoil it, Brother Wells," he said haltingly in English. "I had to find out sometime. I'll go see the Forsgrens as soon as we unload. Who were the others that died?"

"Most were Americans," answered Trevor. "One child got kicked by her father's horse and died instantly. It's been a dreadful time since you've been gone."

"None were people we knew well, Peter," said Maren.

"We can talk about it later," said Wangsgaard.

"I see you and Gunda took good care of my lady, Claus," said Peter, trying to cheer everyone. He put his arm around Maren.

"We watched her every minute," Claus lied.

"I don't know what I'd have done without the Wangsgaards, Peter," said Maren sincerely.

"Where *is* Gunda, by the way?" asked Peter. "I thought she'd be the first one to meet us . . ."

"She's not feeling so well this morning, Peter. She said she'd see you soon enough."

"Let's get the wagons moved into town, Peter!" Eugene Michalas called from across the way. "The people want their merchandise!"

Peter waved, then led Maren the few steps to his wagon and helped her climb aboard. "Come to our cabin later, Brother Wells," he told Trevor. "You and Claus can catch me up on everything."

"I'll be there," said Wells coming alongside the ox team. One of the oxen flipped its head, knocking Trevor aside as if he were a fly. Barely able to stay on his feet, the Englishman exclaimed, "They're not as gentle as they appear!" Top hat askew, Trevor straightened himself and brushed his coat, trying to regain his dignity.

"Easy . . . easy there," Peter said as he took his seat next to Maren. "Are you all right, Brother Wells?"

"I am," said Trevor embarrassedly meeting Peter's inquiring eyes.

Maren had turned around, looking at the millstones and all the boxes stacked behind her.

"Peter," she exclaimed. "Where on earth . . ."

Peter turned around. "See that one in the corner?" he said matter-of-factly. "It contains dishes . . ." A small wooden crate stenciled with the words **S.W. Marks U.S.A.** was wedged into the corner. Through the ribs of the crate could be seen a beautiful but crushed lavender ribbon. "They're for you."

"All this has cost a lot of money, Peter," she said overwhelmed, and facing him squarely added, "Where did you get it?"

An admiring couple was passing within earshot. "They look like a valentine under that canvas arch, don't they, John?" the woman said.

Peter touched Maren's lips with the tip of his finger. "Shuush," he said tenderly. "I'll tell you later . . . Bully . . . Stig," he called out. "Get up!" Maren grabbed her seat as the oxen tightened against their tugs and with a jerk pulled the huge wagon forward.

The wind blew Maren's mussed hair across her face. She smoothed it back behind her ears and took a deep contented breath. "You've named the oxen?" She put an arm around Peter's waist. With the other hand she held the wagon seat.

"That's what the first yoke are called," he answered. "The man I bought them from named them. It's taken a while for them to fully trust me. It's easier to direct them walking alongside of the wagon; sometimes I ride though."

Once they got going, the oxen moved like a huge machine, all parts in unison. Powerful shoulders pistoned smoothly, but the ground beneath their feet being uneven, the wagon rocked side to side as it rolled over the bumps and ruts. Trundling along behind, Michalas' wagon cut Peter's ruts even deeper as the caravan headed slowly for town center. Young boys and girls called out as they ran alongside; adults walked behind in eager pursuit.

"Are all these animals and wagons yours then, Peter?" Maren asked simply.

"Ours," he corrected, and leaned over to kiss her on the cheek. Maren looked concerned but not because of what she'd seen; she was thinking of her prayer the week before.

"You knew when we married that my family had wealth," he said as he looked at her. "Don't let this upset you. Once things settle down I'll tell you everything."

"It all must have cost a fortune," Maren continued.

"We're going to build a grist mill in Zion, Maren," he said dodging her inquiry. "What you see behind you is everything we'll need to do it. Two runs of stones, gears, belting, bolting[2] everything! Everything, that is, except for timber. Or maybe I'll use adobe bricks. Claus said he'd show me how to make them."

Maren wasn't listening. Looking straight ahead, her thoughts were about his not telling her about the money, and wondering how he could have such a large sum and she not know about it. She was a bit confused and maybe a bit angry with him, but Maren didn't show it. So happy to have him back nothing else mattered. Almost nothing.

"So that's what you want to do with your life?" she asked, making conversation. "Make flour?"

"I was born to be a miller, Maren," he answered. "I knew it the moment I entered Brother Michalas' mill. All the smells and feelings of my youth were there." He paused and remembered; there stood Torkil Olsen telling him to get to work. Peter rubbed his hands remembering the soreness.

"Just like Mother's my mill will feed many people, Maren, and it will provide jobs. Flour will flow like water from those stones back there. And the mill will be a gathering place . . . farmers will come from all over bringing their wheat, barley and oats . . . and they'll bring news. My family always knew what was going on in the world and especially Denmark."

"It will take a great deal of work to build a mill, Peter," Maren said somewhat doubtfully. "You certainly can't do it alone."

"I'll have to hire some men, Maren, but I've built that mill in my mind so many times that I can actually see the building. It will be twice the size of my grandfather's and water powered, built by a stream. I've designed it so there will be no double handling of anything."

Amid the noise of thudding hooves and jingling chains, Maren felt herself becoming very excited. She had implicit confidence in Peter. "I'm behind you in everything," she said. "I hope you know that."

He put his hand on hers. "I couldn't do it without you, Maren."

Chapter 27

Herzog

The wagons arrived in the center of town and people were out on the muddy streets waving excitedly. Other wagons tried to move out of the way, but William Herzog glared as the caravan passed, pronounced jealousy surging through his ugly little mind. His little eyes darkened into slits as they met Peter's; he tipped his hat ever so slightly. "Good morning Brother Jensen," he said mockingly so Peter heard it.

Peter returned the salutation with a two fingered salute. "Good morning." He wondered at Herzog's meaning, as the wily former merchant rarely spoke to him.

The wagons stopped, and the people crowded around. Many came in their own wagons and brought the entire family! It seemed like everyone in town had gathered. Those people who hadn't ordered anything stood enviously back on the business boardwalks, while those who did gathered more closely around Eugene and Peter's wagons. A stage coach just leaving town struggled to clear the throng.

It took a while to get organized after they threw back the canvas coverings and began calling out names. "You men who ordered tools and so forth will have to wait; ladies first," Eugene said jovially, catching the spirit of the crowd.

"Sarah Bingham," he called. "I see you there. Please come up and help me with the list."

Sarah made her way around Dewey Farnsworth's stomach and through the crowd as Eugene took a pry bar and the first crate squawked open. He handed the lid down to Peter and handed the order list to Sarah.

"Who's first?" she asked.

"Marjouri Coffey right here on top."

"Why don't you just let us take care of this, Brother Michalas?" Sarah interrupted in a non-threatening but effective way.

"All right," said Michalas. "You men, help me with these tool crates."

Marjouri Coffey and Sarah Bingham began calling names and handing out merchandise as Elizabeth Anne Browne, in a long sleeved indigo dress, hair piled high, ringlets down the sides showing her ears and neck beautifully, sought out Maren. The two women embraced as William Herzog, watching at close proximity, suddenly looked as though he'd swallowed a hot pepper. Was it his imagination or did he just see Elizabeth Anne looking coyly at Peter Jensen!?

"Hilda Hairzog, wher're ya?" Marjouri Coffey's homey Irish brogue called, and when there was no response people started looking around. William Herzog, still preoccupied with jealousy and some anger, staring first at Peter Jensen and then back at Elizabeth Anne, soon felt the eyes of the crowd upon him.

"Hilda's not here," he said, suddenly realizing what was going on. "She's not been feeling well." Smooth as a weasel, Herzog slipped through the crowd, took the bolt of linen from Marjouri Coffey's hand and headed toward his wagon. Hilda was in fact at home and time had quickly arrived to have a serious talk with her.

Soon the wagons were emptied of everything but the millstones. Cloth, yarn, needles, spools of thread, tins of spices, perfume etc. the precious items went first, then came the salt pork and canned goods, and finally dishes, knives, forks and spoons. Excited chatter, making trades and bartering time and talent for goods, the crowd sounded like an auction with everybody acting as auctioneer. In the middle of the noise and ruckus Peter reached down and handed Maren a box he'd been hiding under the seat of his wagon.

"Open it," he urged her excitedly. "Open it."

Taking a beautiful blue gabardine dress from the box, Maren held it high for inspection. White lace collar and fringe, the top tapered in a stylish bodice in the rear, long sleeves puffy in the shoulders, with a long full skirt that could be worn with or without hoops. Practical but beautiful, the dress had pearl buttons down the front, a bustle in the back, the tightest twill and most even machine stitching Maren ever saw! She couldn't imagine herself having something so luxurious.

"Oh, Peter!" she exclaimed pressing it against her bosom. "You shouldn't have." Holding the dress high so as not to allow its hem to drag the muddy street, she did a dainty pirouette. "Where ever will I wear it?"

Elizabeth Anne picked up the hem admiring the fringe while young girls and mothers standing nearby tittered, whispering to each other. Six months pregnant, Maren suddenly felt embarrassed and hastily folded and put the dress back in its box to set it in the wagon near the one from S. W. Marks' jewelry store.

She turned toward Elizabeth Anne and whispered in her ear, "I won't be able to wear this for months."

Finally, with nothing left but millstones, gears and iron gating in the wagons, Peter and Eugene drove them away, parking them next to stock pens to unhitch the weary oxen and horses for feed and water. Neither man wanted to do anything useful the rest of the day; Bishop Plowman being correct, neither did anyone else. But after being in a state of depression for weeks, the town came to life with Peter and Eugene's return; cabin to cabin people gathered to continue trading for needles and thread, buttons and cloth, flatware and joyfully to gossip.

In the Wangsgaard cabin, Gunda made coffee and fixed a plate of buttered bread sprinkled with sugar and cinnamon she'd powdered with a mortar and pestle. Still angry with Claus over his interest in Talitha Kjars, the sugar and cinnamon were ground especially fine!

Having pushed hard since five that morning, Peter, in dire need of rest but glad to see friends come and go, set aside his misery and tried to enjoy himself. Andrew Coffey and his darlin' Marjouri came by as did Trevor Wells, Jergen Madsen, Lyman Thayer, and his wife, Anella. But Terrin and Katrine Forsgren stayed home; the recent death of their child left a pall hovering over their cabin. The child would be theirs in the eternities and they'd accepted the temporary loss with dignity and forbearance, but naturally didn't feel like celebrating.

Likewise, in the Herzog cabin, there was little to celebrate. With the bolt of linen under his arm, William had driven straight home to make it official that he'd be taking an additional wife. No discussion, no opinion from Hilda, the display of riches Peter Jensen's wagons brought to town had triggered him. The mercantile business Herzog sold in England made him wealthy, he dressed himself and family well and during their time in Wyoming City he'd procured an expensive wagon and a fine span of mules for the trek west.

Eastern, rather than of local manufacture, his wagon was less than three years old, so in the area of transportation he put on a fine show, but true prosperity among the Saints, or so he believed, only demonstrated itself when a man had more than one wife and showed he could support them; Bishop Jess Plowman and Eugene Michalas being prime examples.

Herzog's proposal of celestial marriage to Elizabeth Anne Browne being almost two months old, he still hadn't received a commitment from her. One way or the other, today he would, and thus show Wyoming City that he, William Herzog, also had money and prominence.

"Hilda," he began as he stood across from her. "As you know, I have asked the widow Browne for her hand in marriage . . . to join with us in the task the Lord has set before us, that of building up His kingdom." The former merchant looked and sounded like a politician. "Awesome responsibility though it may be, today it has finally come to rest upon this household."

Sitting on their quilted bed, nervously fingering the fringes of the cloth he'd just handed her, Hilda said nothing at first. Playing on a braided oval rug laying before the fireplace, their children, seeing their oppressor on stage, were being especially quiet. "Has Elizabeth Anne agreed?" she asked quietly, dejectedly.

With little interest in his frail wife's opinion one way or the other [3]Herzog moved away from the bed, and oddly enough appeared to be shaking. Forcing his plan upon Hilda not the issue here, his malignity and envy of Peter Jensen, coupled with the fact Elizabeth Anne Browne just may have turned her cap toward the obviously wealthy Dane, was.

"Not yet," he admitted. "But she will today."

Hilda had suffered body and soul because of her husband's intentions concerning the widow Browne, and she knew they were strictly carnal, having nothing to do with love and honor. Elizabeth Anne wasn't the only woman her husband had eyes for. He continuously flirted with younger girls and she despised him for coming home to expound upon them. Being a slightly-built woman, fragile with a delicate constitution, she naturally felt threatened.

Hilda was a righteous woman, but because of her husband's brutish ways she had lost all natural affection toward him sometime after delivering her last child, during which she had suffered a hard delivery and slow recuperation. She knew all her husband wanted from Elizabeth Anne was a sexual partner; therefore she'd been silently, stubbornly opposed.

"It is time to stop dilly-dallying around." Herzog continued, still shaking slightly and acting extremely irritable. "Today I will require an answer of the widow Browne. I only hope I've not waited too long."

"What are you talking about, William?" Hilda asked, deeply troubled.

He turned to the fireplace as if it was now his audience and pointing a finger in the air went on with his speech. "After much thought— and prayer mind you, Hilda," his surly little smile apparent as he turned to her, "I've finally come to this decision: We are going to comply with God's law in this household. After all," he sneered slightly, "you could use a little help around here. Look at you. Sickly, weak . . . always tired . . ."

Five children born in stair-step succession kept Hilda Herzog physically depleted; she'd never quite recovered between pregnancies. But Hilda possessed a mental will of iron and though she seldom felt well, drove herself as a wife and mother. She kept the Herzog flat in England—and now their frontier cabin—clean and orderly, her children well dressed, taught and properly fed, and she always looked comely.

Besides the Church, her children provided her only refuge and joy. She taught them how to read, how to pray, and such skills as sewing and cooking. She taught them how to sing, too. Possessing a lovely voice, Hilda knew many hymns and English Folk songs. Marriage to William Herzog had taken much from the captive little bird, but so far not her voice. She was about to use it.

"You need assistance, Hilda, and with another lady around here you might be able to get back on your feet. On the other hand, she doesn't need to live with us and I'll tell her that, also."

Hilda loved the gospel of Christ, and would willingly sacrifice almost anything for it. Willing to do what God required of her, what she said next set her tyrannical husband back a peg.

"Bring Elizabeth home with you, William," she said. "If she'll come that is. I'll not try and stop you. I'm willing to comply with the teachings of the Church; you know that. But let me say as before," she added, "the purpose of celestial marriage is not for a man to use a woman as chattel, and if you think Elizabeth Anne will bow easily to your physical demands . . ." Hilda felt a wave of nausea pass over her and held to the bedpost to keep from fainting, "you may find yourself quite surprised. Unlike myself, Elizabeth Anne is a very strong person and—"

Herzog stepped toward her, grabbing her thin wrist. "I know exactly what she is!" he screeched. "I know her better than you think!" As if he'd just told himself an amusing story, his dark features contorted into base smile; and he started to snicker. "She's one of the prettiest women in this town, that's what she is . . . for what ever reason she likes me, and I want to get to her before I'm assigned to some fat old cow in Zion."

Hilda had almost passed out, but her indomitable spirit flickered to life. "I've taken about all of your perversion I will!" she erupted. "The Church isn't assigning anyone to anyone! And I'll tell you another thing, William. No marriage will be properly solemnized until we get to Zion and general authorities interview candidates. Mark my words, Elizabeth Anne will find you out by then!"

"You don't know what you're talking about," William snapped back. "I'll be good to her."

"First chance I get I'm talking to the Bishop about all this," said Hilda, standing from the bed, wiping her eyes with her apron and letting the unwanted bolt of cloth fall to the floor.

"If you know what's good for you, you'll keep your mouth shut," he snarled, pushing her back on the bed. Herzog raised his hand as if to strike her if she dared to stand again, when his eight-year-old son quickly came between them.

Trembling, the little fellow squared his shoulders. "You leave our mommy 'lone."

Herzog pushed him aside to join his now whimpering siblings.

"Touch him again and I *will* go to the Bishop," Hilda shouted. He again raised a hand to strike her but thought better of it. "Your soul be damned to hell!" she added defiantly. "That's what I say. Your soul be damned to hell!"

"Now everyone listen to me!" Herzog said, backing off. "This household is about to have two women to run it. I'll show the people of this town a thing or two." He put his face right up to Hilda's. "Now," he hissed. "When I bring Elizabeth Anne back here, see to it she feels welcome. Do you hear me!? If you try and stop this thing from happening I'll break every bone in your body!"

She lowered her head and folded her hands in her lap. Tears quietly splashed, spreading on her dress. Four of the children gathered to her, and not wanting to enrage their illustrious father any further, Hilda kept her peace. When William Herzog started swinging anyone could be a target; it had happened before.

"So that's how it will be," he said as he yanked hard on the lapels of his suit as if pulling himself together. "I will go tell the widow Browne the good news then see if Jess Plowman will perform the civil service tomorrow. The sealing will take place in Zion."

Hilda raised her head one more time. "If you think it will be that easy, William," she said courageously, "then go ahead. But let me ask you this one . . . last . . . question . . ."

He glared at her as one would a stray dog.

"Do you love Elizabeth Anne Browne?"

A mocking smirk crossed the would-be polygamist's face. "What's that you say?" Breathing hard, Herzog seemed amused. "Love her?" He looked at his wife as if she were crazy. "Silly . . . women's . . . foolishness," he said with contempt.

The measured words cut Hilda to the quick and she raised a white little fist and shook it at him. "You don't know a thing about women! What do you think we are . . . cattle?"

"Just remember what I've said," he growled. "Have yourself, and them," he jutted a pointing finger at the children, "presentable!"

Herzog grabbed his top hat and stalked past his offspring, all of them except the baby—who'd been crying—dodging instinctively as he did. "Silly women's foolishness," he repeated mockingly as he turned his back to Hilda.

He tried to slam the door but to his chagrin, so heavy were its footings it hardly made a sound. Herzog's two mules were still hitched to his wagon. It was nearly two miles to Elizabeth Anne Browne's cabin; he'd driven it many times, and as he rolled slowly along, he pondered what he would say to her. If he was indeed competing with Peter Jensen who had a healthy wife and no children, he decided to continue to play upon the widow's sympathy; her caring ways about the only thing left to work with.

Using that strategy in the recent past, Herzog had the comely Elizabeth Anne eating out of his hand, and once she'd almost invited him inside her cabin—the other women she lived with not home that day. Herzog thought he had the makings of a beautiful affair, but from what he'd seen this morning his plans might be all up in smoke.

Chapter 28

The Ploy

A worried look crossed Herzog's face as he saw the object of his deluded affection just stepping outside with two of her friends. In best dress, complete with shawls and bonnets, the women were heading over to Sarah Bingham's to see what she'd received from Chicago.

"Whoa," Herzog called as his mules stopped in front of them. "Good day, ladies," he said, tipping his hat with all the gallantry of a proper English gentleman.

"Good day, Brother Herzog," said Elizabeth Anne cordially, somewhat flushed.

"Could you excuse us," said Herzog abruptly. He was addressing Frieda Olsen and Anella Thayer. "I need to speak with Elizabeth Anne alone for a moment, please."

He jumped down and Elizabeth stared at him. His clothes were well tailored (Hilda being a skilled seamstress) and fit his trim frame nicely, but his attitude troubled her; she felt flustered. There were no doubt feelings of infatuation toward the obviously successful merchant, and not wanting to be rude to him she said, "I'll catch up with you, Frieda and Anella. I shan't be long."

Elizabeth's situation with William the talk of the small settlement, her friends smiled faintly at each other. A crisp afternoon, skies showed patches of blue and the ground remained slightly frozen. Except for Main Street, where heavy traffic churned, the streets of town were generally firm, leaving people's shoes and boots mostly free of mud. Sarah's cabin was just half a mile away and they'd intended to walk.

"That will be fine," said Anella, then she and Frieda quickly departed, leaving a red-faced Elizabeth Anne standing next to her suitor not knowing what to expect.

"What is it, Brother Herzog?" she asked a bit nervously.

"Hilda needs to see you," he lied. "Can you ride with me?"

"Is it something serious? Has she been taking the Laudanum I sent home for her?"

"I'm not sure. I don't think so. She says it makes her listless. She's not well, my dear. Not well at all. Let me help you aboard." It was more of a demand than request. Herzog had an imposing way that caught people off guard and caused them to do things they really didn't want to do, but felt awkward to refuse; an expert at manipulation, laying out small contrivances to the unassuming and amenable until they were in so deep as to cause either confrontation or submission.

Submission to Herzog allowed him to rule, confrontation caused him to hate. There was no in-between with him, no winning.

"Let me get my bag of medicines," said Elizabeth, turning back toward her cabin. "Perhaps some lobelia . . ."

"That won't be necessary," said Herzog taking her arm gently. "I think all she needs is to talk."

Elizabeth frowned but allowed herself to be helped aboard the wagon, and as they rode along, Herzog made his final pitch. He told Elizabeth Anne he'd had a dream and that in it he saw the two of them married. He told her that the time had come for their marriage. When she hesitated he assured her, as he'd done many times before, that he'd make her happy for the rest of her life.

He told her he'd build her a home in the West where she, and her children as they came, would live in peace and contentment. Still mourning the loss of her daughter, Elizabeth wanted children as nothing else in the world; Herzog knew that, played on it.

With kindness and words Shakespeare would have been proud of, Herzog talked on and on and when he parked the wagon out of sight behind his barn and leaned over to kiss Elizabeth Anne, to her shock, she let him. Self-sufficient though she was, Elizabeth Anne was terribly lonely and actually afraid of the wilderness trek. There were no other suitors at present except a boisterous and ugly fellow named Trent who'd come calling.

Herzog's kiss being pleasant, perhaps a bit stiff, nevertheless she was very flattered if not slightly tempted by the man. He helped her down from the wagon.

"You're sure Hilda is behind you then?" she asked nervously.

"Yes, Elizabeth Anne. You'll see that." He put an arm around her. "She's had quite a time of it lately. The unfortunate little thing goes from day to day barely hanging on."

"Poor Hilda," Elizabeth Anne said. "The children must feel the lack."

Herzog nodded his head in mock sorrow. "It's true, my dear." he said ruefully. "But then, we make do. I'd like you to join our family soon, Elizabeth Anne . . . very soon."

She offered him little resistance at this point. She and William were about the same size—he had her by an inch; it felt good to be in his arms. Not the same as it had been with her departed husband, but Elizabeth wasn't repulsed by the well heeled merchant either. She felt protected; after all he held the priesthood.

"It's the Lord's will for us, Elizabeth," Herzog cooed.

She barely felt the pressure he was exerting. "I know you feel that way, Brother Herzog. I've prayed about it and I'm just not sure yet . . ."

He cut her off ever so gently. "Sometimes answers come when we least expect them, my dear. I need you Elizabeth Anne, and Hilda needs you. Some days it's all she can do to make meals. We've discussed it time and again and always your name comes to the surface. We know you're the one. You'll fit into our family like a glove."

"Hilda is completely supportive then?"

Herzog smiled sweetly and nodded.

"I still need time to think, Brother Herzog."

He tried to kiss her again, but she turned her head aside and his lips fell upon her cheek. "You will never have to worry again."

Elizabeth gently pushed away from him. "You've never been quite so insistent," she said, flattered.

"I know my dear, I know, but now I must know. We're leaving for Zion soon and there is so much to do. So much preparation to do in your behalf, I'd like to have your answer." She stiffened at that and he relented slightly, "by tomorrow."

"Tomorrow?" she asked, somewhat perplexed. "Why tomorrow?"

He moved in and gave her a peck on the lips. "Tomorrow," he said softly. "Now let's go in and talk it over with Hilda. I want you to see how supportive she is."

"I will give you an answer tomorrow, Brother Herzog," Elizabeth said firmly, "But I really don't feel like going in and talking to Hilda just now. I believe what you say . . ."

"Father," said the voice of a small boy who'd come up behind them. "Mother wants you to come inside."

Herzog placed his hand roughly on the child's head, pulling his hair with his thumb and forefinger. "I'll be right there," he said firmly. Then trying to neutralize the quickly charged atmosphere, he smiled at Elizabeth Anne drippingly and held the boy next to his leg. "This is Jacob," he said apologetically. "He's barely four years old."

"I know Jacob," Elizabeth said, bending to touch the frightened little boy on his cheek. "I see him each Sunday, don't I, Jacob?" The boy nodded.

"Are you sure you won't come in, Elizabeth Anne?" Herzog implored.

Elizabeth stood up and shook her head. "I want a little more time, Brother Herzog. I think my answer shall be yes, but I must be certain it's the right thing for all concerned." She smiled down at the boy who mirrored the gesture.

Facing Herzog with renewed strength she said, "Could you take me back home now, Brother Herzog . . . please?"

"As you wish, my dear," Herzog said sweetly. "Go along now, Jacob."

As Elizabeth's eyes tenderly followed him, Herzog's sallow-looking offspring shyly retreated around the side of the barn. William noticed this and was immensely grateful to the boy; just the right thing to happen at just the right time.

"I think you can see you're needed here," he said slyly.

"Yes I can," said Elizabeth Anne, sincerely touched. She was a bundle of mixed emotions while her well-to-do suitor was calm as Spring. Herzog knew in his heart he had her, that the answer would be yes, so flaunting his position he drove his team not to hers, but directly to Sarah Bingham's cabin.

Chapter 29

Celebration

*A*n hour later, a message from Jess Plowman came to the Jensen/Wangsgaard cabin. To celebrate the return of Peter and Eugene, the Bishop and his councilors had called for a barn dance to be held that very evening. Home teachers were carrying messages throughout the town requesting food and refreshments, also men to come and help clear out Plowman's huge barn and make it ready for the festivities.

"You're both needed," the youth carrying the Bishop's message stated. "Things are goin' on right now, and after the work is done Bishop Plowman wants to speak to you."

"May as well kill a man one way as another," said Peter wearily.

"Come on," Claus said, pulling him off the bed where he'd been seated comfortably. "You're only young once."

The two of them joined others in Plowman's barn, and after the livestock had been removed and the manure they'd left behind shoveled out and fresh straw put down, Jess called a short meeting of men he intended to call and set apart as leaders for the exodus west. The first, of course, was Philemon Bingham, Jess' first councilor and husband of

Sarah Bingham, the aforementioned women's president. Philemon and Sarah were "up and backers", they having been to the Utah territory twice before. Their first trip was in 1851 and the last in 1859 with a handcart company. Plowman leaned heavily on Bingham's advice.

Next were John Meeks (town blacksmith and Jess' second councilor), Eugene Michalas, Dewey Farnsworth, Andrew Coffey, Claus Wangsgaard, Jergen Madsen, and Peter Jensen. Trevor Wells was there, but only as a courtesy. Everyone knew he was headed back to England as soon as he was able.

It was an informal meeting with the men standing around near an empty stall.

"From the looks of things, your trip was hugely successful," Philemon Bingham was saying. He was leaning against the stall chewing a length of straw like a cowboy on break. "Certainly brought everyone's spirits up, at any rate."

"Ah'll say't 'as," said Andrew Coffey. "But nothin' will cheer up t' ladies like havin' a dance t'night." Coffey's presence seemed to fill the stall. Jess Plowman liked the big Irishman and knew Trevor Wells had made a good choice when he'd called him as a leader of fifty. He didn't care for some of the others, however, and their absence at the meeting was his way of saying it.

"You men returned just in time," Jess Plowman agreed. "The flour mill has been down for a week. That runner stone we were worried about finally came apart. The new procedure wore it smooth out."

"The Jensen process," said Michalas, slapping Peter on the back.

Peter smiled slightly but didn't say anything. Actually he wished he were home. He was so tired he felt like putty.

"Anyway," said Jess, assuming a serious tone. "It's good you brethren are back safe and sound. As you've heard, there's been some problems since you left for Chicago."

"We heard there were a few deaths . . ." Michalas started to say.

"Let me just bring you up to date," said Plowman. "First of all, three days after you left, Julia Russell took off with a drifter who came through town. Left Moses Russell flat. Moses took out after them and when he found them, Julia told him to just turn on around and go back because she wasn't coming. Ol' Mose came back pretty scratched up . . . he got into it with the drifter feller, and he said Julia just sat there and watched them."

"Moses hasn't been much good in the saw pits since then," Trevor Wells mentioned. Trevor didn't particularly like taking a back seat to Plowman, but he was glad he didn't have these kinds of problems to deal with. He'd had his share on the *Wortham*.

"Just a week later, Pinas Chapman ran out on his family," Jess continued. "He just up and disappeared!

"It's been a bad situation; there are ten children between the two families. Julia Russell hadn't been right in the head for quite a while, but to this minute, I can't figure Pinas. Everything seemed right in place in his marriage."

"That's where you're wrong, Bishop," corrected Philemon. "They'd been fighting for months."

"That right?" said Jess. Philemon nodded, but added nothing further.

"Who's got the children?" asked Eugene Michalas.

"Moses still has them," answered Jess. "Maybe that's why he's all wrung out at work, Brother Wells."

"Could be."

"Gunda's been helping with Keziah Chapman's brood," Claus Wangsgaard injected.

"But it looks like she may have to farm out a few of them permanently," Jess added.

"What else has happened around here?" Eugene asked, shaking his head. "Or maybe I shouldn't ask."

"We had two deaths from cholera, Helen Madsdatter and her little son Jens but there doesn't seem to be an outbreak . . . other than that I guess the next worst thing was some Sioux Indians got into our stables and made off with a bunch of horses. We organized a party of men to go after them and found the horses smack in the middle of a herd the Indians keep near the river-bottoms. The old chief denied any were ours, but when we showed him our brands we got most of them back."

"Some renegade braves, or so the chief claimed, took off on eight of them," injected Philemon Bingham. "A group of us chased after them. George Williams' horse hit a gopher hole or something, broke its leg and fell on him, and he died three days ago . . ."

"Musta' busted something inside 'im," commented Andrew Coffey.

"Sounds like you've had a bad time of it around here," said Michalas.

"The town's needed some cheering up that's for sure," said Jess. "Like I said, you men got back just right."

"We didn't need the loss of all those horses," lamented Philemon. "We're short on livestock as it is, and you can't find an ox or horse anywhere near this settlement . . . for a decent price, that is. A few of us went out on a buying trip. Got as far away as Des Moines. We did all right with small animals; sheep, goats, pigs, chickens, and such, but we didn't get many beasts of burden. People wanted an arm and a leg for anything that chews cud."

He took off his hat, scratched his head, and continued. "We did get eighteen oxen pretty reasonable from a widow who was selling out and moving back East. Her husband was killed and she gave up on frontier life. But we're still short. As it looks we're going to have a bunch of folks pullin' handcarts."

"That so, Bishop?" asked Eugene Michalas.

"It looks that way, Brother Michalas," said Jess. "We'll be all right though. After you men get the mill up and running again, you can help with the construction."

"It looks like my sons did a good job while we were gone," bragged Michalas, trying to put out something positive.

"They did, Brother Michalas," said Jess, and now let's change directions here . . . the main reason I called you men here was not to have you clean out the barn for the dance nor to hear about all these problems; my councilors and I are on top of things and everything should be settled down by the time we start west.

"And that's why you brethren are here . . . I'm issuing a call to each of you, excepting Brother Wells here, of course; calling you men as group leaders of fifty. By the time we're organized to leave you'll know the people you're over, but I felt you should know my plans early on. It'll give you all time to think whether or not you want the responsibility.

"Jergen I know you're not a member of the Church, but I've watched you and you're good with people. You're needed among the Scandinavians to replace Terrin Forsgren. He just can't handle it right now."

Jergen understood Jess but just to make sure; Peter repeated what Jess had said. When he'd finished the translation Jess continued.

"We've set a target date for departure to Utah no later than May tenth," he said with no more emotion than if he'd given a church budget report. "That's less than one month away. We want to arrive in the Great Basin in time to help with Summer harvest and also to do a Fall planting for ourselves."

"They get two crops a year?" Peter interrupted. He should have known that by now but he didn't, and this subject piqued his interest. If he was going to build a flour mill "out there" he wanted to know everything about the growing season.

"That's right," Philemon Bingham answered for Jess. "Winters out there are long and cold, so the people take advantage of every moment of sun. The soil in the valley is very responsive. I've seen wheat sprouts when there was still snow on the ground. They also put in a Spring planting, and if frost or crickets don't get it, it's harvested in late Fall."

"They still have crickets?" asked Claus Wangsgaard. "I thought the seagulls got them all."

Bingham laughed loudly. The walls of the barn seemed to echo. "There are grasshoppers and crickets by the millions out there Peter . . . and mice. You should see the mice. You level a piece of ground and next day it's covered with burrows." Bingham grew very serious. "I've seen pests strip the ground bare of anything green."

Peter felt sick to his stomach. If he had the floor, he decided to alter the subject. Back at his cabin and in his wagons were the finest sets of millstones money could buy, but this man was making things sound so bad he doubted whether he'd ever get to use them.

"Are there plenty of rocks in the valley, Brother Bingham? I'll need them for the walls of my mill."

This time Bingham's laughter seemed to begin from the bottom of his feet and traverse up the length of his body until it shook the whole barn. Wiping his eyes and gaining control of himself he answered, "Better you should ask if there's any dirt!"

Now everybody was laughing, including Peter; if he'd asked his question backwards or said something stupid he didn't care. It felt good to laugh. Everything here always seemed so serious.

Jess Plowman took the floor again. "All right now, do you want this man to dessert us?" The mirth subsided quickly. "There's plenty of rocks to build your mill, Peter. Plenty." Bingham was still giggling slightly.

"May tenth is the date, gentleman," Jess repeated. "It's a Tuesday, and those of us heading west, are leaving one way or the other. Anyone not ready . . . well there'll be plenty of vacant cabins. After I make assignments this Sunday, I want you men to see to it everyone in your group is set. If there are any special situations, I want to know about them. If we have to pull men off one job to see to another we'll do it. Most important is that all the wagons and handcarts are sound, ready for the trip.

"Again, there will be those that stay behind to keep the town ready for new converts from Europe and wherever, but the main body will be on its way west."

Plowman's positive tone sent a feeling of confidence through the men.

"Nothing to it," said Philemon Bingham. "Pack up and leave, travel a thousand miles, unpack . . . and start plowing."

Nobody laughed.

"Do you honestly think you'll be ready?" asked Trevor Wells.

"We'll be ready," Jess assured him. "We have to be.

"Well that's all I had, brethren," the youthful Bishop concluded. "If there's no questions, then I've got to go inside and get cleaned up for the dance. I suggest you men do the same." Jess smiled at them, and then went over to Trevor. "Er, Brother Wells," he said in a lower tone. "Could I see you alone for a moment? The rest of you men are free to leave."

There was a serious look upon Jess' face when the barn had cleared, and at first it made Trevor uneasy.

"Brother Wells," he began, "this is very confidential and I didn't want the others to hear. Just before we got together this afternoon, your man Brother Herzog came to me and says he intends to marry the English widow . . . Browne, I think."

"Elizabeth Anne Browne it is," answered Trevor, shaking his head and closing and rubbing his eyes.

"I'm not all that close to your people yet, Brother Wells," Jess continued, "but I'm not sure this Herzog fellow has the widow's best interests at heart."

That's putting it mildly, thought Wells. "I'm quite aware of the situation, Bishop Plowman," he said audibly. "William has been making overtures toward Sister Browne for several weeks now."

"Is that so? How are things between him and his current wife? Would she support such a proposition?"

"I don't know," answered Wells. "I haven't talked to her."

"What's her name?"

"Hilda," replied Wells.

"I vaguely remember her," said Plowman.

"She doesn't get out much," Wells added succinctly. "William Herzog," he went on, "I believe is here for all the wrong reasons, Bishop. The man slipped up on me, actually. For a while I needed him. I even made him a leader of fifty before our voyage."

"I want you to interview all parties in question," Jess said, ignoring things over which he had no control. "Interview them and get back to me. I'd do it myself but you have their confidence. I'll tell you this though . . . all three of them, Herzog and the two ladies must be in total agreement or else I'll not give approval. You can tell Brother Herzog I said so."

"All right," said Wells. "I'll do it."

"After you've seen him, talk to the ladies then get back to me. You and I may have to talk to William Herzog together.

"For the time being, Brother Wells," he concluded, "I'm leaving the situation entirely in your hands. Don't sit on it too long. I told Herzog I'd be getting back to him." He purposely left off the 'Brother' courtesy. "See you at the dance."

Chapter 30

Revelation

*A*s Claus and Peter headed back to their cabin, the puddles of mud in the street had frozen over and shined like mirrors under the rising moon. Temperatures had again dropped below the freezing level and snow patches crunched under the feet.

"You better not be too tired, little brother," Claus was saying as they walked along. "I'm sure Gunda and Maren have many questions about your trip. I have a few myself."

"I can endure a few questions, Claus," Peter sighed. "What I'm wondering is how I can endure the dance. All I want is sleep."

When the two men entered their cabin they found the guests had departed. The cabin itself normally had an earthen smell mingled with grease and smoke, but this night it smelled faintly of women's cologne and talc. Sitting at the table, thoughtfully stroking her long hair with smooth even pulls from her mother's old pearl handled brush, Maren looked up. "How was your meeting?"

"Fine, Peter said wearily. "Just a few details."

"They made us leaders of fifty," Claus beamed, thinking that might impress Gunda, but standing at a mirror tacked on the wall, pinching her cheeks, the little lady showed no interest whatever.

"You'll make them bleed," Claus said, trying to bring in a little humor. Gunda went on pinching.

At the mirror Peter gently ran his hand down the length of Maren's hair. "Beautiful," he said.

"Thank you," she said smiling slightly.

"My goodness," said Gunda wrinkling her nose as she went to stoke the fire, "You men both need a bath!"

Peter had sat on his new bed hanging his head. "Why don't you all go to the dance without me . . . I'm so tired I could die."

Maren stood abruptly. "What ever are you saying? Gunda and I have been cooped up in this cabin so long we're about to go crazy!" She took his hands and pulled him to his feet. "Come on . . . take off your coat and shirt. You'll feel better once you've cleaned up."

"You'd better not let us down," Gunda snapped, glaring at Peter as if she wanted to poke him with her poker. Claus' eyes opened wide.

Peter groaned and took off his coat while Maren unfolded the blanket partition. "Here, Gunda, help me hang this across."

They stretched it out and in the scanty privacy Peter reluctantly undressed to his faded red long-johns. "Whew!" said Maren, picking up his pants and socks with a pinch of her fingers. "These are going outside. I'll wash them tomorrow."

She came back in with a bucket of well water and poured some of it into a porcelain basin. She then handed the rest around to Claus. Taking a wash cloth she dipped it in, wrung it out and rubbed Peter's bare back vigorously.

"You do the rest," she said handing him the cloth. "It'll wake you up. I'll get you some clean underwear." Obedient as a child, Peter washed his face, beard, underarms and the rest of his body, wringing out the wash-rag until the water in the basin splashed murky grey. Finally cleaned and dressed he sat at the table feeling a warm glow of health. Maren smiled at him like a proud mother.

Gunda placed a cup of hot coffee in front of him saying, "Here you go, Peter, it'll do you good."

"Thanks, Gunda," he said his head clearing. The hot ⁴coffee further revived him.

"You should have bought yourself a new coat while you were in the big city," Gunda said as she sat across from him. "That sad thing makes you look like an old man."

"Oh he looks fine, Fru Wangsgaard." Sitting next to Peter, Maren wasn't feeling her best, but still wanted to go to the dance. "Do you feel like telling us a bit about Chicago, Peter?" she asked.

"Of course he does," Gunda said, folding her hands as if she had all night.

"We don't have to be to that dance for an hour or better," Claus said, joining them and pouring himself a cup of Gunda's coffee. His hair lay back with scented pomade, Claus looked freshly scrubbed.

"I hate the smell of that stuff," said Gunda wrinkling her nose.

"I knew you'd say that, Mother," he said cheerfully, his big hands almost hiding his cup. "At least give us a glimpse of what you saw in Chicago, Peter."

Feeling blessed to be in such a cozy setting, Peter smiled warmly. "All right," he said. "Where shall I begin?"

"I still don't like your coat," said Gunda stubbornly.

♥ ♥ ♥

Brightly lit lanterns hung from the rafters of Jess Plowman's huge crowded barn, revealing people all decked out in their Sunday best. Work boots below dress pants and suit coats, the men looked rough around the edges, but women in layers of petticoats covered by long full dresses and high-buttoned Sunday go-to-meeting shoes appeared very civilized, especially with rosy cheeks and hair piled luxuriously.

The Wangsgaards and the Jensens finally arrived amid two violins and a fiddle playing something vaguely resembling "The Blue Danube".

Waltzing around as if the straw-strewn dirt floor were a marble ball-room in Europe, people here and there waved or else smiled a welcome. Everyone knew Peter and Eugene Michalas had caused this fine event.

With only a slight protest, Claus took Gunda in his arms and maneuvered her amongst the crowd; Gunda loved to dance and she soon found herself giving in.

"Peter, my man," said Jergen Madsen as slapped Peter on the back. "It's good to have you back. You've been sorely missed."

"Thank you."

"And Maren, don't you look beautiful." Six months pregnant, her expanding waist and breast pushed relentlessly against her buttons, making her unable to wear a corset. Maren wasn't alone in her dilemma; there were several ⁵expectant ladies in the crowd, but wild horses couldn't have kept them away from this fun event. It had been a long Winter.

"Thank you, Hr Madsen," she said, tersely pulling on Peter's arm. "Let's see what refreshments they have." Jergen followed them to a long table on the west wall of the barn; loaded with homemade bread, butter, honey, sweet cakes, onions, sliced pickles and beets, boiled eggs, cold meats and cider, the table was a miracle of frontier women's genius.

"How did the ladies put this together so fast?" Jergen marveled. Across from the table standing on Jess plowman's wagon were Dewey Farnsworth and two men Peter didn't recognize, all sawing earnestly away at their worn instruments, and all slightly out of tune with each other. Nobody cared; laughter drowned them out anyway.

Maren wished Jergen would go away. She took a small cup of apple cider, sipping it quietly while watching the swirling crowd.

"What an amazing thing the human spirit is," Peter said with wonder. "There are people out there who've lost loved ones and yet are smiling at each other, laughing and talking as if they hadn't a care in the world." He absently waved at a passing friend but his mind was on Maren. She'd stuck very close to him but hadn't said much of anything.

Just then Andrew and Marjouri Coffey danced to a stop.

"Well, Peter," Marjouri said slightly winded. "You decided home was the better place after all, didja?" Marjouri's jet black hair had little curl (except her bangs—she'd curled them with a hot poker) so she braided it, two long braids, one hanging down at each side of her face. Except for traditional Irish dress and milky white skin, the short little woman resembled an Indian.

"How are you, Marjouri?" Peter asked.

"We're fine, ain't we, Andrew?"

"Fair to middlin," he answered.

"I like your hair, Marjouri," said Maren.

"Peter, you and Brothair Michalas burrought back a muoch needed relief," Andrew said, rolling his R's all over the place.

"He's right, Peter," agreed Jergen. "Things have been grim around here."

"If it hadn'a been for me work, ahm sure I'd a gone nuts," Andrew emphasized. "It's been tough. Specially ta' funerals."

"Don't go on so," said Marjouri. "E'll wish e'd 'ave stayed away."

These friends were his family and Peter relished being with them.

"Did you hear me and Andrew are going to be business partners, Peter?" Jergen asked.

"Partners?"

"Coffey n' Madsen Wheel Works," said Andrew proudly.

"Madsen and Coffey," corrected Jergen. "It was my idea."

"It sounds official," said Peter.

"'Tis," said Andrew. "We got a fast system a' makin' wheels and we're settin' up shop soon as we get out West."

The music stopped momentarily, before the mellow strains of another waltz flowed enticingly. Maren took Peter's arm. "Shall we dance, sir?" she urged.

"Excuse us everyone," Peter said, leading Maren on to the spacious barn's floor. She turned into his arms, laying her right hand and head against his chest. Peter held her left hand firmly yet gently, an angel in his arms.

"The music is wonderful," she sighed. "Brother Kartchner and Brother Nichols play as well as Brother Farnsworth."

"Not so bad," he agreed.

Peter became aware of a slight uneasiness with Maren as they waltzed. She wasn't following him as smoothly as in times past. "Is something troubling you?" he asked.

She didn't answer at first but held to him tightly, and Peter felt a tear against his cheek. They made a few more turns and then stopped near a support post in the west corner of the barn. Maren stood on tip-toes, put her mouth close to his ear and whispered, "Do you love me, Peter?"

He moved away from her so he could see her eyes, "Of course I do," he said earnestly, but with concern.

"I mean really love me?" she asked again, not caring if anyone around should hear.

"With all of my heart, Maren," Peter said holding her against his chest. "Why are you crying?" he whispered.

"I don't know," she whispered. "I guess I'm just sad. I must talk to you privately."

The great barn was packed wall to wall with people dancing, talking or else stuffing themselves with food. Some were even laughing, and above it all the music of the violins swelled through the rafters.

"What could be more private?" he asked. "No one is paying any attention to us."

"Could we go outside?" she asked. "I want some fresh air."

"Are you sure you're all right?"

She nodded. "I'm fine. I just need to be alone with you for a moment." Maren wiped her eyes and smiled up at him, but her emotional attitude had Peter baffled.

They maneuvered through the jostling crowd and Peter felt a pat on the back now and again.

"Glad you're back!" called one man after another.

"Welcome home, Peter" said Terrin Forsgren as they passed.

"Thanks, Terrin," said Peter as he waved at him. "I'll be over to see you soon." They made it through the crowd and he added, "The death of their little one . . . I'm surprised to see him and Katrine out, Maren."

She didn't answer. The double doors of the barn were opened a crack for ventilation, and spreading them further apart Peter and led Maren outside, then pushed the doors back to their original position, leaving a thin beam of light cutting across the dark farmyard and into nothingness.

The night air chilled her and Maren pulled her shawl tightly then pulled Peter gently around the side of the barn. Their steamy breath hanging about like fog, ousted livestock penned in corrals waited patiently for the humans to leave their warm habitations so they could get back inside. For now it was mud and frost.

It took a moment for Peter and Maren's eyes to adjust to their surroundings but soon they could see each other clearly. Music wafted through cracks between the boards of the barn, occasional laughter too, but the merriment inside had little effect upon the anxious couple outside. Except for the animals they were indeed alone. Peter held both Maren's hands and looked apprehensively into her eyes.

"Now what's going on?" he asked tenderly.

She went into his arms, shaking gently as she cried. He held her for the longest time, his eyes wonderingly searching the star studded sky. *Who can understand a woman?* He thought protectively.

Her quiet sobs gradually decreased and Maren wiped her face, this time on his coat. "Oh, Peter," she said pleadingly. "You have to love me. You just have to."

"I do . . . I do," he said much perplexed. "More than you'll ever know . . . Maren, what ever is the matter?"

She stood back from him and looked away. "I missed you terribly," she began, "and I wanted everything to be so right between us when you got back. But," and she sighed heavily, "I guess our life together will never be the fairy tale I'd dreamed of as a girl. All it will ever be is work, work and more work. Hardship!" She calmed herself and looked up at him, and Peter noticed a beautiful glow gradually descending upon her. Even in the pale moonlight he could see a lovely, melancholy expression in her countenance, one of deep serenity, and it left him mystified. If she didn't think he loved her, why was her appearance one of such tranquility?

"I want you to marry Elizabeth Ann Browne," Maren said without any hesitation.

"What did you say?"

She was looking straight at him when she said it. No stuttering, and no regret.

Peter was totally dumbfounded. His face contorted from an exhibition of bewilderment, to surrender and then one of understanding.

"I mean it," Maren reiterated unrelentingly. "I want you to ask Elizabeth Anne to join us in this marriage."

Peter took a deep breath and shook his head, letting a gush of air escape his mouth.

"While you were gone I had a great deal of time to reflect upon our future," Maren continued, in complete control of her emotions. "I went for many long walks in the woods, and while there I had time to think and time to pray. I prayed and I prayed. Something heavy was upon me and it wasn't just that I missed you. It was something else."

She balled her small fists together and held them to her breast. "I could see us joining with others out in the West working to build God's kingdom. This curious law of marriage we're expected to live troubled me greatly. It also caused me deep reflection. The Lord must have a mighty purpose in mind to put this people through such a test."

Maren paused and her eyes had a faraway look in them. "Peter, I don't know why this great trial has come to rest upon you and I, but I know Elizabeth Anne is supposed to be part of our family." She paused briefly and looked at him earnestly. "I want for us to go see Bishop Plowman and discuss it with him."

She spoke with conviction, no regret in her voice; some pain but also a hint of pride. "I am prepared to give up, at least partially, that which is most precious to me. That being you . . . and our marriage, as things stand . . . will change. The circumstances between us will never be the same. I am to share you with another. Perhaps several others. Who can say? But for now . . . the Lord has revealed to me that Elizabeth Anne Browne is to be your second wife."

Ever since his long talk with Eugene Michalas in the flour mill, Peter had a similar heaviness hanging over him. Perhaps it had gone way back to Denmark when he'd first heard about celestial marriage. But it seemed so strange that such a thing could be coming his way from Maren, especially at this particular moment. He'd just returned from a long separation from her, and something of this extreme nature should have been the furthest thing from her mind.

He suddenly came to realize what a noble woman he'd married. He knew Maren still loved him but he saw her in a totally new light. Her strength, lack of selfishness and dedication to God were greater than he'd imagined. He'd always known Maren to be a righteous and courageous woman, a person of deep humility, purity, and loyalty; loyalty to the Church and loyalty to her Father in Heaven. Yes he'd always known these things, but now all were magnified.

He didn't own her, in fact he almost felt she owned him; she belonged to God.

"For the first time, Peter, I know exactly what I'm to do with my life," she went on. "I've had goals and desires, expectations . . . some I held in common with your own, some I've compromised for your sake, but mixed in with everything is the fact I'm willing to do what God wants me to.

"I'd prayed this sacrifice wouldn't fall upon me. But it has, Peter. I'd prayed it would go away, but His answer—or that is, His request of me—was personal, was astonishing. I can't say that it didn't surprise me. Other women I know have faced this, and I rebelled at first. But then I thought of Leah and Rachael, I thought of Ruth and Sarah and other women of the Bible. They put God first in their lives, Peter. Obedience to God—and that is what I want to do."

Peter felt a penetrating sense of respect that such a worthy person as Maren actually cared for him as well; that she still prized him in spite of the situation at hand! It wasn't *he* that had imposed another woman upon her, but God. These stark realizations hit him like an sledge hammer and he just stood there, numb for a moment.

"I don't know quite what to say, Maren," he managed at last. "And you're exactly right. We must first talk with Bishop Plowman, but this is the last thing I thought I'd ever hear from you. And then we must talk with Elizabeth Anne. She might well say she's not interested . . ."

"There's that possibility," Maren said knowingly. "You've thought about Elizabeth Anne also, haven't you, my husband?"

He closed his eyes and nodded slightly. The portrait he'd seen in his mind of the young widow standing next to Maren when he and Eugene were out on the prairie, came back and to tell her about it seemed fitting enough, however he decided against it; neither the time nor place. He just stared at her momentarily. "I have, Maren," he admitted finally. "Heaven help me, but I have."

She moved in close to him and he held her tightly. "It is God's will then," she said. "I don't fully understand why He would have it so, but it is His will and I can't deny it."

The occasional moan of an ox or cow in the pens behind them, accented the sounds of gaiety coming from the barn, but Peter and Maren were oblivious. They might well have been a thousand miles away. They stood together in the starry night, feeling the warm embrace of their Father in Heaven.

"It's getting cold, Maren," Peter said at last as he thought he felt her shiver. "Let's go inside." He kissed her, and she kissed him back; surely the sweetest kiss he'd ever experienced. They clung to each other then without speaking headed for the double door.

Barely noticed when they returned inside the barn, violins were still singing, couples still spun on the dance floor and dresses swished about like so many large brooms, sweeping loose straw gently about. Maren and Peter wore a quiet air of dignity and suffering as they waltzed. For her part there was loss, on the other gain. The only way she could live with what she had just done was to trust in God.

Peter on the other hand felt burdened. He had a slight feeling of joy but also a keen sense of anxiety. Now he might have two women to measure up to; what would their expectations of him be?

"We still have much to go over, Maren," he said heavily.

"We do," said she. "But why not just enjoy the rest of the evening?"

He looked at her puzzled. "You're right," he sighed. *What will Elizabeth Anne think of us?* He thought to himself. *And what will she say? She may refuse . . . that would be good. Bishop Plowman may advise against it . . . this is all crazy!*

Peter shook it off and drew Maren close to him, whereupon she laid her head gently against his chest. "It will all work out," he said quietly. Then taking a deep breath repeated to himself, *"Somehow, things will work out."*

♥ ♥ ♥

Two a.m. and still a trace of heat coming from the hearth when the Wangsgaards and Jensens returned to their cabin; both couples retired to their respective sides of the blanket partition and hurriedly undressed for bed. The cabin was cold, and snuggling under the blankets was heavenly. Claus and Gunda knew their roommates hadn't seen each other for a long while, and out of courtesy they promptly said goodnight and turned out the lantern.

Except for a tiny glow struggling to stay alive in the fireplace, the log-walled sanctuary soon became as black as pitch and quiet as a tomb. It had been a momentous day for Peter and Maren, and as they lay silently next to each other their minds were in a state of wonder. Just being back "home" was novel enough for Peter, but Maren's startling revelation to him still had his head swimming. He didn't know exactly what to think. As for Maren, strangely enough she seemed quite content and was curled up next to him like a child.

Soon Claus' snoring and Gunda's open mouthed deep breathing were easily audible and Peter turned to Maren. "Are you still awake?" he whispered.

"Yes," she quietly returned, "I am."

Peter moved closer, took her to him and kissed her longingly, passionately. As usual, their love making was restrained and quiet. Pregnancy, coupled with the Wangsgaard's close proximity, kept the act a gentle affair with neither partner giving to the extent they longed to. Holding her that night invoked unspeakable bliss, and for a long time he gently stroked Maren's back and kissed her softly.

Not long afterward, Peter was dead asleep. His leaded eyes and tired body demanded rest, but Maren remained awake for quite a while. Her husband's safe return greatly eased her mind but the situation involving Elizabeth Anne Browne was hardly narcotic. Still, Maren had told Peter what she knew God wanted of them and he'd accepted. He'd known as well, and that provided confirmation to her. It was right and she knew it.

Maren knew the pressure Elizabeth Anne had been under concerning William Herzog and wondered briefly if that was where her revelation came from. She quickly dismissed the thought. She and Peter and Elizabeth; somehow, someway she just knew it was the will of God.

Chapter 31

Madison, Wisconsin

Torkil's return being a sterile affair—no crowd, not even a small one—he parked Stransen's still-loaded wagon outside his little cheese factory/barn and went inside his cabin. He'd look up his Uncle Sebastian and sons Paul and Emil tomorrow. David Steed, too. Perhaps they'd just show up at work. *What day was it?* He wondered. Since his remarkable meeting with Catherine Jensen in Chicago he'd lost track of everything, including his bearings, even the time—which happened to be two in the morning.

Deeply in love with her, his long trip back to the outskirts of this brave little town had literally flown. He was certain Stransen had been blowing verbal, biblical smoke the entire journey, but Torkil spent the trip within the chambers of his mind—thinking of little else except Catherine's parting kiss—and had come to himself only as Stransen called him up short for being rude.

"You haven't said a thing worth hearin' the whole time," the preacher had complained as he turned his horse toward his own cabin. "Made for one heck of a long haul, I'll tell you. What happened to you back there? Chicago overwhelm you, did it? Nothin' but dirty, big city life, Thor. I can do without it. Personally I'll be glad to see the misses."

Torkil wondered at all that. This man of the cloth had visited a few houses of ill-repute, not to mention several bars, in the big city; but Greta Stransen would kill him if she ever found out what went on. She'd never hear anything from Torkil, that was sure. As far as that went she'd probably seen the last of him, too. He could no more sit through a sermon in Stransen's little church again than fly to the moon.

Cobwebs hit him in the face as he entered the lonely cabin and lit a candle. He wiped his face and grabbed a broom, swinging it at one particularly large web hovering just over his bed. Its sticky silk webbing showed no trace of a spider but after sweeping it away, Torkil banged the broom on both sides just to be sure he'd killed anything that happened to be in it. He then flopped on his straw tick mattress and using both hands as a pillow, gazed at the dimly lit ceiling. There were cobwebs there, too; they showed eerily in the flickering candle light. He'd get them tomorrow.

What am I doing here? He wondered. *Why didn't I just jump on that train with her? Why? Because I didn't have any money that's why, and it will be months before I get any. That is, anything substantial.*

Catherine had him in a daze. *What a fine and complete person she is,* he mused. *Certainly she had some gray in her hair. Didn't he? But her conversation, her conviction, her beauty . . .* he'd gone over every detail of their discussion in the icy park, gone over every lovely detail of her face. He'd barely noticed the cold; in fact to him it was Spring! Her kisses were so moist and tender. So full of longing. They'd generated enough heat to thaw their immediate surroundings. Maybe even the entire park!

Now he'd almost lost the will to build up a cheese business, almost lost the will to remain in Madison at all. *What do I have here anyway?* Thinking about that, actually, he had quite a lot. *Far more worldly wealth than I ever possessed in Denmark . . . a business of my own, this cabin, a barn, even a fine horse. Yes, I have property . . .* "But, who to share it with?" he said out loud. "My sons and their families are here . . ."

What troubled Torkil more than anything that early morning being religion, his thoughts shifted momentarily. *I'm not following after no Joseph Smith,* his mind fairly shouted at him. *If Catherine and I ever get together, we'll have to compromise on that.* "But I'm not following after Darold Stransen either," he said, again aloud. Where could he find what he'd discovered at that tent revival in Ohio? *Pure and clear, easy to understand, I've been forgiven of my sins. I've been saved. Jesus loves me. Where can I find that?* He sighed heavily, and yawned widely. *I'm giving up on the whole religion thing,* he thought. *I'll just have my prayers, read the Bible, and take a walk in the forest once in a while . . .*

The last thing Torkil remembered before blowing out his candle was the look on Catherine's face when she'd given him that Book of Mormon. So sincere, so pleading yet so full of humility and confidence; he'd left the book in his trunk in the wagon but he'd never throw it away. Maybe he'd read it one day, but wasn't the lady who'd given it to him something? Wasn't she just something!? With his mind finally resting upon the beautiful lady from Denmark, Torkil fell asleep with a troubled smile on his face.

Chapter 32

Peter and Maren

"Do you still feel the same as last night?" Peter asked Maren as once more they had taken occasion to be alone. It was evening, and they had gone for a walk on the outskirts of town not far from the woods near the frozen river.

"I do," said Maren somewhat sadly but as resolutely as before.

Peter shook his head in wonder. Two wives. All of a sudden life had become so complex. How he longed for those carefree days in far away Copenhagen. He and Maren were so in love . . . they wandered the paths of Norr Park, never wanting to go home. Now here they were enlisted in a noble and great cause, the gospel of Christ, and there was no turning back. "May God help us," he said.

"He will," said Maren.

Peter looked down at his high topped boots. They were free of mud because the ground was still frozen. He almost looked military. "Some people predict plural marriage will cause the Church its utter destruction," he said as if he hadn't heard her.

"I don't believe that for a minute," she said. "The Church will grow and prosper until the second coming of the Lord. This trial we are taking upon us will be but a moment in time. The Lord knows His purpose and I trust that."

"I hope what you're saying is true, Maren, but I'm afraid the price will be dear. Very dear."

"Nothing worthwhile comes easy, Peter," Maren said calmly. "Having to share everything we have and everything we do with another person will teach us many things; things like sacrifice and unselfishness."

"There can be no jealousy, Maren," Peter interrupted, his voice filled with concern. "If this thing drives a wedge between us I think I will die. You are my life, my love and my first thought Maren. Never doubt that."

She looked into his eyes and smiled at him. "I'll try not to," she said. "And I'll try not to be jealous, though sometimes it might be extremely difficult. You must know this has been no small decision on my part. When it first came to me I rebelled . . . wouldn't accept it and was angry with God. Share my husband? It shook me to the very core. But then as the days came and went, I grew to understand the divine purpose. And please do not ask me to explain what I mean by that. Some things are best left between God and the individual."

"That I *do* understand," he said.

"This could never be explained to a non-member of the Church," she went on. "Never in a hundred years. I could never have conjured up so peculiar an arrangement, and it's a very sacred matter with me."

"God expects so much from us," said Peter.

"He does," she agreed. "But, Peter . . . I've come to love Elizabeth Anne. She is a dear sister and friend. I won't withhold anything from her . . . not even my husband. I do have one condition though," she said, being sensible as well as sacrificial.

Peter looked at her intently, his ears and eyes grasping every word and feeling. "I won't share my house again. This terrible ordeal with the Wangsgaards has convinced me of that. I want a home of my own. Just like Elizabeth Anne will."

Peter nodded. "You've thought about this long and hard, haven't you?"

"Yes I have," she admitted. "I'm willing to do God's will, but I don't think he expects me to give up privacy all my life."

♥   ♥   ♥

April 28, 1866

Today we awakened to what sounded like reports from a rifle coming from the direction of the river. Although we still have a fire at night, during the day the sun is bright, temperatures are warming, and ice is quickly splitting off in giant sections; soon the river will be navigable again and that means Trevor Wells will be leaving us. He has served the Danish people well, but ever since we arrived in Wyoming City he keeps a back seat, letting Bishop Plowman run things. But Trevor's been a good friend to me and I'm going to miss him terribly.

Much has happened since my last entry. I will not attempt to put all the reasons in writing, but one day soon I may take upon me a second wife. Peter paused and looked at the fateful words. In print the thing was no less astounding. Feelings enveloped his soul he could scarcely explain. He shook his head slightly, dipped his quill and continued.

It being an extreme change in my life, if my mother ever found out I'm sure she'd disown me, but Maren has actually encouraged me. Teachings from the Lord plus the fact I genuinely have feelings for the lady—and Maren loves her as a sister—help me know it's the right thing to do, therefore I will at least propose the arrangement. The lady can always say no.

There is everything from joy to fear in my mind. As stated, I care a great deal for the lady in question but wonder where I'll gather the courage to ask for her hand. I did have occasion to shoe her horse yesterday, and as she stood there watching me, we talked about trivials. I'm sure she senses I've got something on my mind—talk of plural marriage becoming more common these days—but how does a man go about asking a lady to be his wife when he is already married?

The only answer I have for myself is that the Lord is in it.

Chapter 33

Finalization

*S*unday morning found William Herzog in his barn feeding his mules. The warm, acrid smell of the animals in their pens gave the air a pungent and foul attitude, similar to Herzog's natural demeanor. He hated the laborious task of caring for these dumb beasts, and in addition, realization was setting in that the widow Browne hadn't been particularly overjoyed with his closing offer of marriage.

"Good Morning, William," came the business-like voice of Trevor Wells as he stepped through the open doorway and walked around Herzog's parked wagon. As a former headmaster, he sounded formal—like he might be addressing a gathering of school teachers back in England. His abrupt entry startled Herzog, making him even more irritable than before. "We missed you at the dance last night."

"What brings you out here, Wells?" growled Herzog as he threw a pitchfork of hay into a stall, the hay spreading over the mule like grass in the wind. Ripples reverberated down the animal's spine as it shook off the hay like a dog doused with water.

The visit was highly unusual, both men knew it, and for his part Trevor didn't know exactly where to begin. "Just stopping by, that's all," he said conversationally.

Herzog leaned upon his pitchfork. "Of course you were, Wells; just happened to be two miles away from your cabin . . . out seeing the neighbors, eh."

That knocked Trevor's wheels off track; his emotions were already running high with the task at hand. He'd known he'd be sparring verbally with his countryman, but didn't think the first cut from the former merchant's bladed tongue would come so early in the match. He should have expected it.

"There were many reasons I agreed to lead the English contingency to America, William," Trevor began tactfully. "The welfare of our branch being primary among them."

Here to discuss women, that is one particular woman, Trevor was instantly reminded that his own marriage being less than happy caused his volunteering to lead the English contingency to America. He'd thought getting away from his wife for an extended period of time might help matters between them. And even though he'd been away for five months he still wasn't especially anxious to return to England.

He hadn't admitted it to himself yet, but during the course of time and events he'd become quite fond of Elizabeth Anne Browne. American Church members such as Jess Plowman had given him a new perspective on plurality of wives; Trevor greatly admired how well the man got along with not just one woman, but three! There were other examples in town, and not all were good, but Eugene Michalas and his two wives also seemed very happy.

Because of what he'd witnessed, Trevor's protective interest concerning Elizabeth Anne had recently increased into much more than that. He'd even found himself daydreaming about her. He wasn't particularly proud of the fact, but couldn't say he didn't enjoy his fantasies either. After all, Elizabeth Anne was a very intelligent and beautiful woman and she seemed fond of him as well. She was compassionate, selfless and had a strong testimony of the gospel; the latter traits he found even more appealing than the former.

But Trevor had to ask himself if Elizabeth Anne admired him because of his leadership position or what? *There's at least ten years between us; she probably feels about me as a young lady does a grandfather,* he'd reminded himself time and again when his daydreams got out of hand. The second posture was distasteful to Trevor, and the first less than enviable. What he hoped was at least Elizabeth Anne had some attraction for him, intellectual or otherwise. He could build from there.

There was much at stake confronting William Herzog that morning. But he was supposed to be talking to the crafty little Englishman not as Elizabeth's Anne's interested beau, but as her priesthood leader, and at the moment Trevor couldn't distinguish which he was.

"You've come here for a specific reason, Wells," interrupted Herzog. "Why don't you just say what's on your mind and be done with it?" The air was suddenly super-charged and the two men faced each other like prizefighters in a ring.

"All right, William," said Trevor, swallowing hard and setting his feet firmly apart. "It has come to my attention that as of late you have been courting the widow Elizabeth Anne Browne . . ."

"Everybody knows that," said Herzog acidly. "Specifically, what business is it of yours? As I understand it, you're going back to England. Jess Plowman is in charge around here."

Trevor set his jaw. William had a quick tongue that could cut him off and he wanted to make sure he got his points across.

"Isn't that right, Wells?" Herzog's attitude showed him well prepared for this confrontation. Rehearsed even.

"I haven't been officially released as Branch President, William. And yes it **is** my duty to discuss this matter with you . . ."

"There's nothing to discuss, Wells," Herzog shot back. "This is strictly between the lady and me."

"You c-can't just enter into celestial marriage on your own whim," stammered Trevor, his anger rising. "It must be approved by your wife, and then you two together go to the Bishop! It begins there . . ."

"And why wouldn't the Bishop approve my marrying her?" asked Herzog arrogantly. "I'm well able to take care of the lady. I'm following correct procedure, Wells, don't concern yourself about that. I've already taken it up with my wife, Hilda . . . *and* for your information, our good Bishop Plowman."

Herzog threw another pitchfork full of hay at his mules. "That's why you're here, isn't it? Plowman sent you, didn't he?"

Trevor wouldn't answer directly. "Why I'm here is . . . I want to know exactly how Hilda feels about your plans. Would she really sanction a union between yourself and Elizabeth Anne?"

Herzog looked at Wells sardonically. "Yes, she sanctions it! Go in and talk to her. Listen, Wells, I'm a busy man. Why don't you just get out of here and let me finish my work?"

With that he turned his back on Trevor, set his pitchfork against the stall gate—which act caused Trevor to visibly relax—and picked up a heavy wooden bucket of water, pouring its contents into a trough. He threw the bucket down and with fumbling fingers untangled a harness hanging on a nearby post.

Trevor was staring at his long bony hands trying to think of what to say next when the graceful figure of a woman moved through the open doorway of the barn. Neither man noticed her shadow pass the wall as neither was looking. She was just about to say something when Trevor raised his head.

"Do you love Elizabeth Anne, William?" he asked pointedly. With that the lady froze in her tracks, slowly crouching behind the parked wagon.

Herzog turned to face his tormenter. "You sound just like my wife," he said sarcastically. Curiously, Herzog was extremely calm. He seemed in control of the situation and it further angered Trevor. "Elizabeth Anne needs a man, Brother Wells, someone to put a roof over her head and to take care of her."

"I've talked to the widow Browne about this, William," Trevor lied.

"I don't think she really has any affection for you. She simply wants to help out with your wife."

"Isn't that the purpose," Herzog barked sensing the lie. "To *help* one another?"

"That's part of it," Wells had to admit. He knew many of the plural marriages had been arranged for exactly that reason. "But love should be paramount in a marriage . . . of any kind."

Herzog's face twisted into his familiar smirk. "Come on now, Wells . . . you're a man, aren't you? Heh, heh."

"What do you mean by that?" Trevor shot back indignantly.

Herzog sniggered again. "They're all the same, aren't they good brother?"

The woman behind the wagon almost gasped; a hot flash of anger embraced her. Trevor's face went crimson, too. "I ought to knock your bloody block off!" he exclaimed.

"You can try it any time you like, Wells," sneered Herzog, reaching over and taking hold of his pitchfork menacingly. "Anytime. What is love anyway!?" he added defiantly, scornfully. "Especially out here. This is survival, man! Elizabeth Anne and I can learn to love each other if it's so all fired important."

He let fly a string of curses. "It's a tough life out here, Wells. Horses kick you, oxen step on your feet, there's manure all over everything (Herzog was used to a softer life) . . . never ending labor. No proper food, nothing ever completely clean. She needs me all right, rather I need her; but like I said when you first walked in here Wells, this affair is none of your business."

"And I tell you it is!" shouted Trevor angrily. "I haven't left for England yet, and I'm still Branch Leader. With your own words you've shown your hand, William!" Trevor was shaking his fist at Herzog, and if it hadn't been for the pitchfork he'd have torn into him. Wisely he held back. "What you really need is a housekeeper. It's quite apparent your intentions for Elizabeth Anne are less than admirable, and if so I'm telling you to withdraw your suit!"

"My intentions are to provide a home for a lonely woman, Wells," Herzog fired back, stabbing the pitchfork directly at him. "And, mind you, to live the law of the Church!"

"And I've come to give you my answer, Brother Herzog," said the voice of Elizabeth Anne Browne as she stepped from behind the wagon and into full view.

Trevor Wells and William Herzog both whirled about. Both could see her plainly. In a dress that lightly touched the ground and highlighted by a cameo at the collar, Elizabeth Anne's shapely Victorian figure showed perfectly in the open barn door. As she bravely stepped forward, her green eyes were on fire, leaving both men to gape at her in hot embarrassment.

Trevor groped for something to say, while Herzog was trying his best to put on a smile. Both men felt like crawling under the haystack.

"I've come to tell you no, Brother Herzog," Elizabeth Anne said icily, directing her words at him like cold air from a dark cave. "I'm not interested in your proposal."

"But . . ."

"I had planned this to be a private interview, but it seems my name has been thrown carelessly about here, so let me speak for myself." Trevor's presence, though it upset her immensely, also gave her courage. She'd become genuinely frightened of Herzog and now knew she had good reason.

"I do want to thank you for your good intentions, Brother Herzog," she said in forced courtesy, and then parroting the words of Gunda Wangsgaard, "and must say I was flattered by your proposal. But I'm afraid I must decline."

Nobody spoke. If a pin fell, it would be heard hitting the dirt floor. Herzog now assumed his gentlemanly attitude and stammered something to the effect of, "V—very well my dear . . . suit yourself. But w-who will take care of you on the journey west?"

"I'll manage just fine, thank you, Brother Herzog," Elizabeth Ann said, turning on her heel. "Good day, gentlemen."

She was out the door and riding side saddle on the quiet old mare she'd ridden before either man knew what happened. They looked at each other and both appeared like they'd been slapped in the face.

"Get out of here, Wells," growled Herzog, pushing against him. "Get out of here before I do something we'll both be sorry for!"

Trevor's visit had achieved a hollow victory, but as he headed toward the open barn doors he worried that any moment he'd be struck in the back by the sharp prongs of a pitchfork. Upon a quick backward glance, what he observed was a jilted little man wildly throwing hay at his penned up livestock.

Chapter 34

Farewell

*A*s April turned to May and temperatures warmed, the center of town turned into an island of mud surrounded by a prairie of budding green. Thin drifts of snow still lined the banks of the Missouri River, but water flowed steady and deep. With each passing day people became more and more anxious to leave the boggy frontier town called Wyoming City.

There were finally enough wagons and handcarts for the journey to Zion, and because of Peter's process and now the new stones, the grist mill had milled feed and flour barrels to capacity. The trek would be long and arduous, but no person or thing would starve.

With the thaw, oxen, mules and horses were put out to pasture. New growth being sparse, the animals had to forage through dead grasses blackened and soggy from frost yet still full of nutrition. Ribs that had become visible during Winter began to smooth over with new layers of fat.

Only the bare necessities of life such as blankets, clothing, food and tools would be taken west. Wagon boxes three feet by twelve feet, with rails barely eighteen inches high, were packed and unpacked diligently and people shared precious space with friends, but in the end much would be left behind.

Pots and pans, spinning wheels, looms, churns, plows, and other cumbersome equipment ate up space in the wagons, and tempers became short among women forced to leave priceless wardrobes and chests of drawers—not to mention the old pot-bellied stove that kept them warm in Winter and made meal planning easy. Weight being the enemy, to spare the animals, many precious things had to be left behind and even though people planned return trips, precious family heirlooms left behind were forever lost.

By the middle of the week temperatures continued to warm, the river eventually freed itself of ice and on May 7th, the blast from the whistle of a riverboat sounded near the dock. People left their cabins and came in from farms to gather along the river banks and watch it pulling up. Churning the river, a mid-sized paddle wheeler sporting two levels and twin stacks was arriving to buy a load of wood and also to pick up any person who might be heading downriver.

The smoke from the riverboat's stacks and the sound of its whistle enlivened the town. It would be docked for at least two hours taking on wood, and as it floated there more and more curious people arrived from scattered homes and farms to catch a glimpse of civilization.

Soon passengers were stepping off the handsome vessel to stretch their legs and mingle with a large crowd welcoming them to Wyoming City. Men in business suits, trimmed goatees and mustaches and ladies in long dresses and fancy hats stepped off the riverboat, but there were plenty of passengers wearing buckskins and moccasins, work britches and blousy shirts with stains. Mostly whites, a few blacks and Indians made up the crowd, but there was also a contingency of gypsies, their brown weathered skin and folk dress readily apparent. Many were heading for New Orleans.

A great stir ensued as the pilot of the craft, along with his first assistant—both dressed in the dark blue uniform of their company—descended the gang plank to meet Jess Plowman and other political figures of Wyoming City. With red and gold trim, their sharp uniforms may as well have been military. Murmurings and a few "ahhs" sounded in the crowd, and while all that was going on, some enterprising women with home-spun clothing and crafts to sell, set up small tables to display their wares.

The two hours passed quickly, as wood the riverboat needed to complete the leg to St. Louis had been purchased and most of it loaded. Shortly, a wagon drawn by two horses carrying Maren and Peter Jensen, Gunda and Claus Wangsgaard along with Terrin Forsgren and Trevor Wells, came rolling up. Pug, Peter's faithful Springer Spaniel who'd trotted behind the wagon, arrived at the same time. With a packed trunk and wearing his ever-present black suit, Trevor resembled an undertaker, and truth be told he felt like one that morning.

Brother Wells had shepherded most of this flock several months; across the Atlantic Ocean, through the Gulf of Mexico all the way to New Orleans, then up the Mississippi to St. Louis and detention on Arsenal Island. Then a winter march along the Missouri River to outfit in Wyoming City.

"With all we've been through together it is heart breaking . . . no, it is *pitiful* to leave such friends!" Trevor announced as they drove up. Tears filled his eyes, as one after another, people came up to pay their respects and embrace him. Trevor would never see them again; he knew it and couldn't maintain composure. Jess Plowman looked on enviously. He should invoke such feelings from the members. He didn't.

Finally Peter sided up to Trevor and put an arm around him. "Leave us then, will you?" he said sadly.

"I don't want to, Peter," said Trevor heavily. "I really don't old man. But I'll be back. I'll fetch my family and be right on your heels. Wherever you fine people settle in Zion, I will find you."

Nobody within earshot believed him. Gunda least of all. "Humph," she snorted. "You'll get back to your cozy little nest in England and forget you ever met us."

Trevor moved free of Peter and put his arms around the fiery little woman and kissed her on the cheek. "I wish all ladies had as much spirit as you, Fru Wangsgaard."

"We'd all be in trouble," stated Claus.

Gunda pushed him away. People were coming up to the wagon to shake hands and wish him well, then Jess Plowman and Eugene Michalas were both there and Jess handed Trevor a yellowed and folded newspaper. "The riverboat brings a precious commodity to us, Brother Wells," he said formally. "I think you should read this. It's several months old but also very interesting."

People stopped talking as Trevor's eyes hastily scanned the smudged and brown stained print. Drinking in the words like a person who'd been without water, he read from a St. Louis newspaper printed nearly three months previously. Dated February 19th, 1866 the bold headline announced:

"ROBERT E. LEE TESTIFIES IN WASHINGTON!"

"Everyone, everyone . . . please," Trevor called to the people standing about. "Please . . . brethren and sisters let me have your attention! The Bishop has handed me some very startling news here. If you don't mind I'll read it aloud. The newspaper I hold was printed in the city of St. Louis and contains some rather shocking information!"

At that moment Eugene Michalas stepped up. "While you read, I'll translate into Danish, Brother Wells."

"Capital idea," Wells ejaculated. "All right then . . . this is something we all should be aware of. Kindly give your attention!"

Men finishing the loading of wood stopped their work and people who'd gone aboard the riverboat to have a look lined up against the railing. Everyone grew quiet. "Harumphh." Trevor cleared his throat and began reading aloud:

"Murder in St. Louis!

"The badly bloated body of city health official, Mr. Arnold K. Schmidt, was found floating face down in a shallow nook of the Mississippi just south of the city. Two hunters following the barking of their dogs made the ghastly discovery! It appeared as if Mr. Schmidt's head had been bashed in!" Trevor's troubled eyes scanned the crowd.

His forehead wrinkled as Michalas repeated everything in Danish, and when finished Wells began again.

"WEAPON FOUND!

"A thorough search of Mr. Schmidt's scattered office turned up a heavy bust of Napoleon Bonaparte matted with dried blood and human skin! Chairs turned over and signs of robbery were everywhere."

Further down the column under the word:

ARREST!

Trevor read on. "Two soldiers detached and assigned to Mr. Schmidt have been detained and no less than two civilian assistants by the name of Ferrell. Brothers it appears, and fingered by the boys in blue as accomplices, both men were arrested in a bar where they were causing a disturbance . . . and taken into custody." Brother Wells lowered the newspaper. He'd just made his final public address to a people he loved. And in a way it seemed fitting. Everything had gone full circle.

"Well there you have it, brothers and sisters," he said finishing up. "Justice was done after all."

The crowd broke into a low rumble. "Isn't that something?!" said Elizabeth Anne Browne to Marjouri Coffey. "Isn't that just something. The little devil got what was coming to him."

Everyone started talking at once. Words crackled through the crowd like popcorn in a giant skillet. "Justice was done" was repeated most often, and details circulated around the crowd, many were not familiar with what had happened back on Arsenal Island, but no survivor was gloating. It was only a bad dream; wasn't it?

Eventually the talk turned to chattered excitement as once again the people of Wyoming City mingled with passengers and bartered what goods they had. A carnival spirit took over, and in the midst of all the commotion Trevor Wells calmly and sadly went back to Peter's wagon to retrieve his trunk.

The former shepherd of nearly a third of the town's residents had hoped this day would never come, but it had and he was very reluctant to leave. Turning, he took one last look at the stores lining the board-walk in town and the scattered log cabins on the outskirts, then Peter came up and took one end of the trunk. "Here, let me help you," he said sorrowfully. The two of them walked up the loading plank and went to find the ticket agent together.

As the paddle wheeler began to gather steam in her boilers, Gunda, Maren, Elizabeth Ann, and Marjouri Coffey went aboard to take Trevor a basket crammed with bread and Danish pastry, the best of Gunda's baking. Maren gave him a pair of wool socks she'd knitted and Marjouri some boiled potatoes and molasses candy. Elizabeth Anne gave him a small bottle of her precious Laudanum.

"For your nerves, Brother Wells," she said. She wanted to say so much more. From England to America this great man had been there for her. "Thank you for standing up for me against that . . . man." With everyone standing around she hesitated to say more, but Elizabeth Anne would be eternally grateful to Trevor, and she gave him a long and full embrace. Trevor languished in the moment; there were deep feelings here, gratitude on her part, but so much more on his!

Then Gunda hugged him, followed by the rest in turn, and after a battery of empty words and promises nobody could keep, his friends eventually left their former leader sitting on his trunk and fondling the socks Maren had knitted.

♥   ♥   ♥

The pendulating red needle in the pressure gauge showed the boil-ers almost up to capacity, and shortly the pilot stepped up and pulled the lanyard of the steam whistle. Screaming loudly into the morning it signaled all un-ticketed passengers to get off the boat, and those coming along to get aboard. As the last of them walked up the gangplank and it was fastened in place, the pilot throttled again this time shooting a black surge of smoke up the tall twin stacks.

By now Trevor stood at the railing waving to the crowd. "I'll never forget you all!" he called above the noise. Tears streamed down his cheeks. "God speed. Save some room out there for me!"

His words were swallowed up in another whistle blast of steam. Mooring ropes were thrown aboard and the huge paddles began to turn, slowly moving the double-decker down river. Brother Wells had completed his task. His charge was securely fixed in the heartland of America ready to begin their trek west. In many ways he felt he'd abandoned them, but he had to return to England—especially now.

May 8, 1866—I have been so busy with life here I've scarcely given my journal much attention, but tonight with my wagons loaded and everything at ready I had a few moments. My mind seems to wander back to Denmark where I see the family estate in Holbaek; the old grist mill, the pond, and our sturdy thatched roof home. And all surrounded by forest. What a beautiful place. What a good life there. How I miss it, and how I miss my dear mother. Each time I open this humble record, she is there giving me strict instructions to record my comings and goings. I've let her down lately.

I sent a letter to Mother with Brother Trevor Wells. He said he'd post it in England and that it will get to Denmark within three or four months. By then we'll be in Zion. In many ways I'm sorry to leave this place. We were just starting to get comfortable. The mill is up and running, we've filled every barrel we can find with flour and corn meal, and we're ready for the trail.

What kind of life awaits us out West? I can't help but think that a great deal of work lies ahead. What an adventure this has all been: the ocean voyage, the riverboat, Chicago and back; all filled with heartache and difficult decisions, and recently Maren and I made the most difficult decision of all.

A few days ago I asked the widow Elizabeth Anne Browne if she would travel along with us to keep an eye on Maren. She has agreed and has placed her trunk in our wagon. Although Claus Wangsgaard will be driving that ox team, Elizabeth said she wants to learn how to do it as well. That is all left to be seen, but she's a very capable lady and I'm sure she can do it.

What would Mother think of me if she knew I might soon be married to two women? She would go through the roof. She'd never understand and I couldn't blame her. Sometimes I don't understand myself, but it appears that's where I'm headed. Since we agreed to be traveling together, Elizabeth has been at our cabin more often than not.

The day after tomorrow we leave for the mountains and my mind is swimming. Sleep seems impossible. Tonight Simensen Kjevelsrud came by and added a further complication. He and his wife have been unable to find animals and are going to pull a handcart. As the handcarts will travel ahead of us, Simensen asked if I would take their crippled daughter and some of their belongings on my wagons.

The girl in question is barely five years old; her name is Natalie, and she has a withered leg. Unlike the many healthy children among us, there is no way she could walk to Zion, and the Kjevelsruds decided just today that she'd be too much extra weight on their handcart. She's a pale little thing and carries a rag doll everywhere she goes. I wouldn't have thought about refusing her but before I could speak, Maren and Elizabeth immediately agreed.

Peter stopped writing and turned to gaze at his kind hearted wife. Fast asleep, shrouded by the flickering yellow glow of the lantern, she looked like an angel, very peaceful. With each breath, the heavy quilt under which she lay rose and fell steadily and her long thick hair, shiny from one hundred brush strokes she gave it each evening before retiring, covered the side of her face and lay on top of the quilt like a glistening tapestry.

Peter turned back to his journal. *What a condition for my Maren to be in for travel. It worries me, but I'm very glad Elizabeth Anne will be around when the baby comes. Between her and Gunda Wangsgaard, Maren should fare well. The child has become a common thought between all three women; they talk about the baby as if it were theirs mutually.*

Claus is snoring away over there on his side of the cabin. I can't say I'll miss that, but I love the old fellow. He's like a father to me. I hear he's getting pretty good with his musket. Expecting the worst along the trail, he and Andrew Coffey were out shooting today.

Before we leave this place there will be a memorial service for the assassinated American President, Abraham Lincoln. An unusual event as far as I'm concerned, but Bishop Plowman almost worships the fallen hero; he says America is in serious trouble because Lincoln isn't alive to lead it through reunification. Due to defeat, there is much poverty in the South and great animosity remains between States.

Bishop Plowman, Philemon Bingham and Eugene Michalas will be speakers at the service. All three men hailing from Northern States, they are profoundly loyal to 'honest Abe' as they call him. I know very little about the martyred President, but from what I hear he was hated by most Americans. Not unlike our King Christian IX of Denmark.

Peter closed the journal and stood to stretch. He yawned, then just as he did every night, removed his coat and folded it into a pillow so the necklace was padded in the center. He then placed the precious wad next to Maren's head, blew out the lantern, and undressed by the dim light from the coals in the hearth.

The next day flew. After the Lincoln memorial service, packing and seeing to last minute details used up the time like the flame of a matchhead. The warming trend continued, and melting snow and mud made everything arduous; washing clothes and hanging them on the line and packing was especially difficult, but soon empty cabins echoed damply as each pot and pan, blanket and curtain were taken down and loaded.

Women and their daughters packed dishes and quilts, jars of preserves, churns full of butter, and extra loaves of bread. It would be a long time before fireplaces with ovens were again part of their lives; and just forget having an iron stove! "Someday in Zion," soon tumbled from the lips of everyone.

Loading went on far into the night; wagons were packed and unpacked as people fought to utilize every precious inch of space. Men and boys crated up pigeons, chickens, ducks, and cats and herded small animals into holding pens, as men gorged their livestock with feasts of wild hay. The bulk of the animals' diet on the plains would wild grasses, growing greener as the days went by. A few more fortunate pioneers had a sack or two of oats on their wagons, but most would have to wait for new grass to give added strength to their cattle and oxen.

Knowing Jess Plowman meant what he said about leaving on May tenth, many people worked far into the night, preferring little or no sleep to not being ready. Then true to his word, Bishop Plowman blew the bugle at five o'clock a.m. sharp and pandemonium ensued. Hasty meals prepared the night before were gulped down, fervent prayers for a safe journey were uttered, and bleary eyed people moved their wagons in line for the march.

The handcart company, which consisted of 28 handcarts and 197 people, left at six a.m. leaving tracks across the prairie consisting of narrow ruts and human foot prints lined on either side of wooden wheel marks going almost single file. These were followed at nine a.m. (seven had been the plan) by a mass exodus of the main body. With herds of animals and people walking alongside the wagons, the churned up earth closely resembled the tracks of a huge army on its way into enemy territory. The procession *sounded* like an army as well.

Yells and shouts, cracks of whips and exuberant expression re-sounded overhead as oxen and mules pulled their sodden loads. Dogs were running about barking and nipping at the hooves of cattle and prancing horses and to add to the confusion, chickens squawked, cattle bellowed and pigs squealed. It took hours for the caravan of wagons to finally stretch a comfortable distance away from each other; until then tempers flared, oxen bawled, and teamsters hollered.

Between companies, including handcarts, there were 753 people (men, women, and children), 204 wagons, 782 oxen, 45 horses, 24 mules, 96 assorted milk cows (the majority being Holstein), 250 sheep, 12 goats, 112 pigs, 309 chickens, 38 rabbits, 46 pigeons, a dozen geese and a similar number of ducks. Added to that were 57 dogs, 23 cats, 4 turkeys and two hives of bees. A modern version of the mass exodus from Egypt slowly poured out of Wyoming City, but Jess Plowman was no Moses.

Shouting orders till he was red in the face—as his horse spun in and out, up and down—the handsome Bishop was about to lose his testimony. "You there, Joshua Mills . . . hold back, hold back! Ferrell Jensen, close up, close up there!"

There'd been no dress rehearsal for this production, and confused though it started out, at the first curve of the river a colossal traffic jam ensued when Richard Stotts—a greenhorn with mules—turned his wagon over. The team survived, but Stotts' lost his entire load and his temper, while scouts riding alongside the wagon train returned with ropes to pull the wreckage back on its wheels. Still in the saddle, Jess Plowman and took on the role of traffic cop. "Move along there, move along," he shouted to no avail. The procession bunch up even more as every passing wagon strained to see what had happened.

"Nobody hurt, move along!" Jess bellowed. "You brethren," he next shouted to a group of four youths in their late teens. "Come over and help this man get loaded up again!" The youthful Bishop had expected no delays in leaving the dreary outfitting settlement of Wyoming City, planning for an orderly exodus, and it hadn't been too bad. A minute before Stotts' wagon overturned he'd even been congratulating himself. "We'll leave a couple of men behind to help you get back on the road," he yelled to Stotts.

Grateful the inexperienced mule skinner hadn't killed himself; Jess spurred his horse and rode to the rear of the train to see how things were progressing. Following obediently behind their walking mothers—the most orderly group on the wagon train—children seemed to be everywhere; clusters of threes and fours being most common. Likewise, goats and sheep clustered together under the guidance of shepherd boys. After finally negotiating the first major curve in the river, the wagon train seemed to lengthen out, settle in, and like a long line of freight cars began functioning as a single unit.

As they strolled alongside the wagons, the white bonnets of women resembled the small sails of boats escorting a large fleet of schooners. With their high topped shoes packed away for some distant church meeting or other social gathering, ladies trudged along in men's (actually boys) boots, long hems brushing over the mud and snow and patches of grass. Many had babes in arm or young children in tow, and looked at first like they were going on a picnic in the country.

Many men and women rode on the wagon seats; others lay out on top of belongings or bunched up under the canvas while some—most— simply walked. Some walked arm in arm, others side by side and filling the long, tedious miles with flavor, oh the conversations! Detailed, rich and satisfying discussions. Love blossomed, friendships deepened as people pulled together.

Rifles in arms, a few men called as guards—some on horseback, some on foot—flanked the wagon train and brought up the rear, while a mile or two—depending on the need—ahead of the procession, including handcarts, scouts on horseback led the way. Of the 753 people, roughly five percent were gentiles and the rest Church members; of those, four were American Indian, three were black, and seven oriental with the rest being of Scandinavian, English, Irish and Scott descent. Americans comprised half the total while the balance, were immigrants. Eighty five Church members ended up staying behind in Wyoming City to assist new converts from wherever.

At first talk was enthusiastic, back and forth, exuberant laughter, some singing and a little shouting, but by lunch time, the wagon train began to take upon the look of hard and tedious work. So early in the season, the road they followed was little used and the terrain at first level. There were few chuck holes or rocks to hamper travel, but low lying meadows full of muck and sandy riverbanks soon became the enemy, especially to the last wagons. Firm areas softened making it easier to bog down, but fortunately no outfit became so stuck it couldn't be pulled out, not even Peter Jensen's ponderous Conestogas carrying the mill stones.

By late afternoon, Wyoming City had become a faded brown spot situated near the river, and as people looked back their voices began to lower along with the temperatures of a graying afternoon sky. They on their way to Zion, and insecurity began to creep in.

The first day wore on, and in the thin snow and muck, leather shoes became soggy and soles swelled against their stitching. With feet so wet and numb they felt as if they didn't exist at all, people walking soon had the illusion of floating along with the wagons; reality wouldn't hit until they sat around campfires later that evening. Not being used to this much exertion, at first legs would stiffen, feet would ache with pins and needles while joints locked as if they'd aged ten years. But each day the people grew stronger and more nimble.

With a thousand miles to go, Peter and Maren Jensen, Elizabeth Anne Browne, Claus and Gunda Wangsgaard, Jess Plowman and all the others of this company had little idea what lay ahead, but with God as their guide and His Son Jesus Christ as their stay, day after day they forged ahead, ready and willing to carve out their place in the history of our nation.

About the Author

Steven D. Nielsen is a history buff and business owner. He and his wife, Susan, are parents of five children and ten grandchildren. Houston, Texas has been home for the past 40 years where Mr. Nielsen has served in two bishoprics, as scout master, early morning seminary teacher, and mission leader, with missionary work being his passion.

Scandinavian roots and pride in Church heritage provided the driving force behind the fifteen-year project, which became the exciting and epic saga, *Two Runs of Stone*.